"A RUNAWAY BESTSELLER."
Time Magazine

"ONE OF THE BEST YARNS YOU HAVE EVER READ IN YOUR LIFE . . . MAGNIFICENT."
The Cleveland Plain Dealer

"Swift-moving, pulse-racing, the story swirls through Paris, pounds across Switzerland . . . and roars to a wild-bullet-streaked climax in Venice. . . . A top spellbinder in the suspense field, Helen MacInnes never has been in finer form than in THE VENETIAN AFFAIR."
Buffalo News

HELEN MacINNES

"A master of the suspense novel."
The Boston Globe

Fawcett Crest Books
by Helen MacInnes:

ABOVE SUSPICION
AGENT IN PLACE
ASSIGNMENT IN BRITTANY
DECISION AT DELPHI
FRIENDS AND LOVERS
THE HIDDEN TARGET
HORIZON
I AND MY TRUE LOVE
MESSAGE FROM MALAGA
NEITHER FIVE NOR THREE
NORTH FROM ROME
PRAY FOR A BRAVE HEART
PRELUDE TO TERROR
REST AND BE THANKFUL
THE SALZBURG CONNECTION
THE SNARE OF THE HUNTER

The Venetian Affair

by Helen MacInnes

FAWCETT CREST • NEW YORK

To Eliot and Keith with love

The Venetian Affair

ONE

TWO MEN sat in a darkened room. Outside was the blare of traffic grinding its way through the brilliant heat of the last day of August. But here in this room, the closed window, the drawn Venetian blinds kept noise and glare to the street. Here in this room, guarded by two locked doors, New York was forgotten.

The two men ignored the spasmodic screech of the dentist's drill from his adjoining room: it was only a jagged part of the blurred background of sound; an annoyance, like the still, stifling air within these four safe walls. One man was talking, the other listening, both concentrating on every spoken word. They had exactly fifteen minutes to conclude their business.

Then the one who was talking would leave by the door that would take him to the service stairs: although he was the one in command, he was dressed in gray shirt and trousers appropriately soiled and wrinkled from a day's work, his electrician's toolbox lying beside a silent electric fan on the bogus mahogany of the dentist's cheap desk. The other looked like a businessman, not too affluent but eminently respectable; he had removed his gray jacket, hung it carefully over the back of his chair, slackened his dark-blue tie, loosened his white collar. When he left, tightened and buttoned up once more, he would unlock the door into the next room, pass the empty dentist's chair, not even glancing at the white-coated man who would be staring blankly out of his window, enter the waiting room, with its huddle of patients concentrating on their own problems. As he closed the front door behind him, he would leave the white-clad receptionist saying "Next please!" with the same crisp boredom she had dealt him only twenty minutes before.

The man who was dressed as an electrician was middle-aged, thin-faced, and angular. He had a voice as smooth as the palms of his hands. It was an educated voice, cool, deliberate, held low, but stressed by urgency. "This evening, you will leave from Idlewild. Your destination is Paris, as you learned from the plane reservation that Thelma delivered to you at noon. There was no difficulty when you met Thelma? No one interested in your movements; in hers?"

The other shook his head. He spoke for the first time. He was a man in his late fifties, thickset, short, with muscles running to fat. Either he found it cooler to sit on the edge of his chair or he was exceedingly deferential. His voice, too, was low, a little hoarsened by the tension of this meeting. "I followed instructions. I walked into the Zoo from Central Park South. I reached the seal pond fifteen minutes before noon. No one followed me. I went into the cafeteria, quickly got a cup of coffee and a sandwich, paid for them with the exact money I had ready. I carried my tray out to the terrace. Thelma was sitting at a table, finishing her lunch. She left, and I took her table. I pushed aside her tray to make way for my own. Under the tray was the envelope with the reservation. I spent half an hour on the terrace. No one was interested in me. No one followed Thelma."

"And no one followed you?"

"I saw no one."

The cool voice sharpened. "Not even the man we call Bruno? He was watching you."

The thickset man moistened his lips.

The other relented. "He kept at a distance. He reports that no one followed you."

The thickset man smiled weakly, dabbed his brow gently with a folded handkerchief, felt his stomach muscles relax again. If they had kept an eye on him when he picked up his flight reservation today, they must also have had someone guarding him when he was collecting his passport yesterday from Bruno in the Museum of Modern Art. So he was in the clear, ready to leave as soon as he got back to his hotel and changed his clothes. He looked at his watch. Half past three. No time to waste.

"This is what you take to Paris," the gray-uniformed man said. He had opened his toolbox and drawn out an envelope. It was a medium-sized opaque envelope, unaddressed, sealed, not much bulkier than if it contained a three-page airmail letter. He threw it across the desk.

The thickset man picked it up, weighing it automatically in his hand, and frowned.

"Unfortunately," the cool quiet voice continued, "its contents cannot be made into a film or a microdot." There was a thin smile on the thin face. "And so we must use you."

The thickset man lifted his jacket and inserted the envelope carefully into a zippered inside pocket. He made no remark.

"You are wondering why we did not use diplomatic channels?" The cool voice had sharpened. It was on the defensive. It disliked even unspoken criticism.

"It would have been simpler."

"On the contrary. This whole operation must not be connected in any way with our embassies in Washington and Paris. Or with any of the consulates. Or with the Mission to the United Nations. No connection whatsoever. That is of highest importance, only second to the importance of the envelope itself. It has taken us four months to prepare that envelope. Only three people besides myself know what it contains."

The thickset man used his folded handkerchief again. Patches of sweat were spreading over his white shirt.

"Actually," the cool voice went on, "we could have sent this envelope by mail. It contains nothing illegal. But we could not risk having the envelope opened by mistake, or being delayed. Its value, incalculable, lies in its surprise. So we send it by safe hand."

"I will take care, great care."

"That is why I chose you," the electrician said sharply. "Because—although there should be no difficulties at Orly; they pay little attention to anyone's baggage—it must be hidden. No risk of discovery, I repeat. You understand?"

The man nodded. He eased his collar open still more. "And after Customs?"

"You will hand the envelope over at once to an intermediary. He will be waiting for you just outside the arrival hall at Orly."

"Identification?"

"We have made that as simple as possible for you. And certain. He met you three years ago, when you arrived in Zurich. Remember him?"

There was a nod. "The meeting will be easy. There won't be any—any delay."

"There won't be *any* mistake." The thin man uttered the

word the other had hesitated over and left unused. "You know each other. You know the method to follow."

"As at Zurich?"

"Why not? It was successful."

Again there was a feeling of hesitation.

"Yes?" The quiet voice was impatient. It didn't even wait for the answer. "It is perfectly safe to let you work together once more. He has been kept out of sight, inactive, for almost two years. Just as you have been kept inactive for the last fourteen months. Both of you have changed your names, your occupations, your countries, your lives. Two different men; except you know each other by sight. To help your eye find him quickly, he will wear a blue shirt and a yellow tie. His hair has become white, and slightly longer. We have told him that your suit will be brown, your tie green, and that you have begun to wear glasses. Is that adequate enough?"

The thickset man ignored the hint of sarcasm. He nodded, rose, put on his jacket. "Thelma—and Bruno—you are sure of them?" He was looking at his watch again. The room was suffocating him.

"Quite sure. They know nothing except that they were asked to help you escape to Europe. Tell an American comrade that he is saving a hero of the revolution, and he will come to the rescue at full gallop on his white horse."

And now they both smiled. On Americans, they agreed completely. They were the professionals, with only contempt for the amateurs.

"You leave first," the electrician said. "I have this fan to fix." He pushed its socket into an outlet. Its slow whirr began, and mounted into an overwhelming whine. "I make a good electrician," he added, but there was no one left to enjoy his heavy humor. The door into the dentist's workroom had closed noiselessly: nothing less than a crash or a shout could be heard over the high falsetto of that damnable contraption. Still, he was grateful for the current of air even if it was stale, even if the sudden coolness was only an illusion made by motion. He waited for five minutes, thinking of the man who had left him. A reliable man, instincts excellent, senses alive, quick wits. Today he had seemed less at ease, overcautious. It could have been the heat: he had felt it badly.

The five minutes were over. The electrician lit a cigarette, caught up the toolbox under his arm, and opened the door into the back corridor. By the time he sauntered into the street, his friend was already in a cab heading south to Pennsylvania Station. There he would take another taxi, then another, and drive to his hotel, the third hotel he had used in the three nights he had spent in New York.

The electrician stopped, almost at the corner of street and avenue, to look at the window of a small delicatessen. Parked cars, moving trucks, bareheaded women with groceries in their arms, screaming children gathered around a fire hydrant hopefully, a bulldozer ending its day's work on the site of some old brownstone houses, workmen in sleeveless singlets and helmets, a pneumatic drill, glare, heat, noise, total confusion. But he was almost sure that no one was following him. He lit another cigarette, timing the traffic lights at the corner. At the last possible second, he turned away from the overcrowded window with its red neon sign, loped swiftly across the avenue just before a four-lane stream of traffic came rushing down on him. No one could follow him now.

He hurried along the crowded sidewalk to the subway entrance. A good operation, he thought with some satisfaction, and it would succeed for one simple reason: the enemy did not know it even existed. Success always lay in surprise.

And failure, too. Although at that moment, surrounded and protected by a sweltering mass of the enemy, he gave it little thought.

TWO

BILL FENNER settled himself comfortably in the plane. There was plenty of space on this flight. It was almost the end of summer, the last day in August, when most people's vacations were over. But it was also the end of summer in a year, 1961, that had produced its crop of alarms. The Wall in Berlin was nearly three weeks old, voices from Eastern Europe were alternating from cold to hot, memories of shoe-thumping and outshouting at the United Nations were still alive. So the average tourist must have decided that life was simpler at home, this year, where he didn't have to depend on strangers or cope with a foreign language if a real emergency blew up in his face. There had been a lot of quiet cancellations. And the plane, ready to take off from Idlewild, was less than half filled.

The other passengers on the flight to Paris were either young enough to be unencumbered with wives and children or determined enough on pleasure—the kind of tourists who would be found climbing Vesuvius on the day that smoke was already forming over the crater; or they were businessmen, soberly optimistic; or they were lone travelers, like Fenner himself, with a job of work to do. At least, he thought, as they waited for take-off, there will be no crying children on this flight, no nervous old ladies fretting about the weight of their luggage, no neighbor crowding my elbow.

Not that Fenner was an antisocial type. He had spent the afternoon over a long luncheon at the club with three of his old friends, who, like himself, had begun as journalists some thirteen years ago, but had since diverged into book publishing, magazine editing, politics. Bill Fenner had stayed with the New York *Chronicle,* and for the last six years he had been its drama critic. Which was exactly what he had wanted to be in the first place: it was the job that would

14

keep him alive, mentally and physically, pay the rent and stimulate his mind and—in the great moments of theater— stir his soul. And in a few years, he would reach his second objective: the play he intended to write.

It hadn't altogether worked out that way though. Perhaps the critical mind was too analytical, too pragmatic, for the creative to be bold enough to assert itself. Here he was, on his way to France for a four-week vacation combined with a job of writing. A play? Not on your life. Two articles for the *Chronicle*'s Sunday edition on the French National Theater, a starter for a book on the European theater, which might be ready by the year 1967. God help me, he thought, perhaps I'd better never begin those articles.

What's delaying us, anyway?

It was hot on the waiting plane. The air conditioning wouldn't start until they were two thousand feet up or more. He glanced at his watch. The man across the aisle was doing the same thing, only more intently. Like Fenner, he was traveling alone; a sturdy individual, with a solid chest expanding into fat under his heavy brown suit, and a red round face looking redder by the minute above his tightly knotted green tie. He was middle-aged. (Fenner, fully thirty-seven, was kinder about other people's advancing years than he once had been.) And in no mood for any talk, thank heavens. For he had glanced across at Fenner, eyes sharp behind his horn-rimmed glasses, and looked quickly away. His fingers tapped on his arm. Nervous about flying? But who wasn't?

Fenner glanced through the window. Two late-comers were joining the flight, looking as cool in their crisp white shirts and neat blue suits as if the hot sunset outside were only an evening mirage. Fenner concealed a smile: he knew the type well from his cub-reporting days, when he had been sent to haunt the law courts. They could give evidence as expertly as they trailed a suspect. What was taking them to Paris— an extradition case, some federal offender who might now start wishing he had not jumped bail? Serious business, certainly, or the plane wouldn't have waited. The delay had been only six minutes, but to those who were impatient to leave, each minute had seemed endless.

The smiling hostess was performing the usual ritual of take-off with a gentle prompting here, a helping hand there. The man across the aisle seemed adept at air travel, after all. He was already secure in his safety belt, and was setting his

watch forward. He certainly wasn't going to be caught una-
wares by a sunrise only a few hours away. He will eat a
large dinner, Fenner surmised, go soundly to sleep, wake up
looking efficient, while the rest of us, having had a nightcap
or two, and read, and talked, will be just about thinking of
bed by the time we arrive. With that he dismissed the man in
the brown suit, a pretty dull and harmless fellow, and began
to look through a copy of *Réalités* to get some French phrases
rolling on his tongue again.

Across the aisle, the man in the brown suit (who considered no one harmless) studied Fenner quietly until dinner arrived. Despite the heat of the day and the tensions of waiting
at Idlewild, he had recovered something of his normal appetite. He ate quickly, greedily. In his youth, he had starved
often enough in Odessa to make him appreciate any free
meal. (He was, his nicely faked passport said, Mr. Albert
Goldsmith, naturalized citizen originally from Frankfurt, resi-
dent of Newark, New Jersey, and an importer of ladies'
handbags.) Just as he had finished his steak and was eying
the blueberry pie appreciatively, one of the efficient-looking
men whose late arrival had delayed the flight six long agonizing minutes chose to walk through the cabin, glancing (an
automatic habit) at his traveling companions as he passed.
He only wanted to chat with someone he knew in the forward
section of the plane. But he stopped Mr. Goldsmith's appetite
cold.

Mr. Goldsmith did not panic. He was too experienced for
that. His mind stayed alert, his thoughts were quick-darting
but intensely rational, his face remained as placid as ever.
Only his digestion betrayed him: the food he had eaten co-
agulated into a heavy, solid lump in his chest. Even the
return of the brisk stranger with the photographic eye to his
own seat didn't help Mr. Goldsmith. A false alarm? Yet no
alarm in Mr. Goldsmith's profession could be treated as false.
He sat quite still, planning emergency countermoves, elabo-
rating his new identity so that his Mr. Albert Goldsmith was
more than a fake name. If there had been any suspicion
about him, surely he would have been stopped as he entered
this plane. No one knew of the contents of the envelope
except the man who had given it to him that afternoon, and
three others. And none of them, if they had been arrested,
would talk. If they could have been interrogated by the
Gestapo or the old NKVD, he might have good reason to
fear. Logically, he was not afraid. Illogically, he was worried.

His instincts would not be quietened. He felt threatened.
By what?

He did not sleep, even with his raincoat safe under his
hand. He felt cold—the air conditioning was as great a curse
as the heat had been—yet beads of sweat kept gathering on
his brow. A tight band seemed laid across his chest. Indigestion, he thought, it was just indigestion. He sat still, his
hand gripping his coat, while his mind held firmly to one
comforting thought: at Orly, it should not be too difficult.
There was a long walk, yes, but no delays, few formalities.
And in the entrance hall his contact would be waiting.

At Orly, the two brisk men in their neat blue suits were
the first to leave the plane. They were joking, laughing, bright
as two polished buttons. Bill Fenner left more slowly, admiring
their resilience. He watched the narrow stream of passengers
trail after the stewardess, the pretty one who swung her hips
a little, toward the right entrance in the huge building of
shining glass. Stiff legs in crumpled clothing began to pick up
pace as the fresh morning air washed night-tired faces. Fresh,
but tinged with the kerosene smell of jet planes. There was
a long line of them, drawn up neatly, beautifully angled,
exactly spaced. A nicely welcoming honour guard, thought
Fenner. Good morning to you, too, gentlemen!

He let the others pass him. Each was determined to be
the first out of the giant airport and on the road to Paris. But
he could enjoy stretching his legs, this feeling of release from
a tightly sealed bullet. There was no hurry: no one meeting
him, no urgent conferences, no brief stay into which Chartres
and Versailles and Montparnasse had to be jammed, no
plane connections to make, no wife to add to the worries of
transport and wrong accommodations. This was one time, at
least, when the solitary bachelor had an advantage. He was
the casual observer, the disengaged, free to wander, free to
do as he liked when he liked. Except, of course, for that
little errand Walt Penneyman had given him. He might as
well clean that off his plate this afternoon, oblige Penneyman
by sending the facts he wanted, and retire into a long lazy
weekend before he even started his own work. An odd kind
of errand that Penneyman had assigned him. Yes, "assigned"
was the word; Walter Penneyman was part owner, part editor, and total energist of the *Chronicle;* he had given Fenner
his first chance at journalism, nursed him through that bad
patch of his life just after Korea, when—

His thoughts were knocked aside as someone, passing him quickly, lurched against his arm. It was the man who had sat across the aisle from him. Extraordinary thing, Fenner thought, that some people can have the whole width of an enormous airfield to walk over and still manage to collide. The man's white face looked at him without a smile. Did he think Fenner had blocked his path purposely? "Excuse me," Fenner said. The man walked on rapidly, almost too much in a straight line to be natural. Was he drunk? Had he spent the night nipping from a flask? He had been slow at coming out of the plane, but he was putting on speed. He stopped to put down the small case he was carrying, shifted his coat to his left arm, picked up the case with his right hand, and was off again. And don't look around at me, Fenner told the departing back, I'm not following you: I'm just going where we're all going. Well, where was I—oh yes, Walt Penneyman. . . .

An odd assignment—an interview with a professor named Vaugiroud, whose interests were entirely political and had nothing to do with the theater. It would be simple enough, something that Fenner would have treated as routine six years ago, when he was a foreign correspondent, but now—unusual. As odd, in fact, as Penneyman's urgency yesterday morning when he had asked Fenner to look in at his office. "You're leaving for Paris tonight, Bill? You're just the man I need." It was always flattering to be needed. Besides, this Vaugiroud character sounded like an interesting type.

He stepped into the glass palace and smiled for the little hostess, who waited worriedly for the last one of her flock. "That way," she showed him, pointing to the cluster of people ahead. He had his passport and landing card all ready, so she forgave him. "The luggage will be examined when it reaches the arrival hall," she told him. Now he saw that her worry was not about him.

"Baggage will be opened?" he asked her in surprise. That wasn't usual at all.

"It won't take long," she said soothingly. "A formality."

The well-trained nurse, he thought. If she knows, she is not telling. Nor was the welcoming committee, waiting patiently in the vast stretch of light-colored wood and glass with the slightly jaundiced eye that French officials keep for those who have time and money to waste on travel.

Fenner's luck was in. He saw his suitcase and weekend bag traveling smoothly along on a moving belt, and signaled to a blue-smocked porter. They were quickly placed on the counter. *"Vous n'avez rien à déclarer, monsieur?"*

Fenner shook his head, produced his keys. "Excuse me," he said to the passenger standing beside him, and moved a couple of feet for elbow room. It was the man in the brown suit, who had been in such a hurry and now was waiting for his luggage. He didn't look well, Fenner noted: he was no longer energetic and businesslike; he was almost listless, withdrawn into some overwhelming worry—he hadn't even noticed he was standing in Fenner's way.

The French officials were serious-faced, silent. The innocent tourist was probably the least of their problems this bright and pleasant morning. Algiers and generals in open revolt had put the peaceable traveler into proper perspective: someone not necessarily likable, but not inimical either. Yet, Fenner noted, the quick fingers examining his luggage were extremely thorough; the eyes glancing over him were equally searching. What interested them?

Nothing, so far. The Customs official saw just another American in a dark-gray suit, blue shirt, dark-blue tie; neatly cut brown hair, gray eyes, well-marked eyebrows, bone structure of his face noticeable and pleasant, an easy smile. He was fairly tall, thin, relaxed. He had a raincoat over one arm, a bundle of newspapers and magazines under the other, a hat which he preferred not to wear, and nothing to declare. Nothing? the sardonic French eyes seemed to ask: no failures, fears, frustrations? "And what is that? In the pocket of your raincoat, monsieur? Thank you. Ah—" An eyebrow was raised in pleased surprise. "You are an admirer of our Comédie-Française?"

Fenner nodded. As it once was, he thought, and as it may be again. But he didn't risk saying it. This, he felt, was not the year for plays upon words or double meanings. Beside him, he heard a hiss of breath—or was it a slow sigh of impatience?—from the man in brown. His suitcase had arrived. He leaned on it heavily. His face was set. "Are you all right?" Fenner asked him. He got no answer. Just a look that told him to mind his own business and get on with it.

"In French," the Customs official observed. He smiled. "You are preparing yourself?"

"That's my homework," Fenner agreed, and jammed the small, thin edition of *Le Misanthrope* back into its hiding place. He dropped his coat on the low counter and began locking his cases. He glanced at the impatient stranger beside him as if to say, "There now, I'm hurrying, can't you see?" He looked more closely. This man is ill, he thought worriedly: he won't admit it, but he is ill. Fenner caught the eye of the Customs official, and nodded toward Mr. Goldsmith's white face. "Where can I find a glass of water?" he asked.

The Frenchman pointed to a gendarme who was patrolling the background in quiet boredom. "He will show you." And then, to Mr. Goldsmith, "Would you like to rest? Please sit down over there." He turned to a woman whose bracelets jangled as she searched for her keys halfheartedly, hoping her sweet smile would save her the trouble. "Open everything, madame."

"No," Mr. Goldsmith said angrily. "No, I am first." And indeed, he had his suitcase unlocked.

At that moment, three short and violent explosions burst savagely into the quiet room. Everyone jumped. Two of the officials ducked automatically. The woman with the bracelets screamed. Fenner spilled the water he was carrying. Mr. Goldsmith, after a violent start, stood rigid. The gendarme, the least perturbed—either he had been the first to realize the explosions were outside on the street or he had become accustomed to such disturbances—noticed Fenner's accident. Quietly, he himself brought another cup of water for the man who stood at the counter. *"Le voici!"* he said crisply, tapping the man's shoulder to draw his attention.

Mr. Goldsmith's head made a slow half-turn. Suddenly, the ridges of agony on his face were no longer controlled. He moaned and slipped to the ground, his eyes staring with incredulity at the ceiling.

"We shall take care of him. Please continue!" the gendarme told Fenner and the woman, and signaled to the nearest porter to help him lift Mr. Goldsmith away from the counter. Fenner obeyed: the order made good sense; those who had been cleared were to move out; those still to be examined were to stay where they were, under the official eye. A little commotion like this one would be made to order for any smuggling. So he looked around for another porter.

The Customs official was repeating "Everything to be opened, madame!" The woman recovered herself sufficiently, bracelets jingling with haste, but first, as her gesture of sympathy to the poor man who had collapsed almost at her feet, she lifted his raincoat from the floor and placed it neatly on the counter beside some luggage.

Mr. Goldsmith's eyes watched her. He tried to speak. He shivered. He managed the word "coat."

"His coat!" the gendarme said to one of his helpers. "He wants his coat over him." The porter moved quickly to the counter—the woman was anxiously explaining the contents of several plastic jars; the Customs official was opening them carefully—and seized a coat lying near the sick man's suitcase, bringing it quickly back to throw over the inert legs. Mr. Goldsmith was quite helpless now, his eyes closed, one hand feebly clutching the edge of his raincoat as if it comforted him.

Fenner had found a young and agile porter. "Over there," he said, pointing. "A brown suitcase, a brown bag, and a raincoat. That's all." The porter darted ahead of him, toward the counter. There, the Customs official was looking dubiously at the contents of a jar, trying to reason out why one woman could need so much face cream for a two weeks' stay in a city that had practically invented cosmetics. The woman was saying anxiously, "It's *only* night cream, the kind I *like*. I didn't *know* if I could get the same brand—" She paused helplessly, watching a penknife gingerly testing the opaque, heavy mess. She paid no attention to the porter, who collected two pieces of luggage and a raincoat with great efficiency and speed.

Mr. Goldsmith was being placed on a stretcher. A doctor, a nurse, an attendant surrounded him. The gendarme, back on normal duty, saw Fenner hesitate and look in the direction of the little group. "Please proceed," he told Fenner, pointing toward the exit. The porter was already there, glancing around impatiently, hurrying on as Fenner started after him into the giant entrance hall, glass and more glass, people and people, arriving, leaving, waiting, searching, talking, looking.

"Want a lift?" a voice asked at his elbow, and laughed.

Fenner swung around. Mike Ballard? Yes, Mike Ballard. Fenner recovered slowly from his several surprises. First, he hadn't expected anyone to meet him, and most certainly not Ballard, whom he had known only slightly in New York before Ballard had come over to work under Keir in the *Chronicle*'s Paris Bureau. That was four, if not five, years ago. Secondly, Ballard had changed. He had added a bulge to his waistline, a jowl to his square-shaped face, and removed a couple of inches from his thatch of dense-black hair. His dark eyes were satisfied, his mouth was soft-lipped and relaxed, he smiled readily. An easy-going type was Mike Ballard, who—judging from his clothes, and they were the third surprise—had come to appreciate the finer arts of dressing as well as the food and wines of France. The fourth surprise was simply that Ballard was not the type to drive all the way out to an airport to meet an early-morning arrival unless something pretty special was involved. For Ballard, since Keir's heart attack last spring, was now acting head of the *Chronicle*'s Paris Bureau. Also, Ballard liked his comforts. "Expecting someone important?" Fenner asked with a grin.

"You," Ballard said, administering the fifth surprise. "What kept you so long in there? Come on, this way. Where's your porter?"

"He guessed the wrong direction, I think. He's over there, just beyond that character in the yellow tie."

Ballard waved his arms, but the porter didn't notice. Fenner started briskly after the man, gave a whistle that stopped the porter in his tracks. It also made several other people look around sharply. Only the man with the yellow tie paid no attention; he didn't even halt his steady pacing. The porter, quick to cover his miscalculation, headed back toward Ballard, whose arm was still signaling. "There's a hired cab waiting in the parking lot across the road," Ballard told him. To Fenner, as he returned, he added, "Seemed easier than bringing my car. I don't drive so well at this time of the morning—not after last night's party."

"You're taking too much trouble," Fenner said. It was the usual polite formula, but he meant it. For the last hour he had been looking forward to arriving in Paris. By himself. He didn't need a conducted tour. All he wanted was to drive, alone, to his favorite hotel on the Left Bank, with a guaranteed view of the Seine from the balcony of his old room. And there he had planned to bathe leisurely (unless a shower had been added since his last visit), shave, and enjoy a second breakfast with the morning sunlight on the trees outside for company. Now he would have to invite Ballard for breakfast, and listen, and talk. He would be lucky if he didn't find his whole day arranged for him.

"No trouble," Ballard lied gallantly. "Besides, someone had to steer you to the right hotel."

"I've got a hotel."

"Not any more. It was bombed yesterday."

"What?"

"Secret Army stuff. Oh, it was bound to spread to Paris. We have had bombs and machine-gunning in the provinces all summer. It was bound to spread. I got you a room at the Crillon."

"Thanks. But isn't that a bit rich for a drama critic's blood?" Certainly too steep for his pocketbook.

"Not after I got a phone call from the old man yesterday, telling me you were coming over."

"From Penneyman?" Fenner gave up counting surprises, this morning.

"Well—he was on the phone about something else. But he mentioned you. Told us to let you have free run of our files if you needed them." There was a look of speculation in Ballard's side glance. "So I figured your expense account was good. Also, I hadn't the time to go shopping around for hotels last night."

Fenner felt churlish. "Sorry I gave you so much trouble." He still couldn't find a reason for it though. "Thanks a lot."

"My pleasure." They had crossed the broad, handsome road. "There's my driver, willing and waiting." And the porter was already stacking Fenner's possessions in the front seat, eager for his tip, impatient for another job. (Ballard had the money out, brushing aside Fenner's arm reaching into his pocket.) "Besides," Ballard said as they settled themselves in the small taxi and were off, "someone had to come out here and identify the pieces."

"What pieces?" Fenner asked absent-mindedly. He was marveling at the speed with which they were negotiating the cloverleaf that led them onto the expressway.

"Yours. There was a bomb threat against Orly this morning. Didn't they tell you? No, I don't suppose they would. I bet they searched the baggage pretty thoroughly though. They always do that when they're jumpy."

"There was a moment when we all jumped," Fenner said with a smile.

"The three explosions? Just a truck expressing its opinion. A plastic bomb has a real bang to it." He shook his head, and his grin faded. "It was bound to spread," he said. "The damn fools."

THREE

ONCE THEY entered the new expressway to Paris, the journey promised to be quick and direct until the immediate approaches to the city were reached. But Ballard's conversation, even if it was headed in one direction as determinedly as this *autoroute*, had as many crossways and detours as any old-fashioned road. It was loaded with questions, asked and unasked. Fenner resigned himself to the inevitable and roused himself from his pleasant after-arrival lethargy. Ballard, after several hours of sleep in a comfortable bed, was expansive. He always had been a compulsive talker: silence worried him.

"How long are you staying?" he asked suddenly.

"In Paris? Probably only a few days, at first. I'll return by mid-September for a couple of weeks."

"That's wise. Not much theater to see in Paris right now. What are your plans?"

Fenner answered as briefly as possible. He had had to explain all this so often in the last few weeks—vacation plus research, plus articles, plus future visits to other countries, plus other articles—that it had become a standard routine. It now embarrassed him to have to listen to himself.

Ballard was smiling, but not so easily as he usually did. "Come off it, Bill. You don't have to tell old Mike all that theater stuff."

"Theater stuff," Fenner said, "is my business."

"You were a newspaperman long before you were a critic."

"Meaning?"

"What story are you after? This Secret Army Organization? Doesn't old Penneyman trust me to handle it?" Ballard was smiling broadly.

Fenner's astonishment gave way to perception. Was this

24

the reason why he had been met at Orly? "I'm after no story. All I'm interested in is a book. Eventually."

"Wish I had time to write a book."

"Yes, that's all it takes."

Ballard glanced at him quickly.

Fenner was studying the invasion of suburban houses, glimpsed briefly before the expressway burrowed more deeply between its high banks. "Am I wrong, or didn't there use to be a lot of woods around here?" That would turn the conversation nicely, he thought.

"There are still plenty of forests around Paris," Ballard said defensively. "We've rented a place out on the Bois. You must come and visit us when Eva and the kids get back from Brittany."

"How many do you have?"

"Three. Four in December."

"Busy man."

"Too busy to take a vacation this year—there's a lot to handle at the office, with Keir sick."

"How is he?"

Ballard shook his head, pursed his lips. "Old Penneyman had better stop hoping." He hesitated. Then, "Keir has been off the job since April. When is Penneyman going to admit that Keir is never going to get back on it?"

"When Keir admits it, probably. Heart attacks aren't always the end of a man's career. Relax, Mike. You're in line for the job when it's declared vacant. By the way, there was a case of heart attack, or something pretty close to it, at Orly this morning. Fellow just folded up—"

"In line for the job—" Ballard laughed briefly, bitterly.

Fenner kept his eyes on the cars they were passing.

"Or perhaps he just likes to keep me dangling," Ballard added, but genial again, as if to sweeten his criticism of Walter Penneyman.

Fenner moved a cramped leg. "He likes Keir a lot," he said uncomfortably. "Keir isn't old. If he makes a good recovery, he could go on for another fifteen years at least. If he were ditched now, he'd probably be dead in six months."

"Sure, sure," Ballard said. He lapsed into unusual silence. When they reached the Porte d'Italie and the beginning of the city proper, he came to life. "Cut left as soon as you can," he told the driver, "and get onto the Boulevard Raspail." But the driver had his own ideas of a quick route.

Ballard didn't argue. He laughed and shook his head. "We'll take almost as long to reach the Place de la Concorde as we took to get here," he predicted. "By the way, did you see Walt Penneyman before you left?"

"Yes."

Ballard's gloom returned.

Fenner said, "But he didn't talk about Keir. Or the Paris office. He is making a speech next week in Washington, and that's filling his mind." But as he spoke he began to wonder why Mike Ballard had not been given the job of visiting Professor Vaugiroud. Or perhaps it wasn't an important-enough assignment. "I have a professor to visit—"

"I've told my secretary to give you all help with the addresses of people you have to see. I'll be out of Paris for the weekend."

"Belgrade?"

Ballard shook his head. "I've got a man there covering that neutralists' conference. Nothing important is going to happen anyway. It will be a nice long weekend with not one screaming headline in sight." The prospect pleased him. He slapped Fenner's knee. "Even the acting head of the Paris Bureau has to get off the chain now and again. Right?"

Perhaps . . . and perhaps not. It depended on how much the acting head wanted to be head.

"So old Penneyman is giving another speech in Washington. What's his subject this time? Don't tell me—I can guess." Ballard struck a pose of upward and onward. "The freedom of the press depends on its integrity!"

"Something like that."

"He never gives up, does he? He was harping on that back in April, when he flew over here for two days. Two days— imagine that—for Paris! I thought he was going to give all of us heart attacks. I'm just getting the office back into shape now."

"I'm not following you."

"He didn't tell you?" There was a look of relief in Ballard's eyes. "Oh, you know—the Great Rumor of April. CIA urging French generals to revolt in Algiers. Remember?"

"Oh yes. That was the rumor an Australian journalist flattened out for us."

"Not quite. He just forced the French into admitting that they had no evidence at all."

But the rumor had been allowed to run wild, gathering momentum, a nasty piece of international suspicion that could have been disastrous. "So Walt Penneyman came over himself to see what it was all about?"

"Found out nothing, of course. None of us could. If he had paid attention to my reports, he could have saved himself a journey."

If Ballard imagined that Penneyman had lost interest in finding out, he couldn't be very much in Penneyman's confidence. It was just as well, Fenner decided, that Mike Ballard's garrulity had interrupted his remark on Professor Vaugiroud. "Well," he said, "Walt Penneyman has always been a great Francophile. You can't blame him for being upset when his favorite foreigners seemed to be spitting right in America's eye."

"Oh," Ballard said with a laugh, "it would have all ironed out anyway." And he really believed that. It made crises easier to bear, perhaps. Certainly it made life simpler "Walt Penneyman fusses too much. Well—here's the hotel. I'll see you in, and if you ask me to stay for a cup of coffee, I won't refuse. Can't wait long, though. I've got to clear some things up at the office and catch a plane by noon. No, this is mine!" He had his black crocodile wallet out with a flourish. Changed days, Fenner thought as Ballard paid their driver, changed days from New York and Ballard's dogged news coverage over at the United Nations when he had always looked as if he needed a good square meal, a haircut, and still more information. "Don't worry about your luggage," Ballard was telling him. "This place really takes care of its guests."

Fenner repressed his amusement. Was he just the New York country boy come to town? He gave a last look at the Place de la Concorde, with its sea of cars flowing in a steady surge, their chrome and glass flickering like the ripple of small dancing waves in the early sunlight. The man-made sea with its man-made roar, he thought: I'll probably end up as a true country boy on a Vermont farm.

"There's no place like it," Ballard said at his elbow as they crossed the broad sidewalk, newly watered and swept. He looked around at his adopted city with proprietary pleasure. "Ever think of coming to work here?"

"No."

But Ballard didn't quite believe him. He is coming up for that cup of coffee, Fenner thought, just to make sure where I stand with Penneyman. How do I make it clear that I've no interest in his job without showing him I know the real

reason why he met me at the airport? This called for more
tact than he felt capable of mustering after a night journey.
Besides, he was handicapped by a qualm of memory: Walt's
words, yesterday, at the end of their meeting. "You used to
be good at finding the threads of a story, Bill. Never feel the
itch to get back to international politics again? No? Well, enjoy your trip. Call me as soon as you've talked with Vaugiroud." He had thought nothing of that casual question at the
time. Now, it had taken on more meaning. So had the Vaugiroud assignment. Was Walt Penneyman trying to make him
feel that itch again?"

"There's no place like it," Ballard was repeating.

"It has its points," Fenner agreed, his eyes following two
pretty girls for a brief but adequate moment. Two very pretty
girls, neatly cinched at the waist, dark hair piled high, slender legs under floating skirts.

Ballard said, "I'm old-fashioned in one thing: I still prefer
blondes. By the way, did you know your wife was living in
Paris?"

Fenner's step hesitated. Then he went in through the giant
doorway, past the elegant waiting rooms and the colonnades
and the elevators. Behind him, Ballard greeted someone in
the lobby, stopped to speak. Fenner had finished all the
usual routine at the reception desk before Ballard rejoined
him.

"Sorry about that," Ballard said awkwardly.

"I had no trouble. You laid it on well."

"About Sandra, I meant." There was no malice, only curiosity glancing out of his dark eyes. "I thought I'd better tip
you off, in case you ran into her."

"It wouldn't matter if I did. And," Fenner added pointedly,
"it is eight years since she was my wife." He moved toward
the elevators. "I may go bankrupt, but I'll do it in comfort,"
he said as he looked around him. Soft rugs underfoot, soft
air, soft voices. Deceptive. "Everyone looks so damned important. Are they?"

Ballard wasn't to be sidetracked. "You know, I've often
wondered why Sandra left America. I know it's none of my
business, but—"

"That's right," Fenner said with a quiet smile. "It was no
one's business. What about that coffee? And I need a shower
and a shave." But both elevator doors were now closed.

"Look"—Ballard was glancing at his watch—"do you mind
if I take a rain check? I've just met a man who has some

good contacts with the Quai d'Orsay. He's waiting for me."
He nodded toward a room near the entrance. "You know
how it is, Bill."

"That's all right. Thanks for delivering me intact."

"Use the office whenever you need it. I'll be back on Monday. And the Embassy is across the street"—the old smile
was back again—"just in case you need to take refuge."

"From a bomb, or Sandra?"

Ballard looked at him. "You don't have to worry about
Sandra. She has no hard feelings about you."

Wasn't that generous of her? "That's kind of her."

"No, believe me. I was at a party last night at her place—
she has a big apartment out on the Avenue d'Iéna, been living there for the last three years—"

"That's nice." Glutinous word, "nice," applicable all the
way from rice pudding to sun tans.

"She entertains a lot, you know. Not theater stuff—she's
given up the stage—only politicians, diplomats, a few journalists, that kind of thing—"

"Policy-making level," Fenner suggested. That sounded
like Sandra, all right. Poor Ballard, didn't he know what he
was getting into?

"Not quite," Ballard said modestly. "But an interesting
bunch." He dropped his voice. "She's the very good friend
of Fernand Lenoir."

"Is she?" And who was Monsieur Lenoir, who rated a
dropped voice? Fenner looked at the returning elevator. "I'd
better take this one," he said. "We can't keep the Quai
d'Orsay waiting, can we?"

Ballard held his arm, his voice hurrying. "Sandra and I
had a little talk last night. She had some pretty nice things to
say about you. In fact, she—"

"Now," Fenner remarked and freed his arm, "that really
is worrying news." Sandra at her sweetest was Sandra at her
most dangerous. "I'll call you," he told Ballard as he stepped
into the car. From the background, one of the assistant-
assistant room clerks, with Fenner's room key in his hand,
moved forward to join him.

"Any time," Ballard said, "any time at all, Bill." He
looked disappointed, as if he still had one more question to
ask. Or perhaps he was disappointed in Fenner, the man
who had never appreciated such a sweet and generous woman as Sandra Fane. The name, Fenner reflected as he came
out of the elevator and followed his guide through half a

mile of carpeted corridors, had been as bogus as her life, and
as carefully planned. He wondered how long Sandra had
stayed in Czechoslovakia? All of the five years between her
quiet exit from America and her descent on Paris? Perhaps
she had changed. People did. But Sandra?

The clerk hurried ahead of him with the key held ready,
an elderly maid with folded towels over her arm moved out
of a pantry to appraise the new arrival discreetly, a door
opened and a waiter pushed a breakfast cart into the corridor. A young woman followed it, calling back to someone
in the room, "All right, I'll have the sketches ready for you
by noon."

"No later, honey," a querulous female voice reminded her.

"No later," the girl said calmly. "Thanks for the breakfast." She closed the door, shaking her pretty blonde head,
almost blocked Fenner's path as she adjusted a large black
portfolio to fit more comfortably under her arm, said "Excuse me" in her charming voice, glanced at him with large
gray eyes, and walked quickly away toward the elevators. It
seemed unfair, Fenner thought, that anyone as young and
decorative as that should have to be so crisp and businesslike
at half past nine in the morning. A waste of natural resources.

His room was comfortable and handsome. There was not
much view—a side street, with some small cafés and shops
topped by two or three stories of nineteenth-century façade
now converted from private homes into offices and dress-
making work-rooms—but there was a shower, in a bathroom as large as his bedroom in New York. His suitcase and
weekend bag were placed on luggage racks; his raincoat was
already in one of the huge wardrobes. He tipped the elderly
porter, thanked the room clerk, locked the door, and began
throwing off his clothes. He ordered breakfast to be sent up
in half an hour, and felt pleasantly efficient. The shaving
lights were excellent. The shower worked. He even burst into
a brief aria from *Tosca*.

He breakfasted in the bathrobe the hotel had so obligingly provided, the warm air floating in from open French windows along with the grind and shriek of buses and cars. If
it hadn't been for them, he might have fallen into a pleasant
sleep: the beds were as soft as everything else in this hotel.
He opened his suitcase and began dressing. Fresh clothes
made a new man. He even decided he would call Professor
Vaugiroud and arrange an appointment for—well, not for this
morning; that was being too damned efficient. This after-

noon would give him time to collect Vaugiroud's remarks, simplify them into basic points, and cable them to Walt Penneyman. It was only the beginning of the day in New York right now. He had at least twelve hours before he need call Penneyman and tell him the information was on its way.

He lit a cigarette (the last one in this pack, he noted with a touch of annoyance), found the telephone number that Penneyman had given him, and got through to Vaugiroud with only reasonable delay. Professor Vaugiroud spoke good English, if a little impatiently. "Yes, yes," he said as soon as Fenner had identified himself. "I had a cable last night to tell me to expect you. Is Mr. Penneyman ill?"

"No. He just could not get away himself."

"I am sorry," Vaugiroud said with marked disappointment. "He was, too. Could I see you this afternoon?"

"Where?"

"Anywhere you like. And whenever it suits you."

Vaugiroud thawed a little. "Come to my apartment at four o'clock. You have my address."

"Yes."

"At four, then."

So that was that. Fenner looked thoughtfully at some of the other addresses in his notebook: most of them he would have to see toward the middle of September, when they were back at work in Paris. There were only three—one a director, another a playwright, one an assistant to the Minister of Cultural Affairs—whom he knew well enough to be able to visit even while they were on vacation. He had their invitations in that folder in his suitcase. He could reach them easily by telephone. No, he decided, today I relax and walk around Paris. I've got to find another hotel anyway, or else I'll have to cut my vacation to a week. For like most Americans abroad, well-dressed, educated, seemingly carefree millionaires from the land of giveaway, Fenner had to keep an eye on his traveler's checks.

He got out a map of Paris and tracked down Vaugiroud's address. It was across the Seine, not far from the Sorbonne, where Vaugiroud had once taught Philosophy. It would make a long, but pleasant, walk among some of his favorite streets. He might even revisit the bullet hole, unless they had plastered it over, although he had still seen it—and the other bullet holes from a Nazi sniper—on his last visit here, in '58. It wasn't every tourist who could look at a wall in Paris and say, "And that was the bullet that nearly got me." My first visit to Paris, he thought, just ten days before the Germans left. He looked around his elegant and peaceful room; and he shook his head slowly.

He rose to find another cigarette. There should be a couple, at least, left in the pack in his raincoat pocket. As his hand touched the coat, he had his first suspicion. He pulled the coat off its hanger, and the suspicion was a fact. It wasn't his.

There was no identification mark, not even the usual label at the back of the collar. He dug his hand into the deep pockets to find some scrap of information, but there were only two folded sheets of blank airmail paper, as if someone had meant to write a letter and never got around to it. And that was all.

He looked at the coat again—same color and same shape, but many raincoats were. Only the texture of the fabric was different. Hell and damnation, he thought, this takes care of my morning. I'll have to start telephoning around. Where do I begin? He stared angrily at the coat, at his shattered plans. One of those efficient prize packages who shuttled luggage in and out of this hotel must have mixed up—no, possibly not. It could have happened back at the airport, with that other efficient prize package of a porter. And Fenner's attention had been wandering; first, with the man who had collapsed; second, with Ballard's unexpected appearance; third, with Ballard's constant stream of questions; fourth, with talk of Sandra.

He cursed himself for an idiot, sighed wearily and telephoned the baggage porter downstairs.

Had any guest returned a wrongly delivered raincoat this morning? No one had.

Would the porter check and find out? The raincoat would have to belong to someone who had arrived or departed around half past nine.

The porter could tell him that right away. There had been several early departures this morning before eight o'clock, and some arrivals around ten o'clock. Only four people had had their luggage moved between nine-fifteen and nine-forty-five. One was Monsieur Fenner, the other three were ladies. He would investigate further if necessary.

"No need, thank you," Fenner said. He was sure in his own mind, now, that the coat had been picked up by mistake at the airport. He had put it down, after jamming the book back into its pocket—yes, that was the last time he had touched it.

The scene at the airport came back to him. The man next to him had had a raincoat, hadn't he? Yes, coming back from that abortive expedition for water, he had seen the man collapse and the coat fall with him. . . . There had been a coat thrown over his legs when they tucked him on the stretcher. So that's how it happened. . . .

He had better start calling Orly. He would probably have to use French, so he must get his story brief and clear. It would be better still to be able to use the man's name: that simplified all explanations. There must be some identification on the raincoat; people did not travel around without identification. Fenner searched the edge of the sleeves and the pockets. No label, no inked name on any part of their lining. But this time, as he thrust the blank folds of airmail paper back into its pocket, roughly, annoyance growing at every defeat, his knuckles felt something. There was a slight thickness between the pocket's loose lining and the heavier lining of the coat itself. A very slight thickness, of cloth possibly, from some hidden welt or seam. He pulled his hand out quickly, with exasperation at his own time-wasting. His impatience had added to the delay: a thread, loose in the pocket's lining, was snagged around the stem of his wrist watch. He tried to free his watch, but it was well caught. He tried to snap the thread, but it was strong, of nylon possibly: he would end by pulling off the stem of his watch. Cut it loose? Easier, in his annoyance, to try to break the thread at its other end in the pocket. It didn't belong to any seam, this thread; it had been drawn out of the lining material itself. So he tugged at it with a quick, firm snap. The thread ran along the lining for a good three inches, and the material parted in a neat line.

There you've done it, he told himself angrily. Then he looked in amazement at the two gaping lips of cloth. He hadn't pulled at a thread; he had opened a secret kind of zipper. His watch was still firmly trapped by the end of thread. With the coat over his arm, he went into the bathroom, found his small folding scissors in his shaving kit, and cut his watch free. After all that trouble, he felt he was owed a look at the secret pocket. Inside, tightly held in place with Scotch tape, was an envelope. It was unaddressed, opaque. There was something inside, not heavy, not bulky; smooth and firm.

Fenner walked back into the bedroom, threw the coat

on the nearer bed, and ripped the envelope open. He was angry and he was troubled. The incredible secrecy of the pocket was much too professional a job for a normal person to have planned. The man in the brown suit had been either a very clever criminal or a canny lunatic.

Fenner's first reaction was embarrassment. He never liked handling someone else's money. All that secrecy for a few dollar bills? He counted them—there were ten—thinking of the complications ahead of him. When he called Orly, he would have some explaining to do. Or would the currency-control people be interested? Ten bills of—he looked again, thinking his eyes had added zeros and a comma. My God, he said to himself. "My God," he said aloud. In his hands he held ten bills, each worth ten thousand dollars.

FOUR

FENNER RECOVERED from the shock. A hundred thousand dollars carried in a raincoat? Of all the crazy places—why not in a money belt hidden around a man's waist? Beyond that first reaction, he did not waste any time trying to fathom the implications of this puzzle for himself. There would be plenty, he knew. He wanted someone else to start on that, someone, too, who would take the ten monstrous bills safely into keeping. Even the thought of a hundred thousand dollars lying on his dressing table was more than disconcerting.

He put them out of sight in the envelope, replaced it in the coat (damn him for an idiot: why hadn't he kept his eyes glued on his luggage like some first-time-aboard tourist, and saved himself this trouble?), hung the coat in the wardrobe once more. He had better start telephoning Orly.

But would they believe him? They would begin by thinking that he was some kind of crank. Perhaps he had better take the coat all the way back to Orly. The idea depressed him. What a damned waste of time, what a— If only he knew someone at the Embassy—no, the Consulate: that was the right place to inquire about this, so that it could be handled for him by the proper people in the proper way. Besides, it would be easier on his temper to be able to explain in English. This was going to take a lot of explaining, he thought gloomily. Surely Mike Ballard knew someone at the Consulate, who'd know someone, who'd know ... The roundabout approach could be the quickest one.

So his first call was to the *Chronicle*'s Paris Office, which was a general headquarters for the collation and distillation of news reports gathered mostly from European sources. (It had been established just before the war, when suspicions were aroused that one of the big European news-gathering agencies had sold out to the Nazis. Today, with the wire serv-

ices doing a reliable job, it might have been disbanded, but
the *Chronicle* maintained it as possible insurance. Walt Penneyman had very firm ideas about news: he wanted not only
accuracy, but accuracy double-checked, with no opinion-mold-
ing additions or subtractions in the presentation of facts.)

But Mike Ballard was not in his office. His secretary was
French, and well trained. She was precise on all the information Fenner did not need, vague on the details he wanted.
Monsieur Ballard had already left to join his friends. They
were flying in a private plane. No, not from Orly. He would
not be back in Paris until Monday afternoon. He would telephone tomorrow and on Sunday, of course, to hear any urgent reports. Could she give Monsieur Ballard any message
from Monsieur Fennaire?

No, Monsieur Fennaire had no message. "But," Fenner
added quickly, "if he is calling for news reports, who is
collecting them?"

"His assistant, Monsieur Spitzaire."

"Spitzer?"

"But yes. André Spitzaire. You would like to talk with
him?"

"But yes."

André Spitzer was French, too, and a sharp journalist. It
was something of a triumph, Fenner reflected as he put down
the receiver, to have managed to extract a name that might
be able to help (or advise, at least) without having actually
satisfied Mr. Spitzer's probing curiosity. Fenner had begun by
explaining that he wanted someone at the Consulate who
could deal with a problem involving an American citizen and
French currency regulations. Oh, nothing serious, but urgent.
No, no, nothing to do with any black market—did the Consulate have a specialist in that, too? (Laughter on the phone.)
Yes, he wanted a specialist in French currency regulations,
currency control. Oh, not currency control at any particular
place, just currency control.

It was only then that Spitzer admitted he didn't know anyone, personally, at the American Consulate. He could, of
course, make inquiries, and let Mr. Fenner know in half an
hour? If Mr. Fenner could be more explicit, it would be
much easier . . .

Fenner resisted the reply that he could make inquiries, too.
"Does Ballard know anyone at the Consulate?" A name is
what I need, he kept telling himself, just a name I can reach
directly without having to explain all the way up, from infor-

mation clerks to secretaries to assistants of assistants. A hundred thousand dollars brought so secretively into France was not exactly his idea of telephone conversation.

"No, only at the Embassy."

"Who?"

"Well, there's a press officer named Dade, Stanfield Dade. And there's—"

"That will do. Thank you. Thanks a lot."

Stanfield Dade. He remembered the name. He remembered its owner from the days when Dade used to haunt the long corridors at the U.N. A tall young man, thin, with glasses and a Haavad Yaad accent? That was eight years ago. Would he remember him? Anyway, remembered or unremembered, Fenner had the name he needed.

Stanfield Dade was eventually tracked to his desk. There was someone with him, for Fenner heard background voices as Dade came onto the phone with a sharp "Who is this?" Fenner was terse and urgent. He identified himself, didn't pause when Dade said in better mood, "Oh yes. And how are you?" but rushed on with his story. Dade kept saying, "Yes, yes," with growing impatience, until Fenner reached the final discovery. "Money? In an envelope? Was it much?" Dade was jolted into attention.

"I'd say yes." It would keep me comfortably alive for at least ten years, Fenner thought wryly, but then, I don't play in the Miami-Vegas circuit.

"Well—" Dade was bemused. He paused. "I was going to suggest that you contact the Consulate, but—" He paused again. "And this envelope was really well hidden?"

"Definitely."

Dade turned his head away, spoke to someone, muffling the receiver as he began, "It's very odd, you know—" Soon he was back again with Fenner. "What did this fellow look like?"

Fenner described the brown suit again.

"He arrived at Orly just after eight this morning?"

"That's right." What goes on here? Fenner wondered.

"Please hang on." The line became silent, with Dade's hand completely smothering the receiver this time. Fenner waited patiently, but gloom and annoyance mounted: this was one hell of a way to spend his first morning in Paris. Then Dade was on the line again. He sounded soothing, like a family doctor who feels his first job is to get the patient calmed down. "Fenner, there's someone here who may be able to advise you. He knows more about this kind of thing than I do. Half a second—"

A stranger's voice spoke from Dade's office; a quiet Midwestern voice, possibly competent. "Mr. Fenner? You have a problem, I hear. I think, as far as you are concerned, it is mostly with the Lost and Found at Orly. And there isn't much the Consulate could do about any American taking currency out of the U.S. There are no restrictions on that. How much did you say the amount was, again?" The voice was so innocent.

Fenner half smiled. He was beginning to feel really assured about the competence of the unemotional voice. "Too much to be carried in dollar bills. A bank transfer would have been simpler."

"It's in an envelope?" The voice was slightly incredulous.

"It's in an envelope."

"Do you think you could drop over here for a few minutes? Bring everything. Ask for Dade's office."

"Yes, I could do that. I'd feel better, though, if I could hire a Brink's truck to get me across the street."

There was a short silence. "In that case, I'll come over and see you in your room. Let's say around noon?"

"I'll be here. Whom do I expect?"

"Someone who is five feet eight, hair light, eyes blue; gray suit, brown tie and shoes. The name is Carlson. Okay?"

"Fine." Fenner grinned. "I'll keep my door barred and bolted." He heard Carlson laugh. "And could you have someone contact Orly? I really would like to get my own coat back."

"We'll make a try," Carlson said. "See you!"

A cheerful type, Fenner thought with relief. And careful. He arrived exactly at twelve o'clock, too. His manner matched his voice, but Fenner had a feeling that he had been examined, classified, and catalogued all in the time that Carlson shook hands, walked briskly into the room, said "Let's get rid of this" as he pushed the breakfast cart into the corridor, and locked the door. He didn't waste a gesture or a word. He took a chair with its back turned to the windows, so that Fenner faced the light. He might be around forty, Fenner decided, and added a few notes of his own to Carlson's description of himself. Medium height, but solidly constructed. Fair hair, thinning away from a high brow. Blue eyes, pale, certainly clever, but highly amused at this moment.

Clothes not expensive, but quiet and neat; the brown shoes good, expertly polished, no high gloss, just the rich gleam of carefully honed leather.

"Doubtful of me?" Carlson asked. He sat easily in his chair, one ankle over the other knee.

"Just curious. You look more like an ex-Marine than State Department."

"I'm neither." Carlson looked at him with disarming frankness. "I'm attached to NATO. Just spending a few weeks in Paris." He hesitated briefly. "My job is Security."

"No official connection with the Embassy?" Fenner asked, worriedly. He wanted someone who could take responsibility, start things moving.

"Oh, the Embassy has given me a temporary corner in someone else's office. You could say that I am attached there. Meanwhile. On a special assignment from NATO." Carlson grinned. "Not specific enough? All right. I go around making sure that everyone has burned the trash in his wastebasket. Just a general errand boy and go-between. Is that better?"

I'll settle for that, Fenner decided. A lot of going-between may be necessary before the problem of this coat is solved. So he pulled it out of the wardrobe, and handed it over. "I hope you are also a puzzle-solver. Frankly, the only reason I can see for carrying a lot of money in a raincoat would be to hand it over to someone else in a public place, easily and quietly."

Carlson let that pass. He studied the coat. "When did you first realize this coat wasn't yours?"

"About twenty of eleven, when I went searching for a cigarette."

Carlson nodded, as if he found that reasonable, and fished out his pack of cigarettes for Fenner. He tossed it over. "Keep them. PX rates. I can afford to be lordly. And when did you discover the envelope?" Carlson was drawing out the two blank sheets of airmail paper.

"I think they're a blind," Fenner suggested. "If anyone was making a quick search, these sheets would distract his attention from the secret pocket—it's just underneath—"

Carlson looked at him, raised an eyebrow. "When did you say you discovered the envelope?"

"Later. You see, when I found the coat wasn't mine, I checked with the porter's desk downstairs. No dice. I thought I'd telephone Orly, and I started searching for some clue to the owner. My watch caught on a thread inside that pocket. I pulled. It held. And—well, I wrenched at it."

"Forceful." Carlson examined the opening that had come apart with the wrenched thread. He ran his finger along its edge; his eyes were thoughtful. "That was just about eleven?" he asked casually.

"Five minutes past, to be exact."

"And you called Stanfield Dade at eleven-twenty-five."

Fenner couldn't help admiring the technique. He explained what happened in that gap of time.

"So that's how you got Stan's name—from Spitzer?" Carlson was amused. "He was sure you had remembered him. Set him up for the day." He had taken out the envelope from the concealed pocket, and looked at its ripped flap. "You were getting madder by the minute, I see." He nodded as if he sympathized thoroughly. "What did you tell Spitzer, by the way?"

"Nothing about the envelope. Or the coat."

"Congratulations. Spitzer likes to know." And then, at last, Carlson drew out the ten bills. His eyes opened wide; his face muscles froze.

"I was waiting for that moment," Fenner said with a wide grin.

"Did it come up to expectations?" Carlson picked up one of the bills. "I've heard of them, but these are the first I've seen. Queer feeling, isn't it, to handle a year's pay in one small piece of paper?"

Fenner pointed his cigarette at the bill's engraved portrait. "Who was Chase? If Washington is on a one-dollar bill, Lincoln on a five, Hamilton on a ten—you really are slipping down the ladder if your head is only worth ten thousand."

"Salmon Portland Chase," Carlson said crisply as he replaced bills and envelope in their hiding place. "Civil War Secretary of the Treasury, and a good one. He had a bankrupt country to prop up." But he was thinking of something else. "May I use your phone?"

He called Dade. "Definitely interesting. And very professional," he reported. "Yes, I think the Embassy should take charge until we can find out more. . . . No, no, it isn't consulate business: our American citizen here isn't in any trouble." He grinned across the room at Fenner. "Don't worry. I'll take the responsibility. After all, the brown suit may tie in with what Rosie told me this morning. You just alert the Treasury boys and Rosie. Do that for me, will you? Tell them I want to see them right away. . . . In your office, why not? Just say we borrowed it. I don't give a damn where we meet as long as it's as soon as possible. . . . Sure, tip off the French if that makes you feel better: get Bernard; he doesn't think all Americans are morons. . . . Fine. Do that now, will you? And save time. Yes, we'll be with you soon. The quicker we get this little package back onto U.S. territory, the happier I'll be. I've got a feeling it should never have left there." He glanced over at Fenner, who was staring at the raincoat as if he could strangle it. "By the way, did you get any reply from my call to Orly?" He listened intently. The news did not please him. "In that case, telephone Bernard first of all. We'll need him." He ended the call.

"Well?" Fenner demanded.

"No coat at Orly. The man took it with him."

"He *left?*"

Carlson nodded. "Nothing is ever made easy for us, is it? I thought we had him nicely wrapped up in bed. But no, he recovered enough to refuse to be sent to any hospital. He rested for almost an hour, and then wandered off, declining all help except for a porter. Last seen following the exit arrows."

"He's crazy. He'll be dead within a week."

"Perhaps that doesn't matter so much as his job," Carlson said softly. He seemed very far away from this green-and-golden room.

"Is it as important as all that?"

Carlson's frown deepened.

"So he didn't notice the exchange? Damnation, I was hoping he would."

Carlson said, "He's too smart not to notice. But he wouldn't ditch your coat. He needs it to find out who you are. Once that's done, he will find out where you are. He wants his own coat back, intact."

"That's going to be difficult." Fenner took a deep breath. "How do you get me off this hook?"

"That's why I'm standing here, wasting time," Carlson said sharply. "The process is known as creative thought."

"He's a sick man," Fenner suggested. "He is in no shape to play detective."

"His friends may be in very good shape."

"If it's any aid to your attack of thought, there's no address in my coat. No telephone numbers. No notebook."

"No name?"

"My initials. And the maker's name, of course. Nothing in

the pockets except cigarettes and a lightweight edition of a Molière play with some notes I was making in the margins. I'm hoping to see a production of it in Avignon. But none of that would tell very much." He looked at Carlson hopefully.

"It tells something. An American who is interested in the French theater. . . . One inquiry at Orly, with a good excuse behind it, will soon add a name to your initials. It isn't a totally unknown name, either. They could find it in one of the *Who's Who* series in any reference library. Next step, the *Chronicle* office. And so—to here."

"A bit awkward for me," Fenner admitted. He liked the idea less and less. "Let's hope he's working alone, with no one to run errands for him."

Carlson's eyes measured Fenner. "I'm going to give it to you straight. If he is alone, he will hire some help. You're in for trouble, friend, unless—" His eyes brightened. He picked up the coat and handed it to Fenner. "On your way out, you are going to stop at the porter's desk to pick up your passport. Tell him not to worry about your lost coat—"

"Like hell he is."

"Because it must be at Orly. So you're taking the wrong coat back and getting your own."

"I can answer that one: he will offer to send a boy out to Orly."

"You have to identify it, haven't you? And be identified? That's why you want your passport. It fits, doesn't it?"

"It fits," Fenner had to admit. "But supposing this fellow and his friends or his hired help go chasing out to Orly?"

"They will. So we'll get the coat out there, after we have finished with it."

"It won't be exactly as they expect to find it. What then?"

"At Orly, they will learn that the Sûreté arrived and confiscated the coat. My friend Bernard is very adept at arranging that kind of thing. In fact, I think he would like one of them to go chasing out to Orly. That would give his boys someone to follow."

Carlson opened the door. "I know it isn't brilliant," he said as Fenner still hesitated, "but can you think of anything better to get them off your back?"

Fenner couldn't.

"Well, what's worrying you?"

"The scene at the porter's desk. I'm no actor." I'll play it loose, keep it brief, he decided. Perhaps the porter will fall for my story.

"You'll do all right," Carlson told him. "Just use the Method."

The baggage porter accepted Fenner's offhand remarks with the impassive, drooped eyelids of a man who saw no other sensible course. Carlson was at Fenner's elbow. "Come on, Bill, we'll never make that lunch date," he was saying with all the sharpness that a very old friend, almost family, could be allowed. "Yes, we'll need a taxi," he told one of the doormen, "for Orly."

As they stood on the sidewalk, a girl came out of the hotel. *The* girl, Fenner saw. She was now wearing a gray linen dress, straight, sleeveless, and simple. Her hands, in short white gloves, were carrying her large black portfolio. She glanced at the two men and looked away, far far away, across the stretch of traffic toward the trees of the Champs-Elysées. "Punctual as well as pretty," Fenner observed. "She had her sketches all finished by noon, I see."

"You know her?"

Fenner shook his head. "Should we offer her this taxi? Better still, share it?" He grinned at the nervous look in Carlson's eyes, and climbed into the cab as the doorman announced their destination to the driver, and the driver announced in turn that he would have to make a detour— one-way streets and don't blame me. He repeated his self-clearance in basic English. A cautious man, this Frenchman, with not much trust in foreigners' comprehension.

"Then detour around by the Faubourg-Saint-Honoré," Carlson said. His French was fluent and authoritative, even if the accent was still Midwest. "I have to buy some shaving cream." He glanced back at the girl. "For a moment, I thought you meant it," he told Fenner.

"I did, but this isn't the day for it." In fact, this wasn't his day at all. "I've got an appointment at four. Unpostponable. If I miss it, I'll never get another." That much he could tell from Vaugiroud's voice on the telephone.

"You'll get there," Carlson promised. They had traveled about five hundred yards, and were now in a narrow street with smart shops. The driver was slowing up in front of an English apothecary, and looked around for approval.

"Fine," Carlson said, paid the man, overtipping handsomely to calm his grumbles about their change in plans. Their visit to the shop was brief. After that, they retraced their route, nicely mingling in the lunch-time stroll of clerks and salesgirls, until they had almost reached the Embassy grounds. "The side entrance is easier," Carlson said, and guided Fenner expertly, quickly. "This won't take long. Just tell your story. Play it straight down the middle. Keep out the jokes. Sign it, and that's that. No sweat."

"It won't take long?" Fenner asked blandly.

"Not for you. You'll be out of all this in an hour."

"In one way, I'm sorry. I've got my feet wet, and the water looks inviting."

"You're an ungrateful son of a gun," Carlson said with a broad smile. "I've been spending the last half hour scrubbing you clean. Stay clean, dammit. Don't waste Auntie's efforts."

FIVE

CARLSON'S EFFORTS were certainly impressive. Fenner had a small, quiet room to himself, with old acquaintance Dade keeping so much in the background that he was practically a crack in the plaster. There was a stenotypist tapping noiselessly on a small machine that obediently sucked in every syllable and spewed out a continuous sheet of paper covered with compressed symbols. It was a magic palaver, Fenner thought, fascinated by its speed. Sometimes it seemed as if the machine were even ahead of him. "Beats Indian sign language, any day," he observed to Dade when the stenotypist left to have fair copies made. Dade smiled faintly. Perhaps he was hungry. Perhaps he wished he could have been in the other room, where four sedate and thoughtful men had gathered. "This will soon be over," Fenner reassured him.

"You know," Dade said with some reproach, "this is not really my line."

"Sorry, but I didn't know anyone else to call around here."

"Oh, that's all right. It has been a devil of a day. Carlson has been digging into my files all morning, my chief is still on vacation, and now this envelope business. Haven't got one stroke of my own work done."

Fenner commiserated with him, tactfully. Dade might really be upset if you took his crying-towel away from him. Fenner made a mental note—he did this periodically in order to tighten up the weak strands in his own character, of which, he was convinced, he had too damn many—never to complain aloud, never to enjoy complaining. "How's the family?" he tried. Everyone had a family, except him.

That launched Dade. He was talking quite happily about German measles and French poodles when the stenotypist

45

returned. He and Fenner read over the copy of the statement (Dade caught a misplaced comma), and Fenner signed.

"All clear?" Fenner asked. "Thanks a lot, Dade."

"We must have lunch someday."

"We must do that." Fenner opened the door and almost walked into a heavy-set, dark-haired man with a beaming smile.

"Just got you in time," the newcomer said. "Hi, Stan!"

Dade said with marked coldness, "Hello, Rosie!" but whether it was for the form of greeting or for Rosie, Fenner couldn't quite guess. "Did you receive my earlier message to you, this morning?"

"Sure, sure. Don't fret. I'll listen to her if she calls me. What's her name?"

"I didn't get it," Dade said stiffly.

Rosie looked hard at him. He turned to Fenner. "For you," he said, "I bring good news." He handed over a slip of paper. "Don't wait for us, Stan. We'll show each other out."

Stanfield Dade and the stenotypist left. "So he didn't get the name," Rosie said pleasantly as the door closed behind them. "Well, that's one way of keeping yourself clean. Cautious son of a." Rosie was amused by some thoughts of his own.

The note, which Fenner was reading, was equally cheerful. *Coat problem solved. Told you, didn't I? Auntie.*

"I'm Frank Rosenfeld," the dark-haired man said. "Can you talk to me for two minutes? Then I'll conduct you to the street. Quietly. No use disturbing the masterminds at the front gate: what never came in can't go out." He observed Fenner looking at him. "Carlson warned me that you're curious. All right, I'll tell you and save time. I don't belong here at all. I come from the big bad world of outside, and Dade doesn't approve of me or it."

"On special assignment from NATO, too?" Fenner tried.

"Do I look like a military type?"

He did not. "Then you are CIA?" persisted Fenner. He wanted to know exactly who was going to talk with him for those two minutes.

There was a slight inclination of Rosenfeld's head, but no direct answer. His smile broadened, splitting his face into two camps: below, was a rounded jaw line, a full underlip, a chin with a marked cleft; above, was a sharp nose, clever brown eyes, a remarkable brow. He said crisply, "I've read your statement. My particular interest is Mr. Goldsmith—the little man in the brown suit. Describe him as exactly as you can. Take your time to remember. Exactly."

Fenner did all that.

"Good. That tallies." He offered Fenner a cigarette, lit it for him. He seemed to be making up his mind. "Let me explain a little," he said at last. "I had word from New York last night about Mr. Goldsmith. So this morning, bright and early, I had someone out at Orly, just to keep Mr. Goldsmith in sight. But he didn't show. My friend waited for almost an hour. He made some tactful inquiries, and heard that our man was ill, would probably be taken to a hospital. He telephoned me. By the time he got back to the first-aid station, Mr. Goldsmith had walked out. My friend was too far away to catch up or get the taxi number. But he did see that there was someone helping Mr. Goldsmith into the cab. I'm telling you about this slip-up for one reason. Did you see, among the people waiting to welcome their friends in the entrance hall at Orly, a man with white hair and a yellow tie?"

Fenner thought back. "Yes."

"Close enough to describe him?"

Fenner considered. "In a way. I wasn't looking much at him—I was trying to get my porter's attention. I remember thinking he was a pretty cool character, not easily jolted or startled. That was strange, come to think of it. He looked like a painter, or a poet. An amateur artist with some money of his own—you know the type."

"I know the color of his clothes—blue shirt, yellow tie, gray suit. And that they looked fairly expensive. And that his white hair was long. But what about his eyes, features, complexion?"

"Eyes blue; features blunt and blob-shaped; complexion very sallow."

"Are you sure?" Rosenfeld was dubious of the quick answer.

"I remember saying to myself, 'Well there's a chap who not only matched his shirt to his eyes, but his face to his tie.' Then I didn't give him another thought."

Rosenfeld was amused. "Just one more question: what is blob-shaped?"

"Sort of—well, a pin-cushion effect. The opposite of taut, tightly drawn. Sponge under the skin instead of bone."

"Thanks. I get the picture. Where did you learn to use your eyes?"

"It's my trade. When I sit in a theater, I have to look as well as listen. But tell me—this character in the yellow tie, why does he interest you? Was he the friend who helped Goldsmith into a taxi? That's not in the tradition, is it?"

"Tradition?" Rosenfeld's eyes opened in bland astonishment.

"If he was waiting to contact Goldsmith, they should never have seemed to meet at all. At least, that's the way I thought those things were worked."

"You go to a lot of movies, too, I see."

"How to be successful in espionage without really trying —just break the accepted patterns?"

"Not funny, my friend. And who said this had anything to do with espionage?"

"Are there other forms of international understanding?" Fenner asked with mock innocence.

Rosenfeld smiled amiably.

Surely the two minutes are almost up, Fenner thought. If he left now, he could have a decent lunch before he saw Vaugiroud. He looked at his watch, and rose. Rosenfeld made no move. Fenner tried some sympathetic talk to ease old Rosie toward the street. "I don't think you should feel too upset about losing Goldsmith. The mistake was in New York."

"Oh?"

"Why did they let him leave? Easier for everyone if they had stopped him at Idlewild."

"On what grounds?"

"They don't know what his business is?"

"No."

"But surely they must know who he is, what he is?"

"Not even that."

"In that case, why alert you to keep an eye on him?"

"Well," said Rosie, with his sharp brown eyes gleaming, "you know how stupid we all are."

Fenner smiled. "That must be the explanation."

Rosenfeld offered him another cigarette. "Since I've answered your questions—well, some of them at least, didn't I?"

Fenner nodded and took the cigarette.

"I'd like you to answer a few of mine," Rosenfeld ended. "Fair enough?"

"If I can answer them."

"Sit down. This will only take a couple of minutes. Did you ever hear of a man called Bruno?"

"Bruno what?"

"Just Bruno."

Fenner shook his head.

"Or of a man called Geoffrey Wills?"

"No."

"Who sometimes used the name of George Williston?"

Fenner's eyes went cold.

"He was a very close friend of your wife's ten years ago." Rosenfeld was lighting his cigarette carefully. "In fact, they both belonged to the same group."

"I was in Korea," Fenner said. "She had many friends I knew nothing about."

"But you did meet Williston?"

"For five minutes, one night. I had the pleasure of throwing him out of my apartment. Him and three others."

Rosenfeld raised an eyebrow.

"Not physically. I just told them pretty forcibly to get out, and stay out."

"Why?"

"Not my type," Fenner said briefly. "A man has the right to decide who is to be invited into his home and who is not. Hasn't he? That's one freedom of choice that hasn't been taken away from us yet."

"A Constitutional right," Rosenfeld agreed. He rose and paced around the small bleak room, as if he were marshaling his thoughts with each even step. "The next question—I hope you'll answer it—did you come to Paris to see Sandra Fane?"

"I didn't even know she was here until Ballard told me this morning."

"Sorry—I just thought—well, after all, there isn't much going on in the theater here at present."

"People connected with the theater are still going on," Fenner reminded him angrily. He mastered his irritation. "I haven't seen Sandra since the night I told Williston to leave."

"Were they having a meeting of some kind in your apartment?"

So Rosenfeld knew about Sandra; more, probably, than I do, Fenner thought. "You might call it that."

"With *you* around?" Rosenfeld was amazed.

"I was supposed to be covering one of those late-night emergency sessions at the U.N.—I had just got back, the week before, from Korea—but I went home at ten o'clock. I felt I was coming down with an attack of grippe. And the emergency session was getting nowhere—" He halted. He was remembering the long dark hall of the apartment, the sound of subdued voices from the living room at its far end. He was standing there pulling off his coat, cursing the idea of a party and people to face, feeling the ache in his bones and his tight throat, wondering if he could slip unnoticed into the bedroom and fall asleep. He needed Scotch and aspirin. He went to get them, quietly, just outside the living-room door. There was one voice speaking, clear, authoritative. My God, he thought, ready to laugh, someone's giving an imitation as his parlor trick; Sandra has developed a strange taste in entertainment since I've been away. But the parlor trick went on and on. My God, he thought, no longer ready to laugh, and what's this about germ warfare, what's this about arranging protests and demonstrations? The voice ended its instructions, and it was Sandra who was talking the same vicious nonsense, with a seriousness, an intensity he had never heard before. He came out of his trance. He could see, even now, the startled faces staring at him in the doorway; and Sandra, reverting automatically from the agitprop activist into the fluttering hostess. "Darling, but how wonderful! You're just in time to hear us read Act Three of George's new play. George Williston—my husband. And this is Jenny— Why, Bill, Bill! Bill, these are my friends, will you shut up?" The sweet hostess words had ended in a shout of anger, but he finished what he had to say. And so began the Grand Exit. Followed by the Great Quarrel. That lasted until three in the morning. It was more than a quarrel: it was, in the unguarded heat of Sandra's anger, a revelation.

And then he had left, his body shivering with fever, head throbbing, heart sick. He spent one day in a hotel, four days in a hospital. When he returned to the apartment to pick up his clothes, it was empty. Sandra had gone. On orders, he thought bitterly, like everything else in her well-controlled career. He had been a useful name to cover her real life; he had become a positive handicap, perhaps even a possible danger.

"Well," Fenner said, "I suppose we have all been fooled one way or another at one time." He mustered a smile. "Yes, I've met George Williston."

"He was in Paris last April for a very brief visit," Rosenfeld said smoothly. "He met Mrs. Fane—that's what she calls herself, these days—at a café over on the Left Bank. It could have been an innocent meeting, from Mrs. Fane's point of view. Perhaps he was trying to pull her back into her old life again; perhaps she was refusing, and chose to meet him far away from the Avenue d'Iéna to save herself embarrassment. The truth is, she's a question mark. She's been living a perfectly normal life since her escape from Czechoslovakia." If, Rosenfeld added to himself, being the mistress of a French government official with private means and a wide circle of friends could be called a normal way to live.

Fenner said nothing. Not even the use of the word "escape" had aroused his interest. He looked at his watch.

"But Williston is no question mark. He hasn't changed his aim in life. So that is what makes the meeting with Mrs. Fane important. Was it real business or was it only an attempt at business that failed? The answer is essential, because of her —of her influence over a certain Monsieur Fernand Lenoir. He's an important guy."

"Another blind idiot?"

Rosenfeld looked nonplussed. But he wasn't defeated. "Won't you even think of accepting her invitation?"

"What?"

"She sent you one last night, by way of Ballard. Didn't he pass it on?"

"He never got the chance. I cut him off when he started talking about Sandra." There was complete disbelief in Fenner's eyes. "She'd never invite me—"

"But she did. Stanfield Dade was there at the time. She was talking to Ballard and him. About you."

"Then she's just using me again." The words had slipped out. He cursed himself under his breath.

"Perhaps. Perhaps not. There's one way we could find out. That would answer the question about her meeting with Williston, too."

Fenner stared at him. "I hope you are not meaning—"

"I'm meaning this. People who reform have anguish and remorse. Right? They feel better if they can give an honest apology to those they have hurt the most. Right? She would talk to you, more than she would talk to anyone else. She would feel she owes you that. Why don't you see her?"

"No."

"But you could be doing her a good turn."

"I'm doing her no kind of turn, either good or bad."

"Look, she proposed seeing you. Why don't you—"

"No," said Fenner quietly. "And no, and no." If Sandra had wanted to see him, it was more likely for quite another reason: she could very well want to gauge how safe she was with him in Paris. She was a much more devious and intricate character than Rosenfeld imagined.

Rosenfeld was saying, "Oh well, it was worth a try. But I'm still curious why she talked about you to Ballard. Either she wants to say she's sorry—she was the reason you ended your career as a news correspondent, wasn't she?"

Fenner studied the leaves in the garden outside. Some were beginning to shrivel at the edges into the first hint of autumn.

"Or," Rosenfeld went on, "she wants to know where you stand. You could do her a lot of damage. Not many people know her history; and you know her better than they do." He noticed the look in Fenner's eyes. "Yes?"

"Oh, just making a mental apology. You're a smart boy."

"Sometimes not smart enough." Rosenfeld wished he had never brought up the subject of Sandra Fane. "Well, let's go. Thanks for the two minutes. They stretched a little. I'm sorry." He paused with his hand on the doorknob. "How's your memory, by the way?"

"At times, it can be very bad. I just can't remember a thing you were talking about. How's that?"

"That's fine." Rosenfeld opened the door. "I'll escort you across the frontier. When you reach France, turn right. You'll be back at the Crillon Bar in no time."

At the side gate, Fenner looked at his watch and decided he would have to settle for a short lunch, after all. He had lost his appetite, anyway. He said good-by to Rosenfeld. They went separate ways.

Fenner crossed a busy narrow street to a small café with a red-striped awning. He was thinking gloomily that the past was never over. As long as you lived, you carried it with you. It shaped your life: what you were, today, depended on all you had seen and felt and heard yesterday; and what you now accepted or rejected would mold your tomorrow. We are, because of what we were.... Shall we be, because of what we are?

Let's try some will power, he told himself, and blot out the ghosts that came rising up this morning. It has worked before, giving long stretches of blessed anesthesia. No good in remembering the hurt and the misery and the damage that was done you: that only nurses your bitterness, and you inflict hurt and misery and damage on yourself. Just remember enough never to be vulnerable again: total forgetting could be as self-destructive as complete remembering.

He settled at a small zinc table outside the café. He disregarded the traffic, the heat, the arms brushing past, the unsuccessful sandwich and the bitter coffee. Will power, he reminded himself wryly, was sometimes necessary for the present as well as for the past. But a small cluster of typists from the Embassy turned his mood. They were young and pretty, trying to be chic and worldly. Their chatter held pleasant no-meaning, more amusing, actually, than most first acts he had sat through this last season. Their laughter won. The traffic became friendly bustle, the heat was tempered by a small breeze, the passing faces were varied and intelligent, the second cup of coffee tasted better. Patient coming out of shock, he told himself almost cheerfully, and could smile. He would sit here and enjoy the Paris sun until it was time to move toward the Left Bank and Professor Vaugiroud.

Only a few streets away from Fenner, in a small restaurant without any outside tables, Neill Carlson was having his third cup of coffee. The place was almost empty: the customers, mostly Frenchmen, had been leaving steadily for the last half hour. He finished reading *Figaro*, slung it back on its hook on the brown paneled wall, took down *Combat*. As he was returning to his isolated table, Frank Rosenfeld joined him.

"About time," Carlson said. "Another five minutes, and I'd have to leave."

"Went back to the office," Rosenfeld explained. "I got a face-to-face description of yellow-tie that was worth sending out."

"So?" Carlson was curious.

"But that was about all I got from Fenner." Rosenfeld broke into a description of his mother-in-law's visit to Paris in July as the waiter approached for his order. An omelet and coffee, Rosenfeld decided.

"You didn't do so well?" Carlson asked when they were left alone again.

"I don't know."

Carlson looked puzzled. "He didn't strike me as an evasive type."

"He wasn't. He answered my questions. And he had a few of his own." Rosenfeld grinned. "Wanted to know if yellow-tie was the friend who had helped Goldsmith into a cab."

"Reasonable deduction, seeing you were asking questions about yellow-tie."

"Then he suggested their meeting wasn't in the tradition, was it?"

"Well, he's a critic. They like to cast doubts."

"He's a bit of a comedian, too. Suggested how to be successful in espionage without really trying."

"How?"

"Just break the accepted patterns."

Carlson laughed. "He might have something there."

"Yes," Rosenfeld admitted. "That open contact and departure was a bit startling. I was beginning to wonder, this early morning, if Goldsmith wasn't just a harmless soul being met by a patient friend. Kind of comic, when you think of it."

"Not for Mr. Goldsmith. It must have been a quick and agonizing reappraisal on his part. He couldn't pass on the wrong coat. Contact needed for explanation, and some reorganization."

"That's what worries me. This business must be pretty important to make him act with such speed. He's a sick man."

"No ideas as yet?"

"Just speculations. And you?"

"Just speculations. Give us all time, Rosie."

"Do we have it to give?"

"Well, the other side is stymied, too, meanwhile. How do they replace those ten bills? It must have taken them weeks to collect them, using carefully chosen people to ask for them at their banks. The Treasury boys can trace them: the banks make a note of that kind of transaction."

"Glad to hear someone can get results."

"You've made a start yourself. You've got an adequate picture of yellow-tie. Bernard's files over at the Sûreté may be of help on that—they're pretty complete on the Communist underground."

"If Bernard will co-operate."

"He smells another of those one-for-all-and-all-for-one situations. Sure, old Bernie will co-operate."

"At least," Rosie said, "I made certain that yellow-tie isn't going to be forgotten by Fenner."

"You think he may be in danger?"

"If this business is as urgent and important as I feel it is, anyone involved is in danger."

"He's back to his own life again, seeing his friends in Paris, going to theatrical parties, talking about Molière and Anouilh and Beckett. His involvement is over."

"Certainly," Rosenfeld said, "he isn't going to let himself be involved with Madame Fane."

"Your suggestion fell flat?"

Rosenfeld saw his waiter approaching. "Flatter than a jalopy's tire running on its rim." He began talking about the Grand Canyon's pitted walls. The omelet was served, and the waiter left, surrounded by Hopi Indians taking refuge in the canyon's holes from a Navajo raiding party striking across the Painted Desert.

"So," Carlson said, "he just clammed up when you started probing?"

"About her, yes. He did say he had met Comrade Bruno. Not as Bruno. Nor as Geoffrey Wills. George Williston was the name he used on the night Fenner threw him out of the apartment."

"Dear old Bruno-Wills-Williston," Carlson murmured, "what would you do without him to lead you to such interesting people?"

Rosenfeld laughed. "You know, that's one question Fenner forgot to ask: why didn't we nail Williston if we knew he was such a bastard? But I agree with you; he has his uses."

"New York will be preening itself on following that hunch. Bruno suddenly turned aesthete, visiting the Museum of Modern Art, standing a long time in front of *Guernica*, very close to a quiet man. Meaning? Nothing. Quiet man unknown, innocent visitor; Bruno just an admirer of Picasso. But next day Bruno turns animal lover, walks in Zoo, seems to be keeping friendly watch. On whom? Same quiet man. Quiet man now interesting. Becomes more interesting when he jigs around town, takes three taxis to get to his hotel from a dentist's office only a few blocks away." He noticed Rosenfeld's deep gloom. "Didn't I get your story right?"

"You tell it better than I do," Rosenfeld said sourly.

"All is not lost, Rosie. After all—"

Rosenfeld said, "Yes, they had a good hunch in New York. They tipped us off. And we missed." He pushed his plate aside. "Never thought a French omelet could taste like a piece of flannel."

"After all," Carlson persisted, "the man wasn't half so interesting as the envelope he carried. And you've got that, Rosie, my boy."

"Through pure luck. Where's the credit?"

"Everything is luck and unluck. We get the credit when we

use them properly. The only thing we can't deal with is the bullet that flattens us out. Stone dead hath no fellow."

Rosenfeld's brooding face looked up. He almost smiled.

"What would you rather have? Someone tailing the puzzling Mr. Goldsmith all over Paris? Or the envelope in good hands?" He had Rosie's frown ironing out. "Well—your little ray of sunshine is about to depart and tend to his own business. Sometimes I wish I were back in West Berlin. Bloomers are made there, all the time, but no one has to be cheered up."

"I see your British contacts in West Berlin have enlarged your vocabulary, anyway. Yes"—Rosenfeld brightened visibly—"that was a real fast-blooming bloomer about the Wall. There ought to have been advance notice on that. Why not, I wonder?"

"It was left lying in someone's in-tray too long," Carlson suggested. He wasn't so amused, but he had old Rosie back to normal.

"They missed you, I guess. When do you return?"

"Soon."

"Oh, you've got everything sewed up on your film producer?"

"Yes and no. I've found out a lot. But it's not enough."

"Who says so?"

"I do. There's something deeper—"

"What? I thought you did a pretty good analysis in depth. You know him better than the men who made out his life history for him."

"Perhaps there's a lot they don't know either."

"You mean he is really a big wheel?"

"If I could find out his real name, I could answer that."

"You can't trace it?" Rosenfeld was astounded. "That really makes him very interesting."

Carlson nodded. "I'll bequeath him to you, once you get the problem of Sandra Fane worked out. By the way, how much did you tell Fenner?"

"A certain amount, to enlist his co-operation. But it wasn't enough, obviously." Rosenfeld frowned and shook his head. "He won't talk, though. He has learned to keep his mouth shut. Don't worry about that."

"So what's worrying you about him?"

"I'm just hurt," Rosenfeld said with a broad grin. "He doesn't take us seriously." He pulled a note from his pocket. "Fenner slipped this into my hand when we said good-by. He thought you'd want it back, so that you could burn it and save yourself extra work in searching Dade's trash basket tonight."

"Indeed?" Carlson's usual quick phrase deserted him. He took the note he had sent Fenner about the coat. He rose, saying, "Keep in touch, will you? I'd like to know how this puzzle ends."

"I'll keep in touch," Rosie promised. "And thanks for the help."

"Thank our critic," said Carlson wryly, and departed.

Rosenfeld glanced at his watch and called for his check. Time to get back to the office and be waiting for that woman's telephone call. Who was she? Dade might have told him. He must have known who she was or else he wouldn't have given her Rosenfeld's number. People had odd ways of figuring out the limits of their actions: I'll give Rosie's number because this may be important; but if she changes her mind—as women do—and doesn't call Rosie, then let's leave her anonymous, and Rosie can't try to reach her. And if that was the way Dade had figured it, the woman must be pretty important, too. For Rosie, happily married, didn't go around trying to telephone women unless they were interesting. And "interesting" in Rosie's vocabulary did not mean glamorous.

SIX

BILL FENNER took a taxi to get him across the Seine and along the stretch of tree-lined quays that marked the river's left bank. He got out near the Ecole de Beaux-Arts, was tempted to loiter among the bookstalls across the street, even sit under the coolness of the green leaves and watch the sun-speckled water swirl past the Louvre's gray eminence. But there were only twenty minutes to Vaugiroud: ten minutes of walking; ten minutes of margin to find Number 7, Rue Jean-Calas. So he turned to his right, and headed south on a street that was long and narrow and, more importantly for his purpose, remarkably straight.

It led him, at a good quick pace, past a sprinkling of antique shops and small studios where art objects were displayed or made. Here and there a bakery, with the sweet warm smell of new loaves; little bookstores to remind man that he did not live by bread alone. And everywhere were the people who lived or worked in this quarter: craftsmen out of their workshops for a breath of air; students with books or portfolios of drawings; thin-waisted housewives clopping along in heelless sandals; thin-legged, button-eyed children, carrying pikes of bread as tall as themselves; two sculptors in clay-smeared smocks; girls with alert faces, fine eyes, tight skirts, loose sweaters, wild hair combed by the winds and washed by the rains. He crossed the Boulevard Saint-Germain, broad and busy. Shortly, he ought to branch off to his left, following a twist of side street which—if his map was accurate—would lead him into the Rue Jean-Calas. His map was correct: there was Vaugiroud's entrance just ahead of him. And he had five minutes to spare.

Fenner strolled past its huge doors, sun-beamed and rain-scrubbed. Like the house itself, they belonged to the eighteenth century, when they no doubt led to porte-cochere, perhaps even to an interior courtyard. They stood closed; the windows above and around them were silent. There was no row of name plates, no indication of how many apartments now lay behind those doors. Fenner walked on, and reached the end of the short street. In front of him there was a small cobbled expansion, which someone had called a square: Place Arouet. It was more of a breathing space, to trap some sunshine, before another little street closed in with its walls of gently decaying houses. All around was the peace of age and forgetfulness, a sense of quiet resignation and retreat from busier streets and a noisy boulevard only a few minutes away.

There were few people in the Place Arouet. Two old men, carefully dressed, had paused to talk in their late-afternoon saunter, a boy jolted over the cobblestones on a bicycle, a car was parked on the shaded side of the square near an antique shop. At the café opposite, marked by four zinc tables under a faded green awning, there was a man comatose over an unfinished drink. It would be pleasant to join him and have a long cool beer: but perhaps not, Fenner decided. The café lay on the sun-drenched side of the Place Arouet. It would be hot under that awning. The man who sat there must be a Finn enjoying a late-summer sauna.

Fenner, his eye on his watch (Professor Vaugiroud's voice, this morning, had been too brisk for unpunctuality), retraced his steps along the Rue Jean-Calas. He pulled the old-fashioned bell, and heard its weak jangle echo its echo, dying, dying into a distant tremor. As he waited, he glanced briefly back to the Place Arouet. The man at the café table was visible from this doorway. He would certainly know Fenner again. But what else had a man to do, who had finished his newspaper and hadn't armed himself with a book and had chosen to sit at a lonely little café, except look? Yet, Fenner thought, I could have sworn he was dozing like a dog in the sun when I stood at the corner of the square. What brought him back to life?

One of the doors half opened. A woman, her short and heavy body covered by a tight black cotton dress, her bare feet thrust into flat-heeled scuffs, looked at him inquiringly from under a dyed, dried fringe of hair.

"Professor Vaugiroud?" he asked.

The door stayed at its forty-five-degree angle. She was middle-aged, sad-faced, distrustful.

"He is expecting me. At four o'clock."

Her sharp brown eyes studied him.

"My name is Fenner," he said clearly. Was his French as difficult to grasp as all that?

She looked over her shoulder quickly, and she scolded someone. "Get back to your work!" She waited, the lines in her face deepened by her annoyance, and at last she swung the door fully open to let Fenner step inside. The depths of the building encased him in a short but massive tunnel, with an entrance to a staircase on either side. Ahead was a shadowed courtyard with a cluster of old bicycles around a covered well, ivy climbing around dark ground-floor windows, a few scraps of clothing drying on a sagging rope. The woman had closed the door behind him and barred it. She was at his elbow, pointing to the staircase entrance on the left. "One flight up," she told him, voice brisk but pleasant enough. She noticed that he seemed fascinated by the courtyard. "Everyone except the professor is away—place is empty until the classes start again—my husband—" She looked at the bicycles, shrugged, and said nothing more. She nodded recognition of his thanks, her eyes looking past him into the courtyard, and clopped off in her loose slippers. As he entered the staircase hall, he could hear her voice, changed back into sharp anger as she called to the child who provoked her so much. Then there was only the sound of his footsteps on the elaborate wooden staircase. Above him, from a small crown of window in the ancient roof, the light and heat streamed down.

A door opened as Fenner reached the second-floor landing. A small man, slight of build, dressed in a neat light-gray suit, cocked his head to one side as his deeply set brown eyes studied the American. "Mr. Fenner? You are punctual." The voice was precise but melodious. "That way!" Professor Vaugiroud raised his walking stick and pointed. Fenner walked through the small hall, jammed with furniture, toward an open door. Behind him, Professor Vaugiroud snapped a bolt into its socket and followed him with a good attempt at speed in spite of his dragging right leg.

The room they entered was a surprise. It looked across the Rue Jean-Calas to the sun-baked houses opposite, but here, on the shadowed side of the street, it was cool. It was airy, light. And it was, in comparison with the crowded hall, almost empty. Large, high-ceilinged, bare-floored, it contained only a large table (serving as a desk), three chairs, a couple of practical reading lamps, a telephone, a small radio, and books. Books everywhere, covering the walls, climbing to the carved scrolls of the ceiling. A filing cabinet was tucked into one corner of the room, a narrow bed into another. It was a neat place, with its piles of magazines and newspapers stacked in orderly fashion on the lower bookshelves. Even the clutter on the desk had a certain logic in its arrangement. Professor Vaugiroud was a busy but well-organized man. Perhaps, to be effective, the two attributes had to be closely married.

He was also an agile man, even with his disabled leg. He had moved quickly to the desk, leaning heavily on his walking stick, and seemed to be absorbed in selecting some papers. He must be almost seventy, Fenner guessed. His hair, thick-thatched, was white and carefully brushed, but one lock insisted on hanging free over his brow. His thin face, with its long nose and strong chin, magnificent eyes, high forehead, gave the impression of alert intelligence and considerable will power.

"Satisfied?" he asked Fenner, looking up with an abrupt smile. "Does Walter Penneyman's description fit me?" His English was fluent and accurate, but strongly accented.

Fenner decided to be equally brusque. "Yes. And here are my credentials." He searched for the note of introduction in his pocket. Vaugiroud took it, but he seemed more interested in studying the American as Fenner moved over to the near window. Fenner glanced at the desk as he passed it, stood at one side of the opened window, looked down at the end of the Rue Jean-Calas and the beginning of the Place Arouet.

Fenner was both embarrassed and amused. On the desk there had been three old copies of the New York *Chronicle* neatly folded back to the drama page. One had a reasonably accurate photograph of Fenner, taken along with other New York critics at the Tony Awards last year. There was also a copy of *Who's Who in the Theatre*. Fenner could imagine Carlson saying: "See how easy it is?" (Come to think of it, Carlson might have been the man to interview Vaugiroud. He would have known how to get this conversation started, at least.) I'll let Vaugiroud make the pace, Fenner thought: he may have decided he doesn't want to talk with me at all.

"Something interesting in the Place Arouet?" Vaugiroud asked.

Fenner shook his head. The café tables were empty. Just as he was about to turn away, he noticed a small titled mirror fixed on the wall outside the window at his elbow level.

He drew a few paces backward and bent his head to see into the mirror. It reflected a stretch of sidewalk in front of the house entrance. "Useful gadget," he remarked as he watched the man who had sat at the café table now standing below, close to the gateway, facing it. Even as Fenner looked; the man stepped back from the door, stared up at the windows above him, turned abruptly away. Instinctively, Fenner drew aside: the man's quick glance had seemed a real confrontation. Then he relaxed, remembering he was invisible from down there. The man might be interested in him, but Fenner had seen more of the man than he had seen of Fenner. Fair hair, light-colored eyes, a strongly boned face with snub features, bluntly handsome, tanned deeply, powerful shoulders under a blue summer shirt. It was a flash impression, yet deeply etched into Fenner's mind: he wasn't accustomed to seeing such a menace as the man's eyes had shown in that brief moment.

Vaugiroud had noticed Fenner's face, and he was puzzled. "Very useful," he conceded, and waited.

"Can you hear the doorbell up here?"

"Not always. Age has dulled its tongue. You seem worried, Mr. Fenner."

"No." Not worried, just on edge. This morning's events were still with him, seemingly. He was tired, of course. Last night's sleep had been broken. When you were tired, everything was exaggerated. In his normal senses, he would never have seen a pair of curious eyes and read menace into them. Had the man actually been talking to someone inside the front doorway? Or was that just imagination, too?

"But not at ease. I am sorry. If I can entice you away from the limited view offered by that window, I shall offer you this chair. Let me find you a cigarette." Vaugiroud looked vaguely around like a typical nonsmoker for the small box of dried-up cigarettes that he kept for visitors.

"I have my own, thanks." But Fenner took the hint, left the man in the process of crossing the street—good strong shoulders and muscular body, Fenner noted, but below average height—and sat down.

Vaugiroud laughed unexpectedly. "I had expected to be distrustful of you, Mr. Fenner; not to be distrusted by you."

"Far from that, sir," Fenner said, smiling, forced into an explanation. "I was only puzzled by a man loitering outside."

"He followed you here?" Vaugiroud asked quickly.

"Of course not."

"How pleasant to be able to say 'Of course not' with such complete certainty."

"Let's say I am reasonably sure. He was already sitting at a café table on the square when I arrived."

"People do sit at café tables."

Fenner nodded and lit his cigarette.

"You think he is watching this house?"

"Perhaps."

"That's always possible, of course," Vaugiroud said evenly, but he limped over to the window and looked toward the Place Arouet. "A fair-haired man in a blue shirt?" He frowned. "We shall let him swelter at his table," he said, and came back to face Fenner. "I have long since ceased to worry about things over which I have no control."

"You have no control over your concierge?"

Vaugiroud eyed him sharply. "I trust Mathilde." That was final. "Now let us begin. First, I have a few questions." Politely, but skillfully, he set out to discover some information about Fenner: could a drama critic, dealing with a world of make-believe, be a serious student of international politics? Fenner had often been probed by experts, but Vaugiroud was the master-prober of them all. Why, wondered Fenner in half-amusement, must he be so sure of me in his own mind? What has he to tell me that makes it so important for him to be sure?

"You must forgive my curiosity, Mr. Fenner," Vaugiroud said, noticing the look in Fenner's eyes, "but you have me at a disadvantage. Walter Penneyman no doubt told you something about me, but he had no way of telling me very much about you."

"Except that he sent me here."

"Trust me, trust my friend?" Vaugiroud seemed amused. "Yet we do not always like the friends of our friends. How far do we trust people if we don't like them? Or, conversely, Fenner, are scarcely a reliable basis for any accurate judgment."

"So I have learned," Fenner said abruptly. His face tightened, became guarded.

Vaugiroud sensed he had touched a nerve center. This was the difficulty in trying to talk with strangers. Even with people you knew, there could be hidden gulfs of experience which you discovered unexpectedly, one foot ready to plunge over just as you caught your balance and took a step back to safer ground. "My curiosity was not aroused by any distrust of you," he said quickly. "I only wondered about your capability for this special job. You see, I cannot talk freely unless I know I am going to be taken seriously. There is an attitude, among some people, of thinking that anything dealing with clandestine politics or conspiracy is—well, either cheaply sensational or comic."

"I think I've learned something about the hidden face of conspiracy," Fenner said stiffly. "It has its comic aspects, sure. But I don't confuse them with reality any more."

Vaugiroud had been watching Fenner carefully, listening, sensing. Suddenly he nodded, pulled the desk chair around, sat down, manipulating his damaged leg with skill, managing to hide a grotesque clutch of pain. "I have several facts to give you for Mr. Penneyman. How do you propose to get them into his hands?"

"He suggested I should cable the main points. In code, of course."

Vaugiroud rejected that idea with a shake of the head. "Your code is meant for brevity, not secrecy. This information must be handled, meanwhile, with—shall we say, discretion? Because there are two parts to my information. The first is a report for Mr. Penneyman. The second is an analysis, made on the basis of the facts I discovered for him, which could be of interest to Washington. He has friends there? I thought so. I want him to get this analysis, this memorandum, into official hands. The memorandum is not for him, you understand? It goes far beyond the facts I gathered for the report he wanted."

"Have you tried sending this memorandum to Washington through our Embassy here in Paris?"

"How? I don't know anyone there personally. Do you think they would send someone to listen to me? Or would he listen to me if he did come? Another—as you would say —another crackpot professor. Might that not be his judgment?" Vaugiroud almost smiled. "It is never easy to gather such information, but it is sometimes still more difficult to communicate it to the proper authorities."

Fenner, remembering this morning, could agree. "I know someone at the Embassy—" He stopped. Would Carlson be interested enough to find the proper authorities? "You have two problems of transmission. First, the report for Walt Penneyman; second, the memorandum for Washington. I can deal with the first. I'll make a breakdown of its main points, and get it over to Penneyman at once."

"How?"

"I'll try to persuade my friend at the Embassy to send it by diplomatic pouch. You have no objection to letting him see what he is sending?"

"None. But the memorandum?"

"It could travel the same way. Provided, of course, it really is urgent. Someone at the Embassy would have to check that, of course."

"Of course." Vaugiroud was not too enthusiastic. "But will they send it quickly, or will they spend weeks in verifying my facts? Of what use is a warning of danger if it is not made before the danger arises?"

"None, except to produce a fine crop of gloom, breast-beating, ashes on the head, and a general state of despondency." Danger, wondered Fenner: how the hell did anyone analyze danger? Was Vaugiroud one of those crackpot prophets, after all? No, not from what Penneyman had told him.

And Vaugiroud, as if he could share all Fenner's mixed emotions, asked quietly, "Do you trust me enough to believe me, Mr. Fenner? That is important, you know. What do you actually know about my life? Or don't you?"

"You were once a professor of Moral Philosophy, and lectured at the Sorbonne." Fenner glanced at a bookshelf where two volumes had caught his eye: Vaugiroud—*Man's Search for the Divine.* "You resigned during the Nazi occupation and"—Fenner glanced at the crippled leg—"became active in the Resistance. At the end of the war, you changed your interests from Moral to Political Philosophy. You are at present working on *A Social History of Violence.* You also write analytical articles on power politics. You live alone" —Fenner avoided looking at the photograph of Vaugiroud's wife on the desk: she had died as a hostage during the Nazi occupation, Walt Penneyman had warned him—"and you haven't left Paris in the last sixteen years." Fenner hesitated. He had also been warned that Vaugiroud disliked visitors, except his own friends and old pupils, and that he had— from some of those friends and old pupils, now highly placed in their professions—developed one of the best amateur intelligence services in Western Europe. But he thought he could omit that. "That's about all, I think."

"Enough, I suppose. But how meager one's life becomes when it is reduced to its basic facts." Vaugiroud shook his head ruefully. "And the last, most complete, reduction is on one's tombstone: a name, two dates. This man was born, and died. And few ask why." His voice dropped away; his sharp, intelligent face became a sculptured head brooding over his own grave. Then, very much alive, he quickly picked up from his desk a sheet of paper covered with fine hand-writing and a batch of newspaper clippings. "Well, here are the items that Mr. Penneyman would like to see. I have called this report the *History of the Planted Lie.*"

Fenner looked sharply at Vaugiroud.

"Last April, Walter Penneyman came over to Paris. He was worried about the truth or untruth of certain current newspaper stories dealing with our Generals' Revolt in Algeria and the alleged backing of that revolt by your Central Intelligence Agency. I was interested, too. Why?" Vaugiroud had not yet handed over the report. He waited for the answer.

Penneyman had been interested in the responsibilities of the press, Fenner knew. But Vaugiroud? "Possibly it's the same reason that made you change from the study of ethics to power politics. Your experience in the Resistance, perhaps?"

Vaugiroud was pleased with the answer. "You are half right. My conversion was a little earlier than that, though. It happened on the day I stood and watched the Nazi tanks roll down the Champs-Elysées." He paused. "I had always a questioning kind of mind. But that day I wept. I had no answers. How could this be happening? How did an enemy break you down before any real war began, so that all your military protections became useless? How did he weaken you, separate you from your friends, divide opinions, destroy your morale and your purpose? I have been trying to find the answers ever since. I gave up my work, my search for the Good, and turned to analyzing the Evil." He looked down at the report he held in his hand. "I have learned several things: without knowing what is menacing us, we cannot protect our safety; in 1940, it was too late for any answer except remorse, and misery, and hidden resistance; in 1935, we could have saved ourselves that agony. For the basic reality of power politics is always this: who is going to control your life—you or your enemy? There is no evasion of that question. If you ignore it, you have lost."

Vaugiroud's voice hardened. "If we were sheep, or pigs, it would scarcely matter who shaped our history. When a sheep, or a pig, can eat and sleep and procreate, it is satisfied. It cannot even imagine tomorrow. But we have more to demand of our lives than that; and more is demanded of us. Unless, of course, we have become two-legged sheep. Or pigs."

He checked his rising anger. "Ah, well—" He shrugged his shoulders. "These are the times that try men's souls, Mr. Fenner."

"And character." Fenner said quietly.

Vaugiroud's eyes, watchful and probing, were suddenly satisfied. "Character—an old-fashioned word nowadays. But still a good one." He handed over the report for Walt Penneyman.

It was in French, very closely written, precisely detailed. Fenner read it carefully, condensing, selecting the main points that were the skeleton of the report. In brief, it began with the date of the Generals' Revolt—April 22, 1961. Within a few hours a story was circulating that the Central Intelligence Agency of the United States had instigated and aided the revolt against France. Within a few days the story was printed as uncontrovertible fact in the Roman newspaper *Il Paese*. Immediately, *Pravda*, Tass, and Radio Moscow were quoting *Il Paese* to Europe and the Middle East. By April 27, the London *Daily Worker* was denouncing America. A non-Communist French newspaper followed suit. So did other French papers. So did some officials in the French government, who talked cautiously, with shrugs and pursed lips, to foreign journalists. The news was even beginning to be accepted by some friends as well as enemies. The storm was rising to hurricane proportions. Americans protested their innocence, but how do you prove innocence? Even the usually accurate, and conservative, newspaper *Le Monde* could begin an attack on the CIA with the daming phrase "It now seems established . . ." But it wasn't. An Australian newsman, reporting for a British paper, challenged a French official at a public luncheon, and the French government issued a statement that no evidence had been discovered that could support the story. The report became what it always had been, a planted lie.

As Fenner finished reading, Vaugiroud handed over the sheaf of newspaper clippings. "Verification," he said. And it was impressive. Vaugiroud had gathered every report from all the European newspapers that had joined in the attack.

"Damning," Fenner conceded. And damnable. Even at this distance, with the lie nailed to the floor, he felt a surge of cold anger.

"As a Frenchman, I find it painful."

"Was that the reason you did so much work on this report?"

"Partly, yes. And partly because I could not make any deductions unless I gathered the facts first. From them, I have been able to make some suggestions in the memorandum"— he reached for a small pile of closely written pages— "very lengthy, I'm afraid: so much documentation, references, additional facts. And names." He hesitated. "You see," he went on, "I learned more than I expected to learn when I first started on that report for Walter Penneyman."

Fenner looked with some awe at the pile of manuscript. His French wasn't as good as all that. This would take him several hours of concentrated work. Still, he was eager to see what Vaugiroud had written. He held out his hand, and then drew it back. "Sorry," he said.

"You are interested?"

"Definitely."

Vaugiroud didn't pass over the memorandum. He said, "It would be safer for you not to see it, Mr. Fenner. But I can tell you, very roughly, at least part of it. So that you can judge if it really is worth all your trouble in helping me send it to Washington."

Fenner hid his disappointment. Even Vaugiroud's phrase "safer for you ... Mr. Fenner" had aroused his curiosity still more: any information that was dangerous was usually worth knowing. As a onetime newsman— He caught himself sharply. Had Walt Penneyman been right? Was the old itch to know all about a story still there? He said, "That's fair enough."

"The memorandum is divided into four sections. First, the purpose behind the planted lie. Second, the means and methods used to spread it. Third, the reason for its failure. And fourth—the next attempt."

"Fenner stared. "You think they will try something like this again?" The question had been jolted out of him.

"I don't think. I know," said Vaugiroud very quietly.

"You *know?*"

"I know that an act of violence is being planned right now. I know that it will take place soon. I know that the same propagandist is already preparing the campaign against America."

"You don't know time or place?"

"Obviously not. Or else you wouldn't be sitting here listening to me. Instead, I would be talking to some Intelligence officers from NATO, or some of the international experts from our own Sûreté."

"Sorry. That was a damned silly question of mine."

Vaugiroud was mollified by the frank statement. "Why shouldn't they try something like that again?" he asked, pointing to the report for Penneyman. "It was a brilliant success, except for one omission. Next time, they won't make that mistake."

"What was it?"

"They did not provide evidence."

"Evidence? A letter, some kind of signed document? But that would have been a forgery, and forgeries can be disproved."

"Disproof takes time. For the last four years, the Russians have been fabricating several letters and memorandums which could have caused serious trouble for the West. Fortunately, our governments had the time to examine them, exchange proof with each other of the falsity of the documents."

"How did they get that time?"

"No headlines in the newspapers, Mr. Fenner," Vaugiroud said with a tactful smile. "The documents were examined and checked, very quietly. I don't expect you will approve of that. But it did save several unpleasant misunderstandings between the NATO allies. Looking back at last April, I now think we were very lucky."

Fenner said thoughtfully, "The revolt broke so quickly, I suppose, that there wasn't time to manufacture evidence?" He could imagine the added effect of some bogus correspondence between a French general and the CIA being published in *Il Paese*.

"They did very well as it was. But if they could have produced some definite evidence—such as a large sum of American dollars found in a general's luggage or house or deposited in his bank account—what then?"

Fenner, who had been lighting a cigarette, looked up quickly.

"That amazes you, Mr. Fenner? Surely you've heard of planted money? What could be more definitive than a large amount of foreign currency? Oh, I grant you that, given time, we could disprove our guilt. But will we have time?"

"Do *they* have time to manufacture our guilt? There are constant crises, God knows, but—like that Algerian revolt —they can break unexpectedly for both East and West. Unless, of course—" Fenner stared at Vaugiroud "—unless they manufactured a crisis, too. Prepared everything, knew what to expect, and exploited it. To the hilt."

"To the hilt," Vaugiroud agreed. He smiled like a professor who was delighted with his pupil's efforts.

Perhaps the interview could have ended with that. But Fenner wouldn't let it. He was interested. He wanted to learn, to know. He was still a newsman, still the man searching for answers. He forgot about time, about his own plans for the evening. And in that moment of sitting back, of lighting another cigarette to replace the one that had gone out, of framing his next sentence most carefully, he changed the whole course of his life.

"So you know," he said, "that a crisis of some kind, an act of violence, is being planned. But how?" We've been doing some sharp deduction, he thought; we have made several acute inferences, but neither deduction nor inference was knowledge, actual knowledge. "You're a trained philosopher. You don't use the word 'know' meaning 'think' or 'expect' or 'feel.' Right?"

Vaugiroud nodded gravely. "I have seen three terrorists meet regularly, twice a week, for the last month. Two weeks ago, they were joined by one of the most skillful Communist propagandists in France. I know enough about these men, their politics, their past history—" He had become deadly serious. He pointed once more to his report for Walt Penneyman. "You read, in there, about the minor officials connected with our government whose gossip helped to make the foreign journalists so bewildered about America. Their connections gave a special significance to any hints or criticisms they passed around. You understand?"

Fenner nodded. Gossip about an international crisis was only speculation if it came from a grocer or bank clerk. But from anyone connected with a Foreign Office or State Department, gossip might seem inside information.

"For that reason, I was alarmed by that crop of rumors last April. So were several of my friends who are in government service themselves. Granted that our national pride was badly hurt by the army revolt, granted that some officials at the Elysée Palace were only too willing to hope for a scapegoat, there still remained the question: did those minor officials who gossiped really believe what they were hinting? Or were they only repeating what had been dropped very skillfully into their ears? If so, by whom? It took time and patience

and tact to find out. My friends did find out. The so-called information of the officials concerned could always be traced
back, eventually, deviously, to one source. To one man and
his own small group of intimates. He is in a position of trust.
Not important, not policy-making level. But he is a man, in
government, with a wide circle of friends and acquaintan-
ces, and many contacts. I have his name. Here." Vaugiroud's fingers tapped the memorandum on his lap. "It has a
special significance for me. Because I knew him once. Under
another name, of course." He paused. "I have been searching for him for sixteen years."

Sixteen years. Since the end of the war, Fenner thought.

"Today," Vaugiroud went on, "his politics seem nicely left
of center, liberal without being rabid; always admirable,
always acceptable. But I knew him when I was in command
of a special unit of the Resistance working here in Paris. He
was known only as Jacques. He was a Communist, very able;
he fought bravely, risked much. A capable and intelligent
young man, interested in psychological warfare. I made him
my second-in-command. I trusted him. And so, on August 11,
1944, eight days before the liberation of Paris, I found myself
in Gestapo hands." Vaugiroud looked down at his crippled
leg.

"Jacques denounced you to the Nazis?"

"He informed secretly."

"Why?"

"The end of the Nazi war was in sight. That was the time
to eliminate any Resistance leaders who would oppose any
Communist attempt to seize power. He was acting under orders, of course. It was part of the pattern, at that time—like
the arms and the money they were beginning to steal and
hide."

"How do you know it was Jacques who informed?"

"If there were only five people called to a most secret
meeting, and four appeared, and the fifth man did not, but the
Gestapo did; and if in subsequent examination of these four,
the Gestapo's questions all centered around the special business
of that meeting; if only two people knew about the exact
business, myself and Jacques; if the Gestapo showed no interest in the fifth member of that small group; if Jacques made no
immediate move to alert other Resistance units about our arrest so that they could have us traced or make an attempt
to help us; if Jacques abandoned us completely, assumed lead-
ership of my section, replaced the four of us with men of his

own choosing—" Vaugiroud's quiet voice didn't finish his long but damningly clear sentence.

"If you only knew him as Jacques, how did you find out who he really was?"

"Life plays its jokes. I searched through Paris for sixteen years, and never could trace him. Then, two weeks ago, he walked into a café to meet a very odd group of men. It's a small restaurant not far from here, just off the Boulevard Saint-Germain, where I lunch each day. He did not recognize me, for two reasons: I have changed a great deal, physically; and I was supposed to have died under Gestapo examination. That was one rumor I have allowed to live."

"And he never knew your real name, or your background?"

"Just as I never knew his. It was a security measure that all our unit shared. It was supposed to mean some safety for our families." He looked at the photograph on his desk. "Life also plays cruel tricks. She was arrested because she was the wife of Professor Pierre Vaugiroud, who was believed to be working with the Free French in London. She never told them that—" He broke off. His face became as lifeless as his voice.

Fenner searched desperately for another question. "What happened to the three others who were captured with you?" he asked sympathetically, drawing Vaugiroud away from that blank stare of grim memory.

"Two died. One stayed barely alive, as I did. The Americans freed us. And a year later—when we were fit enough—we came back to our own identities, Henri Roussin and Pierre Vaugiroud. We both had the same purpose: find Jacques. But he had dropped out of sight long before we were released from the hospital. I began to think that the Communists had transferred him to another city, another country. Or perhaps he was dead. Until two weeks ago—" Vaugiroud began to smile "—when Jacques walked into the Café Racine, which Henri Roussin owns. Jacques is now affluent, handsomely dressed, very confident in manner; a man of position, most respectable, restrained. But he is recognizable. He has aged normally, unlike Henri and myself." Vaugiroud paused. "How old would you say I am, Mr. Fenner? Frankly?"

Fenner hedged. "About sixty-five or so, I guess."

"You are being too polite. Even so, you add eleven years to my age."

Fenner was shocked into silence.

"So," Vaugiroud said, "once we found Jacques, it was easy to discover his present name. It was a double shock for me, I must admit, when that same name was given to me a few days ago as the source from which all rumors flowed."

"He is the propagandist you spoke of?"

"Yes. And the three men whom he joined for luncheon in the highly respectable Café Racine are the terrorists."

Fenner was startled. A highly respectable restaurant?

Vaugiroud did not hide his amusement. "They have been meeting twice a week since the beginning of August. My friend Henri makes a point of knowing his patrons. Most of them are regular visitors—lawyers, professors, judges. These three terrorists seemed very much the same type, well dressed, circumspect, interested in good food. One was a wine merchant, another a retired industrialist, and the third a film producer. But after Jacques met them, we naturally took a closer interest in them."

"Three rather unlikely terrorists." Were they really that? Fenner couldn't help wondering. The word had such supercharged emotion attached to it. Vaugiroud was really floating off the beam there. Why did good men who uncovered twisted politics seem to develop some twist of their own?

"Unlikely? They have money, brains, international contacts, intense convictions, ruthless ambition. The wine merchant is a staunch sympathizer with the Secret Army Organization. The industrialist subsidizes an activist group of right-wing nationalists. And the man who is now a film producer, a propagandist for Communist causes, a naturalized Frenchman, was previously—to my own knowledge, eighteen years ago—an organizer of Communist militants. His work was most secret, and so important that Comrade Jacques took abnormal risks to help smuggle him out of France back to Russia. I saw him only once, briefly, by accident. I didn't remember him until Jacques came into the restaurant. Seeing them together struck some distant memory, brought it to life. Of the four men at that table, he may be the most dangerous. . . . Yes, they are terrorists, for they are the arrangers. They are as guilty as the men who bomb, and kill, and destroy. I believe they are more guilty; because it is their planning, and their money, that can turn vicious impulses into a concerted pattern of violence. They have the means, and purpose. In the most cowardly sense of the word, these four men *are* terrorists. Do I make myself clear?"

"Quite clear." And I apologize: it was I who was wandering off the beam. Only, Fenner thought, only—

"Yes?" Vaugiroud had sensed his puzzlement.

"I suppose they couldn't be arrested, or questioned by the police?"

"On what grounds? For having luncheon together? For having political connections? They've hidden themselves well, Mr. Fenner. My friends and I have had to dig deeply to find out what I have just told you. Even I, until a few days ago, was merely puzzled, interested, worried. It was only when the man Jacques was identified as the source of anti-American propaganda last April that the warning bell sounded for me. I knew then that the threat was real. And I knew the purpose of the threat. But until I know its actual shape, all I can do is to gather facts about these men, analyze, suggest." He passed a hand over his eyes. He added wearily, "And hope that my warning is taken seriously."

"Well, they're not lunching together to finance a new movie, that's certain," Fenner said bitterly. There was a real threat in their meetings. But what? Their objectives must be far apart. What could have brought them together? A fascist and an extreme nationalist sitting down with a hard-shell Stalinist and a hidden Communist propagandist. An unholy alliance. But it had happened before. They'd use each other. Their ends justified any means.

Vaugiroud was looking at him, a little startled. "You know, that is exactly the reason they give for lunching together. Whenever Henri or one of his waiters is near their table, the talk is all about the costs of film making."

Could that be the reason, after all? No, Fenner decided slowly. "A very smooth act," he said. Too damned smooth.

"Like the meeting between Jacques and his old comrade," Vaugiroud said. "They pretended they were strangers. It was the retired industrialist who introduced them, invited Jacques to have lunch with them." That amused Vaugiroud briefly. "Very smooth, as you say, Mr. Fenner. As smooth as the lie that Jacques is now preparing against your country."

"We are again their target?"

"Again and again, until America is eliminated from Europe. I have shown you what could have happened if that last lie had succeeded. America would have been isolated, pilloried. Properly fanned, that fire could have burned out NATO. Or do I exaggerate?"

Fenner shook his head. Distrust, dissension, denunciations.

Bitterness, anger, complete disillusionment with all those who had taken so much help from America, and yet, when we needed friends, had been so willing and eager to believe the worst about us. "We would have been pushed back into isolationism," he said. "NATO would have had its back broken."

"And without NATO, what protects Western Europe? Without a peaceful Western Europe, what protects the growth of the Common Market? And without the Common Market, how could a United States of Free Europe ever develop? And that, Mr. Fenner, is their ultimate target. The Communists think far ahead. The dream of a United States of Europe is the nightmare of the Communist world. They have preached that Western capitalism is doomed, ready for burial; a system breeding wars and economic cannibalism. A collection of prosperous and peaceful nations in Western Europe would be the complete rebuttal to all Communist theories. Who would believe them then?"

Well, thought Fenner, here is a definite disciple of Monnet. Here's another Frenchman who thinks in terms of people instead of nationalities. "The Communists would find their ideas outmoded. They might have to renounce Lenin as well as Stalin," he observed with a smile. Even if Vaugiroud was a Common Market enthusiast, his basic argument was valid. If the Communists feared the prosperity of West Berlin so much that they built a Wall, how much more would they fear a prosperous and peaceful Europe?

"They may be forced to do that," Vaugiroud said soberly. "But before that, they will fight us every step of the way, with every psychological weapon they can find. They don't intend to lose."

Fenner rose, glancing at his watch. "I may just catch my friend at the Embassy. May I use your telephone?"

"You trust him?"

"Yes."

"How well do you know him?"

"Actually, I only met him today."

"Today?" Vaugiroud stared incredulously.

"Yes. He is with NATO. Some kind of security branch, possibly Intelligence?"

"Did he tell you that?"

"No. Just my guess. He is attached to the Embassy, meanwhile. I saw him there."

"Alone?"

"No, no," Fenner said patiently. He restrained a smile.

"There were other Embassy people around who knew him. He wasn't an imposter. Shall I telephone?"

Vaugiroud did not answer. He rose, painfully, placed the memorandum on his desk, and walked over to the window. "If there were any careless talk, any casual handling of that memorandum, then our enemy might learn we were interested in their activities. I do not believe in warning our enemy, Mr. Fenner. Much wiser to make him feel secure, secure enough to be bold, to make one mistake. One, Mr. Fenner, is all that is ever needed." He looked along the street. The furrows on his brow deepened. "Is your friend a careful man?"

"Surely he wouldn't hold down his job if—"

"Wouldn't he? You really trust him a great deal on one day's meeting."

"I trust you. Is that foolish?" And you trusted me; a little, certainly.

"I hope not." Vaugiroud smiled. Then the smile vanished. He drew back slightly from the window. "I think you were right about that man in the blue shirt," he said very quietly.

"He's still there?"

"He is restless. Bored, perhaps." Vaugiroud watched the man strolling along the street again. The stranger's face came into focus.

"Perhaps you haven't had enough visitors today to please him." Fenner started toward the window.

Vaugiroud's upraised hand stopped him.

"Is he coming to check on me again?" Fenner asked jokingly. "He probably thinks I've made an exit through a back basement."

"He checked on you? How?" Vaugiroud asked sharply.

"With Mathilde at your front entrance. I thought he might be finding out my name."

"Why didn't you tell me?"

"Well—it seemed a silly idea at the time: sort of jumping to conclusions."

Vaugiroud turned away from the window, his face set in worry. "Would you telephone your friend at the Embassy and ask him to come here?"

"When?"

"Now."

Fenner made no comment. He moved back to the desk, glanced at his watch again, registered the fact that they had lost four minutes by all that hesitation, hoped that Carlson

would still be in his office at half past five, and began the intricate job of telephoning. There were, of course, various
stages of waiting. He used them to continue talking to Vaugiroud, holding his hand over the phone. There were several
questions that puzzled him. "Is it possible that Jacques did
recognize you in the Café Racine?"

"I am sure he did not. Otherwise, I would have been
watched before now. This flat would have been entered and
my papers searched, to let them know how much or how little
I know."

"And then what?" This man, Fenner thought, may be in
greater danger than he admits. He takes it all so calmly.
"Would they kill you?" he asked sharply. "Would they go as
far as that?"

"I should certainly be very careful in crossing any streets,"
Vaugiroud admitted, and smiled. Then the smile became bitter.
"Monsieur Fernand Lenoir, secure in his career, could hardly
tolerate anyone who could identify him as Jacques."

Fenner stared at Vaugiroud. "Yes," he said into the telephone. "I want Carlson. No, I don't know his first name.
Carlson. That's right. Tell him it's Fenner. And it's important."
He looked back at Vaugiroud. Fernand Lenoir and Sandra
Fane and the pleasant parties on the Avenue d'Iéna . . . That
had been a calculated indiscretion on Vaugiroud's part, slipped
in as skillfully as a hypodermic. Why? Because Vaugiroud
knew that he had once been married to Sandra Fane? Or because Vaugiroud wanted to establish Lenoir as a name to be
remembered if, someday, he wasn't too careful in crossing a
street? At last, Carlson's voice came over the telephone, and
Fenner was speaking with a new sense of urgency.

"This is becoming a habit," Carlson told him. He sounded
far from enthusiastic.

"It's urgent."

"Again?" Carlson asked, and groaned.

"Did I disappoint you this morning? This may be still
bigger news."

"You do get around, don't you?"

"I've got a new angle on those people Rosie was asking
about." And Fenner had Carlson noting down Vaugiroud's
address without any more protests.

Vaugiroud said, as Fenner put down the receiver, "That
was very expeditious. And remarkably cryptic." The unasked question hung in the air.

But I can be discreet, too, Fenner thought. He said,

"Carlson will be here at six-forty-five. I'll wait until he comes." He grinned and added, "I know how you like proper introductions."

"I find them reassuring," Vaugiroud said dryly. He pursed his lips, frowned. "Perhaps you should be waiting downstairs at a quarter to seven, and let your friend enter?"

"Of course. Anything to keep Mathilde from finding out his name. I don't think Carlson would like that."

"Not Mathilde. Her husband is the one who should perhaps be kept ignorant. Was he in the courtyard when you arrived?"

"Someone was there. Out of sight. I thought it was a child."

"No children. Her husband is problem enough. Nothing he does is ever successful. You saw the bicycles? He lost his little repair shop, asked me to let him work in the courtyard until the other tenants come back." Vaugiroud sighed. "It is always the small request that turns out to be the greatest nuisance. Constant visitors, all explained as clients. If he had as many clients as that, I don't think he would ever have had to give up his shop. One thing, Mr. Fenner. When you do leave, you may see him. Mathilde won't be there; she goes out in the late afternoon for her daily shopping. Pay no attention to him at all. And if that man in the blue shirt is still out in the street—do not even look his way. Let him think you have never seen him. Will you do that?"

Fenner nodded. He didn't quite follow Vaugiroud's reasoning, but that was something he could puzzle out later. The quiet voice again amazed him. He said, "You take all this pretty calmly."

"How else?"

How else, indeed? "If I could borrow a corner of your writing desk and some paper, I might start working over the material for Walt Penneyman." He might even have his notes complete to hand over to Carlson for dispatch by the next diplomatic pouch.

My first evening in Paris, he thought, as he settled at the desk and tested his pen.

It was with some amazement that he heard Vaugiroud's voice from across the room saying, "Mr. Fenner, it is twenty minutes to seven."

SEVEN

BILL FENNER left the Rue Jean-Calas with mixed, but pleasant, emotions. There was relief for a job that was over —his report for Walt Penneyman was in Carlson's hands; satisfaction in the way he had convoyed Carlson upstairs, briefing him abruptly on Vaugiroud's past, leaving Vaugiroud's present to be discovered from Vaugiroud himself; and some plain, unabashed glee over his own nicely timed departure. He had waited beside the window for a few minutes after his introduction of Carlson, just long enough to see the curious stranger, sitting once more at the café table in its cool evening shadows, begin to rise and stroll toward the Rue Jean-Calas. Fenner's hasty good-by might have startled Vaugiroud and Carlson if they hadn't been too busy sizing each other up like a pair of circling judo experts, but it got him down the stairs in a quick run to make sure he would be gone before the stranger could reach the house. In the courtyard, darkening rapidly, he had glimpsed a hefty, sausage-eating type in a tight gray suit which had never seen work more arduous than opening a beer bottle. And paid no attention. He had stepped out into the street well ahead of the man sauntering toward the doorway. And paid no attention.

So here he was, no one following, duty done, free. Carlson could handle all the worries from here on out. The fading light of September's first day was broken by the bright splashes of the Boulevard Saint-Germain, just ahead of him. The bookstores and shops were closing, but there were plenty of cafés in all shapes and sizes. This was the time to be meeting a girl; beautiful, of course, and intelligent, naturally; with taste and a sense of humor. Too much to hope for? These things rarely came together in one pleasing package. The intelligent ones were usually too old, the beauties' conversation lasted

79

about fifteen minutes, the ones with taste tried too hard, the ones with humor knew it, alas. My God, he realized, I left out the one ingredient that matters most: honesty, just some decent, reliable, plain old-fashioned honesty. Didn't you have enough of the pretty little finagler, all open innocence, all hidden purpose? And then he wondered wryly, who was he to demand so much anyway? How much would a woman see in him? How much did he deserve? Not so much, he decided, not so much at all.

His speculations about a girl, the girl who always waited just around the corner or in the next room, had begun with a smile and ended in bitter memories. He needed a drink to get the sour taste out of his mouth. Besides, coping with Vaugiroud's French for the concise translation he had sent Penneyman had been an arduous hour. He stood at the edge of the broad boulevard, nineteenth century driving its straight way through the maze of ancient streets, debating where he would have that drink. For here the cafés had their own hard core of constant patrons drinking and talking in chosen groups, while the visitors wandered in to look at the captive poets and would-be philosophers, and went away after an inadequate dinner but at least with another coup notched on their tourist tomahawks. Fenner wondered, as he hesitated, if his eyes had not really been searching for a café called Racine. ("Not far from here," Vaugiroud had said.) It wasn't in sight from where he stood, so he gave up, crossed the boulevard, turned left, deciding to play the complete tourist and head for the Deux Magots, where the existentialists had established their original beach-head. But before he reached the heavy gray stones of the medieval Church of Saint-Germain-des-Prés, the only relic of its green meadows in its name, he saw—just off the boulevard, at the corner of a side street—the sign Café Racine above a quiet little restaurant. Again he hesitated. His job with Vaugiroud was over, but his interest was still alive. One minute he was telling himself it was no longer any of his business, the next minute he was crossing the side street to reach the two long window boxes of prim marigolds that flanked the Racine's open doorway. The narrow sidewalk held no room for outside tables, but, as he realized when he stepped over the threshold, this was a place that took food seriously.

There was a pleasant paneled room in front of him, with a large central display of remarkable cold dishes, cheeses, fruit, over which a large fan revolved slowly. Around the walls were well-spaced tables, covered with white linen, only half filled at this hour. The lights were bright in unshaded globes. Plenty of polished brass, but not an inch of chromium, he noted. Only two women were in sight, and they were both middle-aged, carefully coiffured and dressed, listening with small, correct smiles while their husbands discoursed airily. This was a man's restaurant, most definitely.

No one paid any attention to him except Madame, who sat on a high chair at an old-fashioned desk to one side of the doorway. "Good evening," he said, aware of her careful scrutiny.

"You wish a table, monsieur?"

"Eventually."

"Ah, you are waiting for someone?" She was the quick, clever type who always knew what you wanted before you did.

"Yes." For a glimpse, at least, of Henri Roussin. It was a safe answer, true enough, not committing him to anything.

She gestured to the other side of the door, where the corner opposite her held a group of marble-topped tables against a background of newspapers, each hanging from its wooden spine hooked onto the wall like a medley of medieval banners. Yes, this was the waiting-place, Fenner decided, where strangers warmed cold feet with a tepid *apéritif* until courage was recovered and they could ask if one of those empty dining tables might not possibly be granted to a mere foreigner? He selected a chair that faced the room. Madame's powers of remote control had summoned an ancient waiter, but that was the extent of her interest. She was back to business, checking accounts, concentrating. She was a thin, small-boned woman, about thirty-five, dressed in subdued gray, with intense black hair, pale lips, thick white skin, deep shadows under her sharply observant eyes.

The waiter took his order, showed no visible signs of shock when he was asked to bring a Scotch and soda. He even suggested ice. So some Americans must wander in here occasionally. Fenner felt less of a stray Martian, lit a cigarette, studied the room, with its small islands of complete self-absorption. There was a preponderance of gray and white heads, of double-breasted suits, of lapel decorations. Solid citizens, all of them. There was a mild clatter of heavy silver as some threw themselves into the serious business of eating, a hum of talk from those who waited for food to be cooked. Voices were low, although clear-pitched, brilliant; faces were quiet, clever; gestures were controlled but ex-

pressive. Intelligent citizens, too, but preoccupied with themselves: not one knew, or cared, what was going on around him.
Just the place, thought Fenner, for a clandestine meeting.
All you needed was a double-breasted suit, a long haircut,
and drooping eyelids.

Where's my drink? Fenner wondered, reaching overhead
for a newspaper. And where is Henri Roussin? Madame
was watching him again, and then—as he had looked over
at the desk—not watching. He began to read, but could give the
paper little attention. The puzzle that had drawn him to
the Café Racine was unexplained: if Vaugiroud was being
observed, Roussin would also be under suspicion. Yet there
was no one here who seemed to be interested in anyone else,
except Madame, and that was possibly an occupational disease.
I am not going to snitch any newspapers, he told her under
his breath as he looked up and saw the curious eyes glance
away from him; in fact, I'm just about to leave. But now, from
the back of the restaurant, was *Monsieur le propriétaire*
himself, emanating.

He was a large man, Henri Roussin, an impressive testi-
monial to his chef. He moved slowly along the row of tables,
a small bow here, a few words there, his head always turning
to one side as he paused to speak. Quite naturally it seemed,
he came toward Fenner. "You have not been served, monsieur?" His voice was half muted, hoarse, as if it were
strangled in his throat.

Fenner nodded toward the arriving waiter. He forced himself to keep looking at Roussin politely, tried to banish the
shock from his eyes. Roussin's face carried the traces of his
war. Once, they must have been hideous. Surgeon's clever
fingers had worked hard, but there was still a disfigured look
to the right side of the face in spite of its carefully disguised
scars: an overneatness of the ear, its lobe gone, a drawn
smallness of the eye; the side of the jaw oddly fallen. His
thin gray hair had its long strands brushed carefully over
a bald welt, the continuation of a puckered furrow of white
flesh that ran from the misshapen ear up over the brow onto
the scalp. "Here's my drink," Fenner said awkwardly, glad
of an excuse to drop his eyes. He studied the one small cube
of ice that had been allowed him.

"Monsieur would like a table?"

"Eventually." Fenner was pleased with that word; his
French accent sounded better this time.

"You are waiting for someone? I shall arrange a table for two?"

Fenner said, "Well—I'm not sure—"

Roussin watched him with amusement. "Or perhaps you came to see me, Mr. Fenner?" he asked in English. As Fenner stared up at him, he added, "I'm sorry I was not here when you arrived. I was in my office, speaking on my telephone."

Fenner grinned. "With Professor Vaugiroud? So he called you to expect me. But how did he know?"

"To be exact, he did not telephone. I called him. When we were talking, he mentioned you."

"And described me pretty accurately."

"The professor is always accurate. He notices the essential details. That signet ring on your left hand, for instance; the blue shantung tie; the small lapels of your dark flannel suit. It wasn't difficult to identify you."

"But how did he know I was going to drop in here?"

"He did not know. He only thought what he would do himself if he were you. It was a brilliant guess, don't you think?"

"Are all his guesses as good?"

"Usually, yes."

"Sometimes wrong?" Fenner asked jokingly.

"Not in recent years."

"Not since August 11, 1944?"

It was Henri Roussin's turn to stare. The quick dark eyes in the half-dead face widened for a shocked moment. He recovered. With a smile, he said, "You had an interesting talk with the professor, I see. Excuse me—" He turned away to greet two men who entered the restaurant, delivered them into the care of a waiter, stopped at the desk to speak to Madame, and returned to Fenner. "Will you have dinner with me, Mr. Fenner? My table is just over there."

Fenner looked across at the table. It was the nearest one to Madame's desk, separated from it by a tactful screen of potted plants. "I'd like that very much. But another night. I have a telephone call to make before dinner."

Roussin took that as a rebuff. "You are welcome to use the telephone at the desk," he said stiffly.

"This is a call to New York. If you aren't too busy, why don't you sit down, and we can have a drink together?" Fenner glanced over at Madame.

Roussin noticed his look. His manner had eased again. "No one would be astonished if I did. In fact, they might be astounded if I did not. I like Americans. I like to practice my English. And I like to sit down. These habits are well established. Also, I have already dropped a hint that you were recommended to dine here by one of my old English friends who now lives in New York. So we have much to talk about."

He pulled a chair to face Fenner, and lowered his enormous bulk carefully. All his movements were calculated and slow.

"I have a feeling," Fenner said, "that Madame does not like Americans as much as you do."

"True. We disagree about most things."

"Difficult." Fenner was embarrassed.

"Ah, you think Angélique is my wife? Not at all. She is my sister-in-law. A widow. Her husband was killed in Algiers."

"Oh, one of those OAS attacks."

"No. By the Algerians, in 1958. In an ambush. He was a soldier."

"And that makes your sister-in-law anti-American?"

"That is part of it. She thinks you forget about atrocities unless the Rightists commit them. The other part? Simply that I like Americans."

Does Angélique take opposite sides just to feel she is at least that much independent? Fenner wondered.

"After all," Roussin was saying, "I owe them my life. And they salvaged enough of my face to let me come back into the world. Seventeen years ago, they found me." He fingered his right cheek thoughtfully. "I was more like a lump of hamburger than a man. I never forget the words I heard from the American soldier who first saw me. 'Holy Christ!' he kept saying, just two words over and over again. There was a very encouraging sound in the way he spoke them—with awe and admiration—as if he were pinning medals on my chest. Most flattering. I began to feel that by simply staying alive, I had triumphed. And so, I decided not to die. What man wants to be cheated of his medals?"

"Yet, in one sense, you have cheated yourself."

"That was necessary. I might not be alive to talk with you tonight if the true story of these injuries had been known." He tapped the damaged side of his face. "A bad car accident in a London blackout. I spent the war years in England, didn't you know? Later, when all danger was over, I returned here to inherit my father's restaurant. On the whole, I am considered a lucky man—one who has arranged his life very comfortably, except for a silly accident."

Fenner was beginning to like Henri Roussin. "So that's where you spent the war. I'll remember."

"Please do," Roussin said very quietly, all the humor drained out of his eyes. "This deception is not a joke that the professor and I have played all these years. We had a purpose."

"I know. And you hooked your fish."

Roussin showed frank shock for the second time that evening. Then he narrowed his eyes, studying Fenner's face. "And how did you extract so much information from the professor?"

"Does he let anyone extract anything, unless he wants them to?"

Roussin nodded his agreement on that. "Now I would like to do some extraction. Why did you come here? It did not puzzle the professor. But it puzzles me."

"Oh—just checking on the story I had heard. It becomes a habit with newspapermen."

"And how could I help you to check on the story?" Roussin asked with mock concern. "Shall I point out the table where we hooked our fish, and caught three minnows as well?"

"Minnows—" Fenner repeated the word, searching for some way to turn Roussin's distrust back to amiability once more. "You don't think they are important?"

"To me? No." Roussin's eyes were hard. "First things first. That is my way. My main interest is the man who was the cause of this." Once more his hand went up to his face. "The professor is a philosopher. He thinks mostly of the future. But I am a practical man: I find the past enough to think about."

"So you don't always agree with the professor's ideas?"

There was a pause. "Common Market? European unity? Nonsense! But what are friends for, except to enjoy disagreement? All day, with my guests, I have to agree, agree, agree. It is a relief to disagree. A necessity, perhaps. What are friends for if they can't help?"

Fenner studied his drink. He said lightly, "I guess I'm almost a friend. At least I'm disagreeing with you."

Roussin laughed, a strange, strangled gasp heaving out from his massive chest. "We might be very good friends. Indeed, if I show you the table where one of our minnows is sitting at this minute, will you answer a question I would like to ask you?"

"Right now? I thought they only came here at lunchtime."

"Right now," Roussin repeated firmly, watching only Fenner. "The pattern is broken. Interesting? I do not think our film producer has merely developed a taste for my cuisine. He has postponed ordering. He is waiting, I think." Roussin was enjoying himself. "He arrived only two minutes before you did. In fact, before I went off to telephone the professor about this strange development, I wondered if you might not be following him."

"What?"

"But the professor reassured me about you."

"What worried you?" Fenner asked sharply.

"You could have been on either side: his or ours."

"Watchdog or bloodhound, is that it?"

"Exactly."

"Where is he?"

"Four tables to your right, Mr. Fenner," Roussin said, still keeping his eyes on the American's face.

Fenner looked casually around the room. A well-dressed man, with receding red hair and a handsome profile, sat at the fourth table. He was studying a menu, sipping a glass of wine, looking remarkably at ease. "A most affluent Communist. What's his name?"

"You are a very inquiring journalist, Mr. Fenner."

Yes, thought Fenner, I had better stop being so interested: I am letting myself become too involved in something that goes deeper and farther than Walt Penneyman's assignment. "Thanks for the reminder," he said dryly. "It's none of my affair."

"Most wise. But before you put all this out of your mind, you still owe me an answer. Why did you come here?"

"And that was?"

"Let's say I was trying to find an answer to a question of my own."

"And that was?"

"Who told Jacques that Vaugiroud and you are still alive?" Fenner asked very quietly.

"Jacques—" The name jerked out under Roussin's breath. "So the professor even told you that? He must trust you."

And perhaps that's the reason why I've been worrying about him, Fenner thought. "He is being closely watched."

"So I heard," Roussin said quietly, grimly.

"He is not the man to be panicked by the threat of danger."

"No."

"So he must have recognized some real danger."

"When?"

"This evening." When he so suddenly reversed himself about a telephone call to Carlson.

"Is this a guess, Mr. Fenner?" Roussin asked shrewdly.

"What we call an educated guess. I was given the impression that he felt time might be running out, and that he had better make sure that others knew about Fernand Lenoir."

"Yes," Roussin said slowly. "If Lenoir knew who we were — Yes, there would be real danger for both the professor and myself. But he does not."

"You are sure of that?"

"With this face? With my story about London? I don't even look the right age. I was twenty when the Gestapo caught me. Do I look thirty-seven, Mr. Fenner?"

Fenner shook his head. "I still think Lenoir knows."

"Someone told him? Is that what you have been trying to say? No one could tell him. No one."

Fenner said nothing. Perhaps, he thought, I've said too much. Roussin was angry.

"No one," repeated Roussin. "For the simple reason that the men who worked with me in Paris during the war have died, either then or since. Jacques himself is the only survivor, besides the professor, of those who knew me; and he believes that the Gestapo finished me." Roussin studied Fenner with impatience. "Do not blame me for any carelessness. I learned English to prove I had spent the war years there. I even go back to London every autumn for a week's holiday to see my wartime friends. I leave, in fact, for this year's visit on Monday." The impatience turned to annoyance. "I am not an indiscreet man, Mr. Fenner."

"I didn't think you were."

"Then why blame me for this real danger?"

"There's no blame—"

"Yet you came here thinking you would find the answer to your question. You could have found it in the Rue Jean-Calas. And why? The professor has drawn danger upon himself. All those intellectuals who come to talk with him, all those anti-Communists, anti-fascists, anti-OAS, anti-this, anti-that—"

"Anti-totalitarian," Fenner suggested quietly. "That sums it up."

Roussin paid no attention: the exact meaning within a phrase did not seem important to him. "They have made many enemies for themselves. Why are intelligent men so stupid? It is enough to be clever, and live. Politics! Can a man eat politics, sleep with politics?"

This, thought Fenner, is where all rational discussion ends. Nothing I could say would either impress or change Roussin. His link with Vaugiroud is an emotional one—an old comradeship, loyalties based on danger and sufferings shared. Nothing wrong with that, as far as it goes. But with Roussin, it can't go much farther. He hasn't the mental equipment, clever fellow as he is, to grasp half the implication of Vaugiroud's ideas. No doubt Roussin hates Communists because Jacques was one. When he looks at Jacques, he sees the traitor who caused death to his friends, torture for himself. But Vaugiroud—he sees Jacques not so much as the man from the past who deserves punishment, but, rather, as a clear and present danger that must be fought for the sake of the future. "Well," Fenner said evenly, "it's possible that Professor Vaugiroud believes that men who have learned something about power politics have a special duty to share that knowledge."

Roussin turned his head to eye the clock above Angélique's desk. "Almost eight. The beginning of a very busy hour. The tables will all be filled by nine." He rose to his feet. "I shall reserve one for you, just in case you decide to stay. My private office is at your disposal if you wish to telephone New York. Meanwhile, let me order that other drink. With more ice this time?"

"Thanks," Fenner said, and had to smile.

Roussin snapped his fingers impatiently for a waiter. He dropped one last thought before he turned to the door, where some newcomers had entered. "Look around you, Mr. Fenner. The professor is being watched. But who is watching me?" And then he was moving away, welcoming the arrivals, checking Angélique's list of reservations, a very perfect host.

True, thought Fenner, no one here seems to be watching anything beyond the aphorism on his tongue or the food on his fork. Except Angélique. Perhaps that was part of her job. But why that sullen stare at Roussin's back as he led his guests toward a table? Had he corrected her for some mistake? Not

in front of any customers, Fenner decided. As he watched
her, she looked sharply over at him. For a brief instant,
he could see the tense look on her face, something more
bitter than angry, before she even became aware of him. Her
expression changed, falling back into its pattern of frown
and suspicion.

What was her trouble? Widowhood? Dislike of a job handed out by her husband's brother? Or resentment that this
restaurant had been inherited by her brother-in-law, who was
alive because he had not been a soldier in Algeria? The French
had a strong sense of possession and property. Whatever
Angélique's feelings were, she barely hid a seething contempt
for the world around her. There's a volcano here, Fenner
thought, about to erupt.

The waiter brought him his drink, and—from one extreme
to the other—a bowl of ice. The old man hovered around
anxiously, emptying the ash tray, making sure that monsieur
had the right newspaper. "Everything's fine," Fenner was
reassuring him as another guest arrived—a tall man, distinguished in dress and manner, dark of hair and eyes, thin-
faced. He gave Angélique a pleasant good evening, received a
smile in return, looked around for Roussin, who seemed
much engaged with a recent batch of arrivals, quickly set
out for his table by himself. Angélique's voice sharply summoned the waiter: "Auguste! Conduct Monsieur Lenoir to his
table!"

The old man hurried after Lenoir into the dining room,
catching up with him in time to pull out a chair. It was, of
course, at the fourth table on Fenner's right. So that is
Jacques, he thought, and gave a good pretense of being absorbed by his newspaper. It was hard to believe that anyone
so well groomed, so well dressed, with such a pleasant smile
on his intelligent face could be anything else than what he
wanted the world to believe: a man of honorable career, a
foreign-affairs specialist or perhaps a press officer or a confidential secretary, with government security and private
means to cushion him comfortably against the sharp edges
of life. Fenner had to smile at himself. If those two men
talking so quietly at the fourth table had been poorly or care-
lessly dressed, gaunt, white-faced, intense of eye, bitter-
mouthed, would he have been asking himself if Vaugiroud's
information could be true? The nihilists of the mid-twenti-
eth century had taken a lesson from confidence men: merge,
and you'll be accepted; be accepted, and your battle is half

won. No one bought the Brooklyn Bridge or the Eiffel Tower from a man who looked like a crook. And then his amusement changed to amazement. When he had seen Lenoir, he had immediately remembered Vaugiroud. Only now did he think of Sandra Fane, who entertained so successfully for Lenoir in her apartment on the Avenue d'Iéna. I really am cured of Sandra, he thought, and relief swept over him like a cold clean draft of fresh air.

The doors shook against their anchoring chains in the sudden gust of wind from the street. There was a muted ruffle of drums from the sidewalk. Rain? Fenner looked up at the high window. Rain it was, a thundering downpour. The newest guest had just managed to arrive in time to save her blonde hair and smart black dress. Yes, Fenner thought approvingly as she hesitated within the entrance, you're as neat and pretty a piece of honey cake as I've ever seen, but don't be so scared, my pet; I know how you feel, but they don't chew you into actual pieces; Angélique at the desk is not old Cerberus himself even if— My God, it's the girl I saw at the Crillon!

She stood there, one short white glove smoothing back a lock of hair that the wind had blown wild, hesitating, looking at the dining room. Her eyes swept around to Fenner. There was a spark of recognition, a smile of relief. She came toward him, ignoring Roussin, who was looming up with unusual speed, her hand outstretched. "I am so sorry to be late," she said, her gray eyes pleading from under dark lashes, the smile on her lips widening as he rose to meet her. "Have you been waiting long?"

EIGHT

"I AM CLAIRE CONNOR," she said in a low voice as she took the chair that Fenner offered her. Color was high on her cheeks, her eyes were embarrassed, but otherwise she seemed perfectly natural. She pulled off her white kid gloves, frowned briefly at three rain spots, and said she would prefer Dubonnet. He ordered, talked, and gave her time to catch her breath again. The color subsided in her cheeks, her eyes could meet his, her pretty hands (no nail polish, no rings) were relaxed as he lit her cigarette, she even laughed. But a shadow of worry, of strain still lurked in her eyes.

"Please forgive me," she said when the waiter had come and gone.

"My pleasure." Indeed it was. Close up, her skin was as flawless as he had thought, with a touch of color in her cheeks to give it life. The eyes were large, darkly lashed, warm. Chin and nose and cheek and brow were all molded by some master hand. Fair hair had been piled high to crown her finely shaped head. Her lips—yes, pretty lips that knew how to smile. "And don't explain," he told her quickly. "In fact, you were just the explanation I was needing. Madame at the desk has stopped wondering why I am here."

"Is she the wondering type?"

"That, among other things. My name is Fenner, by the way. Bill Fenner."

"I know. I read your reviews, Mr. Fenner. They tell me what I'm missing by living abroad."

"You haven't missed much in the last year. So you live in Paris?"

"Off and on." She glanced back to her own thoughts. "Actually, I have been doing some work for the *Chronicle* in the last month."

"I'm in luck. Small worlds aren't usually filled with colleagues that look like you."

"But that was only a temporary job—an emergency. I was filling in."

"You got the drawings finished in time?"

She looked a little startled. "You actually noticed—"

"That large portfolio was very impressive."

"Just some illustrations from the latest Paris showings."

I might have guessed that, he thought. Her simple black dress, sleeveless to show slender tanned arms, her pearls at the neck and on her ears, her smooth fair hair once more in perfect place, were all part of the pattern of the fashion world.

"The man who usually draws them for your fashion editor went for a weekend to Switzerland and fell from an alp. Broke his shoulder. So Mike Ballard thought of me."

"Very knowledgeable fellow, Mike Ballard."

"Fashions aren't really my line," she admitted. "But half the battle of getting a job is just to be there. Like Everest."

"What is your regular job?"

"I work for Historical Design and Decoration. It's a New York firm. They sent me to Europe three years ago. I've been here ever since."

"And off and on in Paris?"

She smiled. "Yes."

"Well, I'm glad I met you in an on-period. Or are you off again soon?"

"For a little, perhaps. It depends on what the clients in New York want. I have to travel around a good deal."

"I'm not really following you. What do they want?"

She laughed. "Designs and decorations."

"You mean someone wants her dining room to look like the Taj Mahal, and you go flying out to India?"

"Now, now," she said gently. "Some of our best clients are hardheaded businessmen. They need exact details of certain designs—a ceiling in a Roman *palazzo*, a mosaic floor in a Venetian church, a paneled wall in a French château, an arrangement of seventeenth-century fountains, an eighteenth-century staircase. They have an idea, and no time to travel. We find what they want. Usually, that is. Sometimes ideas seem wonderful in New York but—" She shrugged her shoulders.

"You sound like an enthusiast, anyway."

"Except when some occasional Marie Antoinette wanders

into the New York office, all ready to play milkmaid. Usually it's the swimming pool that brings out the silliest in women. Last month, a lady from Texas wanted some designs of Hadrian's villa—the part that lay around *his* pool." Claire Connor smiled and added, "The nymphs' shrine, she meant."

"Never underestimate the power of an oil well."

"Or what you can save in taxes if you claim depletion."

"So you chased off to Rome and sketched madly?" And I bet, he thought, that her pretty mouth was drawn into that strange little curve of disapproval—not unpleasant to see, but a little unexpected. The age of twenty-five or so (how old was she?) was not usually so critical of the silly season or aesthetic blasphemy.

"No. We talked her out of the idea. She settled for a Japanese tea-garden effect. We didn't have to send anyone to Japan. That's file nine: standard procedure, nowadays."

"But you didn't tell her that? My, my, what deception!"

The long eyelashes flickered. There was a sharp little intake of breath, and then again that wonderful smile. "But beneficial," she insisted. "Our client has taken up flower arrangement and boulder placing. She may become contemplative in the cherry-blossom season. Husband much pleased."

Fenner grinned. "Where did truth end and fantasy begin?"

She opened her gray eyes wide. "What is a story without some embroidery? Just a little, here and there? And you didn't let me finish."

"That," he agreed gravely, "is unforgivable. Please finish."

"I can't! I've lost the pace."

"It was something about her haiku poem for her next barbecue," he prompted.

"Oh yes . . . She began it well enough. 'Peaceful is evening among charred embers.' But she is running into trouble with the end. Can't get the poem into seventeen syllables."

"The next thing you know, her husband will be asking you for a full-color design of an authentic sixteenth-century padded cell, the kind of place they kept for little princes when mama and papa came from a long line of first cousins."

"Perhaps that's what we should have designed for her all along. In fact, I think it could become quite a standard item. There's a need for it nowadays."

"Not only for ladies with wild dreams of grandeur," he agreed, and glanced at the table where Lenoir and his friend were talking. They didn't seem exactly happy with their conversation. Lenoir wasn't even pretending to order from the menu which lay at his elbow. "You'll have dinner with me?" Fenner asked Claire Connor, whose eyes had followed his glance.

She hesitated. "I wish I could—"

"I have a table."

"But—"

"Oh, come on! You blow in here with the wind, all dressed to celebrate the end of an assignment, and then you won't stay. You aren't going to leave me to eat alone, are you?" His tone was joking, but he was mystified. Beautiful girls in smart little black dresses did not go out to dinner by themselves.

"It isn't really like that, you know."

"Isn't it?"

"Well—"

"You have another date? Just my luck."

"No. At least—not exactly—"

He smiled. "You just put on your prettiest dress to run around in the rain."

She looked at the white kid gloves, her small black silk bag. "I got all dressed up for a party. But I changed my mind."

"That's my fault, probably. I sat here conjuring you up. And you arrived."

"It was the fault of the party."

"Food or people?"

"People."

"All of them?" he asked, amused, still puzzled.

"One of them." She gave a little laugh. "When you are faced with certain situations, the only way to deal with them is—run."

"I thought you were a little breathless when you came in here."

"And I had to choose a restaurant like this! If it hadn't been for you, I'd have retreated right out into the rain." She looked around the tables. "Not a woman in sight."

"Two most respectable ladies," he corrected her.

"Firmly attached. Like their hats. Think of all the cafés on the Left Bank where I could have slipped in by myself, ordered an omelet, and not even raised one eyebrow. And I had to choose this one!"

The lady does protest too much, he thought, his interest growing. "I still wish you'd have dinner with me. I'm sure they make wonderful omelets here."

"Sacrilege," she said. "If we don't spend three hours over

dinner, we are barbarians. And that's the reason I can't have dinner with you. I just haven't got three hours tonight. I haven't even got two. I've an appointment at half past nine. That's less than an hour away."

"Back to business so soon?" But she wasn't going to have dinner with him, that was certain. He couldn't keep the disappointment out of his voice, and his disbelief.

That upset her a little, somehow, as if she were being ungracious. "Please forgive me. I wish I could spend the evening with you. I really do." She hesitated. "The truth is that I'm leaving for Venice early tomorrow. I'll be away for a week perhaps. Will you still be here when I get back?"

"No. I'm leaving Paris on Monday. I don't get back until the middle of the month, perhaps later. Will you be here?"

"I don't know." She looked at him quickly. "Honestly, I don't."

"Historical Design and Decoration keeps you busy."

"Yes," she said bleakly. She tried to smile.

"Have another drink, anyway."

"I think I'd better leave," She glanced at the dining room. The gentle smile on her face was still there, but she had become, very suddenly, a thousand miles away.

"I know who you are," he told her, watching her profile. "You're a Greek girl from the fourth century. Scopas saw you walking past in the market place."

Her gray eyes had been startled for a moment. And then they relaxed. Her smile widened. She said softly, "You make it very hard for me to leave." She rose. "If I don't, I'll—" She shrugged her shoulders, held out her hand, as he rose, too. "Thank you, Mr. Fenner."

"I'll see you to the door, at least."

"You'll give the waiter apoplexy."

Fenner grinned and dropped twelve new francs on the table. "That should hold him." Roussin was coming toward them, he noticed. And at the fourth table against the wall, Lenoir was on his feet, still talking eloquently. The red-haired film producer was arranging and rearranging his fork and knife, his eyes cast down, as he listened. Abruptly, he cut off Lenoir with a wave of the hand, and it was he who was now talking. Around them, other tables were complete islands of self-absorption.

"Where do you live, Miss Connor?"

"Just across the Seine. Oh dear, have I lost a glove? No, here it is—"

"Let me take you there." That was one way of getting her address.

Her pace quickened as they reached Angélique's desk. Outside, the heavy thundershower was over, leaving the dark street hosed-down, clean, glistening under its lights. "It really isn't far," she said. "There's no need. I've been enough bother to you for one night."

"Mr. Fenner!" Roussin's voice called quietly.

Fenner half turned. Behind him, he heard a murmured "Good-by," and the light staccato of slender high heels. He swung around again. She had left.

"Mr. Fenner!" Roussin's voice was urgent enough to stop Fenner dead.

Angélique, he noted, was well within earshot. He forced the annoyance out of his voice. "I'm sorry we can't stay for dinner tonight," he told Roussin. "Another time." He took a step toward the door.

"Perhaps I may have the pleasure of having you as my guest for luncheon tomorrow? Is twelve o'clock too early? That allows me some time for my friends before most people arrive."

Lunch with Vaugiroud? Fenner wondered in amazement. Surely Roussin wasn't being serious.

He wasn't. It was only an excuse. For, without being obvious about the little maneuver, he had managed to turn his back to Angélique. He dropped his voice, spoke rapidly. "A message has just come. Mr. Carlson will be at your hotel. Eleven o'clock. Tonight." More normally, he added, "Please give my apologies to the charming young lady for detaining you. I am sorry that tonight has been so busy. Excuse me." He turned away, to bow politely to another departing guest. It was Monsieur Fernand Lenoir, hurrying out with a crisp step, a pleasant smile for everyone, a man of grace and good manners, healthy, happy, and wise. The perfect picture of a discreet and successful man of affairs, Fenner thought, and followed it out into the street.

He could see no sign of Claire Connor. The interchange with Henri Roussin had taken only a matter of seconds, but it had been long enough for her to vanish in the darkness. At the corner, he halted and lit a cigarette to give himself time to study the boulevard. It was crowded and hopeless. There were several pretty blonde heads, many little black dresses. For a minute, he watched the busy traffic, the swarm of people hurrying to make up for the delay of sheltering from the heavy shower of rain, and saw his hopes for a most promising evening disintegrate.

Monsieur Fernand Lenoir, he noticed, had found a taxi. Fenner watched it speed away, thinking gloomily that there was one man who knew where he was going. From the side street behind him, where the Café Racine lay, a gray car came swiftly, turning the corner sharply to take the same direction as Lenoir's taxi. Well, Fenner thought, Lenoir may know where he is going, but does he know he is being followed? The idea amused him. His gloom began to lift. Sure, his evening was shattered, but it had not been planned in the first place. He had better find a cab, himself, and return to the Crillon, let the porter there deal with all the palaver of making a call to New York. After that, a quick supper in the bar, and back to his room by eleven o'clock for Carlson. He'd be half asleep by that time, in any case: this had been a long, long day, and not one of the most restful, either. It would be pleasant to wake up tomorrow and think about his own interests, for a change. Good-by Professor Vaugiroud, good-by Roussin, Lenoir and quiet film producers. And good-by to Claire Connor. That, at least, he regretted to say. She was only a mirage, he decided: a dream shining out from an expanse of desert, thirty minutes of delightful hope, and then nothing. Good-by Claire.

But through the rest of the evening, at odd times, she would keep coming back into his mind. Mike Ballard must know her address. And there was that firm, too—Historical Decoration and Design. Or Design and Decoration. She would be back in Paris some time, wouldn't she?

Not good-by at all, he decided over his cognac and coffee. You just gave up too easily there, he told himself. And felt better.

NINE

ELEVEN O'CLOCK FOUND Bill Fenner, relaxed in pajamas and dressing gown, ready for bed the minute he got rid of Carlson. He wasn't disappointed in Carlson's punctuality. "Hello," he said as he opened the door. "And where have you been? You're five seconds late."

Carlson, looking at Fenner's clothes, had his own question. "What's the idea? I didn't know drama critics went to bed before dawn."

"I've had a hard day. And what's *your* idea? Out with it. Then I'll pitch into that bed and not move an eyelid until noon."

Carlson took the most comfortable chair. He needed it. He said, a little gloomily, "Your raincoat never showed up at the airport."

Was that all? Fenner wondered. "Oh, it's here. It was left at the porter's desk at five o'clock. An exchange was proposed, but our story of returning the other coat to Orly was passed on. Did anyone try to pick it up there?"

Carlson nodded. "A man tried to claim it around seven o'clock. But alas, alack, it had already been impounded by the Sûreté. Which must have made his telephoned report, back to Paris, a little on the somber side."

"I thought that would have made you cheerful."

"It would, except for one thing. Mr. Goldsmith's friends have traced you to this hotel. So my job is to get you out of here."

"What?"

"That's right. Get dressed, pack, and pay your bill. We're moving you out."

"But—"

"You were going to look for another hotel, weren't you?"

98

"Sure, but I haven't got around to finding one."

"I have a friend who has lent me his apartment. You'll like it there. It has a view of the Seine and Notre-Dame and all the rest of the American dream."

"Look—" began Fenner.

"I'm looking. At your safety, friend. Get cracking, will you? I've had a hard day myself."

Fenner stared at the blue eyes that were meeting his with the hardness of cold fact behind them. He began peeling off his dressing gown. "I suppose you've already arranged for a car to meet us at the front door?" he asked with some annoyance.

"That's right," Carlson said blandly. "At eleven-twenty-five, to be exact. Step on it, Bill."

Fenner began to dress. His brows were down, his mouth in a straight line.

"Thank God," Carlson said, "you are not the arguing type."

"I can't be. But you wouldn't be here if you hadn't a good reason."

"Several good reasons. Bill, why the hell did you have to go and see Vaugiroud?"

"Aren't you glad I did?"

"From my point of view, it was fine. But from yours— well, Goldsmith and his coat were trouble enough for one day. And Vaugiroud and that setup over on the Rue Jean-Calas, and you really could be in double trouble. Somewhere tonight, my friend, you are being discussed pretty heavily."

Fenner knotted his tie, brushed his hair, and began packing. "So you think that the ten-thousand-dollar bills may connect with Vaugiroud's idea of fabricated evidence for the next big lie?"

"I didn't say that," Carlson said.

"Well, I'm saying it."

"To me only, I hope."

"Look," Fenner said, amusement returning, "whoever is concocting fantastic plots to shake the West into pieces hasn't much time to worry about one drama critic who wandered on stage at the wrong moment. Besides, I'm off stage now."

"I'm just making sure that you'll stay off," Carlson rose and began checking closet and drawers. "And don't use the word 'fantastic' too lightly, Bill. The only time to laugh at conspiracies is after they have been smashed."

"Then you are taking Vaugiroud seriously?"

Carlson didn't answer that. He moved into the bathroom. "All clear here," he called. "Lucky you didn't spend much time unpacking."

"Well," Fenner said, refusing to be diverted from Vaugiroud, "that's a relief. I began to wonder after I left you at Rue Jean-Calas if I had acted too quickly."

Silence from Carlson.

"I took a chance on calling you. I wasn't shown the memorandum. He just briefed me."

"How much?"

"Just enough, I suppose, to get me sufficiently interested to help him. Say—shouldn't I have called you? I thought you were the expert on that kind of thing."

"Thank you," Carlson said dryly.

"Well, seeing you're so communicative—was your visit worth-while?"

"Interesting."

"No real value?" Fenner asked worriedly. All that trouble for nothing.

"I didn't say that."

"You don't have to be so damned cryptic."

"Bad habit," Carlson agreed. He closed the last wardrobe drawer. "All clear? When you pay your bill, give them American Express as your forwarding address. Say you're spending the weekend with a friend if they seem puzzled by this quick departure. At twenty-four minutes past eleven, start walking out. I'll be in the lobby, keeping an eye on you. The car, at the front entrance, will be a dark-blue Citroën. The driver will be dressed in tweeds, and has gray hair. I'll be just behind you. And the minute you are in the car, I'll join you. Right?"

"Right." Fenner moved over to the telephone to call the desk, hesitated. "Shall I tell them I'm checking out, or do I just surprise them?"

"Best keep to the usual procedure."

"That's what I like about life with Auntie: everything is so nice and normal."

Carlson's tired face relaxed into a grin. He closed the door quietly.

The blue Citroën sped quarterway around the Place de la Concorde, then branched off into the Champs-Elysées. Within a few hundred yards, it stopped near some trees sheltering the driveway to a restaurant, once a private villa, which stood discreetly withdrawn into its own grounds. Quickly, Carlson and Fenner climbed out with the luggage, and crossed over to a gray Renault that was waiting under the trees. Before Carlson had slipped into the driver's seat with Fenner beside him, the Citroën was continuing on its way, up the broad avenue lined with trees and park and restaurant gardens, toward the distant neon lights of the Champs-Elysées' busier section.

Carlson waited. He let a few cars pass before he swung the Renault out of the driveway, and followed the Citroën leisurely. He was gently humming *Get Me to the Church on Time*.

"I'm most impressed," Fenner said. Far ahead, the Citroën had become only one of a weaving pattern of taillights. He was still irritated by the supercaution. "All this split-second timing just for me?"

Carlson stopped humming. "It isn't as comic as you think. Or will you wait, before you take this thing seriously, until you're picked up by one of Kalganov's boys, hauled out to a quiet house on the outskirts of Paris, given the electric treatment so they can find out how much Vaugiroud does know?"

Fenner was shocked into silence.

"I am not playing wild hunches, Bill. There was a guy in the lobby whose eyes popped when he saw you were checking out. He made a quick dash to a telephone, a very quick call, and another quick dash outside just in time to note the Citroën driving off. Fortunately for us, taxis are scarce at this time of night. Since honking was banned, I guess cab drivers have lost some of their incentive. Anyway, our eye-popped friend couldn't quite reach us by the time we changed cars. A taxi did chug past at full tilt, though, before I switched on our engine." Carlson began humming again. This time it was a neatly ordered snatch of Bach.

"And who the hell is Kalganov?" Fenner asked angrily, transferring his annoyance onto the strange name.

Carlson finished humming the last line of *Sheep may safely graze*. "Soothing," he said. "Encouraging, too. Just kill all the bad wolves, and you can eat in peace." Ahead of them was an avenue of giant movie houses, neon lights as bright as day, broad sidewalks with innumerable cafés and tables and people gawking at the slowed automobiles. So they swung left from the Champs-Elysées, and traveled gently through quieter, residential streets in a leisurely detour back toward the Seine.

"Who is Kalganov?" Fenner asked after a silent five minutes.

"A name to remember," Carlson said briefly. "Not to repeat, not to say aloud, just to remember."

"Was Kalganov your business in Paris?"

"And not to ask questions about, either," Carlson told him sharply. "Sorry, Bill—I've got a lot on my mind. I've been spending the last hour talking about Kalganov. It's a name that has haunted many of us for years. There isn't an allied Intelligence unit that hasn't been interested."

And in the last hour, Kalganov was no longer a name but a man, to be found right here in Paris? Fenner studied the small smile on Carlson's lips. "Is he another of those terrorist types?" he asked most innocently.

Carlson's smile broke into a laugh. "That's about it," he said noncommittally. "By the way, how much did Vaugiroud tell you?"

The question was not as idly curious as Carlson's voice made it. It had purpose. Two purposes, Fenner decided: one is to find out what I know, the other to get me off the subject of Kalganov. I've had a quiet warning about that name—why else the calculated indiscretion on Carlson's part? All right, I'll tell him what I know. That may be the quickest way to get back to Kalganov. Any man who thinks he could forcibly kidnap and question me is slightly more than a name to remember, as far as I'm concerned.

Fenner began his answer. He kept it as brief as he could, but factual. Carlson listened intently. By the time they had crossed the Seine, and were heading back to the old center of Paris, the story of Jacques who became Fernand Lenoir was completed. "I still don't know how Lenoir got away with it for all these years," Fenner ended.

"Not too difficult. He has always been Fernand Lenoir except for the three years he worked as Jacques in the Resistance. All he had to worry about was any ghost from that period of his life returning to haunt him. He thought there were none."

"He was born Fernand Lenoir, built up his life as Fernand Lenoir?"

"And a very pleasant life, too."

So Lenoir was not the puzzling Mr. Kalganov. "Does the same go for his friend the film producer?"

"Robert Wahl? He is a very different pattern from Lenoir. He wasn't born here. Didn't grow up here. He arrived in

1946, a survivor from a Nazi concentration camp in East Germany."

"Whose records are all in Russian hands. No family, I suppose?"

"All died in the camp."

"Where was he born and brought up?"

"Leipzig, supposedly."

Also in Russian hands, Fenner thought. "No questions ever asked?"

"As far as many Frenchmen are concerned, a man's life only begins from the instant he arrives in Paris. Besides, he was clever enough to work his way into the intellectual camp. He was interested in writers, started a little magazine."

"That takes money."

"His family had money. Deposited safely in Switzerland, it seems. And everything he touched seemed to make just enough to let him branch out farther."

"One of those lucky guys."

"One of those well-provided guys."

"Subsidized?"

"Must have been. Wahl's projects weren't as successful financially as people think."

"So he began with a little magazine—" Fenner waited. No response. He said jokingly, "You know, I could find out all about his career, as far as my friends in Paris know it."

Carlson shook his head. "I bet you would, too. All right. First, the magazine; a few years later, a small radio station; after that, controlling interests in two provincial newspapers; next, two short films with excellent photography and despairing themes; and now, he wants to make another movie. Scene: American Zone in West Berlin. He has applied for our permission. He has even sent us a copy of the shooting script to show us the story is nonpolitical, harmless."

"West Berlin? Why didn't he choose East Berlin?"

"That is what interested us. We knew Wahl was far to the left. That's no secret. He doesn't like Americans. That's no secret, either. And there are several anti-American Leftists among the French intellectuals: that's their normal conformity. Only, why should one of them choose to make a film in West Berlin?"

"Perhaps," Fenner said, with a grin, "he is a reforming character. Wants to make up and be friends."

"We thought of that. We also knew that if we refused him

without adequate reason, we'd have his friends chanting about American intolerance and hysteria."

"So you came to Paris to find out more about Robert Wahl?"

Carlson nodded. "And kept running up against the same blank wall. Even non-Communists would say, 'Yes, he is obviously in sympathy with the Communists, perhaps he is even a party member. But that isn't against the law. Besides, you know our Communist intellectuals: they talk ideas, make propaganda, but they aren't militant. They may be annoying, but they are harmless. They want peace, not war. They quote *Izvestia*, but they weren't trained under Beria. They don't torture or kill.' Yes, that was always the reaction. Robert Wahl was honest because he did not disguise his opinions. He was sincere. Therefore, he was pure in heart." Carlson's laugh was brief and bitter. "Not trained under Beria! My—" He concentrated on the curve of Seine, its black waters gleaming in golden streaks under the lights edging its banks.

"So until Vaugiroud identified Wahl today, he was in the clear?" That was a depressing thought.

"Not quite," Carlson said sharply. He spoke like a man who had done a good deal of work and saw the credit being taken from him. "I had already made out a report against his project in West Berlin. My reasons were valid. Not based on his opinions, either."

"On what, then?"

"You want to know everything, don't you?" Carlson was amused.

"Not everything," Fenner said, very gently. "Just enough to flesh out the skeleton. If Wahl is as dangerous as Vaugiroud implied—I'd like to know what league I'm playing in."

"You aren't playing in it any longer."

"Who is to decide that? You or Robert Wahl? You know, his name is familiar." Then Fenner remembered, at least, the article that the honest and sincere Mr. Wahl had written. On Cuba. And one some years ago, when Fenner had been interested in the Far East, on Indochina just before the French backed out. "He travels, doesn't he?"

"He gets around," Carlson said. He glanced sharply at Fenner: how much did he really know? Was that only a harmless question about Robert Wahl's travels? "We'll make a little detour here," he said, and swung the car away from the Seine. At this moment, he was a sorely tried security officer, whose own hard-earned triumph of the last few weeks had consisted of a detailed study of Robert Wahl's journeys abroad. Their reasons were always admirable: a search for new talent among foreign writers or actors; original backgrounds for movies (which never got made); material for travel articles; attendance at some international conference. But Wahl's visits abroad, when examined closely, formed a disquieting pattern. He arrived in a time of mounting crisis, and just after he departed there had always been some unexplained troubles added to the general strain: riots which erupted violently, bombings, assassination attempts. Situations always deteriorated after Wahl came on the scene, whether it was to attend a student peace conference or give a series of lectures. This could be coincidence Carlson had noted in his report. But regularly occurring coincidence deserved closer examination. Until that was made, he advised against any visit by Robert Wahl to West Berlin. Period. Triple period, in fact.

"Lot of detours," Fenner observed caustically. And the biggest one, so far, had been around Kalganov. "If we make a left turn here," he suggested humorously as he looked out at the busy boulevard, "we can drop in at the Café Racine for a nightcap."

"No more visits for you there, my friend," Carlson said warningly. "And we'll postpone that left turn for another block. I'm taking you to the Ile Saint-Louis. Any objections?"

"Not to that."

"To what?"

"To being kidnapped." Fenner's grin was wide. "Even one of the best views in Paris won't compensate for a locked door."

Carlson looked shocked. "We're only keeping you safe—"

"Sure. That's easier than telling me what's going on."

"Do you really enjoy making my life miserable?"

"At present," Fenner said, "mine is no sweet-smelling bed of roses."

"It could be worse."

"I planned it quite differently. This, Carlson, is my first night in Paris."

"And this is my last," Carlson said quietly. "Helluva way to celebrate, I agree." He was smiling though. Fenner's complaint had been more cheerful than he had expected. Fenner would cooperate, he was sure. Fairly sure. But how much more will I have to tell him to keep him quiet for a weekend behind a locked door? Of course, it could be less time

than that. The too long and happy career of Robert Wahl
might be ending even now. The quiet hunt was on. Bernard,
at the Sûreté, and his men were on the job. "You were only going to spend it sleeping. Alone, too. You can do that just as
well here."

Fenner looked around him with sudden interest. They were
driving onto the peaceful island of Saint-Louis, turning into
a placid street edged on one side by tall houses, silent and
proud, and on the other by the quick dark current of the
Seine. Across the waters lay a second island, where Notre-
Dame rose with flying buttresses into the pale glow of a
young moon lazing over a cloudless ink-blue sky. "Except,"
he told Carlson, "this is the kind of place where a pretty
girl should be more than a dream."

"You'll find everything else. Running water, electric lights,
all modern comforts, monsieur will be happy here; cheap at
the price." He stopped the car, handed Fenner a key. "Top
floor, front. Marked 4A. You can't miss it."

"Concierge?"

"Expects you. Won't be visible. I'll get the car parked
away from here. See you in ten minutes." As Fenner looked
at him, he added, "Just want to see you tucked up for the
night. I take my kidnapping jobs very seriously. Hey, don't
forget your coat!" He threw it over Fenner's arm. "You'll
find the Scotch in the first cabinet in the pantry." There was
a small salute for a laden Fenner, and the car moved off,
smoothly, into the quiet and gentle shadows.

More than running water had been added to the apartment
on the top floor. There was an efficient kitchen, a gleaming
bathroom, a well-stocked pantry. A clutter of small cubicles
had lost their dividing walls to form a pleasant living room
with three windows and a view toward Notre-Dame. The
room had low, simple furniture, books and pictures on white
walls, white rugs on polished wood floor, white roses in a
green bowl on the desk. Fenner raised an eyebrow and removed his luggage, quickly, into the bedroom at the back of
the apartment. It was marked by simplicity, comfort stripped
down to the essentials, a place to sleep deeply, with no in-
trusions except from the closet (cleared for his use and the
only one left unlocked) which had a haunting scent, faint,
delicate, lingering. Behind the shower curtain in the bathroom, he found a flowered cap, a charming piece of rubber-

ized froth, forgotten on a faucet. The man who lived here had good taste in women as well as in pictures. But white rugs? Fenner raised his eyebrow again.

The Scotch, however, was authentic. There was ice, too, in the refrigerator. Standing at an opened window, looking at the view, he was a reasonably contented man.

TEN

WHEN CARLSON ARRIVED, Bill Fenner was still standing at the window with the living room in darkness. "Another admirer of the old lady, I see." He groped his way expertly to a chair. "She'll still be there tomorrow," he suggested.

Fenner had a last look at Notre-Dame, switched on the lamp at the desk, and pulled the white tweed curtains together. "Big and black and impressive. The proportions never seem quite right, and yet there's something about her. . . . Why didn't they add the spires, I wonder?"

"Spent too much on the gargoyles."

"A couple of centuries to put together, and still here after eight hundred years."

"That's how to build," Carlson agreed. "None of that planned-obsolescence stuff about her."

"Nor was there for St. Paul's or Cologne," Fenner reminded him.

"She was lucky. At a price, though."

Which is still being paid, Fenner thought. He poured two man-sized drinks in outsize glasses. "Hope your friend doesn't object to having his Scotch vanish."

"We'll replace."

"Who is he?"

"An illustrator. Good guy."

"He does all right."

"You like it?"

"I wouldn't mind having an apartment on this island my-self—" Fenner stopped. "Was that why you chose this place? So that I'd stay put for a couple of days without much kicking or screaming?"

"You might as well be comfortable."

"Look, Carlson—"

"Neill is shorter. Saves the breath."

108

"I'm not staying put."

"Give me that drink, Bill. Thanks. Well—" He raised his glass. He began drinking, thirstily.

"Here's to the good guy," Fenner said shortly.

"Here's to all of them, wherever you find them," Carlson added between two long draughts.

"You sound pessimistic about the human race."

"Only about its future. It has been that kind of day." Carlson finished his drink, refused another, and relaxed in his armchair. He was letting his exhaustion show now, and didn't care who saw it. "Sorry to keep going back to Vaugiroud. But how much did he actually tell you?"

"You heard it all in the car."

"All? Come on, Bill, I need to know."

"Everything. It wasn't too much, was it?"

"No. But Robert Wahl may not believe that. We'll have to think up some safe explanation for your visit to the Rue Jean-Calas and pass it around." He paused. "You see, Wahl is definitely interested in Vaugiroud."

"That was Wahl's man, was it—the one who was watching the house?"

"Yes. I had a good look at him when I left Vaugiroud."

"In that case, he had a good look at you."

"A calculated risk. And it paid off. I wanted a close-up of that face. It was the one chance I had, so I took it. Why not?" Carlson was smiling it off. "I'm leaving Paris tomorrow." And they'll be under arrest, he thought, bless their clever little minds.

"Was his face worth that risk?"

Carlson studied Fenner thoughtfully. At last, he said, "I'll make a bargain with you, Bill. I'll tell you what I can, within certain limits, if you will stay here quietly for a couple of days. Will you?"

"That's a hard bargain."

"It's pretty soft, actually. You could have been hidden for those two days in a back room of some dreary small hotel where the plumbing doesn't work and the view consists of a brick wall."

"Hidden? Damn it, Neill, you're taking all this too seriously."

"That's better than taking it too lightly."

"I'll keep my mouth shut. I'll attend to my own business. Isn't that enough?"

"You go wandering around, and you know what? You'll be

just the man to run into one of Kalganov's boys, on the street, in a bar, at a museum—which they use frequently, I assure you."

"They wouldn't know me; I wouldn't know them."

"If you met the man who was watching Vaugiroud's house?" Carlson had scored there. His exasperation faded.

"So he is Kalganov's man, too?" Fenner asked quickly. "Then Kalganov and Wahl are one and the same?"

Carlson only looked at him blankly.

"Who is this Kalganov?" Fenner asked. "What kind of a man—"

"You really are trouble prone, Bill," Carlson said quietly. "That's one sure thing about you."

"I've been trouble prone since I decided I was going to major in French at college."

Carlson was mildly amused. Or perhaps he needed another of his detours. "And didn't you finish college?"

"Eventually. On the G.I. Bill. But first, my weakness for French landed me in North Africa as an interpreter, and got me promoted to Paris before the Germans pulled out. Someday, you must let me show you my bullet hole. Oh, it's not in me. It looks much better decorating a corner building on the Place Saint-Michel."

Carlson had a new look of interest in his eyes. "What were you, in that war? OSS?"

"You might call me an expendable contact man. Strictly minor jobs, but seldom a dull minute."

Carlson showed some quiet astonishment. He seemed relieved, too, and thoughtful. "You didn't tell Vaugiroud you had been working with the French Resistance."

"With *his* record? My few days in Paris, even with a bullet hole—" Fenner shook his head. "That proves two more things about me: I know when to fall flat on my face; and I can keep my trap shut."

There was a deliberate pause. Then Carlson said slowly, "I'll tell you about Kalganov. After that, I don't think you'll argue about staying here for a couple of days—until he and his contacts are safely locked up. Here is what we know about that name. He has used many others at various times, but this is the real one." And Carlson's unemotional voice began pulling the facts out of a well-remembered file.

Alexei Vassilievitch Kalganov, born in Kiev, 1917; taken to Belgrade in 1919 by *émigré* parents; his father an ex-general turned taxi driver. Early years unrecorded. By seventeen, he was taking part in Balkan politics—blowing up bridges, derailing trains, shooting at cabinet ministers. Two years later, he added some ideology to his anarchism and went to Moscow. He had specialized training there, and was sent to Spain—not to fight, but to liquidate. From there, he went to Marseilles and learned how to organize. He went back to Moscow in 1944, traveling through Paris, with a Resistance group (subsequently eliminated) helping his escape. He worked with Beria for a couple of years, in the Ukraine, in eastern Poland. And then he became untraceable.

It was thought he had been liquidated with Beria. Except, in recent years, there were hints of the name Kalganov— from a couple of defectors who had been trained in assassination, from a few of the terrorists who were arrested in some of the disturbances he had possibly organized. Kalganov was, perhaps, dead. Yet the name persisted. Since 1946, it had become a rumor, a myth, a threat, a hidden menace.

Carlson ended. And frowned. "In 1946, just before he disappeared, he stated that he had killed over two thousand people. Two thousand and twenty-nine, to be exact. And don't think he was boasting. Those were the days of the grand massacres. I guess the anarchists and socialists he liquidated in Catalonia, at the end of the civil war, accounted for half of them. And the Free French he finished off, when he was trusted by the *maquis*, added some more. And the Ukrainians, and Poles—" Carlson's frown deepened. "Let's have another drink," he said.

As it was poured, he went on, "Today I learned two interesting facts from Vaugiroud: he identified Wahl as a terrorist who was secretly passed through Paris in 1944, en route to Moscow; he recognized the man watching his house as Robert Wahl's chauffeur. So after I left Vaugiroud, I paid a visit to my friend Bernard, over at the Sûreté. He has been interested in Kalganov ever since those murders in the *maquis*. He has collected a file of photographs—men who have been known to work with Kalganov."

"And none of Kalganov himself?"

"What do you want to do—make our job easy?" But Carlson had made some discovery from the Sûreté files. There was excitement in his eyes, in his voice. "The man who watched Vaugiroud's house is one of Kalganov's men, all right. His name is Jan Aarvan. And that's the boy I want you to avoid, Bill. So you'll stay here. Right?"

Fenner nodded. A bargain was a bargain. Carlson had answered his question. But he still had others to ask. "So Robert Wahl is Kalganov?" *And I wasn't so far wrong,* he thought.

"Possibly."

"Only possibly?"

"Deductions and coincidences don't make a case. But—" Carlson smiled—"this is the first opening in that blank wall. Thanks to Vaugiroud."

"And to calculated risks."

Carlson turned aside the compliment by saying briskly, "We'll have to concentrate on Robert Wahl. When we catch Kalganov, it will be for a crime that Robert Wahl has committed. So far, Wahl hasn't made any mistakes." Carlson thought over that. "So far," he repeated, more optimistically.

"Have you any idea what he is planning now?"

Carlson only looked as ignorant as possible. The briefing session was over. "It certainly isn't just handing out leaflets, organizing pickets." He glanced at his watch and rose. "I'll push off. I probably won't see you again, so—"

"Where shall I leave the apartment key?"

Carlson looked at him sharply.

"I'll stay here for a couple of days—no good adding to your ulcers—but I'm pushing off, too."

"Where?"

"I'll be wandering around the provinces for the next two weeks. I'm doing a couple of articles on the French national theater. I won't be back in Paris until mid-September. Does that make you feel better?"

"No."

Fenner said in amusement, "Hey! Let's keep things in proportion, Neill. Kalganov hasn't taken over France."

"You'd be surprised how much backing he can command from ordinary party members, who won't know what they are doing, or why they are doing it, but who'll obey. Without one question. They're fighting a war—"

"Look, you don't have to exaggerate to make me realize they're a well-organized bunch—"

"Exaggerate? That would be impossible with men like Kalganov. They are hard realists, in the same sense as the top Nazis were realists. Their aim is total victory. And if they speak of total victory, they are at war. Or aren't they?"

"I'm not arguing with you on that. But, at present, they are—well, partly leashed."

"Are they?"

"Or at least marking time."

"And they'll halt smartly—on whose command?"

"They do take orders. That's what you said yourself, wasn't it?"

"Sure," Carlson said wearily, "they'll all take orders. All the way from soft-sell, sweet-talk boys who bloom in the open right down to the hidden things in the undergrowth like Kalganov, they all take orders. That, Bill, is what depresses me."

He worries too much, Fenner thought. He's losing his sense of balance. He will end up not even seeing real peace when it's offered to us. "Relax, Neill, relax. After all, the masters have been talking peace. At Geneva, for three years. They've been getting nowhere fast, I admit, but the thing to remember is that they haven't walked out of the conference room. They are still talking. No bombs exploded for three years. That's my point. There's always some hope while there's talk."

"Only if the two people talking mean the same thing in the words they use. Peace, for instance. There's peace in Hungary, according to the Communists. But who wants that kind of peace? Bill, when both sides have agreed on an exact meaning of an all-important word, such as peace, and start talking from there—I'll not only relax, I'll be able to resign and go back to Iowa, where there's a small-town newspaper I once edited. And on Sundays I could stretch out in my favorite spot under an apple tree I used to know, and I could look up at the sky and say, 'Peace, you're wonderful!' " Carlson's voice had lost its edge. He laughed at himself, at Bill Fenner. "You civilians! You hear an army man worrying aloud about the Russians, and you immediately think he is some jaundiced militant, trigger happy soldier. He is just as much a civilian as you are, only he has probably been reading the documents that don't get published."

There was a slight inclination of Fenner's head. "Okay, okay," he said soothingly.

"Here's one little item that will be published, however. Tomorrow. In headlines right across the front page. The Russians, while still talking at Geneva, have exploded a bomb."

"What?"

"You heard me."

"They've broken the moratorium?"

"Smashed it. This bomb is only the first of a planned series. There's another being popped right this minute. It takes several months to prepare a series like that. What price talk?"

"My God—" Fenner's anger was rising.

"Exactly how I felt," Carlson told him. "Remember that piece of fakery, will you, when you are dealing with the Kalganovs in this world?"

"I've had some experience with them," Fenner reminded him sharply. Perhaps that had been his whole opposition to Carlson in the last half hour: the feeling that Carlson might have studied Communist techniques, but he himself had experienced some of them, first hand, and nothing made up for all the bitterness and anguish of a personal betrayal.

"You haven't. Kalganov is a different type from your ex-wife's friends in New York. He isn't George Williston, alias Geoffrey Wills, alias Bruno."

Fenner could only stare blankly.

"In New York, your wife had two other names, also. Didn't you know?"

Fenner rose. He shook his head. He walked over to the desk, then to a bookshelf, then to a picture.

Carlson's quiet voice, flat and unemotional, followed him. "Kalganov makes George Williston look like a toy balloon you can buy at the Central Park Zoo."

Fenner said slowly, under control again, "What about Fernand Lenoir? Is he another Williston, or is he in Kalganov's league?"

"Kalganov wouldn't lift a finger to help anyone like Williston. So, judging from today's interest in Vaugiroud, Lenoir is Kalganov's man. Kalganov protects his own to protect himself."

Fenner came back to the group of armchairs. "Sandra has really moved up," he said bitterly. "Or gone far down."

For a moment, Carlson hesitated. "You did divorce her?" he asked.

"She divorced me." A small smile played around Fenner's lips. "For desertion. In Mexico."

"You went down there, I hope?" Carlson asked in alarm.

"I sent a lawyer to represent me."

Carlson relaxed. "Then it is legal."

"Quite final." Fenner's voice was final, too.

"I'm glad of that. Especially now." He added, as if his words had sounded too ominous, "Desertion? Of all the damned impudence!"

"I did walk out."

"Into a hospital."

"You pick up a lot of information, don't you?"

"Just an old newspaperman, like yourself." Carlson remembered something. He sat down again. "I'll just have a last cigarette. Sit down. Relax, Bill."

What's next? Fenner wondered. He sat down and lit a cigarette, too.

"Mike Ballard met you at the airport. How well do you know him?"

"Just off and on. What's wrong?"

"Nothing as yet."

"You mean he's enjoying Sandra's parties too much?"

"He is clean politically. Honest enough, that way."

"Then what?"

"Well—he is laying himself wide open for blackmail."

"How?"

"He has a family which he seems to love. He has a career that he likes. Yet the idiot has set up a mistress in an apartment in Paris, with the money that he has made on the stock market by following Lenoir's friendly tips. Could you warn him—tactfully?"

"Me?" Fenner had to laugh. "He thinks I am here to take over his job." And no wonder Walt Penneyman has been worrying about the Paris office. "Good God—Ballard isn't even in town this weekend. He didn't expect any news to break. Left everything in charge of André Spitzer. Let's hope Spitzer can handle it—or else Walt Penneyman will really start his own bomb explosions."

"Spitzer will handle his report on the French reaction to the breaking of the moratorium exactly as Lenoir would like him to. Play it down, muted key. Show no alarm, suggest understanding for Russia's mistrust which makes her sometimes so 'difficult,' drop a reminder of Hiroshima, pull out every psychological stop in the organ accompaniment to the neutralists' hymn."

"Does he think Walt Penneyman is a fool?"

"No. He knows that Penneyman, like the rest of us, will be shocked and bewildered. And angry. Angry, too, with the French, who—from Spitzer's report—seem to equate Soviet Russia and the United States as two similar nuisances. By the time your New York office gets in other reports from Europe, and starts evaluating the news properly, Spitzer's suggestions will have entered into a lot of subconscious minds. Second reports from France, however corrective, won't en-

tirely blot first impressions out of some minds. And in Spitzer's creed, every little helps."

Fenner nodded. He had seen that happen before. It was
one of the nightmares of newspapermen: the dishonest
source, the unsuspected twist. The Nazis had been expert at
that. There was one major news source in Europe that had
scarcely recovered yet from that duplicity. "How the hell did
Spitzer ever edge his way into the *Chronicle?*"

"Ballard needed extra help, and Lenoir recommended Spitzer. He has an enormous capacity for work. Most obliging, and
no complaints. So promotion came. He is now second to Ballard. He also introduced Ballard to his mistress. What you
might call the generally useful type."

"He will be out on his ear after his handling of today's
news."

"Will he send it under his own name?" Carlson asked with
a most disarming smile.

Of course he wouldn't. He would send it under Ballard's
name, with the friendly pretense of covering up his boss's
absence. And Ballard would either have to stand by the report or give himself away.

"Where is he this weekend? Could you reach him?"

"I'd have to ask Spitzer for his address," Fenner said. He
swore under his breath. "Damned if I don't spike Comrade
Spitzer's little gun."

"How?" Carlson was suddenly and most cheerfully interested.

"I'll cable a report to Penneyman myself, say Ballard's in
bed with grippe—"

"Sweet Mademoiselle Grippe," Carlson said reflectively.

"You're recovering fast." And Carlson did look more like
the Carlson of that morning.

He said, "It's pleasant to spike a gun now and then. Perhaps that's all we can do: keep spiking, until they get good
and tired of loading." Carlson thought over that. "Yes, when
our policy is to prove that defense is superior to attack—a
most original policy, which would certainly have lost us the
American Revolution—the only thing we can do is to keep
spiking, call their bluff from the big to the small, let them
get away with nothing, wear the bastards down. Bill—thank
you! You've put life in these old bones. You've inspired
Carlson's Doctrine of Peaceful Persuasion, or Coexistence
without Burial." He watched Fenner searching for some writing paper in the desk drawer. "You really are going to cable

Penneyman?" he asked delightedly. "What authorities have you interviewed, Mr. Fenner?"

"What authorities has Spitzer interviewed?"

Carlson's old grin was back in place. "Well, you could guess the official French reaction easily enough: De Gaulle vindicated in refusal to hold conferences with Russians. As the old Cross of Lorraine proverb runs, 'He who sits in a bed of poison ivy will sleep facing down for a month.' *Vive la France! Et les pommes de terre frites!*"

"You just go home to bed and leave me to work out a short cable to Penneyman."

"And how are you going to send it? The transatlantic wires will be crowded out."

"All right; stay. And take the cable with you. You have ways and means."

"It seems to me I've been doing a lot of work today for Walt Penneyman and his New York *Chronicle*. What would a Congressional committee say?"

"It could be that a Congressional committee may owe him a vote of thanks."

"He certainly started something when he asked Vaugiroud to analyze a planted lie," Carlson conceded, and wandered off in the direction of the bathroom as Fenner sat down at the desk. By the time he came back, Fenner had finished wording the cable. It was brief: Ballard was ill and could not make a full report until Monday; Penneyman was to disregard any substitute report meanwhile which did not emphasize official French justification of De Gaulle's policies or did not credit the French people with the same shock and outraged concern that all free men must feel everywhere.

"Discreet," was Carlson's comment as he pocketed the message. "Can't do anyone any harm except Spitzer." He started on his way to the door. Casually, he looked at Fenner; most casually, he said, "Talking of discretion—does this project of yours on the national theater have to deal solely with France? There are other national theaters in Europe, you know."

"That's for next year, and the year after that. I'm an optimist, it seems. Even in spite of tonight's news—" Fenner shrugged.

"I'm with you there. Keep on planning: it's one form of survival. Provided we keep on spiking those guns, too. But frankly, do you have to stick closely to your plans? Why not switch to England this year? Or Greece? September's a good month there. Sea is fairly flat; sky is cooling off. Or what about Sweden? Have you seen the girls in Stockholm?"

"You sound like a travel folder."

"I can't be a very good one. No interest, Bill?"

Fenner thought of a slender girl with fair hair that fell softly over her brow at the brush of a breeze. Would she wear a little black dress and short white gloves when she sat in the Piazza di San Marco? Whatever she wore, he'd know her. He said, "I wouldn't mind a trip to Venice."

Carlson's slow walk halted. He stood very still. "Venice. Why Venice?" His voice was guarded.

"I like it. September's a good month there, too. The tourist invasion is just about over; the Fenice opens up." He was almost talking himself into a visit to one of his favorite places. He grinned, and clamped down on the idea. "Next year, with luck," Fenner said. "I've planned out this September too well to change now."

"And if you had slipped coming off the plane and broken your leg? What would have happened to your darned plans then?"

Fenner's answer was to clap Carlson's shoulder reassuringly. "Again, where do I leave that key?"

"Anywhere you like. The door's self-locking." Carlson held out his hand. "Good luck with your book."

"Good luck to you. And thank your friend for putting me up for the weekend. I'd like to have met her."

Carlson looked at him.

"Blue-edged writing paper in the desk drawer with blue-lined envelopes, flowered cap behind shower curtain, a scent of jasmine and roses in the closet that took several months to build up. Elementary, my dear Watson."

"Elementary, hell. You are at least high-school level. I guess old Rosie was right about you."

"And what did Rosie have to say?"

"You'll find out if you don't take my advice and clear out," Carlson said blithely. "I tell you, Bill, there are times when the only way to deal with a threat is to run."

The phrase had an echo of Claire Connor. Fenner's thoughts were too easily pushed in her direction. He was both amused and disturbed by that admission. It seemed as if everything she had said, everything she had done—the simplest word, the smallest movement—had struck deep into his memory.

"What's wrong?" Carlson asked.

"Relax, Neill, I was just thinking of the Café Racine."

"I told you before, and I meant it: keep clear of that place. Keep clear of Proprietor Roussin." Carlson guessed Fenner's thought from the unexpected shock in his face. "No, no," he said quickly. "Roussin isn't the one who betrayed Vaugiroud's past. It's the woman, Angélique, who told her fascist friend, the industrialist, who told his new Communist friends about Roussin and Vaugiroud."

"But how did she learn?"

"From her late husband, Roussin's brother. Vaugiroud's unit helped him to escape to North Africa in 1943."

So Roussin had thought that the secret between him and his brother was buried in his brother's grave. "You'd better warn Roussin," Fenner said.

"Vaugiroud is going to do that tomorrow."

That was best. Roussin was not an easy man to persuade.

Carlson was saying, "So you know why I've been losing my sleep over you. Angélique is watching every contact Roussin makes. What do you think she has reported about you, sitting alone, waiting for Roussin to talk to you? No more of that, Bill. Leave—"

"She has reported that I was waiting for a girl."

"And when the girl didn't turn up? Nice going, Bill, but not good enough for Angélique."

"But the girl did turn up."

"You *were* meeting someone?" Carlson's eyes were wide. He had a smile of relief spreading over his face.

"Not exactly. But a pretty girl did join me. Most enthusiastically, I might say, although I'm still wondering why. It would look perfectly natural, even to old hawk-eyed Angélique."

"You have the devil's own luck."

"The trouble with the devil's luck is that it doesn't last long. Instead of a pleasant evening with a beautiful blonde, I've been talking with you."

"Well, well." Carlson was at ease again, his hand reaching to open the door. "I'm glad to hear she was beautiful—while she lasted."

"You saw her today. Outside the Crillon. Remember the girl I wanted to give a lift—"

"Yes," Carlson said, looking at him, "I remember."

"But I saw her first. Remember that, too."

Carlson half smiled.

"She's a pretty high-powered little package in her sweet little way."

"She is, is she?" Carlson shook his head. "I still think you'd be safer in Copenhagen. By the way—Rosie may drop in to see you."

Fenner came out of his dream. "Why?"

"Heaven knows. He has, as they say at Harvard, his own thought processes. Just keep refusing all his bright ideas, and you'll get that book written." He opened the door abruptly to cut off any further questions. "See you, someday. But not too soon, I hope." He looked out at the landing, nodded, gave Fenner a broad grin and another handshake. The door closed gently, surely, and locked automatically.

Bill Fenner went slowly to bed—ten minutes spent wandering restlessly through the apartment; five minutes at the window with its view; some scattered minutes opening his suitcase to free his clothes from creases, searching for toothpaste and hairbrush—not only because he was so exhausted that every movement had become the semiparalysis of a dream, but also because his mind, tired as it was, raced and jumped. He had plenty to think about. Carlson had told him far too much. Why? To impress him enough to lie low, clear out? Carlson wanted that, obviously. Or had Carlson been following orders to put him in the picture as much as was feasible, to give him some ideas to sleep on, to prepare him—for what?

At two o'clock he gave up, stripped off his clothes, fell into a bed that was nicely firm and yet yielding. Linen sheets, no less, ice-cool, smelling of sunlight and clover. Bliss, he thought, the kind of bliss that women think up when they put their minds to it. The owner of this apartment had the right ideas for living, certainly. For a few moments, he wondered what she looked like. Brunette and fastidious, as cool and smooth as this pillow ... And then there was the beginning of a deep slide, steady and gentle, down into the dark caves of sleep.

ELEVEN

FAR AWAY, a small bell rang. And kept ringing. Nearer, louder, nearer, until it echoed at his ear. Fenner came out of his deep sleep as smoothly as he had entered it. Time to wake anyhow. It must be noon. The narrow strips of sunlight stretched from the shuttered window across the floor, a golden ladder pointing to the chair with his tumbled clothes. God, I was tired last night, he thought, as he stretched his spine. The phone rang again on the table beside the bed. As he reached for the receiver, he was astounded to see that his watch said only ten o'clock. He had gained two hours on this day, after all. *"Ici Fenner. Parlez!"*

"You amaze me," Frank Rosenfeld said. "Such geniality at this hour! Had breakfast?"

"Not yet."

"Then I'll bring the *croissants,* and you put on the coffee. Fair division of labor." In spite of the sociable phrases, Rosie sounded sharp-set. He hadn't slept so well, obviously; or, he meant business. He must have telephoned from around the corner, for he arrived in less than five minutes, neatly dressed in a dark-gray suit and a crisp white shirt, *croissants* in a string-tied parcel dangling from one curved finger, an amused smile on his amiable lips, a quick all-over glance from his sharp brown eyes. First they took in Fenner, who had just had time after the brief telephone call to pull on pajama trousers, start the coffee percolating, open shutters and curtains. "Had a good eight hours, I see," Rosie said approvingly. His eyes traveled around the cool, shadowed living room, which faced west toward the towering walls of Notre-Dame, and rested on the vase of white roses. "A House of York sympathizer?"

Fenner hoped he had hidden his flicker of astonishment. It never was very flattering to let a man see you had underestimated him. And why shouldn't an Intelligence agent be interested in history? He helped its shaping, one way or another, just as the soldiers who won, or lost, a battle helped to decide the kind of future their country would face. "She has everything cosily arranged. There's a small table for breakfast set up at the bedroom windows."

But his remark led nowhere. Rosie did not even seem to hear his reference to a woman, far less explain her. He glanced in at the sunlit bedroom, discarded it, and returned to the cold living room. He settled quite definitely in a green armchair by a coffee table, well away from the windows, and began opening the parcel of *croissants*. "These are the best in Paris," he said. "But why the hell haven't they got around to inventing paper bags?"

Fenner relinquished his hope for a pleasant breakfast in front of an open window filled with September sunshine. (The owner of this apartment and he shared some tastes in common, it seemed.) He pulled on his pajama jacket and dressing gown, poured the coffee, found some sugar (she used several American brands, he noticed from his search among the cans on the pantry shelves), and hoped he would be at least granted a peaceful half hour. He disliked any kind of serious politics before his third cup of coffee. Until then, back in his New York apartment, he looked over the theater, book, and sports pages of the *Chronicle, Times,* and *Tribune.* And with food inside him, he felt fortified enough to face the news of the day with all its puzzles and frustrations, alarms and excursions.

Rosie was human, apparently. He allowed Fenner the recovery space of two excellent *croissants* and two cups of strong coffee, chatting affably about the recent governmental reprimand to the Comédie-Française for spending elaborate production on nitwit plays—a situation that the advocates of state-supported theater had never imagined could develop. It had been that anomaly which had first amused Fenner, interested him in writing about national theaters. His own views were objective: he would find out the facts, the good and the bad, and set them down without any covert attack or special pleading.

"You'll be damned by both sides," Rosie predicted.

"There's always a middle ground, where reasonable men can argue."

"Must be nice," Rosie said quietly, watching Fenner light

his cigarette, "to have reasonable men as your opponents."

At last we're getting down to business, Fenner thought. But Rosie was approaching it gently (and when it comes, Fenner thought again, it will be like a bucket of ice water). He lit his own cigarette thoughtfully. "It's a world pretty far removed from what you dipped into yesterday."

Fenner agreed on that. "I prefer my own world," he admitted. He smiled and added, "I'll stay with it."

Rosie shot him a quick, hard glance. "Can you? Can anyone? Sometimes, there is a matter of priority. In a time of crisis, we may find precious little left of the world of art if we don't pay attention to the world of power politics."

Fenner could agree on that, too. "Civilization is a perishable commodity. But still—"

"Still what?"

"Life is short; art is long. That's one way of looking at it."

Rosie exploded. "Long? If an implacable enemy, proud, hard, can force his ideology on art, how long will it live— as we know it? He has got to change it, pull it down to his level. How else can he maintain his authority? He won't allow himself to be shown inferior. If he can't usurp and change a civilization over which he has managed to seize domination, he will be forced to destroy it. What would happen to the freedom in our world of art if we lost this war of power politics?"

I've really stirred up old Rosie, Fenner thought. Surely he doesn't think that I don't know what is at stake. Or has he met so many who ignore it that he has got to assume I may be one of them? And why doesn't he want me to be one of them? What does he want me to do? But I'm not ready to hear it yet; not until I know still more about Rosie. Yesterday he was a quick-witted guy with a droll tongue. Today, even if he is trying to reach me by talking about things that interest me, he is really concerned. About what? Does he really believe what he is saying—he is not just a man who likes the mystery and hidden power of his job? "It would be the first freedom to go," Fenner agreed. "Yet your implacable men, proud and hard, don't win in the long run. How many political systems have come and gone since Sophocles wrote his plays? You can still read them, sometimes even see them produced. But where are the fanatic power groups that thought they had a grip on the world by its throat?"

"How many plays did Sophocles write?"

"About a hundred."

"How many exist today?"

"Seven."

"And the others lost, destroyed?"

"Most thoroughly."

"Like most of the plays by Euripides and Aeschylus, or the poems of Pindar."

Fenner looked at Rosie with interest. He smiled. "You win," he said. "Art is long, provided the barbarians don't get their hands on it."

"And it's the educated barbarian who is the worst: he knows what to destroy. A bunch of illiterate Vandals come blundering in. They'll destroy anything in sight, but what is hidden may escape them. But the educated barbarian knows what to search for. He knows. That's my point, Bill. He is selective in his destruction. He knows what must be destroyed if he is to hold power. He—" Rosie's intensity slackened as he looked at Fenner. He frowned. "When did you stop disagreeing with me?" he asked. "Or didn't you disagree?"

"I tried hard."

"You're a son of a."

"That's right."

"You've wasted three whole minutes by my watch."

"Not wasted, I assure you."

Rosie took a deep and audible breath. He shook his head slowly, a smile growing on his lips. "All right," he said, "we can get down to business. I saw Neill Carlson after he left you, early this morning. He sent your message to Walt Penneyman, all right. By telephone, actually. Cable will follow as verification."

"Whatever did he have to say to Penneyman that made him telephone?" Fenner was alert.

Rosie concentrated on lighting another cigarette. "I did the talking with Penneyman. I've met him. Last April, to be exact, but that little story will have to wait. At the moment, let's concentrate on you. I have been thinking about your situation."

"And it isn't good?"

"From my point of view, it's perfect."

Fenner's amusement ended. "Carlson didn't like it."

"Oh, Neill and I don't always agree on methods. Besides, he feels sort of responsible for you."

"Why? If I hadn't handed over the money to him yesterday, there would have been someone else." But not someone, perhaps, whose judgment I trusted enough to put him in touch with Vaugiroud. Strange in a way, Fenner thought, how Carlson and I got on so well, and so quickly: a rare thing, too, the older one got, and all the more pleasant for that.

"That's how I see it. You did get involved. Of your own free will. Didn't you?"

That was going rather too far. "The money in Goldsmith's raincoat hadn't much to do with my free will."

"But after that?"

Yes. It was true enough. "One thing led to another."

"It always does. That's why I'm here. You've guessed that, of course."

"What are you trying to do? Recruit me?"

Rosie was shocked. "Good heavens, no. There's just a small assignment which you could handle."

"Why me?"

"First, you've learned quite a lot in the last twenty-four hours. Carlson put you in the picture, more or less. I don't have to spend valuable time on arguing about Communist conspiracy. Right? Second, you're a newspaperman—"

"Once upon a time, only."

Rosie shook his head. "Once upon a time and always. You know that. So does Walt Penneyman. You'll find a cable from him waiting for you at the *Chronicle*'s office suggesting that you interview two of the prize neutralists returning from the Belgrade Conference on their reactions to the Russian bomb tests. That will take care of André Spitzer's curiosity about your change of plans and hasty departure."

"And where do I interview the returning neutralists?"

"Oh, they are making quite a jaunt of their visit to Europe. Some will recover from their labors in Rome, Athens. And two—so a rumor says—have decided to relax in Venice. I heard you didn't dislike the place."

"Venice . . ."

"Yes," Rosie said, "that's where you'll find your story. It's big. It's so big, in fact, that Penneyman would certainly not object if you hadn't time for any interviews."

"You'd let me write that story?" Fenner was disbelieving.

"It will be written about. That's for sure. You might as well have first crack at it."

"So it isn't something that's top secret." Or even minimum secret, Fenner thought: Rosie wasn't exactly the type to let anything out of his private files unless it had descended to the common-knowledge level.

"At present, it is highly top secret. It will be for the next week. After that—it's anyone's story. I'm giving you the chance to be able to write it first." He rose, stretched his shoulders, walked over to the window.

Fenner waited, but Rosie was keeping his silence. "Go on," Fenner said.

"Not until I know if you are interested."

"How can I be interested until I know what you are talking about?"

"Were those three minutes wasted, after all?" Rosie asked slowly.

Fenner shook his head. "Far from it. If you ask me to do anything for you, I know that you aren't using me for some quick little advantage of your own. I am not a labor-saving device. I'm not just a lucky opportunity, either, to help someone get a promotion. And here is something for *you* to know: I may do this job, but not for you or your department; not even for your whole organization. I may do it because I just like Americans to be able to go on living their own kind of life. That's why I'm listening to you."

Rosie had walked slowly back to face him, his eyes never leaving Fenner.

"Also," Fenner said, "if I go to Venice, it won't be for the sake of any news story. So you don't have to use that as bait. Just tell me what's at stake. If I can help, I'll do it. If I can't, I'll say no. Will you risk that?"

Rosie said slowly, "Yes, I believe I will." He sat down again. "I'll lay it on the line, Bill. You may not like part of this story, but hear me out, will you? The stakes are high. The highest, in fact. An assassination of the head of a Western state. It's planned for next week."

"An assassination? Who is to be removed—De Gaulle?"

"Quick to guess, aren't you?"

"He's an obvious target, at this moment." And now the meeting of Secret Army backers with Communists at a quiet luncheon table in a respectable restaurant began to show its threat.

"Only at this moment?" Rosie asked wryly. Grimly serious, he added, "This moment is enough for us, anyhow. It's our problem. Definitely."

"But if you know of any attempted assassination—"

"Oh, that? I alerted the French as soon as I heard about it. The assassination will fail, this time."

"Well, what's worrying you?"

"We've been implicated. The United States and Britain will be blamed." Rosie looked like a man whose doctor had just told him he wouldn't last a week.

"Implicated?" Fenner took a deep breath. "So Vaugiroud was right. They've manufactured evidence?"

Rosie came out of his black thoughts. "You saw part of it yesterday morning," he said grimly.

"The money?"

"In most traceable bills. Anyone in the States who asks for a ten-thousand-dollar bill at his bank must register—it's a safeguard against any attempt at income-tax evasion."

"So ten people registered—"

"All of them Americans."

"What are they? Not Communists—they don't register so easily."

"Not Communists. Just ten gullible Americans. Rich sympathizers, perhaps, who could be easily persuaded to back a cause. Or people who were paying blackmail; or contributing to some quick-money scheme; or following the instructions of a confidence man. They wouldn't know that any of these approaches were being directed, remotely but definitely, by a Communist—a foreigner sent into the States specially for this mission. It must have taken his organization some months to gather the cash."

"Well, they haven't got it now."

"No. They'll have to substitute something else—a hundred thousand dollars, deposited in the bank account of the man who hired the killers."

"Couldn't that deposit be proved a fake?"

"It is less conclusive than an envelope of ten-thousand-dollar bills being found in the man's own home," Rosie conceded, "but difficult to disprove unless we had time and a reasonable climate of opinion. Which we won't have. Lenoir has attended to that."

"How?"

"He will publish two letters to prove that the Americans subsidized the Secret Army to assassinate De Gaulle, with the British acting as go-between."

"The letters could be proved a fake, too." If we had time, Fenner thought worriedly, if we had no screaming headlines.

"One is real."

"What?"

"It dealt with quite another subject altogether. It will be taken out of context. And it will lend itself, very neatly, to misinterpretation."

"To aiding and abetting an assassination?" Fenner was incredulous.

"It will be used that way."

"And what damn fool handed the Communists that triumph on a golden platter?"

"He isn't a damn fool. And the triumph wasn't handed to them. They planned it that way."

"Who wrote the letter? Was he American, or British?"

"He's a good Intelligence officer, no fool, far less a damn fool. It could have happened to any of us. In fact, from now on, I'll never write a discreet letter again with any pleasure."

"But this one must have been written to one of the conspirators," Fenner objected. "Otherwise it wouldn't be much use to Lenoir's plan."

"They thought of that, too."

Fenner could only shake his head. "Then we've had it," he said softly.

"We'll see about that." Rosie's lips tightened. "We'll make a damned good try—"

"What man in any Intelligence service would write to a Secret Army sympathizer, and confidentially at that? Surely—"

"He wrote in reply to a wine merchant called Trouin, an authentic businessman with right-wing politics, whose Algerian imports were folding. So Trouin had been closing down two of his European outlets—one in London, one in Warsaw. For that reason, late in July, he visited Poland briefly. And in Warsaw, he picked up some highly secret information. When he came back to Paris, he wrote a letter to the British Embassy. He gave them the information, and he also made a request for the Pole who had told him that information. The Pole wanted to defect on his next secret mission into the British Sector of Berlin. Would the Brits keep his defection secret until his wife and child could join him? They would have to leave all possessions behind them, of course, so would the Americans help him and his family to start a new life in the United States, where he wanted to settle? If the answers were in the affirmative, Trouin would be willing to act as the intermediary. Considering that this Pole was a high-ranking officer in the Polish Secret Service working with the GRU—the Red Army Secret Service, that is—the British and Americans were interested."

"I take it that the piece of information was accurate?"

"Both accurate and valuable. The British Embassy passed the letter along to their Intelligence, who checked everything. The piece of information was real. There is such a Polish officer in Warsaw, who has been sent, twice, on spying missions into West Berlin. Trouin's business visit to Warsaw was authentic. The note paper came from Trouin's office, the typewriter used was Trouin's own portable, the signature seemed genuine. Now, of course, we know it was probably a very clever forgery."

"How?"

"Trouin had asked for an appointment—the place and time to be chosen by the British agent who would meet him discreetly and hear the details about the Pole's plan to escape. Everything had to be arranged with great secrecy and precaution—Trouin even gave a poste restante address for the reply to his letter. He did not want any telephone call to his home or office. The reason for that was obvious: complete security. He had to visit Warsaw once more, quite soon. He didn't want the Russians to learn he had been in communication with the British."

"So the appointment was made, and Trouin didn't turn up?"

A small gleam, perhaps of approval, sparked in Rosie's eye. "You've got it."

"And Lenoir got the British reply at a poste restante."

"That's right."

"And the Brits felt no alarm when Trouin didn't show?"

"He could have had a bad scare or an attack of cold feet. That happens, you know: people do chicken out of situations like that. The secret meeting with a British Intelligence officer was supposed to be yesterday morning. The Brits were going to give Trouin a couple of days to calm down, before they tried approaching him again. Their involvement seemed little enough: just a letter suggesting the time and method of meeting for discussion of his problem. It also assured him that he could report to his friend that all his conditions had been accepted, and the Americans would co-operate fully; he would be given every assistance, with the utmost discretion."

"When did the alarm sound?"

"Last night."

"After Carlson had learned from Vaugiroud that the wine merchant was more than ultraconservative?"

"Partly that. Partly—well, I picked up some extra information, too, yesterday evening." Rosie fell silent: discussion on that point was barred; meanwhile, at least.

Fenner was tactful. "A very double-crossed conspirator," he said, returning to Trouin. "I suppose, when the British reply is published, it will be used with some other letter—not about a man defecting from Poland, but dealing with something really damning."

"That's the plan. The letter about Warsaw will be destroyed: its purpose was achieved in getting a reply out of the British. In its place, Lenoir is substituting a real beauty. I haven't seen it, but I can guess. It will make the British officer who wrote to Trouin look as if he were the intermediary between Trouin and the Americans. The hundred thousand dollars deposited in Trouin's bank account will appear to be the purchase price of an assassination." Rosie took a deep breath. "Neat, isn't it?"

"If I were you," Fenner said slowly, "I'd nail Trouin right away. If he sees he is the sacrificial goat, he may bleat. Come to think of it, I'd nail them all."

"We tried that. Last night. The Sûreté sent men to arrest Wahl. But he walked out of the Café Racine just five minutes after Lenoir, and disappeared completely. It's my guess he has left the country. Trouin had already left—yesterday afternoon. His friend the industrialist is somewhere in Spain. And Lenoir is on the vacation he has been planning for some weeks. They are, in fact, all out of the country."

"Sudden alarm?"

"Only in Wahl's case, perhaps. The others had made their arrangements in advance. This was a scattering by plan."

"And you haven't an idea where any of them can be found?"

"We know where Lenoir is."

"Have him picked up."

"It isn't as simple as that."

"How?" Fenner asked sharply. Then he eased his voice and smiled. "Or is that none of my blasted business?"

"It could be your business in Venice," Rosie said, and wiped the smile from Fenner's face. "I want you to go there. But before you give me an answer on that, there are some things you should know. You see, this concerns Sandra Fane.

Now, now, hold on, hear me out!" Rosie's hand was up, like a traffic policeman, pacifying, bringing order. "We are in debt to Sandra," he told Fenner, "we owe her something."

Bill Fenner stared at the serious face opposite him. "She's lying to you, Rosie," he said warningly.

"I don't think so."

"She never defected. No one who defects can live such a cosy and carefree life as she does on the Avenue d'Iéna. Especially a defector like Sandra. She was important in the party. She still must be. Or she wouldn't be working with Lenoir. She may even be working with Wahl—Kalganov himself, isn't he?" For Rosie hadn't mentioned Kalganov by name.

Rosie nodded. "I believe Wahl is Kalganov. But we've no factual proof, have we? We need someone like Sandra who could identify him for us."

"She wouldn't! Stop kidding yourself, Rosie."

"She has already given me a lot of information. In fact, without her help, we wouldn't have been able to fit the pieces of this puzzle together. I met her yesterday evening near the children's puppet show in the Tuileries."

"She really did defect?" Fenner asked slowly. It was a complete reversal of his guesses.

"No. She is defecting *now*. Next week, to be exact. In Venice. She needs help, a lot of help——"

"Look," Fenner said, "I told you yesterday, and I meant it—I'm not going either to help or to hinder Sandra Fane." He rose abruptly to his feet. "I don't want to see her. Ever. Not even from a distance."

"Why?" Was he still in love with her? Rosie wondered anxiously. Some men could take an awful beating and still be afraid of asking for more.

"Because," Fenner said, with a rush of truth, "I have felt like a big-enough god-damned fool without being reminded of it all over again. She never married me for love. Did you know that? Oh, she liked me. That was lucky, she told me on that last night. I hadn't been repulsive. Most fortunate for her. She had been told to marry me. Get that, Rosie? On orders. For political advantages. I was on my way up, in line for news editor at the *Chronicle*. I could be manipulated. I could be useful." Fenner's voice halted. "No, Rosie, don't keep reminding me of that sleazy little bitch."

"I must."

"No!"

"Hear me out, Bill." Rosie's voice was sympathetic. "Just hear me out, will you?"

Fenner's lips closed tight.

Rosie's mood changed. He began to laugh. And as Fenner looked at him angrily, ready to walk out, Rosie said, "I was just remembering the way the Communists even put sex to work for the revolution."

"That's funny as hell," Fenner said savagely.

"Sure. But it's true. They have a School for Seduction in the Soviet Union. Special Intelligence agents take a course there. They have lectures and practical demonstrations. There's one instructor who shows the class how to make love to seven consecutive women without even staggering. He teaches mind control. It's useful, too, when a student is ordered to make love to a beautiful woman—mustn't enjoy it, might become involved; or to some old bag of lard—no flinching allowed. So they graduate, come out into the big simpleminded world, with a diploma in how to make a woman and influence people. Seduce some women thoroughly, and you've got them: they'll do anything in return—even to borrowing documents, searching files, reporting on their husband's work. That's the theory. In practice? It has worked." Rosie shook his head. "In fact, it has been one of the minor headaches for Counter Intelligence in non-Communist countries. But it also gives us a laugh, now and again. Especially when I think of that instructor. A dedicated man." Rosie's hilarity broke out again, and this time Fenner almost smiled. Rosie noted the improvement, the easing of tension. "Clinical and cynical, and oh, so earnest!"

Fenner shook his head, began to laugh in spite of himself.

"Picture of two men discussing an impending threat to Western unity," Rosie said when their laughter died away. There was no amusement in his eyes, though. "Will you hear me out, Bill?" he asked quietly.

Fenner nodded and sat down. He noticed, then, that he must have upset the ash tray when he had risen. "Clumsy beggar, I've ruined her white rug, damn it!" He picked up the stubs and burned matches, tried to blow the gray ash away. By the time he had finished, he could face Rosenfeld again quite normally. "Go ahead," he said crisply. "But I still don't think Sandra is being honest with you. It's a trick, Rosie. She has fed you some information, yes. But it could be the old confidence game: you hold my money and I'll hold yours."

"I am going to tell you exactly what happened. After that, you can judge. Fair enough?"

"Fair enough."

"Well, it was this way—" Rosie said, and began the story of his meeting with Sandra Fane.

TWELVE

THE STORY, itself, began at Sandra Fane's party on the night before Fenner arrived in Paris.

She had invited Stanfield Dade, along with several other attachés of various embassies, and had asked Mike Ballard to persuade him to accept. Sandra was an expert hostess, with five minutes neatly devoted to each of her forty guests. It was perfectly natural that Dade was given his quota of conversation. Only, what she had to say to him was unexpected. First, she emphasized that it was confidential. Next, she said a friend of hers—an American woman—needed help. The friend was a Communist, on an important mission in France. The friend wanted to get out of the party, get out of Europe. Would the Americans be interested enough to help? In return for their help, Sandra's friend would be willing to tell them something of great interest. Would Dade give her the telephone number and name of anyone who could help her friend? She asked him to think over this—he was speechless with astonishment, actually—and because she must leave him to speak to another guest, he could quietly pass her the name and telephone number later in the evening, when she was talking to Ballard. She left him with the same bright smile with which she had talked—gaily, expressively, but with her voice carefully lowered, a contrast which impressed Dade so much by its technique and desperation that, after an hour of brooding inwardly, he decided to take a chance. Or rather, to let Frank Rosenfeld take a chance; what was there to lose, except the hope of valuable information, if this defector turned out to be less interesting than Sandra Fane had so quietly implied? So when Sandra and Ballard were chitchatting, he had joined them. And when Sandra asked Ballard to bring her another glass of champagne, Dade had

134

given her Frank Rosenfeld's business name and his firm's telephone number.

"So there's Act One of our little drama," Rosie said to Fenner. "The exposition, you would call it. Any comment far?"

"Only that Sandra was always her own best friend," Fenner said wryly.

"Ah!" said Rosie, eyes approving. "You jump ahead of me. I didn't find that out until the next day. Dade sent me a cryptic message; he's a cautious man, doesn't like involvement, just warned me I might get a call sometime from a woman who needed help in escaping from political entanglements. But I was too busy with Mr. Goldsmith's arrival and disappearance to pay much attention. There was nothing urgent in Dade's message."

"He didn't think the woman could be Sandra herself?"

"No. Remember, she is generally supposed to have already defected."

"And he doesn't question that?"

"His not to reason why; his but to do, up to a point. Which was me."

"And when did you get her call?"

"The first one reached my office just after noon, while I was at the Embassy, meeting you. No name was left, only a message that the woman would call again at four o'clock. I was to make sure to be there, because she had to put in the calls from a public telephone. She had vital information to give me. My secretary said the woman sounded urgent and capable—she could mean business. So I was in my office just before four o'clock, cursing Dade for dragging me away from the Goldsmith problem, but curious, too. Information, even if it isn't as vital as its donor thinks, may still be interesting. But as soon as this woman's voice began talking to me, I knew she was someone important. Because, although she was asking my help, she was giving me orders. She couldn't get away from the habit." Rosie laughed softly. "I was told where to meet her, and how. She asked my height and weight and general description: and what was I wearing? I was to carry a newspaper, a copy of *Time*, and a rolled umbrella. Just before five o'clock, I was to stroll around the open-air puppet theater in the Tuileries Gardens, choose a path among the trees in a direction away from the Rue de Rivoli. She would follow me. I was to hire a couple of seats under a tree, and as soon as the attendant was paid and moved away, she would join me. I was to meet her alone. Tell no one. Have no one watching, so that he would not attract attention to us. If I thought I was being followed, I was. to read *Time*. If I was sure it was safe, I was to read my newspaper. And I would easily recognize her from her photograph in our files." Rosie enjoyed that bit. "She has a sense of humor."

That's something new, Fenner thought. But her way of flattering—that had always been peculiarly Sandra's. Even Rosie had been pleased that his powers of deduction were not underestimated. "Where did you find a rolled umbrella?" Fenner asked.

"I called in at the Embassy and borrowed Dade's," Rosie admitted. "Forgot to tell him. I guess he wouldn't like having even his umbrella involved."

"You're too hard on him."

"Why not? If everything turns out well, he'll get all the credit."

"Will he?"

"He'll take it anyway, in his memoirs. He is one of those now-it-can-be-told guys, and wasn't-I-right-all-along?"

Fenner laughed. "Okay. So there you were, with a rolled umbrella, strolling among the neatly spaced trees. Background of children playing, nurses gossiping, mothers comparing clothes and manners, wandering couples holding hands, older people renting chairs to rest their legs for a blessed hour." And the time was almost five o'clock, and Vaugiroud and I were talking.

"Not bad, not bad at all. Just add some spotty sunlight, distant shrieks of laughter from the open-air Punch and Judy show, two chairs nicely protected by several prim trees, and you've got me waiting, reading a newspaper. She didn't take long. It was Sandra Fane, all right, although I didn't recognize her until she had almost reached me. She was dressed in black, unrelieved; and she wore no jewelry, no make-up. That makes a big difference in her type. She was just a white-faced, faded blonde with no eyes or lips. A ghost in mourning."

"She'd have make-up and earrings in her purse, all ready to doll her up once the meeting was over."

"No doubt. She did say she was on her way to an art-gallery opening, where she'd meet Fernand Lenoir. Cool customer," Rosie said admiringly. "Our meeting was fairly brief, no more than thirty-five minutes, but her thoughts were well organized. She didn't waste any time. And she had several surprises to deal out. Several . . ."

Sandra Fane had begun with a very direct question. "How," she asked, in a low, calm voice, "could I get back to America?"

"Take the first plane." Rosenfeld wasn't even troubling to be polite: he might admire her technique, but he hadn't any sympathy for her problem.

"You know it isn't as easy as that."

"Perhaps not, but your chief difficulty will be in leaving the Avenue d'Iéna. Or is your friend Lenoir behind this idea?"

"No. Could you help me reach America?"

"Why should we?"

"I'm getting out. I'm no longer a Communist."

"Since when?"

"I've been thinking about it for the last six weeks. I was supposed to have quit the party three years ago, when I came to Paris. It was only a cover story. You knew that, didn't you?"

"Why are you deciding to leave, just at this time?"

"Two reasons. I'm getting in too deeply, the kind of thing"—she looked at him frankly, her blue eyes pale and tired under the uncolored eyebrows and lashes—"that I never have been involved in, don't want to be involved with."

"Turned squeamish?"

"And also," she said, ignoring that, "I have been recalled to Moscow." She had kept her voice calm, but her eyes looked away. Her hands tightened on her bag. Their knuckles, under the black gloves, would be white.

"When do you leave?"

"Next week. From Venice, where Fernand and I are supposed to be on vacation. He has engaged a suite at the Danieli. The plan is this: he will be out of France when the assassination takes place; then return at once to Paris to take full advantage of the situation."

"What assassination?" Rosenfeld asked quickly.

But she wanted his promise first. She had merely ensured he would listen to her. "Will you help me escape from Venice? I leave Paris tonight with Fernand. I'll spend this weekend with him; and on Monday, I escape. Monday evening. The assassination attempt is late in the week. That's how I've calculated it. Because Fernand plans to return to Paris by next Friday. He must be here as soon as the assassination is a *fait accompli*, but not before."

"What assassination?" Rosenfeld repeated.

"I am not in their confidence."

Like hell you aren't, Rosenfeld thought. "Who are they aiming at? De Gaulle?"

"Perhaps. Their plans are big enough for that."

"When? Where?"

"I don't know exactly. I'll know by Monday. I can tell you then."

She knows all right, Rosie thought. She is safeguarding herself, wants to establish that she isn't guilty of conspiring to assassinate. He restrained his impatience, his shock and excitement. He shrugged his shoulders. "You haven't left us much time to arrange an escape. It will take some planning. You are important to them: they won't let you just walk out."

"I know. That is why I ask you for help. It is the only way. I would have asked you before, except"—and the pale lips half smiled—"I had nothing to bargain with. I have no illusions. If I buy help from you, the price will be steep. Ordinary information would not be enough—not to get the kind of immunity I want."

"No one could promise you complete immunity."

"But if I make this gesture—surely I'll be given some consideration? I am thirty-five. By the time I am fifty, perhaps even before, I shall have a new name, a new life. Some quiet, some safety . . . I'll have earned that, I think."

"So far," he reminded her pointedly, "your information isn't worth much. An assassination, with no date, no place, and a big perhaps around the victim's name."

Quickly she said, "I know who has planned it. I know who is implicated. Why else do you think I'm being recalled?"

"You know too much?"

She dodged that answer. "Once it is over, Lenoir doesn't need me to do any more entertaining for him. He has other plans." She looked at him. "Are you interested in helping me?"

"As you said, ordinary information will not be enough. Why did you wait so long before you contacted us? An assassination isn't planned in a week." Not even in a month. Not this kind of job, obviously.

"I told you. I needed bargaining power."

"Show me it."

"Are you interested in helping me, if I do?"

"Yes."

"Can you persuade Washington to be equally interested?"

"I think so."

"The escape and transport to America could be arranged—even at such short notice?"

"Yes."

"I'll take your word," she said softly. "And you have mine. I'll tell you what I know, what I can do for you. And you'll do your best for me. A bargain?"

Rosenfeld nodded.

"The assassination is to be entrusted to the OAS. It was planned by Robert Wahl, a naturalized Frenchman, a Communist. He is supplying money—in American dollars, a large amount but easily handled, which came into the country this morning. This will be used as part evidence of American complicity. The other part is being provided by Fernand Lenoir, also a Communist, in the shape of a letter that will implicate the British and the Americans."

"A letter?"

"It will look like part of a correspondence between Trouin, a wine merchant and secret backer of the OAS, and a British Intelligence agent named Holland. That correspondence exists: I have brought copies of Trouin's letter and Holland's reply, so that you can check with the British on my story."

"And the implicating letter that Lenoir is concocting?"

"It will be substituted for Trouin's letter. It will appear to be the letter that received the British reply."

"And where is this fake letter?"

"I shall have it for you in Venice." Something almost amused her. "I shall have the original fake itself."

"How can you be sure that Lenoir will take it there?"

"Why else are we vacationing in Venice? There he will meet several of his prize neutralists, some of his pet pro-Communists. As soon as the news of the assassination breaks, he will show them two letters: the one he invented and the British reply. He will show the originals, and give them copies for publication." She smiled. "Lenoir's 'original' will certainly be in Venice. I know. Now about my escape—"

"First, what about that money you mentioned? Has it been delivered to you?" Rosenfeld asked, interested in the shape of the lie he expected.

But she was telling the truth, at least in this. "There has

been some delay. It was to have been delivered at my apartment by my masseur, who visits me regularly. Instead, it will be handed to me, this evening, at an art-gallery reception for a new showing of pictures which"—she pulled back her glove and glanced at her wrist watch—"I'll attend, after I leave you and spend half an hour in the Métro." Her sense of humor was returning with her confidence. "How I am going to miss dodging back and forth in the subway just when I have perfected the art! In Venice—"

"You're way ahead," Rosenfeld cut in, and brought back her tense look again. "Is Lenoir going to be at this art gallery?"

"I meet him there. Then we leave for Venice."

"Taking the money with you?"

"No. Fernand Lenoir will see that it is hidden in the wine merchant's private safe."

"And the wine merchant?"

"He doesn't know. And when it's found, he may have already committed suicide. Of course, that's only a guess—I don't *know*."

That's right, Rosenfield thought: you know nothing about any form of murder. Bright girl, aren't you? "Who is delivering the money to you at the gallery?"

"The owner. His present name is Anton Mehr." She spelled his second name carefully.

"What does he look like?"

She said impatiently, "He is of no importance. White hair, blue eyes, yellow complexion. Liver trouble. He worked for many years in French Indochina."

Rosenfeld studied his hands. Blue eyes, yellow skin, and a blob-shaped face, I bet. "Why don't I have the Sûreté pick you all up at the gallery? Right there and then? That's one simple way of arranging your escape from them."

"Yes. You would get Mehr, Lenoir, and the money. And me. But you would not get the letter. You would not get Wahl. You would never get him. One warning, and he would disappear, go underground, work from there. You would not stop the assassination. You would not stop other money being used—oh, it would take a less dramatic form, perhaps a bank deposit in Trouin's account—but it still could be dynamite when used with the fake letter asking for one hundred thousand dollars as expenses." She knew she had made a good point there. Very quietly, she added, "You need that letter, don't you?"

"You can't hand it over now?"

"If I could, I'd walk away with you. Wouldn't I? So it has to be Venice. Here is how I escape. I stroll into the Piazza San Marco on Monday, just before half past six. And you will have someone waiting there for the letter. You must send someone I know, someone I might stop and talk to, quite naturally, without arousing any suspicion. I have three names to suggest: Mike Ballard, who would do it if you promised him first rights to the story; your little moon-struck blonde, who has come to my last parties with various attachés attached—she's on your team, isn't she? The one whose husband was killed in Indochina some years ago? She always was a straight-down-the-middle little patriot. Oh, don't look so worried—I didn't share my suspicions with Fernand Lenoir, who finds her delightful but stupid. Why should I, when I might need her help someday?"

"Uh-huh," said Rosenfeld noncommittally. "And the third suggestion?"

"My ex-husband, William Fenner, who is in Paris and might be persuaded. Not because of me; because of America. He has a quiet sense of patriotism, which once I found amusing. Now, I see it as—well, a little touching, too."

"His beliefs seem to have lasted longer than yours."

Her eyes stared at the empty path lying between the trees. Then, abruptly, she said, "Have one of them meet me. On Monday. In the Piazza, at Florian's Café at half past six. We meet, we talk briefly. I pass the letter. When I start to leave, your other operators, the serious professionals, can pick me up. There will be several around, I'm sure." She smiled. "But how they do it, how they get me out of Venice—that I leave to their ingenuity. They can appear to intercept me, kidnap me, arrest me—anything that seems most convincing. I don't care. Do you agree to all that?"

"Agreed. We'll get you out. But what about the time and place of the assassination attempt? Will you pass that along with the letter?"

She looked at him, amused.

"You may not have that information?" he insisted. The Sûreté would want this most of all. They'd have their agents in Venice, if they could be sure of that. The Italians would help, too: they never approved of foreign conspiracies being hatched on their soil. The British were already in, of course, with that reply of theirs to Trouin— My God, thought Rosenfeld, I am actually believing her.

"I shall have it. I give the letter to the amateur help. But the other information can wait—for the professionals."

"Once you are safe, you'll give it to us?"

"Is that unreasonable?" She lifted his magazine, pretended to look at it, laid it on her lap.

"No. You are a very cautious woman."

"I have to be."

"You seem to be taking a very big chance today." He glanced around at the trees, at the other chairs within seeing distance.

She opened her handbag as if she needed her handkerchief. "I had a lot of last-minute shopping for my vacation. Even Wahl's men lose their quarry between the beachwear and lingerie departments. Besides, his best man of all is on another job this afternoon." Her fingers pulled out two letters from her bag, slipped them quietly between the pages of *Time*.

"Wahl doesn't trust you?"

"Robert Wahl is much too important to trust anyone."

"Thanks for that tip. Who is he, actually?"

"I may even tell you that, someday."

"When you reach America? And we deposit twenty-five thousand dollars in your new name?"

"And a passport to match the name. I shan't bother America very long. Or in any way. I have had my dream. I have had my beliefs." She closed her eyes wearily, the lines at the sides of her mouth deepened, her lips drooped. "Robert Wahl does not know that I have learned about my recall to Moscow. He intends to catch me off guard in Venice, no doubt. So he does not expect trouble from me. And don't you make him expect trouble! Keep the French from gossiping about an assassination plot. Stop the American leaks and the English hints. Handle this with the greatest care. If you don't, you will never see me on Monday. Robert Wahl will make sure of that." She rose. "Don't forget your magazine," she said. She walked away, a fragile woman dressed in unrelieved black like so many French-women in mourning, taking her late-afternoon stroll under the shade of the trees.

Rosenfeld let her drift out of sight before he rose and sauntered away in the opposite direction. He did not forget his magazine. He almost forgot Dade's umbrella, though. He didn't waste any time on returning it to the Embassy. He had much too much to do. Besides, it did rain, that evening.

"Well?" Rosie asked, after he had given Fenner the main points of that meeting.

"She is hiding a lot."

"She is safeguarding herself."

"You think she will tell you Wahl's true name, for instance?"

"Yes. And more quickly than she plans. We can bargain, too. The French might just be willing to drop extradition charges against her if she can identify Wahl as Kalganov. He is the man we all want to get."

"Extradition—she hadn't thought of that."

"Oh yes, she had. She took care to give the impression that she is not one of the actual conspiracy."

"Is she?" Fenner asked.

"Of course she is. Wahl, Lenoir, Fane: Committee of Three. If she hadn't been recalled, she would still be with them. And don't ask me why she has been recalled. Wahl's responsible, I think. It may be some personal clash between them. And if he *is* Kalganov, he certainly has the power to have her silenced permanently. These people live in such a surrealist world. . . ." Rosie shook his head. "Well?" he asked again.

Fenner had risen. He moved restlessly around the room. He stopped at the desk and looked at the clock. Ten past eleven, he noted. He could feel Rosie's impatience reach across to nudge his shoulder. "You can't send Ballard."

"No. His mistress would have the story out of him before he could turn on the pillow. Bed is a place where men let down their defenses."

"Sandra Fane didn't know about that mistress, obviously."

"Nor does she know the girl was recruited by Lenoir."

"Anything else that Sandra slipped up on?"

"No. We've checked her story. Anton Mehr, for instance, is the man who met Goldsmith yesterday morning. And Lenoir did join her at Mehr's art gallery, as she said he would. He arrived in good spirits, but—after a telephone call around twelve minutes past seven, just the right time to let a report about a missing coat come from Orly—he left in a decidedly grim mood. He even let Sandra find her own taxi. He changed his, three times, and eventually arrived at the Café Racine. He stayed there, briefly, just long enough to tell Robert Wahl the bad news. No ten-thousand-dollar notes. Scratch play one, start play two. When he left, he went straight to

Le Bourget, where Sandra was waiting for him with their baggage. She had plenty, too."

"It would have seemed simpler to telephone the Racine." Rosie raised one eyebrow.

Fenner reconsidered quickly. "He knows Angélique is not a trustworthy type?" And there would be new instructions to receive, perhaps, before leaving for Venice. Fenner remembered the way Wahl had had the last word. "He took a risk, though."

"How much risk did he actually take? People saw him and Wahl chatting together. Did anyone know what they really were, or what they could have been talking about?"

Fenner shook his head.

"Risk develops when people have some idea of what you are, and why you are there. If they don't know, they may be puzzled. They may even be suspicious. But they can't start adding two and two. And that is what counts; knowing the exact factors that make the correct total." Rosie looked at him with a touch of humor. "That works for our side, too."

"You're saying that you think I could risk going to Venice?" Fenner asked with a grin.

"Yes. But it's up to you—"

"Like hell it is. The choice is between me and some little blonde, charming but stupid. Good God, you can't send her, Rosie, even if that stupidity was only a bit of play-acting for Lenoir's appreciation."

"You want to go?"

"That question should be, do we really trust Sandra?"

"We have to. We want the letter. And we want Sandra Fane. She's the only person who could, and would, point to Robert Wahl and say 'That's Kalganov!' So, you see—" Rosie threw up his hands.

"Well, we can't have any moon-struck blonde sitting alone at Florian's, like a pretty little pet lamb staked out for the wolves." Here goes sweet Sir Walter with that damned cloak of his again, Fenner thought morosely. "Who is she? Sandra's counterpart, but playing on our side of the fence?"

"No more than you are Lenoir's counterpart," Rosie said with sudden and real anger. "Have you ever betrayed a friend, or even an enemy, to the Gestapo? Nor would you."

I suppose I deserved that, Fenner thought. "I apologize to the lady," he said stiffly.

"She's someone who got caught up in this whole business by a quirk of fate. She's like you, in many ways. Her life would be much more comfortable if she hadn't listened to me." Rosie sighed. "Come on, Bill—what's your answer? Yes. Or no. Definitely."

"I thought I said yes."

"Just wanted to be sure. And you didn't have to worry about our little pet lamb of a blonde being naked out alone at one of Florian's café tables. No, as I see it, you and she are going to be sitting there together."

"What?"

"Eliminates some of that risk we have been talking about. The two of you are having a week together in Venice. Reasonable?"

"If I'm having a week in Venice with a girl, I don't want it reasonable."

"Now, now," Rosie said, good humor returning, "and after we've planned such a pleasant little jaunt for you!"

"You sound like Carlson."

"I don't think so. She's his girl."

Fenner raised his eyebrows. His smile was forced. "My luck, as usual."

"About money," Rosie said, ending the topic of Carlson's girl. "You'll have an expense account. Seemingly from the *Chronicle*. So first thing you do is call at the Paris office and find a cable from Walt Penneyman with your Venice assignment. Drop a small remark that it's the right place to combine business and pleasure, and start phoning for reservations for two, on the train this evening—there's the Simplon Express, which leaves at seven-twenty-eight. Also telephone the Hotel Vittoria in Venice for two rooms."

"And will I get them? Venice is still pretty crowded."

"You'll get them," Rosie said most definitely, but didn't explain. "You do all that from the office, and call this number, too." He handed over a slip of paper. "It's hers. Tell her, again within earshot of Spitzer, that you've got a surprise for her—a week in Venice, and she can start packing. You'll pick her up in time to catch the train."

"Why by train?"

"What is cosier than a private room on a train? Or would you prefer a quick flight surrounded by strangers?"

"You can stop leering, Rosie. You know this will be no damn picnic for any of us."

"No. But—as far as you two are concerned—we've kept it fairly easy. All you have to do—"

"—is wander around Venice together, have a drink at Florian's on Monday evening, meet Sandra, get the letter, wait

for Carlson to contact us. Nothing to it." Fenner's voice was
bitter. "I wish to God this girl wasn't being drawn into all
this. I can handle this alone. Why involve her?"

"It's safer this way. Believe me, I've given that some
thought." Rosie's voice came out of its momentary gloom, and
turned humorous. "She'll act as a restraint on you. No daring improvisations if you are responsible for her."

"I'll stick to instructions," Fenner promised grimly.

"Good. Play it safe. Take no chances. If you are baffled, do nothing. Let us solve any problems."

Fenner nodded. "What's the girl's name?"

"Langley. Mrs. James Langley. Her husband was killed eight
years ago—"

"Yes, so I gathered."

"You've a sharp ear," Rosie said approvingly. "I hope you
can remember everything I told you, until Monday evening.
Afterward, I want you to forget everything just as completely. Can you?"

"I've had some training in the art of forgetting," Fenner
reminded him. "How much does Mrs. Langley know about
this mission?"

"She knows a good deal about Sandra Fane and Lenoir. She
has heard of Wahl. She knows that a man called Kalganov
was responsible for the terrorism in Saigon when her husband
was killed. She knows nothing about the money, or Goldsmith.
About Vaugiroud? Possibly his name, but little else. She knows
about the letter, but not about its contents. In fact, she
knows just enough to understand that something of major importance is at stake."

Rosie had kept a lot from her. "You trust her?"

"Completely. I wish we could have told you as little, but
you forced our hand. You're a hard man to persuade, Bill."

I wonder how much he kept from me, too, thought Fenner. "Why is she doing this for you?"

"Why are you?" Rosie hoisted himself slowly out of the
comfortable armchair. "She is doing it, not for me, not for
Carlson, not for anyone. She has a concern, as the Quakers
say. A concern about the shape of the future. She has seen
a heart-breaking sample of Kalganov's work. She doesn't believe that there is any peace for the rest of us as long as
the Kalganovs are loose." Rosie paused. "You know, in spite
of Sandra's sneer, there is still a lot of quiet patriotism around.
The Kalganovs may be in for a surprise. . . . They won't bury
us so easily."

"Where do I meet Mrs. Langley?" Fenner asked, a little quietened.

"Here. About six o'clock?"

"Here?"

"She lives here, when she doesn't move out for a night to help a stranger in trouble."

Fenner recovered. "Full of surprises, aren't you?"

"Let's say, when things break naturally, it is a pity not to use them."

Meaning? Fenner wondered. That he had spent the night in Mrs. Langley's apartment, that it would be logical to take her to Venice? "It's hard on her," he said, disliking the role he was helping her to play.

"Appearance is *not* reality. That's how she feels. Just you remember that, too!"

"All right, all right. What do I do with the letter when Sandra hands it over?"

"You won't have it long. Someone will contact you at once. Someone you know. Saves time, saves tension."

"And mistakes."

"There will be no slip-ups. Don't even let yourself think of that. Remember Sandra's guess: we are going to have plenty of professionals in the background. Carlson insists on being among them."

"Sort of expected he wouldn't be too far away from his girl. Well, that's about everything." Except for my doubts about Sandra's good faith, but they have possibly become a conditioned reflex. "I'll get shaved, and start thinking of lunch."

Rosie held out his hand. Its grip was encouraging. "Just stick to the script and Act Three will end happily ever after."

"What happened to Act Two?"

"It began in the Tuileries and ended on the Ile Saint-Louis."

"You should write a play someday. I'll review it."

"Thanks for the warning. By the way, have that lunch before you call at the *Chronicle*'s office. Penneyman's cable will certainly be there by this time, but we'll give Mr. Spitzer a little time to digest it."

Fenner paused at the bedroom door. "As a matter of fact, I do have an invitation to lunch at noon. At the Café Racine, mine host's table no less, with Roussin and Vaugiroud."

"You aren't serious?" Rosie was shocked. He looked as if he had been struck by the hideous doubt whether Fenner was really the man to send to Venice. Then he saw Fenner's smile widening. "Don't *do* that!" he said testily.

"Oh, it will be a pretty grim luncheon, anyway. I suppose Vaugiroud has already warned Roussin about Angélique."

"We left that to him."

"A difficult job. This is one day they won't enjoy their daily bread. In France, that's a crime."

Something caught Rosie's attention. He swung around. "How often do they lunch together?"

"Every day."

"At the same table? It's a fixed date?"

"Yes. Twelve o'clock prompt."

"Go and shave," Rosie said. He headed toward the telephone on the desk. "Can you remember Vaugiroud's damned number?" he called, his voice sharp with worry.

Fenner shaved, showered, and dressed quickly. But Rosenfeld had left by the time he came back into the room. There was a note propped against the clock. *His telephone doesn't answer. Will call him at the restaurant. Have a nice vacation. Bring me back a pigeon.*

Fenner burned the message, reminding himself wryly that he was behaving in the very best tradition. While he was being security-minded, he might as well memorize Mrs. Langley's telephone number and get rid of that slip of paper, too. Also, he would call the *Chronicle* on some pretense, and let Spitzer tell him that there was a cable from New York waiting to be picked up. That was better than walking in, asking, "Has a cable by some chance arrived?" This was a game not too difficult to learn, he thought. A game? A game in deadly earnest. A vacation in Venice that was grim business. A girl constantly beside him who wasn't his. How the hell had he walked into this upside-down world? His first mistake had been to play the good Samaritan at Orly, to leave his raincoat unattended. If he hadn't gone rushing off for a glass of water, there would have been no Carlson, no Rosie, and only that wish-I-could-help-you good-by to Vaugiroud.

And no problems, no cause and effect, not one thing leading to another . . .

Where, he wondered suddenly, would Venice lead?

THIRTEEN

SO HE HAD picked up Penneyman's cable at the *Chronicle*'s small office—one large room, one private cubicle, and a switchboard—where two different women and one plump-faced boy were keeping Spitzer dutiful but not enthusiastic company on a bright but bomb-shocked Saturday afternoon.

The cable was good. (Fenner even wondered if Rosie's fine hand had not carefully sprinkled the chosen pieces of information over the text; if Carlson had not signed it in Walt Penneyman's name.) It was clear and exact. First, congratulations on persuading Vaugiroud to write a piece on the Common Market for the *Chronicle*'s Sunday, October 15, edition. Proposed length (three thousand words) and rate (seven hundred dollars) agreeable. Next, could Fenner fit a trip to Italy into his existing schedule for two interviews (five hundred dollars each, plus simple expenses) written in his old U.N. style? Subjects: two rival neutralists returning from the Belgrade Conference, recharging their batteries in Venice on Monday. Topic: the Bomb. Spitzer, a thin-faced, intelligent-eyed man, with a large forehead and a small chin, must have read the cable, but he pretended appropriate interest and surprise. Play it loose, Fenner reminded himself. Sure, he agreed with Spitzer, this shot his immediate plans to hell, but you know Walt Penneyman, always thinking up some job for little hands to do, besides—once the idea was suggested, it began to have possibilities. After all, Venice. With expenses.

So he had made the call to the number Rosie had given him.

The conversation, even if somewhat one-sided, wasn't too bad an effort. A woman's voice answered, but he hoped it didn't belong to Mrs. James Langley—too flat, too routine, not even bothering to return his enthusiasm. "Look, darling," he began softly, "remember that talk we had last night? . . . I know you said Avignon was too hot at this time of year. . . . No, no, I'm not trying to make you change your mind about Avignon. What about Venice? . . . Yes, I thought you'd like Venice. Sure, I'm brilliant. . . . I'll set it up at once. I'll collect you around six—okay? Yes, honey, I remember you don't like to fly. We'll go by train. There's no rush, is there? . . . Oh, about a week, I'd say. Can you manage that? . . . Yes, I love you, too, darling." And the woman's noncommittal voice said, "How nice." Spitzer, head bent over some copy, looked up casually. "A week in Venice?" he asked with thin amusement. Fenner grinned like a happy idiot who had just settled a very smart deal. "On an expense account, too," said Fenner. That was the phrase that would really twist the hook into Spitzer's gullet: wasn't the weakness of capitalists their constant thought of money money money?

So he had made the train and hotel reservations, too, growing cheerier by the minute.

Spitzer was making some work for himself with a blue pencil when he received the biggest shock of the day. Even Fenner, in the middle of his call to Venice, faltered for an amazed moment when Mike Ballard walked in. Ballard was haphazardly dressed, a green cotton-mesh shirt with white stripes, no tie, a natural-colored linen jacket (crumpled at the back), faded red trousers, loafers on his feet. His temper was foul. He scowled at Fenner by way of greeting as he marched to Spitzer's desk. "Why the hell didn't you call me? The Russians start exploding bombs and you don't even pick up a telephone," he began, and went on with increasing vividness.

Fenner completed his call and drifted over to the two men. "Nice beach?" he asked with a grin, looking at Ballard's clothes.

Ballard was studying a copy of Spitzer's report to New York on the Soviet bomb tests. He snapped, "That's where I've come from. Heard the news at eleven. Caught the plane with ten seconds to spare. Now I feel like a refugee from a circus. What are you doing here?" He was eying the cable, with Penneyman's name clearly visible, that still lay casually on Spitzer's desk.

"Picking up a cable." Fenner reached over and lifted it.

"Venice?"

"That's right."

"Why there?"

"I don't think it's any of your damned business," Fenner said gently.

"Isn't it?" Ballard asked, after a startled pause. He went back to reading Spitzer's report. "No good, no good. Scrap it!" he told Spitzer angrily.

"It went out, this morning. I did my best. I thought—"

"You sent this garbage under my name?" Ballard demanded.

"Good-by, chaps," Fenner said, and made for the door.

"Hold on, Bill." Ballard followed him quickly. "What is all this about Venice?"

"Do you want to read it again?" Fenner handed him the cable.

Ballard waved it away. "It is my business, you know," he said, no longer aggressive but openly worried. "And why send you to see this Vaugiroud when I'm here?"

"But you weren't, Mike. Don't worry. I covered up for you."

"And took the Vaugiroud assignment," Ballard said bitterly. "When did Penneyman telephone about it? Yesterday morning?"

Fenner dodged a lie. "You had already gone. So I told him you had grippe, wouldn't be on your feet until Monday." He glanced definitely at Spitzer. "It's a good out for you. Every way. Use it."

The idea had begun to glimmer in Ballard's eyes. He said, mollified, "Who is this Vaugiroud?"

"A retired professor of Moral Philosophy."

"How did Penneyman hear about him?"

"He's an old World War II buddy."

"Oh, one of those." Ballard relaxed visibly.

"Have a nice weekend with your typewriter," Fenner said, leaving. Ballard grunted, stripped off his jacket as he headed for his private cubicle, and threw the two women into a frenzy of work as he yelled for the boy to get coffee. Spitzer, bent over the copy he was checking, looked like a man who had miscalculated and didn't know how.

So all that was over, the first steps taken, no retreat possible. Fenner studied the last hour's performance from every angle as he walked briskly down the broad and spruce Avenue de l'Opéra. On the whole, good. His credentials had been established. Strange how a little evasion here, a little play-acting there, had changed the accounting of his thirty-odd hours in Paris. He hadn't actually liked that skirting of the truth, so why should he be enjoying this feeling of petty triumph? He could almost hear Rosie's probable comment: "Petty? What's petty about Robert Wahl's plans? What's petty about the smallest success against them? And another thing— drop that word 'triumph,' even if you use it ironically. Especially when you use it ironically. Cut out the comic heroics and concentrate on survival. And it's not only *your* survival I'm talking about, either. You know what's at stake."

Yes, I know what's at stake, Fenner thought grimly. Even Vaugiroud, ethics and all, must have put philosophical questions of right and wrong aside in his resistance to the Nazis. How had he equated argument and action? Strength in one could mean weakness in the other. Carlson had guessed something of this conflict in Fenner: that explained, perhaps, why he had wanted Fenner out of this whole business. Yet Rosie, who was in several ways a less sympathetic character, had disagreed with Carlson: did he see Fenner less clearly? Or more deeply? Let's hope it's the latter, Fenner thought: I like feeling flattered as much as any man. And if I laugh at cloaks and daggers, I don't laugh very much at treason, stratagems, and spoils.

He suddenly realized that he was striding down the avenue looking like a man with a fixed destination ahead of him. Not good, that, he warned himself with mock seriousness. He eased off his pace, stopped now and again at the shop windows, some smart, some cheap, glanced casually at the more interesting faces that passed him, as if he were enjoying a normal walk through Paris. The streets became more crowded as he reached the Louvre. He thought of dropping in—he had the theory that the only way to see a museum was in brief visits, no longer than an hour each, when you could choose what you felt like seeing and spare your mind wild indigestion: whoever ate his way through a menu from top to bottom, missing no dish? But he recalled Carlson's hint, much in line with the shenanigans in all the espionage movies he had attended: museums were excellent meeting places for agents. So—with another touch of levity—he kept himself clear of suspicion (if he were being followed) by skirting the old palace and sauntering across the Seine. He could imagine Carlson's shake of the head, telling him he was doing the right thing but with the wrong attitude.

Fenner's jocularity turned into quick and complete depression.

He was not too far from the Ile Saint-Louis, but there were almost two hours to kill before he met Mrs. James Langley. Had that voice on the telephone really been hers? Perhaps that was why he felt so damn depressed. With that voice at his elbow, even Venice would be ruined. If he had to share Venice with a woman, he'd like her soft-spoken, laughing, interested; and, at very least, agreeable to look at. I've become too much of the successful bachelor, he thought, wanting everything just my way. Master of my fate, captain of my soul? Like hell I am!

He stopped at a couple of the bookstalls on the quay to find out if he was being followed. (See, Carlson? I'm learning.) He reasoned that he could expect that from now on: his movements would be checked just to make sure that they'd tally with the story that had been built up around him. But after fifteen minutes of looking at battered books, old prints, and bargain seekers, he felt sure that no one was interested in him at all. He walked farther into the Left Bank area, still more convinced that he wasn't being followed, beginning to wonder if Carlson's caution had not been excessive, a sort of occupational disease. He came to the Boulevard Saint-Germain. There was no breach of security in walking along it, in the direction of the Boul' Miche, where he could have a beer and relax before he headed for the Ile Saint-Louis. There was no breach of security, either, in glancing down the street where the Café Racine retired so modestly from the busy traffic of Saint-Germain. Today it was a crowded corner, jammed. And quiet. Fenner halted abruptly, became one of a group pressed together, staring across at the Café Racine.

The restaurant's front had a jagged gape. There had been a fire, too. Blackened stone, dark water deep in the gutter, smashed glass on the sidewalk, the acrid smell of disaster still hanging over the quietened little street. Policemen were on duty; some firemen were walking in and out of the ruined restaurant. All action was over.

"Terrible, terrible," the woman beside Fenner kept repeating. "The filthy pigs. Assassins! Two children dead. They lived on the floor upstairs." She saw she had caught a listener. She was normally a fat, jolly woman, but anger and excitement had turned her into a hoarse phonograph. She had seen it all. Been walking along this street. Poor little innocents. Their mother had just left them to buy some olive oil at the

shop around the corner. Some women didn't even know how
to keep house, nowadays, running out of olive oil—

"What happened?" Fenner asked abruptly.

"A fire. And the two little—"

"How did it start?"

"A bomb. Then the fire. Spreading. I saw it as I walked
along the street. I could have been struck by flying glass. It
was terrible. They lived on the floor upstairs—"

Fenner turned away quickly from the grim evidence of
smoke-stained walls, of smashed and blackened windows, leaving the woman in search of a new listener. The bewildered
face of an old man caught his attention. It was the waiter
who had served him yesterday in the Café Racine. "Auguste?"
Fenner asked, catching the thin, frail arm.

Auguste looked slowly around, with no recognition. "Terrible," he said, "terrible ..."

"What happened?"

The old man shook his head slowly, as if he still couldn't
believe it. "Both dead," he said at last. His white hair was
soot-streaked; his threadbare alpaca jacket was smeared and
stained. One sleeve was charred.

"I know," Fenner said. Did terrorists never think of two
children when they packed their ideals into a bomb? All
and everything for the cause, including two children. "Did
anyone get hurt in the restaurant?"

"Both dead," Auguste repeated dully. "Monsieur Henri.
Madame Angélique. Both. They were at his table. The bomb
was there. I had just left." The red-rimmed, watering eyes
looked at Fenner. They still could not understand his escape.
The others were dead; he was alive.

"Was there no one else at the table?" Fenner asked
quickly.

"The professor had left, too. To talk on the telephone. He
was at the desk. Madame Angélique's desk. And she was at
the table. Monsieur Henri was talking to her." Auguste sighed.
"And so they are both dead."

"Was the professor hurt?"

"An arm broken. A little burned. He tried to reach Monsieur Henri. They took him to the hospital. Three waiters,
too. No guests were there. It was early, you see. Twelve
o'clock. I had just left to fetch a bottle of wine—" Again
the white head was shaking, slowly, wonderingly.

"No good standing here," Fenner said. "Come away.

Where do you live?" I'll get Auguste into a taxi, he thought, and deliver him home: he has lost the will to move.

But Auguste would have none of it. He drew his thin shoulders, almost angrily, back from Fenner and resumed his staring at the Café Racine, his eyes dull again, not seeing, only remembering that he, counting the months to his own death, had stayed alive today. All right, Fenner thought, I shan't cheat you of your miracle. He left the old man, then.

So Wahl and Lenoir had silenced Henri Roussin. And if Rosie hadn't telephoned, they would have silenced Vaugiroud, too. And Angélique—she had been expendable. So were the two children who had nothing to do with anything. ... Fenner's shock gave way to anger. It deepened with his sense of personal failure. Somehow, he ought to have warned Roussin in time. Even Rosie came in for a touch of blame: why hadn't he got hold of Vaugiroud before he had left his apartment? But Fenner's recrimination collapsed: it certainly wasn't Rosie's fault; he hadn't known Vaugiroud's daily routine; he hadn't known about any bomb. He had only followed an instinct, a suspicion, when he had telephoned Vaugiroud. "It's a fixed date?" Rosie had asked unexpectedly. Now, Fenner knew just how worried he must have been. And there I was, Fenner thought bitterly, not realizing what danger could really mean, just thinking of it as a big vague threat, even making light reference to Roussin's invitation to lunch— Good God, *I* could have been there when the bomb went off!

He reached the Ile Saint-Louis almost twenty minutes early. He hadn't stopped for any beer—he had forgotten about it, in fact. He unlocked the door, and stepped into the small recess that formed the entrance hall. The white-and-green living room was softly bright in the afternoon's sunshine. There was a grouping of suitcase, overnight case, red handbag, near an armchair where a dark-blue cashmere coat had been thrown along with a pair of white gloves. So Mrs. Langley was already here, and ready to go. She was in the bedroom, for he heard a door close sharply, and then, "Who's that?"

"Bill Fenner," he called back. "Sorry if I frightened you." Stupid oaf, he thought, I ought to have rung the bell.

"That's all right," she said, coming into the room, high heels tapping lightly. He knew the voice, even knew the footstep, before he saw the fair hair falling softly over her brow and the large gray eyes looking at him hesitantly from under long black lashes. The smile on the rose-pink lips was uncertain. "My name really *is* Claire Connor Langley. I hope that answers your question."

He recovered himself. "One of them." He tried to smile. "When are you which?" She was wearing a light-gray suit with one of those stand-away necklines that emphasized a slender neck.

"Professionally, I use Claire Connor." She noticed the slight lift of his eyebrow. "By profession, I mean an illustrator and designer," she added severely.

He looked at the small automatic she had carried into the room. "A new type of pencil? Splatter effect, perhaps, in the Pollock manner."

"Oh, this?" She laughed, embarrassed. "I was just getting it out of a closet. I keep it in a hatbox." She crossed over to the armchair and picked up her large red handbag and slipped the automatic inside. "You think it's pretty silly, don't you? Perhaps it is. But it's a comfort, too. Especially when a door was unlocked twenty minutes before I expected anyone —no voice, just a man's footsteps."

"I don't think it is silly at all." And he meant that.

She shook her head in mock wonder. "Neill Carlson will never believe it." She noticed his face more closely. "Is something wrong? Did anything happen to you?"

"Just an initiation. My first terrorist bomb."

"Near you?"

"No, no. I only saw the results. But I could have been there. If Carlson and Rosie hadn't told me to keep clear of the place, I—" He paused. "It was the Café Racine. Roussin and his sister-in-law—"

"I heard about that on the radio. An OAS bomb, wasn't it?"

"Not OAS this time. At least, I think not."

"They'll get the blame, anyhow."

"Four dead—two of them just kids, burned alive—"

"Don't," she said, "don't keep thinking about it." The gray eyes seemed to have darkened. Then she brushed aside the invasion of grim memories. "You look like a man who needs a a quick shower and a long drink." She glanced at her small wrist watch, compared it with the clock on the desk. "We have plenty of time." She adjusted her watch and wound it. "Did you collect the tickets?"

"No." And blast me, he thought, for not remembering. "We'll pick them up at the station."

"That will cut down our time. I think we better take only twenty minutes here. Can you manage?"

"If you fix me that drink." The Gare de Lyon wasn't far from here. "Aren't we going to be a trifle early?"

"It's nice to look around and see who is traveling with us," she said. She was already in the pantry, pulling out an ice tray. "I really am sorry for last night. Truly. You see—"

"Forget it," he said, and headed for the shower. Last night . . . This wasn't the same girl at all. This wasn't the the helpless little blonde that had been blown into the restaurant. This was someone who needed no help, capable and cool. This one would check her watch, see that they got to the station on time; the other one invented fanciful and funny stories. Which was the real girl, he wondered, or were they two sides of the same girl? Whatever she was, she had made sure of one thing: the fireproof asbestos curtain had been definitely lowered between them.

"Hell!" he said, as the cold water turned to scalding.

"All right?" she called through. "Cold runs hot and hot runs cold. Faucets are marked wrong. Sorry! And it wasn't a lie, last night—about going to Venice this morning. I really was. But the plans were changed, and I—" She gave it up. The hiss of water blotted out her voice. She went back to pouring the Scotch, making it a good stiff drink. He needed it, on every count.

She placed the glass on the bureau outside the bathroom door, selected a fresh shirt and socks from his suitcase, folded up his pajamas and last night's tie, and packed them away neatly along with his other clothes. The water had stopped hissing. "All clear," she called, and went back into the living room. She was waiting at the telephone when he came to join her. She picked up the receiver. "I'll just let our taxi know that we are ready to leave," she told him. She was still keeping her role of capable secretary. But, he noted, she had added a pair of pearl earrings, and a gold pin to her jacket.

"Our taxi? This is service."

"Shall I say we'll be downstairs in five minutes?"

"Fine." He carried his luggage into the room as she telephoned. He was still thinking about the carefully arranged taxi. He remembered the pistol, too, so innocently hidden inside her handbag. "Are you expecting trouble to begin so soon?"

"You never can tell." She looked around the room, checked

windows, drew the curtains. She propped a note she had written for the concierge against the clock.

"I'm pretty sure they didn't follow me," he remarked, picking up her coat and handing her the gloves. "Can you take your overnight case? I'll manage the rest. Ready?" I can be casually businesslike, too, he thought.

"They didn't need to follow you. They knew you were collecting me here. Spitzer would tell them."

"And from here on we can expect to be followed?"

"Or to have a check made on our story. They have to know whether this trip is what we say it is." She hesitated, but added nothing more. There was the faint pink of embarrassment on her cheeks. She avoided his eyes.

"We'll make a good pretense. It won't be hard—not for me."

She looked at him. There was the beginning of a soft smile on her lips. "You have forgiven me for last night?"

It really worried her, he thought, and was somehow pleased by that. "We start afresh," he told her. "In future, we tell each other the truth. Right?"

"Yes." She suddenly relaxed. Even her voice changed from polite worry to warmth, hinting at laughter. "That will be a pleasant change—to have someone who can tell me all the truth, quite frankly."

"Doesn't Neill Carlson?"

Her large eyes widened, guessing and a little amused. "Now, Bill," she said gently, "how can he?" Her eyes became thoughtful; she half sighed. It might have been for Neill Carlson.

He opened the door. "Well, here we go. Good luck to us."

We'll need it, she thought. But she smiled and said, "We'll manage."

FOURTEEN

AT THE Gare de Lyon, in spite of the usual hustle and bustle and small delays, they had almost half an hour to spare. Tactfully, Fenner said nothing. Their luggage had been hauled through the windows of their adjoining compartments and stowed as far out of reach as possible; the blue-smocked porter, inclining an eyelid as a thank-you for a generous tip, had huffed away to pastures new and other sheep for the shearing; the *wagon-lit* attendant, either, a Frenchman who spoke brilliant Italian or an Italian who spoke impeccable French, had shown them how the lights went on and all the mysteries of the concealed cabinets. He also had presented them with several forms to fill in detail for the two invasions—one just after midnight, when the Swiss passport control would board the train, the other for Italian Customs officers at three-fifteen in the merry morning.

"Shall we write these up while the train is stationary?" Fenner asked. "Or do you want a stroll?"

She wanted that stroll of inspection. So they walked back down the long platform, slowly, arm in arm. "Sorry about my train fever," she said, "but this is pleasant, isn't it?"

"Comforting, too?" he teased her, looking at the large red handbag slung over her arm.

She nodded, pretending to study the length of the train with admiration. "I always like to know the worst."

"That saves you from nasty surprises?"

She smiled. "Sometimes." She gestured to the train. "Look at our tame monster, getting up strength to pull us over the fields and forests of France, push us through the mountains of Switzerland and spill us out on the plains of Lombardy." She seemed only to be talking for him, an astonishingly pretty creature whose complexion attracted other women's eyes like a magnet, while their men, after an appreciative stare, would turn their speculation on Fenner.

159

Listening to Claire, he was thinking that this would not be exactly an unnoticed journey. Perhaps that was the idea, perhaps that gave them a small margin of safety: who could imagine that any man traveling with this girl had anything on his mind except her?

"Help me talk, Bill," she said pleadingly.

"But I like listening to you."

"Don't make me more nervous than I am!"

"You, nervous?"

"Tell me the worst play you saw last season. And why."

"That would take exactly thirty seconds. What about turning back? We're pretty far from our base." Talk about the theater when he himself was so damned nervous by this open-view walk? It was all he could do to keep his mind on the crowded platform. Left to himself, he'd have been skulking in his own compartment, reading, with the door firmly closed. Which possibly would have been the wrong thing to do. Their role was complete unawareness wasn't it? The happy travelers . . . Like the hundreds around them, installed in their places, standing at their windows to enjoy the rush of those who still struggled with suitcases and porters on the platform, or to call to the rolling food trolleys for sandwiches and drinks, stretching out their arms, snapping their fingers. Babel of tongues, of wheels, of excited talk of darting movement.

And at that instant he saw Jan Aarvan. The man was standing at a crowded window, laying in a supply of rolls and red wine from a trolley below him. He was reaching down, too engrossed in being served before his neighbor to notice Fenner's recognition. When he looked up, the food in his hands, Fenner was walking on at the same strolling pace, talking, smiling down at the girl beside him.

"We could turn back," she was saying.

"Walk on," he said quickly. "Just another carriage or two."

"You saw someone?"

"I think so. Wahl's chauffeur. He doesn't look quite the same. His hair is darker, cut shorter." But the intent face, caught off guard, had been the same one Fenner had seen glancing up at Vaugiroud's house yesterday. There was the same bone structure, the same powerful shoulders, the same heavy neck. Now he was dressed in a mid-blue suit, neat white collar, neat tie, to make him look like a *petit fonctionnaire* traveling to visit his family back in the Jura, or a country lawyer from Provence who had been on a business trip to Paris. There were a hundred like that on this train.

"He must have spent an hour with his barber this afternoon," she said lightly.

"If that's Jan Aarvan, he's a wanted man. The Sûreté—"

"Let them take care of it." A shadow of worry flitted over her face. She forced a laugh, as if he had made a funny remark.

"We do nothing?"

"Nothing."

"What about using a telephone? Getting a message through to the Sûreté, or to Rosie? That would let them pick up Aarvan somewhere along the line—before we reach the border."

"No," she said. "I wish we could, but—no. He might see us. One of his friends might see us. No, Bill, that isn't the kind of risk we take."

She was right, of course. "Better get back to our own car." They turned and started the long walk forward to the Venice section. "He's waiting for us to pass," Fenner reported.

"Waiting for you to recognize him," she said in a low voice. "He is testing you, Bill." And then, when they had walked a hundred yards or more along the platform, she said, "Congratulations. I couldn't even tell from your eyes which was his window. You are sure he didn't notice you the first time?"

"Quite sure. I caught him at a vulnerable moment. He likes his food." But perhaps, as Dr. Johnson maintained, a man who does not mind his belly will hardly mind anything else. "Cool customer, isn't he?"

"Cool and quick." And I missed him, she thought with sharp annoyance. I saw no one who looked in the least like Jan Aarvan as he appeared in Inspector Bernard's files. Poor Neill, wasting all those good hours this morning on briefing me! Either my eyes are failing or that was a very old photograph of Jan Aarvan. No wonder the man is so confident. "Cool, quick, and confident. That has always been his reputation." She added, encouragingly, "Don't worry—I saw Neill and Chris. Separate, of course. We aren't traveling alone."

"Who is Chris?" And where had Neill Carlson been? Damn, thought Fenner, I missed him: my eyes must be failing.

"An Englishman. Neill's friend. He's in NATO, too. He has been on leave in Paris for the last three weeks. He—"

"Look out, Claire!" Fenner pulled her aside from the headlong charge of two empty luggage carriers.

"So it's to be Claire," she said. He has forgiven me. "I thought I was going to be the nameless one." She smiled and climbed up the steps to their *wagon-lit*.

The attendant was there to help. His indignation about the carelessness of the porters who drove the luggage carriers seemed excessive, but perhaps it was one outlet for his annoyance over two workmen in crumpled overalls who were elbowing him aside as they climbed off the train. The attendant brushed the sleeve of his neat, dark-blue uniform with marked emphasis as he went to Claire's compartment to switch off and on the lights. He shrugged. He repeated the performance in Fenner's room. "All perfect," he assured Fenner.

"What was wrong?"

"The electricians were checking the lights. Always at the last minute—"

"The lights seemed all right to me."

"I know," the attendant agreed wearily. His thin, sallow-skinned face was both tired and annoyed. "Seemingly there was some complaint. They wait all day. They remember their job just as I wanted to make the beds ready. It is always the same with these workmen. Always at the wrong time, always at the last minute."

Everyone loved a good grumble, Fenner thought. But he was grateful to the electricians that the beds had not been made ready for the night. Claire and he could at least have a couch to sit on until dinner. "Let's wait in here," he suggested to Claire, pointing to his room. "This is the time I miss the good old Pullman parlor car."

"First service is very soon," the attendant hinted, dark eyes worriedly calculating the number of beds he had to prepare. "And the dining car is very far away."

"And I am hungry," Claire said, unexpectedly taking the man's side. "I'll just freshen up, Bill. See you in two minutes." She went into her own compartment and closed its door. It was actually four minutes before she reappeared. She looked a little disappointed, but as far as lipstick and smooth hair went, very much the same.

They began the long walk to the dining car, past three first-class sleepers and seven second-class coaches, through swaying corridors where people stood at opened windows. Wandering through the train were several tight blue suits, which gave Fenner several false alarms, but the man who had watched Vaugiroud's house (Kalganov's man, Carlson had said) was keeping out of sight, probably chewing on his hard-crusted sandwiches, preparing to sit out the night like so many others in the crowded compartments. Except in the *wagon-lit* section, there wasn't an inch of spare room on this train. Fenner couldn't see Carlson, either. If Claire did, she gave no sign. As for friend Chris, there were several Englishmen in view. And Italians, and Swedes, and Americans, and Germans, and people talking a strange language which might be Serbo-Croat, for the forward section of the Simplon Express would eventually reach Zagreb. And because the make-up of the train was carefully planned to let its different sections drop off at various stages in its journey across Europe, Fenner wasn't too surprised when they entered a freight car, half filled with crates and sacks, where the train's wheels rattled and clattered frenetically under the jumping wooden floor. One of the sliding panels of the side loading door had been left open to let the cold air whistle in. Practical refrigeration, Fenner thought. He halted. This deserted car made as good a talking place as any. It was the nearest they'd come to privacy on this train.

Claire had stopped, too. She was looking at the opened panel just ahead of them. "Do we have to pass that?" She asked in horror.

He nodded, steadied her with his arm as they lurched together, bent his head so that she could hear him against the background of creaks and clatter and groans. "Electricians?" he asked softly.

"Perhaps they were. Perhaps not." They were jolted together. She caught her balance, laughed, tried to smooth down her wind-blown hair. "Rough journey, isn't it?"

"Seriously, Claire—" he began worriedly.

"I did try to find if they had concealed anything in my compartment, but I hadn't enough time. We'll find out when we get back."

"Will we?" His worry was growing. Microphones and midget recorders were easily installed nowadays, but how did you find them without tearing the place apart? "How long could any small recorder run? A couple of hours?" But how could it be turned on, when they arrived back in Claire's room? Or was it fed through to the next compart-

ment? Why bother to speculate, anyhow? He just did not
know one damned thing about the working of any supersecret recorders, except that they were miniature, powerful,
and fantastically ingenious. Only the very best would be good
enough for Kalganov and his boys—of that, he was sure.

"I've no idea how these things work. They do, though."

"But you know what to look for?"

"This morning, Neill briefed me on several little tricks
that could be played on us. Don't worry, Bill. If we think
any gadget is tucked away somewhere in my compartment, we'll just have to play up to it. That's all."

One false word, one giveaway phrase—he looked at the
large gray eyes so close to his, and he felt fear for this
girl. And he thought of poor old Carlson—he couldn't have
enjoyed himself very much this morning.

"Don't worry about me," she said, guessing at the look
on his face. "Please, Bill!" Doesn't he know, she wondered,
that I was sent to get him safely to that café table on
the Piazza San Marco? Wisely, she didn't tell him. And
it was a pleasant feeling to have someone beside her who
thought he ought to be responsible for her.

"Why did they have to send you?"

"Because no one has to explain to me what a man like
Kalganov is. Or means. Or can do."

"You think that he—"

She touched his arm. "Later," she said, and looked back
to the carriage they had passed through. "We can talk seriously in Venice."

"They'll think up some way of bugging our rooms even
there," he said gloomily.

"Well, they can't eavesdrop on *every* gondola." And
with a smile, she drew away from him as three other passengers came laughing and lurching into the freight car from
the corridor. "Oh Lord," she said in dismay, looking at the
open doorway, hesitating.

He took a firm grip of her wrist, felt the cold rush of air
whip around them as he led her past the five-foot stretch
of gaping wall. Outside, the darkening fields rushed along.
Some thoughtful trainman, he noticed, had fastened a chain
as a handgrip across the opening in case anyone staggered
too much at a curve in the line. "It's safe enough," he told
her reassuringly, thinking of the return journey.

She tried to laugh at herself as she smoothed her hair
back into place once more. She was glad to hear a high-

pitched squeal from one of the passengers behind them. "I suppose that's the trouble," she said, pointing to a wooden crate stamped *Pont l'Evêque* over which a faint smell of cheese hovered.

Fenner grinned. "If that door wasn't left open, none of us would be able to face any dinner. How's your appetite?"

"Still good. How much farther?"

"We're almost there. Roast lamb, I think?"

It was an excellent dinner, too. Only the French could prepare and serve five courses on a fast-moving train. There was no choice: the menu was set. And so were the diners. Those who arrived late would have to wait for the second sitting. Claire and Fenner sat next to the window, facing each other, sharing the table with a solid Frenchman and his silent wife, who followed their conversation with as much critical attention as they examined the texture, size, and taste of each course. Perhaps they were interested in the sounds of a strange language. Or perhaps it was an overwhelming shock for the voluble French to discover that foreigners could enjoy conversation, too. But even if they did understand English, they certainly didn't understand any of the light talk, wild gambits, happy *non sequiturs* that flowed so freely between Claire and Fenner.

Fenner was having the best dinner he could remember. It wasn't just the effect of good food and pleasant Beaujolais, or even of the smooth cognac sliding down so benevolently with his coffee, that made him raise his glass to her. "A thousand years!"

"A little optimistic. Even the head Lama in Shangri-La didn't last as long as that. In any case, a thousand sounds much too wrinkled."

Fenner's eyes had flickered toward a man who was coming down the aisle between the tables. It was Neill Carlson, ignoring Fenner completely, looking like a man who had enjoyed his dinner and was on his way forward to his own carriage. "Well," Fenner said slowly, "there is *She*, isn't there?"

"Who?" She caught sight of Neill Carlson's back. "Oh, *She*? Rider Haggard's *She*?" Neill had run into a traffic jam at the doorway, where the second shift had already started to line up for its dinner. An attendant was telling them to go away, without much response.

"She lasted two thousand years, give or take—" He studied

the small glass in his hand so that the man in the blue suit, who was following Carlson from the rear of the car, might not notice he had been seen. Fenner's lips went dry. "Give or take a few years," he ended.

Claire had sensed something worried him. She smiled brightly, said, "You know, I always thought that was the silliest of titles."

"She?" Jan Aarvan was coming nearer. "Why?"

"Imagine being a critic who is very sensitive to grammar—"

"As what critic is not?"

"And his wife says, making sweet dinner conversation, 'What good books did you review today, darling?' I suppose that someone does call a critic darling, now and again—"

"And he replies, 'None, as usual.' " Jan Aarvan, passing their table, almost collided with a hurrying attendant and halted.

"Will you please stop the obbligato? This is one story I am going to finish my way. He says—oh dear, let me get this right—" Neill Carlson was now making his way with difficulty through the doorway. The attendant had lost his argument with the second sitting: the hungry people were determined to wait there.

"He says that?" Fenner asked, smiling broadly. Beside their table, Jan Aarvan was lighting a cigarette, leaving slowly.

Claire shook her head. "Our sensitive critic says with a shudder, 'Pour me another drink, honey. I've just had to write three thousand words about *She*.' And his wife, who went to Vassar, raises her eyebrows and says gently, 'About her, darling, about *her*. And I think you have already had one drink too many.' "

Fenner drained his glass, even if it was sip-worthy cognac.

"Was it as bad as all that?" she asked. She let her eyes rest on the massive blue-clad back of a brown-haired man who was pushing his way through the waiting crowd at the door. He was in a great hurry, whoever he was. Abominable manners, she thought: the sharp-elbow-and-shoulder-aside type.

"On the contrary," Fenner told her, signaling for the chief attendant wandering up the aisle with his cashbox tucked under his arm, "you were superb."

But I didn't ask about me, she thought. And are we leaving? She concealed her surprise, finished her coffee with some difficulty, for the train was gathering tremendous speed, reached for her handbag and lipstick. And she wondered at

Bill Fenner's growing impatience as the chief attendant added, made a mistake, added again, apologized, counted the change with great exactness from his little tin box. Monsieur Solidity and Madame Silence rose to let them pass. "Not at all," the Frenchman said in perfectly good English. Madame was still too shocked by the tip Fenner had added to the bill to say anything.

"It was only fifteen per cent," Fenner reassured Claire as they eased themselves past the group at the door.

"I wonder what he made of our conversation? I could have sworn that he couldn't understand one word we were saying. Which only goes to prove—" She smiled at him.

"That all foreigners are crazy." But from the quick look he gave her, he showed that her point was well made. He opened the door that led to the freight car. Someone had turned on the lights, obligingly—two bare small bulbs swung from two cords. The wooden floor jiggled and jumped; the rattles and creaks, the shrieks and groans multiplied. "Glad we didn't have dinner here," Fenner yelled at her ear. "Not much hope for the soup." He took a firm grip of her arm.

Claire nodded, averted her eyes from the black yawn of night at the opened door, shivered as the cold wind whipped bitterly at their shoulders. Why this hurry? she wondered. But he didn't stop to explain. They walked more slowly through the interminable corridors: it was almost as if he were looking for someone, trying to keep it unnoticeable. Twice they stopped and looked out at black walls of hills rising steeply, and still he didn't talk. The corridors were becoming empty. Most people were settling in for the night. The compartments' lights had already been dimmed, some were even turned off completely. This was no good, she decided: we can't worry separately. And we can't risk any real talk in our rooms, either. As the train roared out of a long tunnel, she stopped by one of the open windows, grasped its brass rail, let the wind tear her hair to pieces. "Where do you think we are?" Outside, she could see black masses of trees, black stretches of fields, black ground steeply sloping. Here was a downward stretch, and the train, released from the hills it had traveled through, was running free into a valley. The noise of wheels was lessening. One could talk without raising one's voice.

Fenner looked at his watch. It was almost ten o'clock. "We are due at Dijon in twelve minutes." It was a one-minute stop. No one got on or off the train there. "Come on, Claire, only two more cars to go."

But she didn't move. She rested her head against his shoulder. They were just a romantic couple looking out at the rushing night. She looked up at him, saying blithely, "Sorry. You'll just have to get used to this." Her mood changed. Quietly, she asked, "Is something wrong?"

"Carlson was being followed." He slipped an arm around her waist. His voice was equally low.

"Does he know the man?"

"Yes. And the man could recognize him, too."

"The man in the blue suit, with the powerful shoulders?"

"Yes."

"Aarvan?"

"That's right."

She bit her lip. "Can he connect you with Neill in any way?" If so, she thought, our mission is over.

"He saw us visit the same address, but he didn't see us together."

"Do many people visit that address?"

"Yes, I suppose so." Vaugiroud must have a constant procession of ex-pupils and friends.

Beginners always worry too much, she thought. She said gently, "Then there is no definite link. We haven't been spotted. Forget it, Bill."

"But why should he be following Carlson so openly?"

"He could have been trying to see if Neill had any contacts on the train. One word, one small sign would have been enough. Chris was just two tables away from us, you know: the well-tailored suit talking Italian like mad to some Milanese friends. He didn't blink an eyelid as Neill passed him. And you didn't either."

Claire could be right, he thought: Jan Aarvan might have wanted to note any sign of recognition between Chris, or us, and Carlson. And yet——he kept remembering Aarvan and the way he had followed. Fenner stared at the black countryside, dark shadow piled on darker shadow, outlines suspicioned rather than glimpsed, swirls of treetops eddying into a thick mass of night. "I just can't figure it out," he said slowly.

"Don't try." It was meant to encourage him. "Let Neill figure it. He will." She smiled, thinking of Carlson. "Someone's coming," she said, and drew still closer to him.

It was an elderly shirt-sleeved man, suspenders undone

and flapping. He crushed past them, with unsteady legs and sleep-heavy eyes. *"Scusa, scusa!"* he said irritably, and lurched on toward the lavatory.

"Night traffic begins," Fenner said. "Let's move." The train's speed was tapering off.

She nodded. "When you next see Aarvan, point him out. Talk about shoulders, if he is close to us. I'll get it." As a woman, clutching her tweed coat over her slip, poked her head into the corridor and hesitated, Claire raised her voice to normal again. "You're right—it's chilly. I suppose we ought to start thinking of sleep, like everyone else."

"Forms to be filled out," he reminded her.

"Oh, heavens!"

"Sh!" said someone angrily from a darkened compartment.

The brakes were on. The express was beginning its long slide into the station of Dijon as Fenner left Claire in her compartment. "See you in five minutes," he told her. "I'll get those forms. And a nightcap."

"Yes, darling." She smiled as he glanced sharply at her. You never know, her eyes seemed to say as she gestured comically at the four small walls around her.

He entered his own compartment, and pulled up the window shade. The station was modern; the platform was long and broad, brightly lighted. He forced his window down from the top and looked out. Neither Carlson nor Jan Aarvan appeared, so they were both still on the train. But three men, waiting quietly on the platform, caught his eye. They were dressed in civilian clothes; they carried no bags, not even a briefcase. And they were the only people on that long platform to board the train. They moved in a tight little group, as if they knew exactly what they wanted. Well, thought Fenner as the minute's stop at Dijon was over, it seems as if someone did get a message to the Sûreté from the Gare de Lyon. He pulled down the shade, thoughtful, but somehow reassured by his guess.

Claire had made good use of those five minutes. He found her standing on her bed, the pillow pushed aside, reaching up to one of the heavy brackets on the wall just under the high luggage rack. She gave him a smile of triumph. She had found what she had been looking for. But what do we do? he wondered. He suddenly felt useless and stupid, just standing there speechless.

Claire moved silently back from the luggage rack, and

lowered herself carefully to sit on the bed. "Darling, how wonderful, you did find your flask! I'm completely refrigerated. It wouldn't really be much fun to arrive sneezing in Venice."

"Better put more clothes on, honey."

She gave him an indignant look, and said nothing. Let him get out of *that* one, she thought.

"You have the prettiest legs, even when they are turning blue. Here, drink this—" He stepped over her shoes and reached for the tumbler on the washbasin.

"Bill—please—stop that! How can I drink if you—I'll spill it, Bill. Bill!" She began to laugh.

Perhaps it was the astonishment on his face that amused her so much. Her laugh sounded merry, carefree, happy. All is jollity, he thought grimly as he went on pouring the drink. Silently, he offered it to her. She shook her head. So he swallowed it himself, and looking bitterly at the bracket, high on the wall, above the pillow. I'll yank it out from its hiding place, he thought, and let us talk naturally. No, I can't do that either: it's the proof of our innocence. Who was going to listen to its recording, and judge? Robert Wahl? Fernand Lenoir? Lenoir was the expert with words, wasn't he? Damn him, damn them all, damn—

Claire had caught his hand, tugging at it gently to bring him back to the present. "Dear Bill," she said quietly, and she wasn't acting.

He sat down beside her. "Claire, I've been thinking about us."

"Don't! Just let's enjoy ourselves—"

"Yes, that too. But when Venice is over, what then?"

"What then . . ." she repeated, at a loss for words.

"Would you throw up your job and come back to New York? With me?"

She stared at him, her gray eyes widening. She had almost believed him. Why, she thought as her alarm subsided, he can act my head off! "Bill, you promised me—you said you would give me time. That's why I'm going to Venice with you." She glanced up at the hidden microphone. "You know that, darling."

He said nothing.

Again she felt that strange alarm.

He was smiling. "Yes, I know. I'll wait."

"And no more thinking about us?"

"Just occasionally."

"Kiss me, Bill." She was lighting a cigarette. She offered him one from her case.

He pushed it aside, took the cigarette away from her lips, tossed it into the hand basin, and kissed her. Her body went rigid; she tried to push him away, but he kissed her long and hard. "There!" he said softly, as he let her go. "Feeling warmer, honey?"

She just kept looking at him. He was very careful not to touch her again.

"Hell!" he said. "I've just remembered—we've got these forms to fill out. Come on, my pet, duty before pleasure. Sit up and start reading the questions."

"Must we do it now?"

"Now," he said firmly. "Or do you want to be stuck at the border in a black chiffon nightie? It would be much admired, but—"

"That's what I like about men," she murmured, pulling her gray wool jacket neatly into place, "you can always depend on their taste: it's so catholic. All right, darling. If I tell you the facts, will you be the recording angel? Claire Connor Langley—is there room for all that? Born: May 20, 1933, Sheridan, Wyoming. Father and mother: John and Agnes Connor. What next? Heavens, they want just about everything. When did I leave the U.S.? When was my last visit to Italy? Why am I going there? Oh dear, would they accept the truth? For the purpose of making up my mind."

"You'll have to be more specific than that."

"What's that you've written? Pleasure."

"Well, isn't it?"

"I also have a little job to do."

He looked up, shook his head even if he was amused. She enjoyed sailing close to the wind, this girl. "I thought you were leaving your work behind, just for once. Don't tell me a client wants a copy of Saint Mark's horses for her front gate in Beverly Hills?"

"My client is a very impressive and well-known magazine, Mr. Fenner, and it wants some details on the upper hall of the Scuolo di San Rocco. Do you know it? It's the large building put up by the Venetian guilds, decorated by Tintoretto, just to show that the trade unions could keep up with the Doges."

"Sounds a pretty big job to me."

"Darling, don't look so upset. This is only a small assignment: it won't take long. I have just to make some suggestions, as a guide for the photographers who will be arriving in October. Of course, if the Editorial Brains like my ideas, that could lead to something bigger— Bill, please don't look so depressed. You have a job to do in Venice, too. How long will your interviews take?"

"Not so long, once they are arranged."

"You see? Arranging them might take you two or three days. And what would I do meanwhile?"

"Just sit around and look beautiful, my pet. Besides, Penneyman has probably made most of the arrangements. His cable sounded as if everything was all laid on."

"You used to do some good interviews," she said. She was serious again. "You know, I think Mr. Penneyman is trying to entice you back into news reporting."

"Could be. But I have a book I want to write."

"Why don't you write a play?"

He stared at her.

"You could, you know," she said.

He tried to laugh the idea away. "And what shall it be— comedy or tragedy?"

"That's the problem, isn't it? You're essentially an optimist, Bill. But you wrap yourself in pessimism."

"Just an old cynic," he agreed.

"No, no. Not that. You are a romantic with your guard up against the realists."

"Just an old, battered, beaten-up idealist?" he asked with a grin.

"Do you always underrate yourself, Bill?"

"I think I've overrated myself with you. I ask the prettiest girl I know to come jaunting in Venice. And what do I find? Does she want to be kissed or cajoled? No. She's too busy analyzing my psyche."

"Darling," she said softly. "I'm just helping you fill out forms. Oh, let's finish them, shall we? And after that's over, we can—" She yawned.

"Don't fall asleep!"

"Of course not," she said drowsily. It was a good act, a nice prelude to his departure, a reasonable explanation for the microphone when all sounds ceased. "Where do I sign? Oh Lord, so many places. You know, Bill, there's one aspect of the population explosion that has no solution."

"Only one?"

"Where are they going to file the forms that everyone will have to fill up?"

"There's always outer space," he suggested, trying to concentrate on his own answers. Date of birth: December 17, 1923. You're old, Father William. You're thirty-seven, and she is twenty-eight.

"The brakes are going on," Claire said. "Another station so soon?"

"Probably Dôle. There's a six-minute stop here. Would you like some hot coffee?" He was already on his feet. The train gave one last lurch and came to rest.

"It might be one way to keep me awake," she said with a low laugh, and made a comical face up at the hidden microphone. Fenner was smiling broadly as he entered the corridor: that's the idea, he was thinking, don't let the beggars grind us down.

The attendant blocked the door to the platform. He wasn't enthusiastic about anyone leaving the train. There was no food cart in sight; the station café was distant and possibly closed. Fenner didn't argue with these suggestions: he had a good-enough view of the platform from the door. Some people got off, some got on; a few people in more countrified clothes still sat on bulging suitcases, hugged paper parcels, waited for other local connections. Two policemen in dark-blue uniforms walked smartly along the train. Abruptly, they halted, as if they had seen someone at one of the carriage doors, and climbed on board.

The attendant had been watching, too.

"Looks as if somebody is going to be arrested," Fenner said hopefully.

The man shrugged his shoulders; his white, tired face was blank. Perhaps he was unwilling to admit to any foreigner that anything could be wrong. He stared along the platform. The policemen did not get off.

"They're traveling with us," Fenner said, taken aback as the train's wheels started moving again.

The attendant said, "You'll have no trouble, monsieur. If you hand me your documents and passports, I shall answer any questions. You will not be disturbed at the frontiers, either."

That was as close as Fenner would get to an admission that the train might be searched. "Thanks," he said. "You're going to have a sleepless night."

"The documents are all ready?"

"I'm just completing them. You'll have them in ten minutes." Fenner went back to the compartment. He was making no more guesses about the Sûreté having been alerted just before the train left the Gare de Lyon. If they had been, wouldn't Jan Aarvan have been hauled off the train at Dôle? After all, plenty of criminals traveled: trains and liners and airplanes carried them. Ordinary travelers forgot that. There could be others on this train who were wanted by the Sûreté. "Disappointment," he told Claire. "No coffee. Our attendant wouldn't trust me out on the platform. He has lost some passengers that way, I gather. And I've got to get these forms ready."

If he was disappointed, she thought, it wasn't about the coffee. What is puzzling him? But she sighed deeply and said, "Red tape is very hard on romance."

"Shan't be long, honey." He began printing his name, et cetera et cetera. Red tape was strong on et ceteras.

Claire let the magazine she had been reading drop on her knees. She curled her legs under her thighs for warmth, pulled over the pillow to soften the hard wall for her shoulder blades. She yawned again. She had never been more wide awake.

She watched him as he worked on the small folding table near the window. Intelligent eyes, lips serious in concentration, a well-shaped head; no flabbiness, either physically or mentally. The movements of his hands with paper and pen were neat and capable. Capable—yes, he was all of that. She remembered Rosie's words when he was persuading her into this trip: "Fenner is all right. I wouldn't send you with him if he wasn't on the beam. Just get to know each other before you arrive in Venice, so as you'll feel natural. No strain. You can't be stiff or stilted. Don't worry, Claire, he's a dependable guy." Yes, Rosie had been right: she could always work with someone she liked, someone she trusted. She had liked Bill from the very first meeting. (That would have startled Rosie. It had startled her.) Now, on this strange journey, she was learning to trust him. Or why should she be feeling more confident? We'll make a good job of this little assignment, she thought happily. Little? Only her part in it was small, and so was Bill's. How many others were converging on Venice, each with his own job to do? Add up all those assignments, big and small, and the sum total must be enormous. And all this effort, which she could sense but not see, all this for one letter? A letter, one faked letter— could it really pack so much possible destruction within one page? Rosie had told her the minimum, naturally, but there was no law against thinking. The letter was only one part of the problem; why else would the French be interested? Why else was Rosie asking for the Italians' help? And the English were involved, too. This was going to be quite a party in Venice. A surprise party. That was the only chance of success, Rosie had said: complete surprise. Keep them unsuspecting, she told herself, and glanced defiantly at the bracket overhead.

"Oh, *darling*," she said, "you are taking for*ever*."

"Won't be long, pet." Fenner seemed a little amused by the warmth of the interruption. "Just four last questions, damn them."

"What was the color of your grandmother's eyes?" she asked sleepily, still looking at the concealed microphone. And what do you make of that, Comrade Lenoir? Lenoir and Wahl: psychological-warfare expert and organizer of terrorism. A very complete combination, a real threat. Yes, much more than a letter must be involved. This was something really big. Not that size mattered when it came to threats against peace. Even the smallest could grow.... Again she remembered Rosie's words: "Nothing is negligible, nothing—if it can shift the delicate balance of peace." He wasn't making a phrase to win some votes or impress a television audience. Old Rosie believed that. So did Neill and Chris Holland. So did Bill Fenner—or he wouldn't be here. And so must I—or I wouldn't be here, either.

She looked back at Bill Fenner. He was reading over the four sets of forms with a strange smile on his face, as if to say, "How the hell do I get into this kind of situation?" What did he really think about her? Someone who made this kind of journey quite nonchalantly? Regularly? Some kind of a sublimated nymphomaniac, treating life as the great and gay adventure? Heavens, she thought in distress.

Fenner turned his head to find her watching him, with her cheeks flushed, her eyes troubled. "Finished," he said. "I'll hand everything over to the attendant. He will deal with the—" He rose, and let his voice change. "Claire! Claire—wake up!"

Had she been waiting for this cue? The worry, certainly, vanished from her eyes. "I'm all right, Bill—all right, really—" Her voice drifted away.

He wondered if they had play-acted themselves into a corner. How was she going to lock her door once he left? And how did he say an adequate good night? She was leav-

ing it all to him, this time: no more invitations to a kiss.
Just as well. When he kissed a girl like Claire, he stopped
all pretending. "Good night, Claire," he said gently. He ruffled her hair, raised her hand to his lips. Just a gentleman of
the old school, he thought wryly, and kissed her hand twice.
Then, on impulse, he added, *"Mes hommages."* His eyes
were serious. So were hers. He remembered to switch off the
main lights as he left.

Claire cautiously slipped off her jacket and skirt. That
was all she could risk. She'd have to go to bed half dressed.
She couldn't risk any sounds of washing or brushing, either.
She was fast asleep, wasn't she? I'll look awful tomorrow,
she predicted as she slid carefully between the sheets. Her
handbag was close to the pillow, luckily. Her hand searched
quietly and found the small automatic. It reassured her, at
least, about the unlocked door. Strange how people who
thought they knew you understood so little. "Steel-lined
nerves," Neill Carlson used to tease her. And Rosie, in a
moment of weakness, had told her that her strongest asset
was her calm competence. Even Bill Fenner had said, *"Mes
hommages,"* as if he had been saluting her. But this, she
thought as she slipped the automatic under her pillow, is the
real me: someone who is doing a job because it's necessary,
because she can do it; someone who feels so frightened that
she is afraid to admit it, even to herself. Except now and
again, in the lonely hours. The hours like those that stretched
ahead of her, as cold and bleak as the mountain air whistling
against the window.

FIFTEEN

VENICE WELCOMED them with blue sky and high clouds, little trails and folds and careless gathers of white silk draped high above the fresh breeze that blew in from the Adriatic and set the waters of the lagoon dancing in the morning sunlight. In the Grand Canal, the ripples slapped at mooring poles and jostled the black gondolas, nudged cellar walls and dared to mount the green-stained steps toward a palace door.

It was a city of contrast. Colors were bright, yet soft: gamboge, yellow ocher, raspberry, terra cotta were bleached into gold, pink, russet; faded, muted, and streaked. Shapes were large and bold, yet decorative, even fragile. Solid walls of high houses rose out of the canal; balconies and windows were carved and fretted, fluted and laced. Stone floated on water.

Bill Fenner, high on the narrow terrace that linked the four topmost rooms of the placid Hotel Vittoria, was waiting for Claire. Directly below him, five floors down to the Grand Canal, was the small landing stage that formed the front, and slightly swaying, approach to the hotel, where they had arrived this morning—Claire, white-faced and tired saying, "Just give me a couple of hours, Bill, and I'll start appreciating like mad." She hadn't even looked at the view from this balcony; no doubt she had done what she had promised herself—dropped into bed and fallen asleep. She had insisted she would join him by eleven. It was now fully half past, but there wasn't a pleasanter place to pass a Sunday morning than a terrace over the Grand Canal. There was sun on his face, a gentle breeze. He had breakfasted heartily; shaved, showered, read the papers, and dressed leisurely. And as he watched the busy waterway below him, the worries of last night receded into better proportion. (But, he reminded himself, he had slept well on the train.)

He hadn't seen Carlson, or any Englishman who might be called Chris, in the Venice station, but it was unlikely that all four of them would arrive together. More probably, Neill Carlson and Chris had got off at Milan, and would travel here by bus or local train. As for Claire and himself— they had two days to wait. Tomorrow evening the mission would be over, and they could relax and enjoy themselves. Or would Carlson collect Claire as well as the letter? I may never meet her again after tomorrow night, he thought bleakly: she may vanish out of my life as quickly as she came into it. We'll see about that, he decided, we'll see. . . . He stared down at the Grand Canal.

New-looking motorboats, brightly varnished, swept across the path of water-buses, the *vaporetti*, crammed fore and aft with Sunday travelers. Delicately balancing gondolas, in deep mourning for their lost Republic, moved with the grace and majestic silence of black swans. There was much maneuvering, no slackening of anyone's speed, hoarse calls of warning from the gondoliers, the rushing sound of water sliced through by the heavy fast-moving *vaporetti*, the roar of a brash engine cutting into power. Across the canal, there were seventeenth-century buildings—a customs house, a large-domed church; and a sixteenth-century palace turned business office, but so restrained, so appropriately faded and gently restored that it was hard to tell from the other Gothic palaces housing museums or real *contessas*.

He heard Claire's light step and turned to meet her. The three other people who sat on the terrace were noting her arrival with interest. The middle-aged German couple, who sat over their late breakfast at a small table just outside their bedroom's French windows, stopped all conversation and watched her with unflinching curiosity. The obvious Englishman, passing fifty, gaunt-featured, gray-haired, his long thin body draped at ease over a wicker chair, stopped reading and seemed to be only admiring the balustrade's boxes of trailing geraniums and sprightly verbena. "Observed and approved," Fenner told Claire, taking her arm and leading her to his small corner of the terrace.

"Venice?" she asked. She looked as if she had slept a solid eight hours and spent two more in dressing.

"You." He studied her openly. Her eyes were rested, her skin glowed. She was wearing a blue linen dress, a light blue that matched the Venetian sky. Her legs and arms were bare, tanned, slender. Pretty feet, he noticed, in flat-heeled sandals. Hair brushed smooth, a neat golden cap on a neatly shaped head.

She laughed and played down his compliment. "Oh, the shower worked, the bed is comfortable, and we have a view. Last time I was here—the only other time, in fact—I had a narrow window facing a line of laundry strung over a small canal."

"The one with the squeezed oranges floating in it?"

"And melon rinds. And a nest of gondoliers just underneath my window. They talk all the time, did you know that?"

"About moonlight and pretty girls—"

"No. About the price of gondolas, new housing developments and rheumatism. And if curses could sink anything, all these newfangled motorboats would be on the bottom of the canal." She looked over the balustrade, up the grand curve of water, then down its sweep. Her eyes rested on the little island of San Giorgio, rising with Palladian balance from the shallow waters, and she fell silent.

"I agree," Fenner said, watching her face. "Sky by Tiepolo, vista by Guardi, foreground by Canaletto, all set to music by Vivaldi."

She glanced at him, catching him off guard. "What else were you thinking about as you stood here so quietly for the last twenty minutes?" She smiled. "I looked out twice. You were watching the canal and thinking—?"

About you, and Venice, and you and Carlson. He said, "About Venice."

"What about her?"

"She's the aging beauty who comes to breakfast wearing all her jewels, a lace turban covering the pins in her hair, powder uneven, bright lipstick a flow of silk and velvet to disguise her arms and thighs."

"But her hands and feet are still elegant."

"Yes. And her profile is magnificent."

"Wrinkles, though, which she can't disguise. Wrinkles from laughter and tears. She has had plenty of both."

"Why should she hide them? On the contrary, she wears them proudly."

"Besides," Claire said, "her eyes outshine the candles."

"Candles at breakfast?"

"Behind half-closed shutters? Naturally."

"Naturally." He looked down at her. Their laughter faded. "At this moment," she said, quickly glancing back to San

Giorgio, "there's an anti-candle man who is planning to fill up the Grand Canal with concrete, and run an eight-lane highway right down to Saint Mark's Basin."

"In that case, we had better wander out and enjoy Venice while we can." Certainly the others on the terrace had staked their claims. The Englishman was settling back to read: he had propped his feet on one chair, and covered another with a clutter of newspapers. The German couple had expanded their beachhead with chairs for their legs, too.

As they walked along the narrow terrace to Claire's room, she was asking, "What about your interviews?" Her voice was casual, clear.

"They arrive tonight."

"Heavens—when did you find that out?"

"I telephoned the Danieli when you were testing the shower." And possibly some other things, too, he thought, such as the existence of automated eavesdroppers. From the gaiety of her mood he could guess she had found nothing to worry her so far.

"So we have today to ourselves?" she asked delightedly.

"And most of tomorrow. I'll try to see them tomorrow night."

"That means you'll be writing on Tuesday. Wednesday, too?"

"We'll have the rest of the week to ourselves." Shall we? he wondered. I can make a damned good try.

"I shan't keep you waiting," she promised him as they reached her room. "I'll get my bathing suit and meet you in two minutes at the elevator." She reached up and brushed his chin with her cheek. "Appropriate?" she murmured.

"Two minutes," he said, smiling, and freed her arm. He turned and began the walk past the Germans and the Englishman to his own room. So they were going out to the Lido and find themselves a few square feet of free sand? It was hardly the way he had planned their first afternoon in Venice. Still, the journey across the lagoon was short, and packed with enough panorama and local color to keep him happy. And two people could be very much alone in a crowd.

The German couple were talking once more—about prices and qualities of decorated leather wallets. Their comparative shopping was driving the Englishman away: he was gathering his papers together, with a pained look and excessive neatness as if to remind the voices of the trouble he had taken to establish himself comfortably. But the voices, delighting in being left in possession of the terrace, only surged louder. They even followed Fenner into his room. He closed the French windows quickly.

His swimming trunks were somewhere at the bottom of his suitcase. He found them under a folder of correspondence: letters from two producers, three directors, a playwright, several actors—all of them working in the French theater, some of them introduced by American friends, others who had become his own friends during their visits to New York. He closed the folder. Letters from another world, he thought. Man was an adaptable animal: he might curse and complain about having the pattern of his life broken up, even temporarily; but within a couple of days, he could be so immersed in his new problems that the old projects became something postponable, to be dealt with once the present urgency was over. And there, relegated to the bottom of a suitcase, the folder lay like some pathetic waif with dumb reproving eyes. He locked up the case securely, shutting away his own life, and left. First things first, was all he allowed himself to think.

As they dropped their keys at the hall desk, the assistant manager came over to ask if their rooms were satisfactory. He was a smooth and pleasant-faced Italian, correct in dark suit and English accent. Anything, he assured them, to oblige Mr. Stephen York: delighted that Mr. York's friends found their rooms comfortable; what a pity that Mr. York couldn't make his usual visit to Venice this year for the Lido film festival; Mr. York always liked that terrace; please give Mr. York his good wishes when they saw Mr. York.

Fenner looked at Claire. "It's a most likable terrace," was all she said.

"And it will be less crowded tomorrow," the Italian assured her. "The honeymoon couple is leaving—"

"Honeymooners?" Claire stared, and then recovered herself.

"—so you will have the terrace to yourself, except for Sir Felix Tarns. He is—" The assistant manager froze, smile in place, eyes immediately veiled to hide his embarrassment. He bowed to the tall thin man in well-cut, fine-checked tweed who was passing them on his way through the long dark hall toward the distant front entrance, where the sunshine rippled in, over polished floor and gleaming brass, from the canal. The Italian retrieved his balance. "He is a very quiet gentleman. It will be as if you had the terrace to yourselves." He bowed and left. He looked as if he would like to mop his brow. Sir Felix Tarns was certainly a most quiet gentleman.

"Quiet but quick," Fenner observed. "It didn't take him long to slip into his sharp tweeds, knot his old school tie, and get down here." I've seen him somewhere, Fenner thought. Some place. Where, when? Then the name and the face came together. United Nations, debates over Korea, 1953. Sir Felix had come over to New York as one of those free-lance observers who were going to write a series of articles, give some lectures to finance their visits. The professional journalists paid little attention to them. Fenner's memory of Sir Felix was dim. But at that time Fenner had discovered plenty of trouble in his own life. Trouble . . . why did he associate that word with Tarns?

Claire was standing very still. "Was he interested in our reactions to Stephen York?"

"He was leaving his key at the desk, just behind you and the assistant manager, for a full minute." But interested in us? Fenner felt a touch of annoyance. There she goes, he thought, slipping back into Carlson's world. "By the way, is Stephen York—"

She didn't seem to be listening. She had glanced along the dark, gleaming hall to the square of sunshine at its end. For a brief second, she studied the black silhouette of Sir Felix. As he stepped onto the moored platform outside, very much the austere admiral on a swaying deck waiting for his boat to come alongside, she said quickly, "Let's look at the gondolas."

So they walked along the stretch of silent carpet to the front entrance, past empty chairs and writing tables and flowers in polished brass vases and a solitary man who was reading peacefully. His eyesight is better than mine, Fenner thought, or perhaps he is the type who only glances at a magazine's pictures. Even so, there were better glancing-places in the hotel than this hall, lit only by a scattering of subdued lamps on the writing tables.

"What about Stephen York?" Claire asked as they approached the shimmer of reflected light from the canal.

"Is he a friend of yours?"

"No such luck!"

"Come, Mrs. Langley, don't tell me a woman of your mature judgment is impressed by a film star!"

"Come, Mr. Fenner, don't tell me you think the only great actors belong in the theater." As they stepped out into the glare of sunshine, she asked, very softly, "So he isn't a friend of yours, either?"

"No."

"That's interesting, isn't it?" But meanwhile, she seemed more interested in Tarns.

"Who is he?" Fenner asked, as Sir Felix, sitting erect on a small black leather armchair, floated away, his gondolier shouting a hoarse warning to two workmen in a heavy unpolished gondola filled with vegetables. For a split second, it looked as if Sir Felix and the zucchini might become a very mixed salad marinating in the Grand Canal. But, with strenuous back-oaring the gondolas scarcely grazed, drew apart, the two workmen now expressing their view of the situation. Everyone, from the terraced bar nearby to the balconies above and around, watched the scene with amusement or admiration. Only Sir Felix, Fenner noticed, paid no attention whatsoever. We should be flattered, Fenner decided, that he had paid any attention to us at all. Claire could have been right.

She hadn't answered his question. Instead, she had placed a hand on his arm as if to steady herself as one of the water-buses, a large steam launch with its captain's wheel amidships under its small funnel, cut quickly down canal toward a pier and sent the hotel landing stage rocking gently. The man who could read so blissfully in the shadowed hall had come out to see the fun, too. He was standing near them, a pink-cheeked, round-faced little man, smooth and well fed, neatly dressed in a sedate brown suit, innocuous enough, blinking disapprovingly at the workmen's exchange of oratory with the hotel doorman. "Let's get a motorboat," Fenner said, and signaled.

"No," she said quickly.

"But a gondola will take a couple of hours," he reminded her, making an exaggerated guess if only to sound authoritative. Who was in charge here, he'd like to know? "Or do we swim?"

"Please, Bill." Her eyes were pleading. She smiled for the doorman. "Later," she told him. "I've forgotten something." She turned back toward the hotel. "I've forgotten my sun-tan lotion," she said to Fenner. "Isn't it stupid of me?"

"Yes."

"Oh, Bill—"

"You could always buy some out at the Lido. If we are ever going to get there."

"Of course we are. But I like my own special brand."

There was no answer to that. He followed her, still annoyed. The hall was empty except for the cluster of people at its far end near the porter's desk. "What's the bright idea?" he asked her quietly. "We walk out, we walk back in." And I feel like a damned fool who can't even hire a motorboat.

"Well, we found out two things."

"Did we?" Carlson's girl, he reminded himself, in Carlson's world.

She restrained her excitement. "That was a private gondola. Didn't you notice the special uniform of the gondolier, the throne effect of its chair, the polished brass coat of arms? So it was sent here specially for Sir Felix. And he kept it waiting."

"Likes to show his authority, no doubt."

"Perhaps. Or perhaps he was delayed on the terrace. Why did he have to waste time up there, hurry his dressing to get down here, waste more time at the desk?"

"Must have found our conversation fascinating."

"You aren't being exactly helpful." Her small sense of discovery ebbed.

"But aren't we beginning to exaggerate?" He was smiling. His voice was gentle. "Really, Claire—" Sir Felix Tarns, after all ... "I can't see him snooping around."

"When he does," she said with marked coldness, "it is called perceptive observation."

Fenner had to laugh.

"I am not being funny. And I am not being silly," she said.

"Well," he said with maddening equanimity, "what was the second thing we found out?"

There was a short, but marked, silence. A spot of brilliant carmine stained each cheekbone, faded to delicate pink as it spread over the fair skin. "Him!" she said abruptly, not even looking over her shoulder to confirm her guess. "Little Mr. Brown Suit is back at his post again. Isn't he?"

He was. "It is possible," Fenner tried, "that the gondoliers' shouts drew him outside. Perhaps he hoped to see a really bang-up accident."

"Perhaps, indeed," she agreed. She halted at the porter's

desk for her room key. "Shan't be long," she told Fenner.
The delicate flush had vanished. But her eyes were too
bright, almost close to tears.

Fenner stared after her. What did I do? he asked himself,
retreating behind his own defensive wall. But he knew
damned well, and the cigarette he had lit tasted like straw
swept from a barn floor. It was possible, he justified himself, to exaggerate conjecture and suspicions. All shadows
were not necessarily sinister. Last night, on the train, he had
gone through a couple of hours of supercaution, clothing
mystery with more mystery. Let's keep our balance, let's
not invent worries, he told himself, glancing again at the distant figure in the brown suit. The man was probably dozing
gently, or just staring vacantly into space while he waited
for Sunday luncheon to be served in the dining room.

Four minutes went by. Five. At last, Claire stepped out of
the elevator, carrying a camera, a white sweater, and sun-
tan lotion as her excuses. She looked calm and poised, and
was smiling charmingly. "And this time, I remembered my
camera, too," she told him. "I couldn't find any film, though.
I can buy that on our way to catch a water-bus. Do you
mind?"

"Wouldn't a motorboat be simpler?"

"But not so much fun." The gray eyes held a hint of
alarm, as if they feared he was going to start arguing again.
So he stopped trying to take control. He went along, with
no comment. A *vaporetto* it would be, jammed to the gun-
wales with a couple of hundred other people. With marked
politeness, he offered to carry her camera; and with equal
politeness, she accepted and offered to put his swimming
trunks along with her things in her oversized handbag. "That's
much better, isn't it?" she asked, with a small smile dawn-
ing at the back of her eyes.

It was. He would no longer feel like an idiot parading
through Venice with plaid swimming trunks dangling from
one hand. "Do you always think of everything?" he asked.
She had possibly been right about the man in the brown suit:
he had left his chair, at least, and was sauntering down
the hall toward the porter's desk.

"I wish I could." Fleetingly, the strained look of worry
appeared on her face; just as quickly, she banished it,
and resumed that calm, oblivious-to-everything exterior.

He took her hand as they approached the large, ornate
back door of the Vittoria. It was his way of saying he was

sorry. She looked up in surprise, and smiled. He had chased some of the worry away, at least. "I wasn't much help to you there," he admitted. "Was I?"

She laughed in her relief. "You did let me get my own way," she reminded him. Kicking and screaming, she thought. What had made him so ornery all of a sudden?

"Do you get your way with every damned man you meet?"

The large gray eyes widened. The pink lips parted as if to speak, closed in a firm line.

"I am sorry," he said, ashamed of the resentment that had slipped out into the open and betrayed him. She was Carlson's girl. He kept forgetting that. He had forgotten it at dinner last night. He had forgotten it on the terrace high above the Grand Canal. But now they had come down to the ground floor, and he was being reminded of Carlson constantly. The hell of it was, he liked Carlson. If he didn't like him, it would all be simpler. "I am sorry," he said again. "I guess things just seem out of my control." And that is not the way I like them, he thought, not one bit.

They were passing through the small courtyard that lay at the back of the hotel, a square of worn paving stones surrounded by the tall walls of other houses. He noted the chipping plaster, the streaked colors, under the heavy ropes of wisteria. Board shutters, unpainted, bleached into greenish brown, closed the silent windows away from the world as the buildings themselves enclosed this courtyard. The only exit was by a narrow crevasse at one corner, dark even by daylight, leading them between more high shuttered houses. "I never knew a place that could be so crowded and yet so private," Claire was saying. She looked around her, and upward, as if measuring the safety of this alley, and halted. She spoke in a low quick murmur. Fenner bent his head to catch what she was saying. Here we go again, he thought, as he slipped his arm around the soft, yet firm waist. And I wish to heaven she wouldn't use that perfume, either.

Claire was saying, "When I went back to my room, I telephoned Neill. He had given me a number where I could check with him if necessary. But he hasn't arrived yet."

"He may have stayed in the Rome section of the train. Perhaps he is flying here this evening," Fenner said, to drive away the frown of anxiety over her eyes.

"Perhaps. Or perhaps he had someone to see in Milan.

Anyhow, I wrote a note for Chris and asked him for some advice. We'll leave the note at a camera shop. It's quite near—"

"Are you sure of that camera shop?" It seemed an additional risk to Fenner.

"Rosie gave me that address for any emergencies."

"You think we have an emergency on our hands?" He was startled. But grave.

"I don't like the rooms we've been given. Perhaps Rosie arranged them, but I don't think so. I just want to be sure we aren't sitting in a pretty little trap."

His arm tightened around her. Someone had just stepped from the courtyard into this dark passage. The footsteps faltered, stopped. "This might be the time to drop a nice, brotherly kiss on your brow," he suggested. And did it.

"And I can laugh coyly, like this." She had a very pretty laugh, even when it was pretense. She hates this as much as I do, he thought suddenly, and felt an enormous relief. She drew away, raised her voice back to normal. "Darling, not here! Someone will see us—" She looked around, as women do.

"Just a man lighting his cigarette," Fenner said with male nonchalance. They walked on, close together, their shoulders almost brushing the house walls on either side of them, much to the relief of the man in the brown suit who seemed to be having so much trouble with his matches. Claire was pointing out a wrought-iron decoration around the lamp on the wall overhead. That was what she loved about Venice: the small ordinary things made into little works of art, tucked away in hidden corners, not even demanding attention, just there to be seen by accident. Behind them, Fenner heard the slow footsteps begin again.

Abruptly, the narrow alley ended. They were beside a canal, walking under a *sotto portico* for a short distance, then out into the open. Ahead of them was a busy Venetian street that crossed the canal by a gentle slope of bridge, a main thoroughfare all of twelve feet in width, lined with shops, above which flower boxes and shuttered windows rose to three or four tight stories. There was a feeling of lightheartedness, of gaiety, in this stretch of sunlight and movement. And the only sounds in the city street were those of voices, of lightly pacing feet. "At this moment," Fenner told Claire, "your anti-candle man is planning to introduce a fleet of Vespas. What's a street without gasoline fumes and the roar of exhausts?"

"Only Vespas?" She dropped her voice. "We go across the bridge, Bill."

The brown suit was very close to them now. Fenner went on talking. "Oh, that's just the thin edge. Once he conditions people to being pushed to the walls, he will bring in cars— small cars, at first, of course—and people can retreat to the roofs. It's the technique of gradualism. Accustom people to retreating, and you can not only push them to the walls, but they'll even begin to believe that climbing across the roofs is really much better than strolling along a street."

She was amused until she thought about it. "That really isn't a joke," she said gravely.

"Not when you think of the Communists." Let's give Brown Suit a bolt and a jolt, he thought. "They really are much cleverer than the Nazis. Hitler's patience was too easily exhausted. He wanted everything all at once: a thousand-year Reich in ten years. But the Communists think of politics as the art of the impossible: just take everything in thin slices, little by little."

"The art of the impossible . . ." she repeated slowly. "Like getting away with bomb tests while you sit at a disarmament conference. You know, Bill, I wish I could listen in to your interviews tomorrow. What do you expect from your neu-tralists—a retreat to the wall?"

"They are already up on the tiles."

"Will they give you a real interview, or will they just hum a little song to themselves?"

"They'll play it safe by putting on a performance, the holier-than-thou act, black is white and white is black, and gray isn't tattletale. After all, they're the kind who are always polishing their Public Image. Do you think they would pass up a chance to get free advertisement in the *Chronicle?*"

"They may wish they had," she murmured, "once you get through with them."

"If my interviews get published," he said as he remembered that they were entirely the brain children of Rosie. He had forgotten that. Here he was, discussing two ambitious, second-rate politicians as if the *Chronicle* wanted to publish their polished clichés. Well, he thought, when Rosie picks a cover for me, he picks a good one: he has even got me believing in it. He began to laugh.

"That's a good sound," Claire said. They had halted on

the crest of the bridge. From here, they could look right down the narrow strip of water, edged with houses, all the way to the Grand Canal. Just below them was a mooring place for gondolas, where their owners polished and scoured their black, gleaming craft from sharp Viking prow to curved stern, talking in hoarse, amiable shouts as they worked. "Can you see the man in the brown suit at all?"

The gondoliers had certainly seen them. "Gondola, gondola?"

"No thanks," Fenner called back. "He passed us when we were discussing Communists," he told her.

"And now he is waiting for us to pass him?"

"Shouldn't be surprised. He is fascinated by a camera shop just across the bridge."

"Oh dear!" Claire said, keeping her eyes fixed on the distant sliver of the Grand Canal.

"Gondola, gondola?" came the renewed invitation. One of the gondoliers was even waving his arms wildly, in hopeful enthusiasm, looking at Claire with a wide smile.

"No!" Fenner hoped he sounded definite enough this time. "Our shop?" he asked Claire.

"It would have to be, wouldn't it?"

"I have a feeling you can cope," he told her, smiling. "I won't even offer a suggestion."

She said quickly, "You'll have to take full charge later. But at present—well, there was so little time before we left Paris —while Rosie was talking with you, Neill was briefing me. That's the only reason—well, you see how it is?"

She was so anxious for him to understand that he felt— pleased, relieved, reassured? There was a strange mixture of emotions, certainly, in his reaction. He smiled, mostly at himself, and nodded. "By the way, what made you so interested in Sir Felix Tarns?"

"Chris Holland will tell you about him."

"I'll be meeting Holland?"

"That's the idea of our message." She glanced casually toward the camera shop. "He is still there. We'll just have to risk it. Let's—"

"La biondina! La biondina!" the gondolier shouted, waving his arms still more wildly.

Claire halted and looked back at him.

"La biondina!" he called up to her, with absolute certainty.

"Zorzi!" Claire said, and waved back.

"Well, well," said Fenner, "and did Giorgio teach you that ripe Venetian accent?"

"Gondola, gondola?" The appeal was directed to Fenner as keeper of the purse.

"Later," Fenner told the broadly smiling hawk-face looking up at him.

"Tonight? When the moon is up?" Giorgio shouted. "I wait here. What time?"

Fenner looked at Claire. "Ten o'clock?"

She nodded. She was as delighted as if he had given her a Christmas present all wrapped in shining paper and bright ribbons. She looked nine years old at this moment.

"Ten o'clock," Fenner called down.

"I wait here," Giorgio shouted back, and saluted nonchalantly.

"And so he will," Claire said as they left the bridge. "We had better keep that promise." She was still very much Alice-in-Wonderland. "Imagine! *Imagine* Zorzi remembering me! It's three years since I was here."

"What really astounds me is the fact that you remembered him."

"Would you forget that old sea raider's face?"

"Perhaps not. But it wasn't the answer Fenner had gone fishing for. "Old? He's younger than I am, I bet. He hasn't reached the age of discussing rheumatism, has he?"

"Only the first twinges." She may have guessed Fenner's feelings, for she smiled and said, "I hired him for a week, last time I was here."

"Opulent."

"It was the cheapest and quickest way to explore the little canals and back waterways. I was sketching all the decorations—windows, balconies, doorways, lanterns—that caught my eye. There was a Venetian phase in Grand Rapids, that year. My first assignment abroad. Zorzi thought I was crazy at first. Then he began to think I was really in earnest. That pleased him. He's a true Venetian."

"Remembering some of those smaller canals, I'd say you really suffer for the sake of your art."

"Oh, I had some luck with cool weather. And a large bottle of Eau de Cologne helped." She was smiling at the memory. Quietly she said, "Remind me to buy some film, will you, Bill?"

"And after that, I shut up. Right? No suggestions, I promise." The brown suit seemed glued to the Kodachrome window. "He is going to have a front-row seat for the next act. Want to postpone it?"

"We haven't the time. Let's show him what innocent travelers we are. Don't worry, Bill"—she was really encouraging herself—"it will be simple enough if we just follow the rules."

They almost passed the display windows. Fenner stopped, catching her arm. "What about that film you need?"

"Why, Bill—I nearly forgot."

They brushed past the waiting man and entered the shop.

SIXTEEN

NEAT ITALIAN cursive over the shop's entrance told them it was owned by V. Arnaldi. It was small, dark, but authentic. On either side were two glass-topped counters, displaying filters and light meters in considerable profusion. There were shelves of Leicas and Rolleiflexes, all bargains at the cheap Venetian price; stacks of varied film; many excellent photographs showing how you could do it, too, if you got up at six in the morning or lived in a city without people. There was one assistant, very young and very martyred, who obviously disapproved of the prominent notice in four languages stating that this shop was open for business every day, all day. For this was a bright, warm Sunday, when reasonable places were either firmly closed or at least putting up their shutters for a pleasant three-hour lunch.

"I need some thirty-five-millimeter color film," Claire said in English. "Seven rolls of K135-38."

The boy stared at her blankly. Fenner sympathized with him. Claire had asked for a film with thirty-eight exposures, and there was just no such thing.

"Uno momento," the boy said, jolted out of his apathy. (He wasn't stupid, Fenner decided; just bored). Quickly he went to a curtained door at the back of the shop. A chair scraped, a limping step dragged on the wooden floor; and a white-haired man appeared, wiping his mouth from an interrupted dinner. His movements were slow, deliberate, calm.

"Mr. Arnaldi?" Claire asked.

The proprietor nodded, his eyes as blank as the boy's had been. Outside, a second man had halted beside the brown suit, to look at the window's display.

Claire repeated her request, with a slight emphasis on the seven. Arnaldi listened placidly, but he had noted the tightening of Fenner's lips as he watched the street. The man in the brown suit was moving on; it was the other, a

192

thin man, much younger, who was coming into the shop.

"Certainly," Arnaldi said as the man entered, and selected three boxes of standard K135-36 film from the shelf behind him. He placed them in a neat pyramid on the counter in front of Claire. "Anything else today, signorina?"

"No thank you. That's perfect." Claire relaxed visibly as she looked at the three boxes. So Arnaldi was the right man to deal with, Fenner decided, quickly changing his mind about mistakes. "I think I'll load the camera here," she said, holding out her hand for it, smiling reassuringly.

Fenner gave it to her, tried to pay no attention to the strange man who had walked over to stand beside them instead of choosing the other counter. Perhaps he was lonely, wanted company, the Coney Island-Brighton Beach type. Why wasn't he out at the Lido? That should suit him perfectly. "Need any help?" Fenner asked.

"Have you ever used a Stereo-Realist?"

"No," he lied gallantly.

Claire began examining the camera's back. "I ought to have brought the book of directions," she said, half to herself.

Mr. Arnaldi was trying to serve the newcomer, but the man was in no hurry. He wanted a yellow filter; he needed time to choose one. He looked down vaguely, at the boxes displayed near Claire. He liked to work close, this fellow: he was missing nothing.

"A filter for what camera?" Arnaldi was asking patiently.

The stranger hesitated for a fraction of a second. "Leica," he said briefly. His eyes flickered over the three boxes of film that Claire had bought, still lying on the counter. "And I want some of these." He picked them up.

"Here!" began Fenner, ready to put on an act of indignation. But Claire was unworried. She was much more preoccupied with the back of her camera, which seemed to have stuck.

Arnaldi took quick command. "That film is not made for a Leica," he told the man. "You need—"

"I have other cameras."

Arnaldi's expression did not change. He merely reached to the shelf for three more yellow boxes, and stacked them into another pyramid before Claire. He drew out a pencil, opened a drawer for a piece of paper, and began calculating the cost. "I shall be with you shortly," he told the man. "My son will help you meanwhile. Luigi! Show this gentleman the yellow filters." He pointed his pencil at the other counter.

Luigi's boredom vanished. "Over here," he insisted, and led the way quickly. The man hesitated looking down at the filters beside Claire. "Not for a Leica," Luigi told him firmly, and drew him, still holding his prize of three boxes, to the other counter.

Claire said, "This has got stuck again. I had it fixed only last week. Can you help?" She handed over the camera to Mr. Arnaldi, who placed it flat on the counter, lifted its back just enough to extract a folded slip of paper, which disappeared into the open drawer. He had the camera closed and locked even as he pushed the drawer shut.

"I am sorry," Arnaldi was saying all through this small operation, "The back of your camera is not working properly. I am afraid you will not be able to load it here." He shook his head.

"Let me try again," Claire said, taking it from him. "Imagine walking through Venice with an empty camera."

"Frustrating," Fenner agreed.

"Oh, I'm sorry," Claire said to the stranger, who had come back to stand beside her. "Am I in your way?" Then she laughed delightedly. "Look, I've managed it!" She told Fenner, freeing the back of the camera, holding it up in triumph.

"Next time, you'd better carry a hammer as well as a book of directions." He reached for his wallet—he was good for that, at least—while Claire started to load the camera right under the stranger's inquiring nose. The man's suspicions were dying down. He watched Claire's fingers, his interest shifting to gadgetry.

And what kind of a man is this? Fenner wondered. He is about my age, about my height, dressed in a gray suit and white shirt. Shoes and tie are not my taste. Apart from that, he might be another version of me or my friends. His face is just the ordinary face of an ordinary man, a mixture of small worries and pleasures, hopes and disappointments, a few simple longings, several deep frustrations. Yet his business is far from ordinary, and so is his power. If Claire or Arnaldi has made one small slip, he can destroy us all: an adverse report to the men who hire him, and that might be the last mistake any of us would ever make. Does he do this for money to buy a gray suit, pay his rent, get promotion? Or does he call himself dedicated: everything, anything for the cause? Complete obedience, blind belief? . . . Possibly he would think of me in the same way: I'm an American, he would reason, so I do what American interests tell me to do. But he is wrong there: I am not in the middle of this fantastic game because I was given an order by Rosie or anyone else. I am here because my beliefs are shaped by my own thoughts; and a man's thoughts are shaped by his conscience. That is what gives me my orders, and I may damn it to high heaven, but I'll listen to it. That's why I'm standing here. Can he say the same? Did he really choose Kalganov's way—the bomb that burns two children to death in an apartment over a restaurant? Or is he a totally ignorant man, a know-nothing who'll lend himself to anything? Or—even more depressing—would he enjoy seeing hate and dissension spread over Western Europe; would he gloat over anarchy?

"All ready," Claire's soft voice said at his elbow. "You look depressed. I'm sorry I was so slow—"

"No, no," he reassured her quickly, and smiled. "Just hungry, I guess."

"Would you like to lunch here?" she asked as she fastened the camera back into its leather carrier.

"And forget the Lido?"

"It doesn't really matter. . . . I just thought some sun and sea would iron out the travel creases."

Was that a hint? He took it as such. "They probably would. We can dine at Quadri's tonight, or perhaps we might try The Resuscitated Louse. You know it?" They said good day to Mr. Arnaldi. The man in the gray suit was watching them carefully, his interest again bleakly calculating, reverting to duty either hired or dedicated.

The boy Luigi darted to open the door and bow them out with a brilliant smile. He could guess from the way they were talking so easily, from the quiet look in his father's eyes, that the difficult customer had somehow been defeated. There he was, complaining about the price of the film he had wanted so badly and which—in any case—wouldn't fit any camera he was likely to use. He wasn't even waiting to choose a filter, either. Hurry, hurry, hurry, Luigi's mocking eyes told him as the man left. He would almost be too late to follow the Americans. Or was he going to follow them? No, he looked as if he would be going to pass them over to a woman who had been window-gazing at the shoe store across the street. A very dull-looking woman she was, dressed in blue: not chic, not young, not beautiful.

"Luigi!" his father called quietly. He was sealing an envelope. Luigi came back into the shop. "Take this to Pietro," his father said. Luigi placed the envelope carefully inside his jacket pocket. He didn't need to be told to be quick and careful, or to leave by the back door that led into a wandering alley, or that the envelope contained an urgent message. He had learned all these things even as a child of seven, before he and his father had managed to escape from the Yugoslav zone of Trieste. He didn't need to be told about Communist control, either. His mother, two uncles, his older brother . . . Even at seven, you remembered that.

"Simple," Fenner reminded Claire as they joined the stream of pedestrians outside Arnaldi's door. "Did we follow the rules?"

"With a few improvisations," she admitted. "There are always complications."

"I suppose," he said too gravely.

"One follows one's instinct, that's all."

"*La biondina* is not quite the helpless little blonde that Zorzi thought she was, is she?"

"I can be very helpless, very silly, very stupid. Why do you keep worrying about what I am and what I am not?"

Why indeed? She was Carlson's girl, he reminded himself. He forced a smile and a light voice. "The trouble about *la biondina* is that she brings out all my protective urges—and she couldn't need them less."

"Doesn't she?" Her voice softened. I know what's really troubling him, she thought: he wonders if I am another Sandra Fane, even if I am on the other side, his side. But I'm not. I am not Sandra. I have never hurt any man the way she hurt him. I have never pretended love, or used it. How do I prove that to him? I can't. And I don't. Because I'll probably never see him again once we have finished this job. He'll be back in his own life, and I to mine. They overlapped for a few days. That's all. She sighed.

He glanced down at the large gray eyes watching him so sadly. This was no way to spend their short time together, he told himself. "I take it all back, Claire. You look as lost and bewildered as any tourist."

"I am."

"This way—if we *are* trying to find a pier." He held her arm, guiding her into a narrow *calle* that led to the Grand Canal. He glanced briefly over his shoulder as they turned the corner. He saw a Hindu girl in six yards of floating sari walking the usual two paces behind a paunchy, splay-footed husband; a couple of clear-eyed, fair-skinned Swedes stepping out bravely; a group of sauntering Venetians, carefully dressed; a dour-faced woman in blue; three English students, needing a haircut, in stained and uncreased flannel trousers; a collection of Austrians with rucksacks and *Lederhosen;* a French couple in loose shirts and flopping sandals; heads, and more heads, bobbing and floating along in the human tide. Useless to worry, he decided. "I'll always remember our theme song in Venice," he told Claire.

"And what's that?" She waited expectantly. She was beginning to know him.

"I wonder who's trailing us now ..."

She burst into a peal of laughter, then silenced it to something more restrained, with a hand at her lips. "I made the ladies jump," she said, and looked at three proper Venetians in hats and gloves.

"You and Papa Haydn." She has forgiven me, he thought in relief as he watched the delight on her face. He has forgotten Sandra Fane, she was thinking happily.

SEVENTEEN

THE WATER-BUS was crowded. Claire and Bill Fenner had to stand well for'ard, but nothing could dampen Claire's high spirits—not even the fine spray from the prow of the ship cutting through the lagoon's blue water, nor the salt breeze tangling her hair, nor the squeeze and jostle as more passengers were gathered up at other miniature piers. She loved it all. "It's like traveling on the open back of the old Paris buses, where you swing and sway through narrow streets. I always feel there ought to be music playing—Offenbach done with a rush—something that sweeps along and hurries your heartbeat."

"You're a strange girl." He was thinking of her elegant white room, restrained and remote, under the shadow of Notre-Dame. "Difficult to please, but easy to amuse."

She laughed. "I have that out-of-school feeling. We took our first examination, and I think we passed."

"I don't see our examiner around," he said quietly.

"Oh, there will be someone else." She glanced casually over the little ship's passengers. Venetians plus ten other nationalities; you name them, we carry them. "Shall we make bets on him?"

"It could be a she this time," he said very quietly, and then remembered Rider Haggard and grinned widely, in spite of the solemn-faced woman in a dull-blue dress who had been edging forward toward them. Will she really try it? he wondered in amazement, and was answered as the woman plumped a hip down on a fraction of a seat near them. A patient Italian lifted his small daughter and her dog onto his lap, and the woman's second hip secured her position.

Claire's amused eyes met his, looked back at the widening lagoon as their water-bus now headed out to the long, low sand bar called the Lido. "This is the way to travel. It would be a pleasure going into the office at eight every morning if you could think of sailing back again at five."

"Beats the Lexington Avenue subway, any day," Fenner agreed, watching a liner floating in from the Adriatic, a towering bulk easing its way along the marked channel toward the Giudecca Canal where the heavy ships could dock. A large freighter was already there. He could see its yellow funnels jutting up in the distance among the red tiled roofs like two fat periscopes.

Claire was saying, almost to herself, "Pink-and-white palaces, silvered towers and golden domes..."

"Rising like Venice from the foam."

She laughed again. "At this moment," she told him, "I am really and truly happy." She said it with a kind of wonder. He looked at her and fell silent. He was far from unhappy himself.

Beside them, the solemn-faced woman stared straight ahead in deepest boredom.

From the Lido's lagoon side, they took a taxi across the narrow island to its Adriatic shore by way of its main street, an odd mixture of Cannes and Atlantic City with a hint of Miami. There, they drove along an interminable esplanade of trees and gardens, lined on one side by hotels the size of Pennsylvania Station, on the other by an endless stretch of cabins and bathhouses that blocked all view of the beaches. Fenner could imagine them, one after another, each with its blanket of bodies.

"Don't be so depressed," she told him with amusement. "You look like *Death in Venice.*"

"How do you know I'm depressed?" He thought of the white sands along the lonely eastern dunes on Long Island, miles and miles of them, with only the thundering waves for company.

"Because you get politer and politer. Cheer up, Bill. We're going to the end of the line, so far out that most people give up. There's a beach there that's only three quarters filled, usually. It's just beyond the Excelsior."

"Is that good?" he asked morosely. It was one of those enormous hotels, mink-lined and gold-plated.

She dropped her voice, even if their driver was screened off by glass from them. "A small canal runs in from the lagoon just behind the Excelsior. There's a private landing place. Very useful for a quick exit."

"When?"

"After we have had our swim and lunch. Around four, or four-thirty."

"And the swim and lunch? Any reason for them? Or are they just an innocent diversion?"

"Establishing our sweet, pleasure-seeking characters," she said, and giggled. She glanced past the pleated silk curtain covering the cab's rear window. "I think our lady in blue had to take a taxi, too. I hope her expense account is as ample as her hips."

"I wonder what she looks like in a swimsuit."

"That really should cheer you up," she said, sharing his vision.

They stretched out on the milk-chocolate sand, and talked. About themselves, mostly. There was no one near enough to hear them. The lady in blue kept at a distance, perhaps only interested in anyone they might meet. She sat, fully dressed, with her shoes and stockings off, near the bathhouse where they had rented cubicles for their clothes. But the doors of the cubicles were solid and strongly locked, and the owners of the bathhouse—a smiling Venetian couple, scoured by wind and sun, as fresh and clean, in their sparkling white clothes, as the wooden buildings—were dependable watchdogs. Claire was sure of that. "Which solves several problems," she told Bill Fenner when she joined him on the beach.

"Yes, I wondered what you were going to do about your Little Comforter," he remarked, and stretched his spine luxuriously on the warm sand. "There isn't much room left for it in that swimsuit." It was a white *maillot,* as perfect in its cut as the body it molded. He stopped looking at her, rolled over on his elbows, and glanced at the people around them. Their nearest neighbors were a pleasant Italian family: a black-haired man devoted to his three children, a gentle-faced wife who smiled on all of them. Next came three French girls in bikinis; four young boys throwing a rubber ball around to develop their minds; two older men who were having themselves spaded into the sand, with only their heads left popping up from their anti-rheumatism caskets. "All shapes and sizes," he said. "What does your instinct say, Claire?"

"We can relax." She arranged her white towel beside his, and lay down.

"That's a pleasant change."

"Our guardian lady watched to see if I used the telephone at the bathhouse. I didn't. I talked to no one. No one talked to me. She seems pacified. So"—Claire stretched herself happily—"we relax and wait."

"For what?"

"A message. I told Chris we'd be here. The rest is up to him."

"If he doesn't get in touch with us?"

"That means there are no additional instructions. We just spend the day enjoying ourselves."

"Enjoying?" He glanced briefly at the woman in blue.

"That won't last forever. Once they feel sure we are harmless, they'll call off the bloodhounds. By tomorrow, we'll be free of them."

"We had better be." He was thinking of tomorrow evening and a table at Florian's Café, of Sandra handing over a letter. "Did Rosie calculate we'd raise all this interest? I doubt it." Rosie had made a mistake, he thought gloomily.

"Yes, he did. And we are raising less interest than any of his agents might. We aren't in any files, Bill. Two complete unknowns, you and I. That's why Sandra chose us. One reason, at least. The other—well, she will see us at once. Makes identification quick and sure. Saves her a lot of strain."

"Did Rosie know we met at the Café Racine?"

"I told him."

"And he saw it as the beginning of a good cover story," Fenner said bitterly.

"Well, it was, you know," she said quietly. "Are you sorry I met you there?"

"No."

"Truly?"

"Truly," he said, smiling at the feminine word.

She relaxed again. "I'm sorry about the way it happened though."

"It had a certain mysterious charm."

"You couldn't figure me out?"

"You made no sense whatsoever," he told her.

"I was pretty shaken," she admitted.

"Were you following Fernand Lenoir?"

"In a way—yes. You see, Neill and I were going to have a last-night dinner together. I was leaving in the morning for Venice on the San Rocco job I told you about. Neill was about to go back to Berlin. Then Neill was called out, on some emergency, around six o'clock—"

After I telephoned from Vaugiroud's flat, Fenner thought. "—and he asked Chris to take charge of me until he was free. So you see, I *was* all dressed for a party."

"I see."

"But Chris had a small job to do—he had to drop in at some art gallery briefly. I waited outside in his car. Then Lenoir came out of the gallery in a very great hurry. And so did Chris, and we followed him. To the Café Racine. Do I begin to make sense?"

Fenner nodded. "Chris didn't want Lenoir to see him again, and so he sent you."

"No, that was my bright idea. And it would have been a blunder if I hadn't met you. You saved me, Bill."

"I didn't give Chris much time to argue. And it did seem so simple—a little Left Bank restaurant, lots of crush and bustle, men *and* women." She smiled, remembering the formal Racine. "I was going to wait five minutes for a friend, and then leave. Five minutes is long enough for a girl to wait, isn't it?"

"Long enough for a pretty girl to wait."

"So that's the way it was."

"Chris Holland is British Army, isn't he?" Attached to NATO, Fenner remembered.

Claire nodded. "You'll get along. He's a humorous type. Like Neill. They've been close friends for years. Met away back in the days when. That kind of thing."

"And they work together?"

"Not actually. They came to Paris on separate assignments. But somehow everything seems to be overlapping. There's a slight emergency, I think. Have you any idea what's—"

"Where does Rosie stand?"

She smiled at the way he had dodged her uncompleted question; and let it go. "Rosie sells refrigeration plants, didn't you know? He is a deep-freeze specialist. Very appropriate for the cold war—keeps things at safe temperatures." Her little joke pleased her. She waited for him to share it, add to it. "No comment?" she asked.

He was looking at her, wondering again. He tried not to ask her the question that puzzled him most. Then it came blurting out. "How did you get into this kind of work?"

She sat up, dusted the sand off her shoulders.

"Sorry," he said.

"Do you really want to listen to the story of my life?"

she asked with mock concern. But her eyes held real surprise.

He thought of Neill Carlson. "I suppose it's none of my business."

There was a flicker of disappointment in the polite little smile. "I suppose not."

There was a small silence. Then one of the bikini girls strolled past in Grand Duchess fashion, seeing nothing, aware of everyone. Some French girls always walked as if they were coming down the runway at the Tabarin, Fenner thought. "All she needs is a three-foot stretch of ostrich feathers on top of that little pinhead," he said. There was reaction, too, from the neighboring Italian family: the pretty wife, scandalized, drew her bathrobe more closely around her in silent protest; the man, intrigued but embarrassed, devoted himself hastily and too emphatically to his three children. The four handsome boys lost interest in catching and throwing. Even the distant lady in blue seemed startled out of her boredom into stiff-spined contempt.

Claire was saying, very softly, "I just can't believe it...." She was on her feet, slender and lithe. "Come on, Bill," she urged him, clear-voiced, "let's test the water." She picked up her cap, tagged his shoulder and ran, laughing as he picked himself up and raced after her. They overtook the bikini girl, swerved past her, reached the calm sea. They waded out into the warm shallow water, beyond the shrieks of the bobbers and dunkers, avoided the little paddle-bicycles, the flotilla of water wings, and still were only waist deep. "Just a few minutes here," Claire said, as she stopped beside a group of young men, "before we swim out to the raft."

He smothered his amazement. Claire, he had discovered, did nothing without a reason. He ducked away from a shower of water—the bikini girl had somehow become entangled with the group near him. She had suddenly come to life, Grand Duchess turned *gamine*, as she splashed back at two handsome hairy-chested Italians who scooped water over her. She was fair game, Fenner thought as he watched the running battle. Miss Bikini decided to retreat, turned and fell with a little shriek, came up beside Fenner, gasping as if she had taken a high dive from a twenty-foot board, floundering in panic. He reached out and caught her arm. "Steady, there!" he said.

She regained her feet, pushed her seaweed hair away from her eyes, seemed to thank him briefly, and really let

her two admirers have a full swipe of water. Masculine guf-
faws, swirls of feminine giggles, amused voices, a babble
of general jollity. And where was Claire? He saw her white-
capped head already halfway to the raft.

They reached it together. He hauled her up beside him.
Claire caught her breath, looked back toward the beach
where the sea battle had reached gigantic proportions, with
splash-reinforcements joining in from all sides. Wading at
the water's edge, skirt held up with one hand, shoes and
handbag safely clutched in the other, was a lonely figure in
dull blue.

"And what had Miss Bikini of 1961 to say?" Claire asked
softly. They were alone on the raft, but there were other
swimmers around, and voices carried very easily over water.

"Half past four. Take the Hotel Vittoria boat."

"So Chris did get my message," Claire said thankfully.

"Who is his friend, do you know?" Fenner counted three
swimmers who were definitely heading in this direction.

"I thought she was a filing clerk in Inspector Bernard's
office, yesterday morning. At least, she brought photographs
for me to study. I didn't know she was studying me."

"Well, that's co-operation." Fenner was impressed.

"Must be quite an emergency," she said thoughtfully.
"Rosie really has pushed the panic button. What do you—"

"Look out for boarders," Fenner warned her as two men
and a woman came to join them on the raft. And then, swimming up to hoist himself on board, too, was a dark-haired
man who had been floating peacefully nearby. He apologized pleasantly to Fenner as he stepped, dripping, over his
legs to reach a vacant space. Close up, the face was handsome, with bold blue eyes and strong white teeth displayed
in a friendly smile. His shoulders were massive, his torso
firmly muscled, his neck strong and thick.

"That's all right," Fenner said not too enthusiastically,
and went on talking to Claire. She had not recognized Jan
Aarvan at all: the photograph in Inspector Bernard's file
could not have been either clear or recent. The man's hair
was darker than it had been on the Simplon Express. But the
eyes were the same hard blue, the nose and cheekbones were
of the same blunt cut, and the same speculative expression
was still there to remind Fenner of the face glancing up at
Vaugiroud's window. Stop thinking about him, Fenner's instincts warned him: go on talking to Claire, or listen to the
discussion behind you about the cost of water-skiing, but don't

think about Kalganov's man stretched out so peacefully just three feet away. This was certainly not the time to warn Claire; just let her talk on, he thought. She wouldn't stay long here anyhow. Their use for the raft was over.

"I'm hungry," she said suddenly. "What about lunch?"

They dived, and swam until they grounded. As they waded ashore hand in hand, he said very quietly, "I wanted to talk about your shoulders on the raft, but I didn't want to see them stiffen."

She got the allusion. She pulled off her cap and shook her hair loose. "He will know us again, all right," she said worriedly. "He's very confident, isn't he? You could feel that, even as he lay there. I thought he was one of those lone superwolves." She paused. "I'm glad you didn't talk about my shoulders. He's the animal who can sense—" She didn't finish. She tried to smile. "What would you have said about my shoulders?"

"Oh, something conventional—the prettiest shoulders I've seen today, even when slightly broiled. But I like them rare. With mustard."

"They can't be!"

"We'll know tonight, just around dinnertime. I hope you weren't thinking of wearing an orange dress, Mrs. Langley?"

She was laughing, which was a good way to walk up the beach, past the rows of private tents where darkly tanned people lay and looked all day.

As she picked up her towel, she was back to worrying again. "He stared straight at you, Bill—" She bit her lip.

"And I stared right back at the gobs of water he was sloshing around. Okay?"

"Good," she admitted. She rubbed the back of her head where her hair was wet. "I suppose a man would do that."

"Completely authentic," he assured her, "when ladies are present. Alone, I'd have said, 'Hey you, watch where you're putting your so-and-so feet, you such-and-such!' Stop worrying, my pet. You're just a hungry girl. How do *scampi* and some chilled Soave Verona sound?"

She was smiling again. "Find them for me," she said, and went to dress.

He did find them, by asking the advice of the bathhouse couple, whose cousins—it just so happened, Italian-style—ran a small garden restaurant behind the beach. Half of its little tables were empty by this time, allowing them privacy, at least. Underfoot was hard-packed earth floor; overhead, a trellis of vine leaves with colored lights waiting (merciful- ly, thought Fenner) for evening gaiety. The checked table- cloths were clean, and the fish—straight from the Adriatic onto the charcoal grill—excellent. Greatest triumph of all was Claire, who thought he was a magician to have pulled this place out of his hat, and Fenner, bronzed by the sun and strong sea air, incredibly refreshed by a warm-water swim, felt relaxed and even-tempered for the first time in twenty-four hours.

As they drank the bitter black coffee, he settled back to watch the sunlight spilling through the leaves over Claire's golden hair. "There is only one thing for you to do," he said quietly. "Get out of all this business. Marry Neill and take him out, too."

The gray eyes under their long dark lashes looked up in astonishment. "I'll get out, when I finish this job. But Neill?" She was half puzzled, half embarrassed.

"He was a country newspaper editor before he was a soldier."

"Go back to that?" She shook her head. "He would de- velop ulcers wondering what really lay behind the headlines." There was a long pause. "And marry him? Why did you say that?" Her eyes dropped to the twist of lemon peel she had picked up.

"Well—you're his girl. Aren't you?"

Again she fell silent. Under the sun-kissed skin, a soft glow spread over the beautifully molded cheekbones. She said, "Neill didn't tell you that."

"No."

She looked up again, in relief. "So it was—" She halted out of caution, although their nearest neighbor was four tables away.

"Our deep-freeze expert," Fenner conceded.

"He would." The embarrassment had cleared from her face. She smiled, treating it as a joke.

And was it only a joke, Rosie's little invention to keep Fenner's mind from wandering off into romance when hard business had to be dealt with? "It isn't true?"

Claire hesitated. "I don't know," she said slowly. "At least—" He was looking at her, unbelieving. "Why do you ask?"

It was he who hesitated now. He had known this girl, apart from seeing her twice in the distance and one brief meeting on Friday evening, exactly twenty-one hours and fifty· minutes. A very concentrated twenty-one hours and fifty minutes, it was true. He was thirty-seven, practically touching thirty-eight; a veteran of several wars, declared and undeclared; a man who thought he knew, at last, the direction his life was taking. Not the kind of man, his friends would have sworn, who would be tripped up by a pair of sparkling eyes. But these had him sprawling. He told her the truth, however impolite it might be. "Because your answer is important."

She didn't ask why. She was neither amused nor flustered nor embarrassed. She simply repeated, "I don't know." She noticed the expression on his face. "You can scarcely believe that, can you?"

"Not in you. You're a woman who has a mind, and uses it."

"My mind tells me that—I'm bad for Neill."

"Bad for him?" He shook his head. "How?"

"I've known him for about six weeks. I saw him a lot. He could relax with me, trust me. . . . But now he talks of getting out of the army, of giving up his work in Intelligence, of returning to Iowa." She was worried, unhappy. "Because of me, Bill."

He agreed with Carlson: it would be a hard life for any woman to be married to a man in his profession. "Nonsense," he said very gently. "Carlson wants to get back to Iowa."

"To that apple tree?" She shook her head. "We all talk that way, now and again. We mean it for a month. And then?" She sighed. "No. Men like Neill are needed—here, in Europe. He knows that. He would begin to feel like a deserter. That's no good. No good at all. Some men could argue themselves into believing that life owes them their own pleasure. Not Neill."

"You have told him all this?"

"Yes. We had a small fight over it yesterday."

"Who won?"

"Who wins in a quarrel with someone he likes? We both lost something." Her head drooped. "The truth is that he is one of the kindest men I've ever met. And I can't bear to hurt him." And the truth is, she told herself painfully, you can't really be in love with Neill Carlson or else you'd have married him right away, whatever his job, wherever he worked. And the truth is you might have drifted from affection and trust into love, into marriage, if you hadn't met Bill Fenner on Friday evening. How could one short meeting with a stranger have had any meaning at all? It had none. Except that it made you uncertain. And if you are really in love, there is no uncertainty: there must not be, or else your marriage would always be vulnerable, a gamble. . . . She looked up at Bill Fenner. I should hate this man, she thought, for having destroyed my pleasant drifting dream. Yet I don't.

"But you don't marry anyone out of a sense of obligation," Fenner said worriedly. "Do you?"

"I don't know—I don't even know that, any more."

"Claire—"

"What time is it?" she asked quickly.

"Quarter of four. If we leave here by four-fifteen, we should have plenty of leeway."

"Ample," she agreed. She stared at her fingers. They had shredded the sliver of lemon peel into a yellow pulp.

"More coffee?" he asked. He took her hands and wiped their finger tips with his handerkerchief. "And this time, we'll ask for several twists of lemon." He signaled to the waiter.

She had to smile. She was relieved, too, to retreat away from her painful moment of truth. "How is our theme song?"

"The lady in blue is still with us. Far behind you, trying to make a plate of spaghetti last a full hour. No more interest in our conversation, apparently. I don't think she even expects us, now, to meet anyone. We have wasted her day."

"How nice!"

"But of course if we concentrate on her, we might not notice anyone else. That could be the idea, couldn't it? It's pretty silly the way she has kept haunting us—too obvious."

"You catch on very quickly."

"Slowly," he corrected. "I only thought of it."

"You are doing beautifully," she told him gently, "for a man who lost his raincoat only two days ago."

"You know about that?"

"You look startled. Too startled," she reminded him. No one could hear them. But they were certainly in clear view of at least fifteen people.

He put his hand over hers as it lay beside her coffee cup. "As startled as if you had just promised to go back to America with me?"

She tried to draw her hand away, then—as his tightened—she let it lie under his. "You *are* doing beautifully," she told him again. "This looks perfect."

"You aren't blushing enough."

"I'm a hard case."

"Are you?"

"Not with you, it seems. I shouldn't have let that slip— about your coat."

"How did you learn?"

"I wanted to find out how you got mixed up in all this."

"Why?"

She tried to evade that, and didn't succeed. "Because, oh— just because I was interested." She fell silent, thankfully, as the waiter brought another pot of *espresso* and left.

"I told you I wasn't good for Neill," she reminded him. And in quick defense of Carlson, she added, "He didn't say too much. Just a phrase about meeting you in search of a coat. But there was a report in one of the Paris newspapers yesterday that the French had tracked down a currency smuggler at Orly—at least, they were in possession of his coat, and an arrest was imminent. Didn't you read about it?"

He shook his head. "I didn't get around to reading many newspapers yesterday. And I wish you hadn't."

"Why?"

"The less you know, the safer you'll be."

"And what about you? Or is it all right for men to know, and be placed in danger?"

"Yes."

"You are looking much too serious," she said, her eyes glancing at the rest of the garden.

"I am serious." He uncovered her hand, held it, looked at it, at last released it. "You worry the hell out of me."

"I wouldn't have been sent here if I had to be worried over." She tested the drip coffeepot, and poured carefully.

"How did you get mixed up in all this?" he asked her.

"Two reasons. I knew Sandra Fane long ago in New York. And Frank Rosenfeld knew me in Indochina. Two separate little points in my life which traveled a long long way until their lines crossed, here in Venice."

"You knew Sandra—" He broke off. Their young waiter was returning with some strips of lemon peel.

"We both had small parts in a Broadway play. I was the little maid who brought in the breakfast tray to a glamorous screen star and opened her bedroom curtains each morning. I looked out at a blank backstage wall and the tired face of a stagehand, and spoke my immortal line: 'It's going to be a lovely day, Miss Julie.'" The waiter was clearing away the dishes. He'd be back for the glasses and wine bottle. "She was the disapproving secretary who found Miss Julie on the terrace in Act Three. Suicide. Oh, it was a very pregnant play, filled with deep inner meanings about the empty shell of success." Here came the waiter for the glasses and last crumbs. "It ran for two months—that was in 1951, when you were in Korea, weren't you?—and by the time it ended, I decided my brain was being turned into cream cheese. So I thought I'd try art school instead. And then I met Jim Langley" (and fell in love, really in love, she thought) "and we got married and went out to Indochina. That was in 1953."

The waiter had left. But Fenner still remained silent. He concentrated on melting a lump of sugar in his coffee cup.

"I didn't know Sandra well. She was older, mixed with a different crowd." She paused, wondering if he was even listening.

"I guess she did," he said. The white sugar turned brown and crumpled slowly. "So—when Rosie heard you were going to one of her parties in Paris, he asked you to talk to her, find out whether she had changed politics." Insistent boy, old Rosie.

"How did you guess?"

"He asked me to do the same thing. What did you find?"

"I thought she was putting on the best act of her life. I was wrong—obviously."

"I wonder."

"You mean you don't think she is honestly defecting?"

"I think she's quitting the party because she has no other choice left." He shook his head. "That was the last small hope I had. That one day she'd make a clean and honest break—something she needn't be ashamed of." He looked up and saw Claire's expression. "For her own sake," he said. "Her life is hers to arrange. Her conscience is her job, not mine. And thank God for that." He drank the coffee, a bitter brew.

"You never tried to reason with her, persuade her?"

"We were together four weeks after we were married in 1950, and there seemed nothing much to argue about, then. After that, I was away from New York a great deal. On assignments. Alone. She couldn't leave the theater—all these great dramatic roles discovering bodies in Act Three. Or she had to go on tour. Or appear in country stock. She even tried Hollywood. I was actually glad of that long stint in Korea. And when the *Chronicle* brought me home—well, we had a fairly cross-purpose week together before the final break came. I blamed myself for having given her such an empty marriage. I think I would have reasoned with her, tried to persuade her, argued and explained and—" He broke off. From this distance, he could smile at such innocence. Innocence or ignorance? "But she had left. For good. And I was spared a lot of wasted breath. You just can't reason with any dedicated missionary."

"You think she still is?"

"Let's put it this way—she's been quarreling with a bishop, or archbishop. She's leaving her church, but she has still got her religion. She sees us as the benighted reactionaries who'll give her refuge. She'll use us for protection. She has a will to live. Because if she doesn't live, she never can make that comeback, someday, somehow, into her church. When there has been a change in bishops, of course. Communists have patience. We count in months; they count in years." He looked at Claire. "Too cruel?" he asked her.

"You ought to know her better than most." Claire was shaken, though. "You're saying that a conversion out of necessity is not real, not honest?" And when he nodded, she asked, "Did you tell this to Rosie?"

"No. You're the only one I've ever—" He broke off, forced a good imitation of a smile, and went back to Rosie. "He knows a lot about people, that guy. And Communists are people—a pretty mean type of people at that, unless one admires liars and traitors, or the kind of man who keeps silent when his neighbors or family are carted off to torture or execution. As has happened. By the millions."

"I still think Rosie would be interested."

"Anything I tell him would sound like someone in high school analyzing Spinoza. Very worthy, but not exactly contributive to the cause of advanced scholarship. How did Rosie come to know you, by the way?"

"By the way?" She almost smiled at his careful casualness. And then all hint of amusement vanished. "By way of a bombing—a terrorist bombing of a café in Saigon where Jim was killed." She frowned down at the checked tablecloth. "We had been married just five months."

"This was a political bombing?"

"Yes. But those who were killed and mutilated were just ordinary people—all Vietnamese, except for Jim who was waiting for me to meet him at the café." She raised her eyes. "I had chosen the meeting place. We were going furniture-hunting. There was an inlaid table I wanted him to see—it cost more than we had planned—before I bought it." Even at this distance of eight years, there was self-reproach in the simple words.

Fenner said, "Claire, please—"

"I have to tell you. Briefly. Because it is the main reason that brought me into all this business. That bombing killed Jim and four men. It crippled three children and two women. It wounded nine others. I saw them—I saw them all." She paused, hurried on. "So that was what one bomb meant, thrown from a passing truck. No one seemed to know who was responsible. I kept asking who and why, and got no real answers. People were very kind and gentle. But their sympathy was driving me numb with despair. Because everyone seemed so helpless and ignorant; and the bombings went on. So did the anti-American propaganda. No one knew how the rumors spread, but for a time they were believed by people who ought to have had a little more faith in us. They whispered that the Americans were responsible, that we were trying to undermine the French, intimidate the Vietnamese, blame the Communists because we always blamed the poor Communists. Jim's death, you'd think, might have ended the rumors, but it was whispered around that there had been a small slip-up in American planning: they hadn't warned Jim to keep away from that café on that day at that hour. It sounds ridiculous, doesn't it? Yet at the time, the results of that propaganda weren't ridiculous at all. They were deadly.

"So Rosie appeared in Saigon. And he came to see me along with some friends—he was called Frank Rennie then. It was just a sympathy visit. Poor old Jim, poor little widow. It wasn't much of a success. I think Rosie knew why. He seemed to understand that kindly platitudes were no answer at all to my questions. Look, Bill, when a man dies, we try to learn what caused his death, don't we? That's the law in civilized countries, isn't it? And here were civilized people who were shocked and sorry but didn't even know why bombs were being thrown or who had paid and organized the terrorists. Most of them didn't even link the bombs to the anti-American propaganda: they thought the propaganda was only silly talk and no one who really knew Americans would believe it; they thought the bombings were the foolish work of dissidents or madmen on the loose, or a matter of local gangsters trying to shake down the café owners. Except Rosie. When the others left that afternoon, he stayed for an hour.

He explained the propaganda campaign and the bombings, all part of the same story being built up around us. Americans were aggressive and ruthless and stupid, who'd turn any crisis into a war. In Korea—but, you remember all that—"

"I remember." A lot of us remember, he thought. We don't all push history into limbo.

"So Rosie made sense. And that was what I needed. Sense, not sympathy. Because that's the only way to stop men like Kalganov. You'll never stop them if you don't know, or won't admit, that they exist. It's knowledge and action, not sympathy and kind words, that will save us from Kalganov's world."

"Rosie actually told you about Kalganov?"

"Not directly. I didn't even know Rosie's job—I thought he was just another businessman visiting Saigon." She smiled and added, "But one who used his brains."

"So he didn't recruit you there?"

"Heavens, no. He just helped me when I needed help. I got a grip on myself and went back to New York and art school. And later, much later, when all the facts had been discovered, he sent me a newspaper clipping about the bombing. The men who threw the bomb from a passing truck were irregulars—bandits calling themselves soldiers. Their war lord, no politics, had been paid for the job. The men who had paid him were Chinese, no politics, who themselves had been paid by other Chinese, who were Communists, plenty of politics. They did it because they were instructed. And who gave them orders, planned everything? A man called Kalganov. He was the only one who wasn't caught."

"He had protected himself pretty well, I must say."

"That's his way. Usually his name doesn't appear in print. In fact, that's the only time I ever saw it. So Rosie and his friends came very close to him."

"And when did Rosie get in touch with you again?"

She laughed. "He *isn't* a sinister old spider, Bill. We met in Paris, as Americans do. When he asked my help, I gave him it. I have seen the enemy, and what he's willing to do to get what he wants. And that's why I'm here. Not because of my own memories, but because of what I learned. That bomb was a threat to all of us—not just a personal tragedy for me. Do you see?"

He nodded.

"If I could help, in the smallest way, to upset any Communist conspiracy—" She stopped, laughed off her tightening emotion. "Let's say I declared war on Kalganov a long time ago. It's my way of fighting for peace. Peace through active discouragement of all peace-breakers."

"Kalganov may need more than active discouragement to end his career."

"His record is black enough. That will take care of him."

"So all we have to do is catch him." Fenner was smiling.

"Not us! That's a job for the professionals. Neill or Chris or some of Rosie's agents. Or perhaps the Sûreté—"

"You think he's in Venice?"

"You saw Jan Aarvan."

"And that means Kalganov is here?"

"He won't be far behind."

"Protecting himself as usual," Fenner suggested. Very casually, he added, "Was Robert Wahl in Saigon around the time of the bombing?"

She stared at him. "Yes," she said slowly. "He was going to make a film out there. But it came to nothing. Bill—"

But he hid his rising worry by glancing at his watch and saying briskly, "There's just time to put on some lipstick and pay the check."

"Heavens!" said Claire, noticing her own small watch and the emptied restaurant. There were only three customers left, far distant. Even their blue ghost had vanished. "Whatever happened—oh, I know, I was explaining myself. Briefly." She smiled at herself, and searched hurriedly for a powder puff and lipstick in her bag. Carefully, she outlined her lips in soft pink. "My nose is going to peel," she told him.

"It wouldn't do anything so indelicate." He watched her, and all her neat feminine motions. She was even remembering to gather their swimsuits from a nearby chair, shaking her head over their dampness, deciding to carry them.

"You're the strangest mixture," he told her. She was ten, twenty different women. Enough to keep a man chasing them all his life. Infinite variety. Poor old Carlson. Poor old Mark Antony, too. "Come on, Cleopatra." She looked up, charming and wide-eyed. "Let's go, my little front-line fighter for peace," he said, and draped her soft ridiculous cardigan around her suntanned shoulders. "And give me those blasted swimsuits."

They walked up a sheltered path, a tangle of vines and rough pergola, toward the main road, passing the restaurant's bad-weather dining room, which now lay neglected. They were alone except for three barefooted, bronzed children, who chased long-legged pullets in and out of a kitchen door.

They were almost at the street. "Drop something," he told her. The cardigan slipped off her shoulders. He halted, took a step back to where it lay, shaking it as he picked it up to free it of dust and a withered leaf. She hadn't looked around. "Our friend in the brown suit has joined us again. He must have been in the dining room." They had fallen into step, arm in arm, the cardigan slung through the strap of her red handbag. "Are they trying to scare us into a false move?" Either these people were damned well organized or he was crediting them with too many brains. "Jan Aarvan, for instance—" (how had he managed to be floating around on their part of the swimming beach?) "—was he also on the water-bus we took? I didn't see him. I was too busy watching the woman."

"It doesn't matter," Claire said as they came out into the street. "As long as Aarvan didn't feel either of us recognized him, it doesn't matter."

Fenner noticed two taxis waiting near the lane's exit. "How convenient," he said, and looked at the street, a long straight line stretching for miles, edged with gardens and bathhouses and hotels. It seemed uninhabited, except—a little distance away—for a small group of ex-bathers and sun-worshipers waiting for a trolley-bus to start back into town. Claire looked at him with brief alarm, and relaxed. They weren't going to take any too-convenient taxi. I can let Bill take charge, she thought thankfully; and the feeling of re-assurance, of safety, which had fallen over her like a soft and silken cloak in that dusty, vine-shaded lane, was wrapped around her again.

One of the taxis moved forward. Its door was open, as in-viting as its driver's wide grin. "Taxi, taxi! Very quick, very quick!"

"He'd make a successful playwright, that one," Fenner observed as they walked on, the taxi cruising gently behind them, "emphasizing the obvious, repeating everything twice." The man's face had been remarkably untanned for someone who lived on this wind-scoured, sun-baked sand bar. No doubt he had quick ears, a good memory, too. And he knew English. I may be oversuspicious, Fenner thought, but— He looked at Claire, who was letting him handle this completely. "No thanks," he called to the taxi, which had drawn along-side again.

The bus ahead of them would leave any minute, and among the swarm of passengers climbing on board by the rear door, he saw a woman dressed in dull blue, her somber face not at all amused by the good-natured jostling around her. Better avoid the bus, he thought. But the taxi was creeping along, cajoling. Its driver would certainly keep following, if only to wear down their resistance. The Excelsior was only a few minutes away. Fenner could see it, even from here, along that stretch of empty road. The woman in the bus would notice them get off, but she could hardly follow them as blatantly as that. At the moment, she was the lesser of two dangers. "Run, Claire!" he said, catching her hand. They sprinted wildly, and reached the bus as it moved slowly away from the curb. He swung her onto its step, and scrambled after her as the bus went into high speed. "And you can run," he told her, regaining his breath.

"You can pull," she said, breathless herself. She looked back at their line of flight. The insistent taxi had given up. Or perhaps it was waiting for further instructions from the other cab, which the man in brown was entering. "You can guess right, too," she told Fenner as he found some small change for their short ride. There was no need to search for a seat. They'd leave at the next stop.

Which made the blue lady's reactions all the funnier. First she had been startled: was *she* being followed? Then she had become suspicious: they must be meeting someone on this bus. So she moved to a side seat near the front, uncomfortable as it was, from which she could watch everyone with that blank, stolid gaze. And just as she was settling, dutifully, at her vantage post, the bus swerved toward the sidewalk for its next halt.

Claire and Fenner slipped off quietly by the rear door, their exit blurred by the rush of oncoming passengers crowding into the aisle. They crossed the street toward the lagoon, walking smartly. "We've got one minute left," Fenner said. He glanced along the road. The two taxis were still standing together, some five hundred yards away. Quickly, they started forward. "Not a chance," Fenner told them under his breath, as Claire, much amused, and he, feeling pretty good, came into the anchorage.

It was a sheltered place—a large and glorified swimming pool, Fenner thought—with a few highly polished motorboats drawn close to one edge. Their owners were not grouped together, talking and scouring, as the gondoliers had been. They wore natty tweed jackets, correct collars and ties, nautical caps at a jaunty angle on good haircuts, and a proud look. "The jet pilots of the lagoon," Fenner said with a grin. "And which is ours?" He didn't wait for Claire's guess, but started toward a boat, lying a little apart, whose owner seemed only interested in lighting a cigarette. "Hotel Vittoria?" Fenner called to him.

"Right here," the man said, and waved them casually on board. He was a young, dark-haired Italian, with interested brown eyes even if the manner was cool and nonchalant. Amidships, there was the usual glass-enclosed cabin with pleated curtains, sashed and befringed, giving privacy. A good deal of privacy, Fenner realized as he handed Claire through the small front door and ducked inside after her. There was a man sitting in one of the neat red leather armchairs. From the jetty, the cabin had seemed empty.

"Fasten your seat belts," the stranger said as the engine roared, the boat curved sharply toward a narrow tree-lined canal, and they were jolted wildly together. "Hello, Claire. You've had a pleasant day in the sun, I see."

"Hello, Chris. Where's Neill?"

"I like boat rides, so I am here. And is this Mr. Fenner? How do you do?" The English voice was cold. "I'm Holland."

EIGHTEEN

THERE WAS TENSION in the small cabin. Claire glanced anxiously at Chris Holland, as much as to say, "Come on, make one of your funny remarks. I've talked you up. Don't let me down!" But the Englishman was making no further remarks at all. He shook hands briefly, lit another cigarette. He was, in spite of his concentration with his lighter, studying Fenner critically.

Of course, Fenner remembered, I was Rosie's choice for this little expedition. Neill Carlson had been against it. No doubt Holland was, too. In his phrase, but in my New England accent, I am the bloody amateur who clutters up the landscape. So I'll keep quiet, he decided, let Holland talk; and if I have to talk, I'll do it in short questions and not flat statements. The opinion of an amateur was not worth too much around here.

Fenner settled himself comfortably in the chair opposite Claire. He lit a cigarette, too, and studied the Englishman in turn. An amateur could do that, at least. Christopher Holland was of medium height, weight, and age; his features, even, pleasant, but unremarkable; his hair, neatly cut, well brushed, graying brown; eyes, an indeterminate mixture of gray and brown, but certainly observant; lightly tanned, unlined skin; his clothes of brownish-gray mixed tweed, worn most casually. A medium kind of man in every way, Fenner thought, one you'd scarcely notice in an empty street, and quickly forget. A man without worries or troubles, you would guess, even meeting him as closely as this, until you noticed the ash tray beside him, filled with half-smoked cigarettes.

Claire was reporting. "They are definitely interested in us, Chris. We have been watched and monitored ever since we left Paris."

"One minute—" Holland said in his quiet, even voice. They were zooming into the lagoon, two scimitar-shaped waves curving up and out from the boat's sharp prow. He slid open the rear door's panel. "Dammit," he bellowed, "what's the rush, Pietro?"

Pietro grinned cheerfully. He had had his flying start. He eased the speed of the boat and shouted back something that blew away in the wind. Holland shook his head, closed the door again.

"First," Holland said, "let's talk about the message you sent me. Your rooms are no good. No good at all. Change them." He was looking at Claire. Claire looked at Fenner.

"So Rosie did not book those two rooms on the terrace?" Fenner asked.

"No. He arranged for two rooms on the second floor, no connecting balcony with any other rooms. Also, two of his men have rooms on that floor, close by. We've been out-maneuvered"—he smiled, thinly—"by film producer Wahl who could very safely use the name of Mr. Stephen York."

"Are they friends?"

"Not at all. But it was safe to use York's name. He is making a picture in deepest Africa. We checked." Again there was a touch of acid amusement. "Wahl was never known for his lack of impudence."

"Wahl," Fenner said reflectively. "Not Kalganov?"

Holland was startled, certainly less diffident in manner. He looked at Fenner thoughtfully. "We don't know that Wahl *is* Kalganov, do we?"

"Where is Wahl?"

"Switzerland, they tell me."

"Not Venice?"

"Holland's quiet stare asked for an explanation.

"Claire thinks Kalganov is in Venice. We saw Jan Aarvan today."

"Where?"

"On a raft." Fenner relented and grinned. "About a couple of hours ago, or more."

"You are sure?" Holland looked at Claire for confirmation.

"Bill recognized him. I didn't. Really, Chris, that's an awful photograph in Inspector Bernard's files. Aarvan has thinned down, for one thing. And he must be fifteen years older."

"Also," Fenner said, "he is dyeing his hair. It was brown

yesterday on the train. It's almost black today. Miracles of modern science. When I first saw him, from Vaugiroud's window, he was blond. How is Vaugiroud, by the way? His arm was broken, I heard."

"You must introduce me to your sources," Holland said. "They sound more accurate than mine."

"Is he all right?"

"He is all right. He escaped the second attempt on his life, too."

"There was *another* one?"

"We can talk about that later." Holland stared at his cigarette stub, let it drop into the ash tray with distaste. His thoughts had drifted onto something unpleasant. He tried to pull them away from it, said, "Now, about your message, Claire——" He was half lost in his own thoughts again.

Claire looked astounded. She exchanged a puzzled glance with Fenner. "Yes," she said. "I was beginning to wonder if it had fallen flat on its funny little face. There were three questions in it. We haven't even finished with the first one. Rooms to be changed. How? That isn't easy, without warning Comrade Wahl that we are suspicious."

Holland said, a little sharply, "That's your problem, old girl."

"I'll take care of it," Fenner said quietly. "What was the second point in your note, Claire?" The sooner Claire's note was dealt with, the more quickly he'd learn about Vaugiroud. There was something wrong. That, he could sense.

Claire was watching Holland curiously. "It dealt with the coat of arms on the gondola that collected Sir Felix Tarns."

Holland was in control of his thoughts again. He even produced an unexpected smile. "You described the coat of arms as either a crocodile rampant or a sea horse sitting on its tail, with either a thin pineapple or a fat palm tree in support."

"Well," Claire said, "I only had a quick glimpse. You know how gondolas float away."

Fenner looked at her blankly. He hadn't paid any attention to the coat of arms. He had been too busy thinking, as they stood on the Vittoria's landing stage, what a damned silly piece of nonsense it all was, following Tarns out there.

"Crocodile and palm tree," Holland was saying, "the most useful piece of information we've had today." He seemed to enjoy the expression on Fenner's face. He explained, with some slight amusement, "We lost Lenoir and Fane last night, after they arrived at Lido Airport. Their launch behaved very much in the way that Pietro is steering our boat at present: most erratic, very difficult to follow. They vanished somewhere in Saint Mark's Basin; never docked at the Danieli, where we expected them to stay. And since then, there's been a bloody flap. Not a clue where they were until"—he gave Claire a nod of approval—"your crocodile and palm tree reached us. After that it was easy, of course."

"Of course," said Fenner. "A crocodile and palm tree, after all."

"It's the coat of arms of the Longhi family, who own a retiring little *palazzo* known as Ca' Longhi just off the Grand Canal," Holland clarified. "It was leased for the summer— the Longhi family is down to one survivor and none of the cash it made in Near Eastern trade three centuries ago—to an American, who calls herself—" He broke off, and then murmured apologetically, "I'm afraid she went back to using your name, old boy."

"What?"

"Yes. Mrs. William Fenner. She has almost as much impudence as Wahl. Or perhaps it was another of his comic touches. I suppose her old passport was easy to bring up to date for the agent who leased the place, last May. So, crocodile and palm tree saved us a lot of time, a lot of investigation.

"You'd have tracked down Ca' Longhi—" Claire began. She was taking her small triumph well Fenner thought. There hadn't been even a flicker of an eyelash in his direction saying "See?"

"Yes," agreed Holland. "With some co-operation from the Italians, we would have. But even with all hands on deck, Ca' Longhi might have taken a full day's work to uncover. Instead, we could set up a close watch on the place early this afternoon. Most rewarding. There has been a series of visitors for Fernand Lenoir since our noble Sir Felix left him at half past two." Holland's voice was icily contemptuous for that one reference. He dropped Tarns there. "It seems as if the briefing session has begun at Ca' Longhi," he said, watching Fenner.

"Already?"

"Yes."

"I don't get it," Fenner said worriedly. Sandra would deliver the letter and make her escape, tomorrow evening, well ahead of either the attempted assassination or the big lie. She had told Rosie that the crisis could be expected Friday.

And here was Lenoir, meeting his contacts today. "I'd have thought the later Lenoir left that briefing session, the safer for them all. Or is he just preparing the ground before he starts planting the lies?"

"Frankly," Holland said, watching Fenner with growing interest, "I don't get in either. Unless—as you say—the ground needs a good deal of preparation. Tell me, how much do you think we can trust Sandra Fane?"

Fenner hesitated. He phrased his answer carefully. "At present—I think we can."

"But in the long run—not at all?" Holland asked quietly. He was a sharp character, Fenner decided. The question had been only rhetorical: the unspoken agreement spared Fenner an answer. Strange, he was thinking, that Claire is the only one with whom I've discussed Sandra quite willingly. He looked at Claire, and Holland noticed it. (What have we here? Holland wondered: whatever is it, I don't think I like it; nor will Rosie.) Quickly, he said, "About that third point in your message, Claire: the man in the brown suit. Not to worry. He has been noted. So have the others. We have marked them all, once they showed an interest in you."

Fenner was amused. "So we've been watched by our experts, too?" To Claire, he said, "You know what we are? A couple of lambs staked out for the tigers."

Holland almost smiled. "Cheer up, chum. You've been very useful. Rosie sends his thanks."

"Is Rosie *here*?" Claire asked, suddenly grave.

"Arrived an hour ago."

"But why—"

"Rosie wants you both to play things very loose indeed. No strain. Just get through the next twenty-four hours as normally as possible. Leave the problems to us. Except the change of rooms. You'll do that right away?"

"First thing," Fenner assured him.

"Good. I remember, in Budapest, we had the same situation. Bloody balcony connecting several rooms. We lost a good man that way." He glanced out through the glass panel in the cabin's rear door, opened it, signaled to Pietro, who if he couldn't make high speed, had at least been having a merry time criss-crossing the lagoon's Sunday traffic, mingling and disentangling skillfully from various groupings of boats. "Ten more minutes and then up the Giudecca Canal," Holland shouted. "Drop me at San Sebastiano."

Pietro nodded, shouted back cheerfully. Holland shut the

door, pulled its curtains securely together. In fact, Fenner noted, all the windows around Holland were thoroughly screened.

"We are getting close in," Holland said. "Keep together, you two. Don't look at me. Look as if you were chatting only to each other. Any further problems?"

Fenner shook his head.

"Then we can talk about Vaugiroud." He would make as good a bridge passage as any, Holland thought. His voice became quite emotionless. "Just around noon yesterday, when that bomb went off in the Café Racine, Vaugiroud's flat was entered and searched. Rather violently. The concierge says her husband allowed a man to go upstairs to the flat. She thinks it was the same man who loitered in front of the house on Friday afternoon. Her husband has been arrested; so far, he is sticking to his story. He swears he allowed only a telephone repairman to go upstairs. Once we get Aarvan, of course, and have a little confrontation scene, the husband may decide it's wiser to tell the truth."

Holland pulled a folded sheet of newspaper out of a jacket pocket. He unfolded it slowly, spoke rapidly. "So, with all this attention on Vaugiroud, we expected there might be another attempt on his life. We announced he was being transferred from one hospital to another, and sent out an empty ambulance to make that journey. A truck smashed into its rear. Truck driver jumped, was caught, pleaded brakes had not worked properly. Ambulance a mess."

"I hope its driver jumped, too," Fenner said to Claire.

"He is one of our very best jumpers," Holland said dryly. "Here's the newspaper story. We thought it a good idea to announce that Vaugiroud had been killed. Saves us a lot of bother in the next few days."

"Where is he?"

"Much hidden." Holland handed over the unfolded sheet to Fenner, and Claire changed her seat to read, too. "It's from the early-morning edition. Rosie brought it with him. I circled the paragraph for you."

"Vaugiroud's friends are going to be in an uproar," Fenner said, after he and Claire had read a brief but highly vivid account of the accident.

"For a few days," the calm voice said. "There will be a retraction, a plea of mistaken identity, a blushing apology and general thanksgiving."

"And what does the poor journalist do who wrote these immortal lines? Cut his throat?"

"He was overdescriptive for a man who didn't arrive on the scene until the two bodies were taken away," Holland said coldly. As Claire looked at him, he added, "Keep your attention on Fenner! And for bodies, read dummies."

Claire addressed Fenner obediently. "What's wrong?" she asked frankly. Chris was usually good company with a string of bright remarks. He could turn any situation, however grim, into comedy. Normally, he would have taken Bill's gruesome joke and expanded it to something really hideously funny. "Chris—" She was inexplicably, and deeply, worried.

"I circled another paragraph, too," he said, "on the next page."

Fenner turned over the sheet quickly. He heard Claire's sudden gasp as she saw the ten lines of close type, headed FATAL ACCIDENT ON PARIS-ZAGREB EXPRESS. She drew back from him, her body rigid. Fenner stared at the lines. He knew, before he read them. He knew, and he didn't want to read. But he read.

Last night, Emile Daubenton and Jean Lacordaire, cousins, both from the village of Darcey, discovered the body of a man lying beside the railway line over which the Simplon Express had passed less than one hour previously. From the contents of his pockets, the man has been identified as John McNally of New York City, traveling to Milan. It is thought that M. McNally slipped, or fell, from the express, about eleven kilometers east of Les Laumes, as it traveled at highest speed before starting the ascent through the Côte-d'Or. M. McNally was traveling alone, and his tragic accident was unobserved.

Claire's face had bleached white under its sun tan as she watched Fenner. At last she said, "It's about Neill, isn't it?" She held out her hand for the paper. She read it, her face masked; and when the reading was over she let the sheet of newspaper drop. She rose, looking at neither Fenner nor Holland, abruptly opening the small door that led to the prow of the boat.

"Let her be," Holland's quiet voice said, stopping Fenner as he rose, too. Claire was sitting, numbed and still, on a wooden bench, her body half turned away from the cabin.

Fenner came back to his armchair. The two men faced each other grimly. Holland said, "We have been able to cal-

culate the time of Neill's death: I glanced at my watch
when I saw him walking through the dining car, and the
engine driver could give us the exact time the train passed
eleven kilometers east of Les Laumes. It's a lonely spot, just
before the line starts climbing the Côte-d'Or hills. If it hadn't
been for a couple of poachers taking a short cut along the
rails, we'd still be searching for Neill." He paused, frowning
down at the spilling ash tray.

"When was he killed?"

"Soon after he left the dining car. Who followed him into
that goods van—did you see?"

The freight car, with its opened side door, with the cold
wind rushing past . . . "Jan Aarvan."

"You are sure?" Holland asked quickly.

Fenner nodded. "Didn't you recognize him?"

"From where I sat, I could only see his back. I didn't
know he was on the train. Neill had made no contact with me
at all. That was our arrangement: raise no suspicion, no
alarm. It seemed safer—for everyone."

For us, Fenner thought, for Claire and me and our innocent journey. But not for Neill Carlson. "He must have warned
someone that he had seen Aarvan. I noticed some plain-
clothes police board the train at Dijon."

Holland nodded. "Neill did get a message through to Rosie,
just before the train pulled out of the Gare de Lyon. He
told Rosie to alert the Sûreté that he would be waiting for
its agents on board the train at Dijon. He could identify
Aarvan for them." Holland frowned again. "I saw them get
on the train. And wondered. And could do nothing—not even
identify myself." He looked at Fenner. "Jan Aarvan didn't
know you had recognized him?"

"I think not."

"I hope not," Holland said softly. "Be alert, will you, Fenner? At any other time, I'd be amused by the situation. Of
all the people we've got here in Venice, you're the only one
who could pick out Jan Aarvan in a crowd without any
hesitation." He remembered Claire's remarks about Aarvan.
Worriedly, he asked, "When did you tell Claire about Aarvan?"

"When we were well clear of the raft. I'm not such a fool
as that, Holland." He looked toward Claire. "I'm not going
to leave her alone out there," he said, and started to rise.

"Wait—what are your plans for this evening?"

"A drink at Florian's around six-thirty. Then dinner at

Quadri's. At ten, we take a gondola ride with an old friend of Claire's—his name is Zorzi. He parks his gondola at the bridge near your camera shop."

"Zorzi," Holland repeated. "I'll let Rosie know." He glanced out of the window. "Better bring Claire inside before we start cruising up the Giudecca. And take a look at the Soviet freighter that is docked there. She's supposed to sail on Thursday." Holland studied his hands. "She has been loading all day."

"You think Sandra—" Fenner hesitated. A clever act put on for Rosie's benefit in the Tuileries. A trick, a trap? "More lies?" he asked quietly.

"Not altogether. There must be some truth in her warning. Why else would Aarvan want to stop Neill from reaching Venice?"

Yes, there was that. But couldn't Sandra tell the whole truth, honestly, just once in her life?

"Aarvan—" began Holland, and stopped. He was beginning to sound emotional, and that wouldn't do, that wouldn't do at all. We'll get him yet, Holland thought, we'll get him. He stared impassively ahead.

"How did Aarvan murder Neill before he threw him off the train? With a bullet in the back?"

Holland's quiet mask slipped. He looked at Fenner. "Yes," he said, watching the American with a new respect.

It would have to be a bullet, or a knife, in the back. Carlson hadn't been the type to be pushed off a train, Fenner thought as he stepped through the door to reach Claire.

The motorboat was leaving the lagoon, making one last sweep around the small island of San Giorgio before it cut up the Giudecca Canal. He took Claire's hands between his and sat down beside her. She had been crying silently, sitting so still, her face turned blindly toward the roofs of Venice. "Come," he said gently, "back into the cabin. You'll be frozen." She didn't seem to hear him. "Please, Claire," he said very softly. At that, she looked at him, the tears ignored. When he pulled her to her feet, she didn't resist. He steadied her with his arm firmly around her waist, and she didn't notice. The broad waters of the Giudecca stretched before them. At its long quay, backed by antique houses, he could see the liner safely docked. And beyond it, a freighter, large, clean, efficient. And it was still loading.

He brought Claire into the cabin before they reached the freighter. Holland, making ready for his quick exit, only signed his approval. He had shredded the sheet of newspaper, and dropped it along with his cigarette stubs into the canal. His hand was on the rear door, his eyes watching the quay. "Change those rooms," he reminded Fenner again, as his parting word.

Fenner nodded. Whatever had happened in Budapest had really seared itself into Holland's mind. "Does Sir Felix shoot people in the back, too?"

"He does everything short of pulling the trigger. That," Christopher Holland said bitterly, "would be against his principles." His eyes were still on the quay. The freighter was safely passed.

I'll take that warning about Tarns, Fenner thought, watching the freighter, too. Claire noticed nothing. She hadn't even heard their voices.

As the boat curved around into a small canal, Holland pulled the door open. "Good-by," he told them, "good luck!" He was out. "Quick as you like!" he said to Pietro as he climbed onto the broad stretch of quay. The boat backed into the Giudecca, pointed to the lagoon again, gathering the speed that delighted Pietro. Chris Holland was already out of sight.

They swept around the island of San Giorgio again, and entered the Grand Canal, slowing down for the increased traffic. Fenner looked at Claire anxiously. He couldn't bring himself to remind her that they'd have to land in a few minutes, all smiles and general jollity, a happy couple returning from an afternoon in the sun. "There's the Vittoria," was all he said.

She nodded, opened her handbag, stared at a small mirror, combed her hair. Her normal color had partly returned to give some life to her face. The pitiful bleached look had gone. She added lipstick. She looked up at him. "Will this do?" she asked bitterly.

"Very well," he said gently. He remembered to pick up the swimsuits. Nothing else left, except his five cigarette stubs. "Ready?" he asked, and handed her out of the cabin.

"I'll go straight to my room, do you mind?"

"No you don't. You stay with me. I'm going to have the rooms changed immediately. We pack together. We keep together." I can take a warning, he thought. And Chris Holland gave me several in his own quiet way.

"All right," she said, capitulating. "Now," she added, watching the crowded hotel terrace as the boat eased broadside against the floating landing stage, "we smile, and smile and smile." Oh, God!

The assistant manager was just about to leave. He looked at the two sun-reddened faces and the damp swimsuits. "Did you have a pleasant day?" he began politely, wondering what had brought this handsome couple to his office.

"Marvelous," the lady said. Mrs. Langley, that was her name; a widow. And so young, so beautiful. Life was sad.

"It's about out rooms," the tall American said.

The assistant manager stopped looking at his clock. "Is something wrong?" And he must not be late, he thought worriedly. This evening he was entertaining his bank manager at his house.

"Not wrong. But not exactly right, either."

"Please?"

"There must have been a mistake."

"How—a mistake?"

"About Mr. York telephoning—"

"His secretary telephoned me. This morning. From Zurich."

"Yes, yes, I'm sure he did. But he didn't telephone you about us. There must have been some mistake in the names. I'm afraid we have these rooms on false pretenses."

The assistant manager's English failed him. *"Prego?"*

"We don't know Mr. York. When you spoke to us this morning, I assumed he was a friend of Mrs. Langley's. She thought he must be one of mine. It was only when we were on our way to the Lido that we discovered neither of us knew Mr. York."

The assistant manager relaxed. He could even glance at the clock again. He said gaily, starting to shepherd them to the door of his office, "Ah, it is all a little comedy of errors? But if you like the rooms—"

"They are excellent." The American was standing his ground.

"In that case, what is there to worry about?"

"Two things. First, Mr. York's friends will expect to have these rooms when they arrive."

The assistant manager's dark eyes dropped tactfully. There had been no mistake about the names, he told himself. What was behind all this? "And secondly?" he asked.

The American lowered his voice, spoke with considerable embarrassment. "I'm afraid these rooms will be too expensive for me. I did, you know, book two rooms from Paris yesterday afternoon. I think they'll suit my expense account."

The assistant manager's eyes opened wide. So there was the true explanation. Film stars were lordly and impulsive creatures, but they forgot that their friends' expense accounts rarely measured up to theirs. "In that case," he said, "let me see if your original rooms are still available. One second, please." He picked up his telephone and made contact with the reception desk. There was a sharp volley of rapid Italian. The assistant manager was the winner. He replaced the telephone, eying the clock, and said, "If you will go to the desk, Mr. Fenner, they will be able to help you, I think."

"Thank you," the American said briefly as they left. But then, to be embarrassed, in this way, in front of the beautiful Mrs. Langley did not help any man to be voluble in his expression of gratitude. The assistant manager followed them at a tactful distance, in a thoroughly good humor: so there were some Americans who had to worry about money, too.

"Neat," Claire said, after Fenner had arranged the transfer of rooms at the desk, and they were on their way to remove their possessions from the terrace view.

"Easy," he told her. "All I did was to lose face." It was little enough, he thought grimly. That ought to make them believe our story, even if nothing else does. How much *is* believed, by this time: all the story we have so carefully built up around ourselves, half of it, none of it? Are all our precautions quite useless? If so, we are in a completely comic situation bound for a tragic ending. We shall have as small a chance as poor old Neill Carlson.

"I'm coming in while you pack," he said as they reached her room. She's going to break down again, he thought worriedly, she's really going to let down every guard this time. He closed the door behind them. "Claire!" she was standing at the French windows, looking out on the terrace, seeing hearing nothing. "Claire," he said, coming over to her. She turned to him blindly, and he put his arms around her, holding her closely. He could feel the silent sobs racking through her body. He held her like that, saying nothing, letting the seconds slip away while he kept his arms tightly around her.

She took a deep, steadying breath. "It's my fault." She tried to wipe away the tears with the back of her hand. "He is dead. It's my fault."

"No."

"But it *is*," she cried out. His assignment in Paris was over, she thought in anguish. He was going back to Germany. "He didn't have to come to Venice. He wouldn't have come if I hadn't been here. He wouldn't—"

"He would have," Fenner insisted. He glanced around him worriedly, wondering if some visitor to Tarns's room this afternoon had been able to come in here and plant another of those hellish contraptions to trap their words. So he didn't risk speaking what he wanted her to hear: Neill Carlson had known what was at stake; he had come to Venice for the same reason that Chris Holland was here. More was involved than a letter, or Sandra's escape. Much more. "Believe me, Claire!" he said. "Please believe me."

Claire saw his glance, his worried eyes. She heard the intensity of his voice. And she left her private world of regret and remorse, and came back to reality. She nodded. "I believe you," she said at last. "I'll start packing." Her eyes, too, searched the room quickly. And then they met Fenner's. "All right," she said, "let's get this job finished."

"We'll finish it," he said quietly.

NINETEEN

TWO MEN sat in a darkened room. Outside was the shadowed stillness of a narrow canal threading its cold, black way between the high walls and barred windows of quiet houses toward the warm glow of sunset on the broad and bustling Rialto. But here, in this room, the drawn shutters cut off the distant sounds of life. Here, behind locked doors, Venice was forgotten.

The two men were on board the Simplon Express. They listened to the rattle of its wheels, to the voices of a man and a woman talking happily, clearly audible except when the brakes screeched to give warning of a curve ahead on the railroad track. They might have been sitting in a neighboring room of the sleeping car, with a connecting door left ajar to let them overhear Claire Langley and William Fenner discussing themselves in between filling out details in Customs declarations.

They listened intently. They were both men in their middle forties, obviously affluent by their excellent clothes and careful grooming. One was Fernand Lenoir, dark-haired, tall, thin, with the diplomatic manner, now permanently established even if it was far from natural, of a government official whose career depended on politeness to his equals and deference to his superiors. The other was shorter, more heavily built. His brow was heightened by thinning reddish hair, which had receded in an even line; his face, blunt-featured and broad, was sallow and coarse-skinned, unprepossessing from a close front view—the eyes were small, closely set, clever-quick; the mouth was wide, thin-lipped, determined—but in profile, with the expression lost and only the strong bone structure showing, it could be called handsome. He was a man of many names, many interests, and one ambition.

231

For the last fifteen years he had been known to most people
as Robert Wahl.

Robert Wahl ... Naturalized Frenchman, a clever writer
turned subsidized businessman, with money made in publishing and in radio, and, in recent years, a small but valuable
reputation as an original in the film world. His real name?
Alexei Kalganov, a name that existed more in top-secret
files than on people's tongues. His face had appeared only
twice in print. The first time was in a photograph taken at
a May Day celebration in Moscow when Kalganov had stood
third from the left behind Stalin, and the foreign experts on
Soviet affairs had wondered for four days—until another international crisis had sent them prognosticating in wider fields
—whether this unknown (identified by Tass as an agricultural
expert named Shakhov) would be a rising star in the variable
Russian firmament. The second appearance was in a photograph, highly unauthorized, hastily taken by a Freedom
Fighter in Budapest, of a group of smiling Soviet officials
clustered around a benevolent Mikoyan, with an oversized
tank as appropriate background. (Kalganov's hand had instinctively covered the lower half of his face. He was the
only one in the group to be unidentified. The Freedom
Fighter was arrested and shot that same day.)

Even Fernand Lenoir, who had been working under his
direction as far back as 1944 when Vaugiroud had been
marked for liquidation—an intransigent bourgeois intellectual
who would always rally to any resistance, a potential leader
who must be eliminated with the Nazi retreat—never mentioned the name of Kalganov. Or addressed him as Kalganov. It was an identity he guarded, like the neolithic men
who hunted and fought and died as Running Wolf, Sitting
Bear, Bird-in-the-Grass, but whose real names were kept hidden to give them secret strength, to protect them from their
enemies. Kalganov would have been the first to scoff at reli-
gious superstition, but he clung to the practice of supersecrecy
as the first law of self-preservation; and in this he was not far
removed from those he sneered at. Only in the form of his
self-perpetuation did he differ from those who aimed, by their
deeds, at a Happy Hunting Ground, a Paradise beyond this
life: his deeds, if successful, would be the shaping of history,
and that was something which could never be undone.
He would have his own kind of immortality.

Lenoir rose impatiently. They were coming to the end of

the recorded conversation. "Good night, Claire," the American's voice was saying, *"Mes hommages."* After that, there would only be the interminable sounds of a train, its passengers silenced by sleep, climbing its way up toward Switzerland. Lenoir moved to turn off the machine. "That's all," he said.

"Leave it!"

Lenoir's hand hesitated and stopped. He didn't show his annoyance. He lit a cigarette, and walked around the room, stretching his shoulders. Gold and cream and faded green—the room's elegance was a piece of the past, like the dust-smeared candelabra and the chipped teardrops of the crystal lamps; a place only fit to be rented to some antique-crazy American who has replaced the English as upholders of what was finished and over. Still, it was a strongly built house, well silenced, remote from the busy little streets and square behind it, yet central enough to be useful.

"Keep quiet!" Wahl commanded, and listened intently to a sound track recording the nothings of an empty night journey.

He is always thorough, too thorough, Lenoir thought. A virtue, of course. But does he never become bored with his virtues? Lenoir studied Wahl's expressionless face. Never, he decided. He moved with his crisp step toward the room's communicating door, heavily ornate with late Renaissance panels and tarnished silver handles. He unlocked it quietly and slipped through into the adjoining library, where Sandra was at work. He closed the door gently behind him.

She was sitting at the large writing table, transformed—with a portable typewriter, a bright light, scattered sheets of paper, inks and pens—into an island of efficiency in a sea of high-backed chairs, dim lamps, and ornamented bookcases that reached the painted ceiling. She looked, as she glanced toward him, a little tired. She pushed her glasses up onto her brow. In her plain black dress, sleeves rolled up, bracelets and rings and earrings in a discarded heap near an overfull ash tray, her hair twisted behind her ears, a cardigan over her shoulders to protect her from the damp chill in the air, a pair of white cotton gloves on her hands, she was far removed from the elegant hostesss in Dessès chiffon of only three nights ago. Now she was the efficient and most private secretary, completing the final piece of top-secret work. The last, in every way. Perhaps he should be glad that Wahl had turned up in Venice: let him break the news of her re-call. "You look cold. Why don't you light the fire?"

"I have tried. It smoked. Why don't we have the furnace turned on? Or does it smoke, too?"

"Heating in September? You have still kept some of your American habits, Sandra."

"In July, this place could feel like November. Oh well, I'll soon be finished here—just checking the copies of the letter. You wanted seven in all?" And if he counts them, how am I going to explain the eight copies I've made? But he didn't, and she talked on to distract his attention. "Five for the men you meet today, and two for your pet neutralists. When do you see them?"

"Tomorrow. Is this the original letter?" He stretched out his hand to pick it up.

"Careful!" She lifted it with her gloved fingers. "I'll hold it, while you read."

"It looks very good," he said with real pleasure. "You notice I placed the main emphasis on the Americans, making the English more of a go-between. The style is just right, don't you think?"

"It could be the wine merchant himself. How do you like his signature?"

"Most authentic. You would have made an excellent forger, Sandra."

You've given me enough practice, she thought.

He had a criticism, of course. "The type jumps a little."

"It's Trouin's own typewriter, isn't it? If it jumps, it jumps."

"So typical of him to tolerate the imperfect."

"I hope he hasn't discovered it's missing." Carefully, she laid the perfectly faked original on the desk before her.

"No more than he noticed the missing sheets of his writing paper. He was too busy preparing to leave for Switzerland."

"How did you borrow the typewriter? Bribe or make love to his secretary? Or was it stolen by a cleaning woman?"

He joined in her laughter, without much humor. "You must not pry out all my little secrets. Actually—it was very simple."

"You're too modest, Fernand." That pleased him and brought real warmth to his face. "It's a brilliant idea. I just hope this sheet of Trouin's writing paper has at least one sample of his fingerprints."

"I can assure you it has. You've been very careful with it?"

"Didn't take the gloves off once. Let's finish this job. I'd like to see the original safely in its envelope, just in case anyone is forgetful enough to pick it up without gloves. If it's spoiled, we are out of luck. Completely."

"I gave you three sheets of his writing paper," he said sharply.

"I had to destroy two. The signature wasn't good enough," she lied most innocently. "I don't think much of the type of nib that our wine merchant likes to use. It's too soft."

"Typical," Lenoir said. He was still annoyed.

"When does he commit suicide?"

Lenoir stared at her, forgetting nibs and two wasted sheets of paper. "You know, Sandra, you really are indiscreet at times."

"Only with you, darling." Her blue eyes were large and sad. "You used to enjoy my little jokes."

"This is hardly the time for any joke."

"Especially when it hits on the truth."

"Sandra!" he said quietly, warningly. He glanced at the door to the sitting room.

"Oh, forget it," she said wearily. She pulled her glasses back in place, not caring how she looked. "Shall I fold the original in three, or does Trouin usually quarter his letters?" She had lifted the letter again, studying Trouin's embossed letterhead across its top. She noticed Lenoir's second glance at the connecting door. "This is *your* department, Fernand. Isn't it?"

"Yes. But Wahl will insist on seeing the letter."

"Did he bring gloves?" She was half laughing.

Lenoir made a gesture of impatience.

"Too bad. He will just have to read one of the copies. You don't supervise his work. Why should you let him interfere with yours?"

Lenoir looked at her quickly. Her face was as expressionless as her voice.

"What's he doing now?" she asked.

"Listening to a recording."

"Oh!" She shrugged. "How shall I fold this letter? In three? Or four?"

"In three." That was Trouin's custom. He watched her fold the sheet most carefully, and search for the two envelopes she had addressed, one long, one square in shape.

She chose the long one. It looked as if it had been handled, crushed in a pocket. "I managed to get plenty of finger marks on this, all untraceable, I hope. You'd better destroy the

other one, Fernand. You'll find matches over on the table
by that red velvet chair."

"You are remarkably thorough," he told her, taking the
discarded envelope over to the fireplace. He studied its
typed address: Major Christopher Holland, Paris 6°, Boulevard Raspail, Hotel Saint-Denis. "Yes, we'd better get rid of
this."

She talked on in the same light voice. Adroitly, she slipped
the original under a box of carbon paper, picked up one of
the copies and folded it silently, inserting it into the long
envelope. "I suppose you can explain why there was no
postmark? That may be the one weak point."

"Not so weak. The letter was intercepted before it could
be mailed." He cursed quietly. "The matches are damp."

They ought to be, she thought grimly. She said, "Oh,
everything is damp around here. I don't know how these
books survive." Her fingers trembled on the long envelope
she had just sealed. "Try my lighter." She reached for her
handbag, placing it beside the box of carbon paper. She
opened it, searched inside with one hand. With the other, she
slipped the original out of its hiding place into her bag.
She snapped it shut.

"These matches are useless!" Lenior exploded as the third
one flared and died.

"Here's the lighter," she said, bringing it to him.

I really shall miss her, he thought. I have come to depend
on her a great deal. That wasn't good, of course. That could
be the reason she was being recalled. "It's all right," he said,
striking another match. Yes, he was being disciplined more
than she was. It was Wahl's way of reminding him who held
the power. The idea displeased him. He frowned angrily.

"Wouldn't this be quicker?" she asked, holding out the
lighter. He will begin to realize I dampened those matches,
she thought anxiously.

"It's all right," he told her sharply, and the match, miracu-
lously, flared and caught. The envelope curled slowly into black
tissue. Once the address was destroyed, he dropped it into
the fireplace and ground it into dust with his foot. "Where's
the original?" he asked, excessively efficient now, avoiding her eyes. Quickly, he skirted the heavy armchairs and
reached the writing table, pushed her handbag aside and
picked up the sealed envelope. He pointed to seven copies.
"Better get them into envelopes, too," he said as he crossed
over to a wall of bookcases.

She came back to her chair, and as she sat down again she felt her legs tremble for a brief moment. She dropped her handbag back on the floor and began folding the copies. She didn't look at Lenoir. She could hear him swinging open three bogus shelves to reach the wall-safe behind them. It was part of the Ca' Longhi furnishings, to match the heavy inch-wide bars on the downstairs windows and the huge bolts on the doors. The Longhi family must have been almost as security-minded as Fernand, she thought. That was why he had chosen to rent this hideous place. No garden, or terrace; just thick walls rising at the junction of two canals, one big, one small. The main entrance was on the dreary little canal, with slimy steps to reach the massive, nail-studded door. And at the back of the huge house, two more doors equally sturdy: one leading into a street so narrow and shadowed that even Fernand had joked about an assassin's lane; the other opening into a small square with flagstones uneven and tilting and the surrounding houses so covered with cracked and stripped plaster that they seemed to be sinking, too. And let's not forget the washing, she reminded herself, strung out from windows: all our neighbors' nightshirts and underpants. Venice. . . . She began sealing the letters, angrily. She felt cheated. Venice could be so many things, and she had been given its worst for her last few days.

"I know what happened to the Longhi family," she said, sealing the fourth envelope. "They all died of galloping consumption. I'm chilled to the bone. What about setting the dining room on fire to get some warmth into these walls?"

Lenoir was smiling as he turned away from the safe and swung the bookshelves back into place. Quickly, the smile vanished. Coldly, he said, "The Longhi clan? Bourgeois capitalists adopting the trappings of feudalism. Twice damned, my dear Sandra. Their death was merely a matter of historical inevitability: the self-elimination of the obsolete."

I know who has just come in, she told herself. She forced herself to glance up casually. Robert Wahl stood just inside the room. Everything he does, she thought angrily, is for an effect. Can't he enter a room normally? We are supposed to be his friends. Friends? No, we are his comrades. His behavior is correct. For comrades. Eternal distrust, hidden faces, smothered voices. Comrades. How bitter I have become, she thought as she watched the man who had made her bitter. She wished, suddenly, she were eight years younger, filled with hope and belief. There had been rapture and excitement eight years ago, lifting, sustaining. . . . The worst thing I ever did was to leave America: I would still have been a good Communist if I had stayed there, happily drugged with my hopes and beliefs that were never put to the real test. But here in Europe, I was promoted. I met the elite group, the gray eminence behind the commissar's chair. And hopes have been replaced by fears. Beliefs are tortured ghosts haunting every waking hour, driving me back. Back to a new beginning? Shall I find it in America? Probably not. It will be enough if I can stop fearing.

Robert Wahl said nothing. He walked over to the desk, picked up one of the unsealed copies, read it—Fernand dancing attendance, explaining that the original was locked safely away, all under control, everything according to plan. Oh shut up, Fernand, just *tell* him and stop accusing yourself! And she looked at Wahl and she was pleading, silently, "Give me back those eight years." Aloud, she said, "Good evening, Comrade Wahl."

"So punctilious?" he asked. "And very busy, I see." His eyes noted everything, even the little heap of jewelry on the table. "You do act your part, Sandra. A most efficient secretary."

"I hope so," she said, with marked modesty.

He let the copy fall, drift back onto the table. "When you have finished, please come into the next room," he told her. The smile was as meaningless as his "please."

She nodded, and went on with her work. The two men left, Fernand casting a look over his shoulder that told her quite plainly, "And no more jokes!"

Strange, she thought, as she cleared the table, pulled off her gloves and straightened her sleeves, fastened her jewelry in place again, strange that I seem to make so many bitter jokes nowadays. Because when I lived in America, and had my hopes and beliefs and paid my dues and did what I was told, I never made any jokes at all. That was one of the things Bill used to tease me about: no sense of humor. Perhaps I ought to be grateful to Wahl and Fernand and all those others—in Czechoslovakia, Moscow, East Germany —for one thing at least: developing a sense of humor in me, even if it is sour. She picked up her handbag to find a comb and her powder box. From the drawer of the writing table, she drew out the folded map of Venice she had placed there carefully that morning. She slipped it into her opened bag, seemingly searching for her lipstick as her fingers inserted the letter deep and safe, into the map's fold. She colored her lips with a bold red, closed her handbag (the map looked innocuous), slung it over her forearm nonchalantly. She gathered up the little bundle of seven envelopes with seven copies of Fernand's masterpiece. I'm ready, she thought as she went toward the connecting door. What have they been discussing, those two? Me, no doubt.

Yes.

"I'm going to miss Sandra," Fernand Lenoir had begun. And regretted his frankness. So he qualified his regret. "She has been useful in many ways. Why don't you trust her?"

"Because she cannot be trusted," Robert Wahl told him shortly, and left it there. The full answer was, "Because anyone who could betray her country, as she has done for fourteen years, could betray us, too." But he couldn't give the blunt truth: Lenoir was in the same category—a Frenchman who worked for Soviet Russia. That was something these people never understood: no matter how well they work there was always that initial stain of treason, recorded deep in the memories of those who had to work with them. All was grist for the mill; but the mill separated the wheat from the chaff.

Lenoir felt the silent criticism emanating from the small, sharp eyes. That had been a mistake to ask why she wasn't trusted, a dangerous error. He, working so closely with her, ought to have been the first to become suspicious. "I only asked to see if your reason coincided with mine."

"You don't trust Comrade Fane either?" Wahl asked smoothly.

"Recently—well, she is too restless, too cynical. Paris has been bad for her." He paused, phrasing a tactful denunciation which would not be marked permanently against him, in case Sandra's rehabilitation in Moscow's purer air might even set her over him at some future date. "It is an unsettling place for those who do not belong there." As I do. And he looked at Wahl.

"Only temporarily unsettling, we hope. The role she played, these last three years, brought her into contact with our enemies. They have been sympathetic, admiring. Her vanity is inflated. Very dangerous. Her judgment is not as detached as it once was. Life has become too soft, too pleasant. Weakening."

"Yes, I've felt that she was forgetting the realities of the situation. In fact, I had prepared a report on her behavior, but it's hardly necessary now."

"Why?"

"Well—your report to Moscow must have covered all my points."

"No doubt. Still, I would like to read them. You would see the development of her deterioration more closely than most."

"You'll have that report." He could write it late tonight. Denunciation must be firm, tempered with sadness over the falling from grace, with hope for quick and complete rehabilitation. That should cover every possibility: past, present, and future.

"How much have you told her in this last week?"

"Only the necessary. No more than that."

"You placed that letter in the safe yourself?"

"Of course."

"Its signature is completely adequate?"

"It is practically authentic." Lenoir was becoming impatient. "I hope everything else goes as well," he said pointedly. Not one compliment about the wording of the letter, not one small admission of its excellence.

"I hope so, too," Wahl murmured with ironic modesty.

It was one of the little habits he had adopted in the West. It irritated Lenoir: the tone of voice was wrong, the smile unnecessary. Wahl's subtleties lay in a different sphere. Lenoir looked at the machine still lying on the table at Wahl's elbow. "Did you find anything remarkable in the rest of the journey?"

"Fenner never returned to Langley's room."

"You seem surprised." And I could have told you that. I listened to a quick run-through of all three recorded wires this morning. The only part worth slowing down to hear was at the beginning of the second wire, an hour of talk between ten and eleven last night. The rest— Lenoir shrugged at the waste of three precisely timed microphones. He allowed himself a touch of sarcasm. "The girl fell asleep. That does happen, you know."

"But does an American give up so easily? Was he aware that they were being recorded? If so, this was an excellent plan to guard their tongues."

Lenoir heard the library door open behind him. "Sandra can tell you more about Fenner's love-making than I can."

"Come in!" Wahl said. She had halted at the sneer in Lenoir's voice. Stupid pig, Wahl thought, he has warned her. Damn all those clever Frenchmen; they can't resist the right tone of voice at the wrong time. "Come in, Sandra, we need your advice. Sit over there. I am going to play a little recording for you. It was made last night. On a train. Listen!" She nodded, handed the envelopes to Lenoir, took the chair opposite Wahl. He turned on the machine, watching her face. Into the quiet room came the sound of a door opening, a man's voice (distant, blurred) saying, "See you in five minutes. I'll get those forms. And a nightcap." The door rattled shut. Movements and rustle and a sighing yawn.

Sandra Fane waited patiently, obediently, conscious of Wahl's eyes. Lenoir was restless. And at last, there was the sound of a door opening, closing. A woman's voice welcomed the man with "Darling, how wonderful..."

Sandra's eyes widened. Could that be Claire Langley? And the man answering her—yes, that was Bill Fenner. She let an amused smile lift one corner of her mouth, raised her eyebrows slightly. Wahl motioned abruptly for silence, for attention. And he kept watching her. At last, the voices ended. There was nothing but the rhythm and rattle of the hurrying train.

Lenoir glanced covertly at his watch. It was half past six. He had two more men to see this evening—the Roman newspaperman, then Mike Ballard. He would have to snatch a bite to eat in between these appointments: Ballard would need careful handling—that unexpected return to Paris yesterday, and the quarrel with Spitzer raised new difficulties. Still, he could be handled. He was the fish that was hooked but had to be played carefully before he could be gaffed and netted. After that, there was the final co-ordination of his story, and the report on Sandra to write. She was losing interest, now, in the steady pounding of train wheels. Wahl was listening intently. Lenoir wondered at his infinite patience.

Wahl switched off the machine. "Et cetera, et cetera," he said lightly. He was pleased. He looked at them both and smiled. "That was the most important part of the whole recording." And as both of them kept silent, he added, "Because, *if* their whole conversation had been a performance, if there had been no black nightdress, no attack of sleep—" he paused for emphasis—"that was the time, once Fenner had left her, for the Langley woman to prepare for bed and lock her door. There was a slight rustle, I thought, but it stopped. Not enough to explain any undressing. Possibly she was turning in her sleep."

Lenoir sat corrected. Sandra looked at the emerald on her third finger. So Rosenfeld had sent not only Fenner, but Claire Langley with him. Rosenfeld had taken her seriously, that was certain. She almost sighed in relief. She studied the deep green of her ring: how much would it bring her?

Wahl said, watching her, "Does your ex-husband sound quite natural?"

She looked up at him, openly amazed. "Really—" She shrugged her shoulders. "I haven't seen him in eight years. I'm no longer any judge—"

"But from your memory of him?"

"He is interested in Claire Langley definitely—for the next few weeks."

Lenoir glanced at her sharply. Could she be jealous? There had been a touch of the cat's claw there.

"Would he have let you fall asleep?" Wahl insisted.

Lenoir said, "Sandra is not the type to fall asleep."

"I am serious!" Wahl warned them. "Answer me, Sandra."

"It would depend on his mood," she said evasively.

"Was he impulsive about women?"

"It's eight years—look, I haven't been following his career."

"When did he meet this woman?"

"I've no idea."

"Not in New York then?"

"He could have met her there. It has been eight years—"

"So we've heard," Wahl said sharply. "You knew her in New York?"

"Yes."

"Her politics?"

Sandra could smile. "Politically immature."

"Why did you invite her to your parties?"

"She came with a friend from the British Embassy."

"You had no suspicions about her?"

"Why should I? She's one of those ornamental girls without a notion of politics."

"You once gave that same appearance, my dear Sandra, when you first lived in New York." He studied her with cold eyes. "So she accepted your story in Paris. How?"

"She asked the same polite questions that everyone asked, and I gave the same sincere, sad answer. It was all part of my return to the West."

"Did you ever think, or feel, that she could be possibly working for American Intelligence?"

"Langley?" Sandra looked amused. "She is totally brainless. Of course, that might be a recommendation for the CIA to pick her."

Lenoir was smiling. "Not altogether brainless. She holds an important job as a designer. Spitzer sent me a report—"

"That's merely being artistic," Sandra cut in. "Since when did either of you credit artists with brain power?"

"True," Wahl said, "but what did Spitzer report?"

"Her firm is completely legitimate. She heads its European branch, lives in Paris. Spitzer tells me that Fenner stayed at her flat on Friday night.

"Does she have many visitors? And who?"

"There hasn't been time to check on the details of her life in Paris. Spitzer reports she is a widow. Her husband was killed in Saigon. In 1953."

"Langley." Wahl was searching his memory. "James Langley. Yes, I remember." What he remembered did not please him. "There was an investigation, a very close investigation." Too close, he thought. That newspaper report with his name boldly printed . . . What was the name of the CIA man who had leaked Kalganov to the press? Rennie. Frank Rennie, a so-called businessman. He had known Langley's widow. Yes, they had become friends. . . . "So," he said pleasantly, aware that Sandra and Lenoir were watching him curiously, "you found nothing that puzzled you in the train conversation?"

Sandra said, "The only puzzle was that you should have been interested in those two."

"Indeed." He half smiled. To Lenoir, he said "And Fenner?"

"We've checked his movements since he arrived in Paris. There are explanations and reasons for all of them. Still, he could be a very clever operator. The girl is harmless, I think. But he may be dangerous."

Sandra Fane was aware of Wahl's eyes on her face. Were his ears as quick? Had he heard the missed beat in her heart? "Bill Fenner?" She began to laugh. "Bill as an agent of the CIA?"

"Or Military Intelligence. Carlson was seen at his hotel."

"With him?" she asked in alarm.

"They both left the Crillon on Friday evening about the same time."

"Together?" Sandra's heart missed a second beat. Stupid, stupid fools.

Wahl did not answer that.

"Not exactly," Lenoir said. "We can't be sure though. That is the trouble with Fenner. We can't be sure of anything about him. Did he intercept the money? Or was the exchanged coat a completely innocent mistake? I'm inclined to think it wasn't—"

"Perhaps you are inclined to read too much into his actions," Wahl said coldly. "There is no room in our work for emotions." He looked angrily at Sandra Fane. Had she thought she would safeguard herself by making Lenoir fall in love with her? Yes, it was time for her to be disciplined. Did she guess what he was thinking? For she had turned pale. She was sitting too still.

Sandra recovered herself. "What's this—about the coat and the money?" She asked Lenoir, "Do you mean Fenner was there when the money disappeared at Orly?"

"It was his coat that was exchanged with Goldsmith's."

She stared at him. And I had to choose Fenner as my contact in Venice, she thought: I had to suggest his name to Rosenfeld. This time, she couldn't control her laughter. This time, it was real. It pealed on, and on, uncontrolled, uncontrollable.

Wahl raised his voice. "Stop that! Stop it!" Was the idea of Fenner as an Intelligence agent so absurd? "This is no time for hysteria," he said acidly, well aware that Lenoir was as startled by her outburst as he had been. She was not a woman who behaved like this normally. Yet the laughter was normal in the sense that it was natural, unpretended. She had not been acting; of that, he was sure. He rose and crossed quickly to where she sat. She got control of herself. She opened her handbag and searched for her handkerchief to wipe the tears of laughter from her eyes. Her fingers touched the map, and the thought of its contents—of her careful plans and calculated risks, of Rosenfeld seeking out Fenner at her suggestion, Fenner the natural suspect for the master of suspicion now standing over her—set her laughing once more. Wahl struck a smart blow at her cheek. There was a sudden silence, ended by the snap of her handbag as she closed it.

Lenoir was saying indignantly, "I see nothing comic in my remark, Sandra."

"But you do not know Fenner as she does," Wahl said thoughtfully. "Have today's reports come in yet?"

"There was nothing in them."

"Let me see them."

Lenoir left the room. Wahl sat down again, pulling his cuff back into place.

Sandra Fane was rubbing her cheek. "What has gone wrong, Comrade Wahl?"

He stared at her. "Nothing. All is in order."

"But why are you worrying so much about Fenner and Claire Langley? I thought Venice was to be a place where we could wait safely until the Big Bang went off."

"We do not need flippancy."

"Just a circumlocution. In case," she was smiling, "Bill Fenner has installed a microphone in this room."

"You take this too lightly, I think."

One could never tell, she thought, how this man would react. She had been wrong, there, to joke about Fenner. "No," she said quickly, seriously, "I am worried."

"Why?"

"Because you are."

"Very sympathetic of you." From sardonic irony, he passed to outright challenge. "But perhaps *your* mistakes are really the cause of your worry?"

"Mistakes?"

"Such as sending the gondola that belongs to the Ca' Longhi to pick up Sir Felix Tarns today. Was that necessary?"

"He—he expected it," she said weakly. "Last spring we sent the gondola for him. He assumed—" Her eyes turned thankfully to the door, to watch Lenoir's return.

"He assumes too much. Pamper his vanity, yes—but not when it could endanger this house. That was a very foolish, a very stupid mistake. We pay for his hotel. Let him pay for his own transportation." He took the two sheets of paper that Lenoir held out to him. "Is this all?"

"My condensed notes," Lenoir explained.

Wahl glanced down the page. He pursed his lips. "Sir Felix thinks they are two simple-minded Americans. That almost makes me believe they are as clever as I thought they might be." He read on. "Nothing much here," he conceded. "No contact with anyone except the gondolier—who is this Zorzi?"

"Just a gondolier who knew the girl from a previous visit. He offered them a ride, but they were going to the Lido—"

"I can read. So"—he turned the page—"they are planning to hire his gondola tonight? At ten."

"That was too openly discussed to be significant."

Wahl said nothing, read on. "No contacts at all. Completely absorbed in each other," he observed. Then he saw something that really impressed him. "Aarvan says that Fenner showed no sign whatsoever of recognition." But he didn't like the way they had to run for a bus and refused his taxi. Or the way they had left the Lido by motorboat before they could be followed. He read those items aloud, interspersed with his own opinions on stupidity. "And what's so funny about that?" he asked Sandra Fane sharply, catching her off guard.

She rallied quickly. "It's all so normal. If a bus is leaving, you have to run for it. And why take a taxi for the few blocks to the Excelsior?" She couldn't tell whether this suggestion was accepted. A bigger furrow was gathering on his brow as he read the last item on Lenoir's report sheet.

"So they changed their rooms, did they? Too expensive—" He rose abruptly, and swore.

"That sounds the truth," Sandra said. "Fenner isn't a rich man. And his expense account from the *Chronicle* wouldn't keep Fernand in shirts. It's just as I told you: he is—" She flinched as Wahl turned on her, stood looking down at her. And so she changed her tactics. "Oh, why don't you get rid of him and save all this argument? You are wasting time, Comrade Wahl."

Lenoir agreed. "One call to Aarvan, and this problem would be solved."

"And create a bigger problem for ourselves? Perhaps needlessly? For the next twenty-four hours, we do not want any more violence. Nothing to stir up the Venetian police—so far, we have broken no Italian law. And as for our other opponents—they have no idea that I am in Venice. Or that Aarvan is here."

"They know I am here," Lenoir said worriedly. "That is no secret."

"They don't know this address. And what could they possibly have against you? Nothing. You had no connection with the bombing of the Café Racine. Or with the American's death on the Simplon Express."

"Why did Aarvan have to—" Lenoir began.

"Carlson was an Intelligence agent much too interested in Robert Wahl. He was also much too interested in Aarvan. He had to be eliminated for our safety. Just as Vaugiroud and Roussin had to be eliminated for your safety, my friend." He looked pointedly at Lenoir, reminding him of an assignment in 1944 that had not been properly finished. "You are needed in France. We have spent too many years in establishing you there to let anything destroy you now."

Lenoir nodded. He had no more criticisms.

"And so, Fenner's death would certainly cause us more trouble than it's worth. Unless he threatened our safety, of course. I don't think he can. Not for the next twenty-four hours, at least. And that is all that matters."

Twenty-four hours? Sandra's mind groped for an explanation.

"One more day is all we need," Wahl said quietly.

"You mean—" she began, and couldn't finish.

"We are ready, aren't we? The longer we wait, the greater the danger. So I have moved our timetable forward."

Lenoir's eyes were brilliant with excitement. He couldn't resist saying to Sandra, "You see why we worked so hard today?"

Wahl silenced him with a sharp gesture. He made the announcement himself. "The assassination will take place tomorrow evening as De Gaulle leaves Paris for his country house. I saw Trouin in Zurich last night. I had him make the telephone call to Montpellier to give the signal to his friends, who have been waiting there for the last two days. They are, at this very minute, en route to Paris. Separately."

Sandra Fane's mind went completely blank. And then it raced madly along on its own train of thought, while she sat calmly smiling. Tomorrow was Monday, the day she had chosen to meet Fenner in the Piazza San Marco. Tomorrow evening. Tomorrow. Dimly, in the background of her crumbling hopes, she was aware of Lenoir's anxious questions about Trouin, the go-between, the man who knew them. Vaguely she heard Wahl's impatient reassurances: Trouin's bank account was swollen by a hundred-thousand-dollar check; Trouin's suicide would be staged at the time of the publication of the letter, with Major Holland's supposed reply; and Trouin's friend the industrialist would not return from his vacation in Spain. But there was one thing that worried Wahl, and that was Lenoir's story about the interception of Trouin's letter to Holland. He wanted it altered.

That brought Sandra out of her half-attention. "Altered?" So he was finding some excuse to look at the original letter.

"It is inadequate."

"What?" asked Lenoir indignantly. "It's excellent."

"Your present story, Fernand, is that you were much perturbed by the American backing of the Generals' Revolt last April in Algeria; that you had heard rumors of Trouin's connections with American and British agents which aroused your suspicions; that you arranged to meet him casually at a small restaurant; that you came away from that meeting with your suspicions increased; that you hired a detective to watch him and make contacts in his office; that one of those contacts, a secretary, intercepted a letter on Friday just before it was mailed—the address made her suspicious; that your detective sent this letter to you in Venice; that you decided it ought to be turned over to the Sûreté but, just as you were telephoning Paris, the news of the assassination came through."

"And what's wrong with that story? Within a week, I don't think any questions will be asked at all. That is the great advantage of victory: those who win can write the history books."

Were they so sure of victory? Sandra wondered. They must be strong to speak so confidently. How many years had Wahl planned for such a complete take-over? Dismay attacked her; she felt new doubts, a sense of stupidity. I've chosen the losing side, she thought bitterly. I threw everything away in one small mistake. I thought that Wahl had overstepped his authority, that his ambition would be disciplined, that, as a Stalinist and Leftist opportunist, his days were shortening. They will be, if he fails: he will be disowned, denounced, recalled, sent to Mongolia or the Arctic in some minor job. But if he produces a *fait accompli*? It will be called the inevitability of history. It will be accepted; his methods will be ignored. And he will be a hero of the revolution.

Wahl was repeating, "It is inadequate. It would seem that either your detective delayed in sending the letter to you or that you delayed in calling the Sûreté."

"I can explain the delay—a matter of embarrassment that a hired detective went far beyond my instructions and actually intercepted—"

Wahl was deeply amused. "Always the gentleman, Fernand. In that case, you will like my suggestion: your detective photographed the letter in Trouin's office, and sent you the negative of the film. You needed time to have it developed. And in this way, no explanation will be needed."

"And the letter itself?" Lenoir asked.

Sandra Fane kept her face calm, but interested. As she

should be. Wahl was watching her. Stay out of this discussion, her instinct warned her.

"I shall send it to Paris tonight, and have it placed in Major Holland's hotel room. The Sûreté will discover it there."

"But Holland?" Lenoir objected.

"He is away for the weekend. The English habits are ingrained."

"Leaving the letter behind him?"

"Leaving it very safely concealed. You wouldn't expect him to travel with it?"

"It's a good idea," Lenoir admitted slowly, "but it's a big job. If I were in Paris, I would have reliable help to photograph the letter, develop the film. Here? We'd have to do it ourselves." His resentment grew. Everything had been perfect. Why had this change to be made? "And all Sandra's typed copies will be useless. We'll need prints to distribute, won't we? And we can't let the letter leave for Paris until we are sure the prints are clear."

Sandra said nothing at all. Clever, clever Wahl, she was thinking: he wants to see the original letter. He wants it out of the safe, and into his own hands. For a moment, she almost abdicated everything was lost, not only escape, but life itself. She almost opened her handbag and drew out the map; almost said, "Here is what you want, Comrade Kalganov."

"Any objections, Sandra?" Wahl asked.

I won't give up my life so easily, she thought. "None. It will be a lot of extra trouble, but we can do it—if we work all evening."

"Sandra!" Lenoir said. "You know I can't—"

"We've been trained for this kind of job," she told him. "It's only a matter of time. We have the equipment and the supplies."

"You know that I—"

"You could manage it if you started work on it right away."

"I have two appointments," Lenoir said in rising anger.

"You can cancel them.' Her voice sharpened, too.

"Impossible!" he exploded. "I must see these men tonight, and you know that!"

She stormed back, "I can't do this job alone. I'm willing to work all night, if necessary, if Comrade Wahl wants the letter treated his way—"

"Not," said Wahl, breaking into the argument, "to the point of having you two quarrel about it." He looked at Lenoir. "That was scarcely your diplomatic best."

Lenoir's thin face flushed. "Sandra," he said severely, regaining control of the situation, "there was no need to scream at me."

"I'm sorry." Her voice was still on edge. "I'm tired. You know that. I've been chained to that damned desk all day."

"*All* day?"

"Most of it," she snapped back. Lenoir was completely silenced this time: his eyes were childlike in their astonishment. She waited, thinking, I have given Wahl his cue: will he use it, will he tell me that I obviously need a vacation, a sea voyage? Or a nice trip by plane? Let him tell me, she willed: I have to know what time I have left, what I can plan. I'm fighting for my life. At least, I made a point there, and Wahl has taken it: I do not seem to be afraid of having the safe opened, the envelope taken out, the exchange noticed; and he has dropped his suggestion, his bright little idea to interfere and check and probe. He has his instincts, this man: he feels something is wrong. And he is searching. Attack and retreat, that was his technique to confuse and frighten. He has retreated about the letter. Now he is going to attack again. But even if my nerves are at snapping point, I still have enough control left to seize a small advantage, to avoid a definite danger: my instincts are as good as his. We are well matched. Beside us, Fernand—who is the most brilliant man I have ever met, more intelligent than this clever animal opposite me—is stupid and slow thinking. He hasn't sensed yet that I have made him look as if he were the one who did not want the envelope opened. For a split second, she had the vision of getting rid of the letter in her bag by slipping it into one of Fernand's suitcases: the fleeting idea amused her. Generously, she smiled at Lenoir. "I am sorry, Fernand. I was not complaining. Can't I be tired—just a little?"

Wahl said slowly, as if she had left the room, "Sandra is worrying too much. She needs a rest. A change of air. There is a ship sailing from here—a pleasant voyage through the Corinth Canal, the Greek islands, to Istanbul." He paused. "And to Odessa." He paused again. "Sandra will sail on it. Tomorrow morning at eight. From the Giudecca."

"Tomorrow morning?" Her voice faltered. She looked at Lenoir, who avoided her eyes. "Hasn't my work pleased you?"

The telephone rang. Lenoir jumped to his feet. "I'll take the call next door," he said. "And put these safely away." He lifted the seven envelopes, and hurried from the room.

"My dear Sandra," Wahl said, "your recall is in no way a reprimand. It will lead to promotion." He watched her carefully. "Don't you want to return to Russia?"

"It's—it's just so unexpected."

There was no doubt of her blank astonishment, numbed shock. Wahl was well pleased. We'll have her safely on board before she realizes all the implications, he thought. "I think you should leave here when it's dark. Around midnight."

Tonight. Leave tonight . . . She could only stare at him.

"There will be a motorboat waiting for you at the canal door. Twelve o'clock. You will be ready?"

She nodded. Lenoir had returned to the room. She looked down at the emerald ring. I have until midnight, she was thinking. Until midnight.

Wahl was asking Lenoir about the call. It had been a report on a brief conversation between Fenner and Langley in her terrace room at the Vittoria. "Nothing very much," Lenoir judged. "The girl was very upset about some other man. I've given orders to stop watching them. We are wasting our—"

"Upset?" Wahl asked quickly. That was always a vulnerable time. "Did you make a transcript?"

"Of course." Lenoir handed over a few scrawled sentences. Wahl frowned over them.

"A lover's quarrel, perhaps," Lenoir suggested.

"As meaningless as most," Wahl agreed. Who didn't have to come to Venice? he wondered. Who wouldn't have—if it hadn't been for Claire Langley? Whose death was her fault? Death. Had she known Carlson? If only we had time to check on all her past history, he thought. "I'll take this with me," he said, pocketing the piece of paper. "I must leave. The gondola is waiting?"

"For the last hour. But that's quite usual in Venice."

"And it isn't your private gondola," he told Sandra, smiling. He patted her shoulder. "My congratulations. And a very pleasant journey."

Congratulations? On the promotion he had dangled before her? She could have struck these smirking lips. "Good-by, Comrade Kalganov," she said. He stopped, looked at her, his face frozen for one brief instant. Then he was walking to the door, his arm around Lenoir's shoulders. They were talking of other matters.

"She took it very well," Lenoir remarked as they went

down the curving sweep of grand staircase into the dark, flagstoned hall.

"Just treat her normally. Keep her calm. Arouse no animosity. Women have long claws."

"She'll give no trouble," Lenoir assured him.

"I wish we could say the same for that American newspaperman, Ballard. I thought it was rash of you, Fernand, to bring him to Venice."

"Not too rash. He tried to discharge André Spitzer yesterday. So I have no choice. I had to make direct personal contact with him. Don't worry, Robert. I know how to approach that type of man."

"It might help if Aarvan were to make the first approach, so that by the time you see Ballard tonight, he would be more—malleable. At least you would know what to expect from him. If he is totally intransigent with Aarvan, I would advise you do not see him at all. We'll deal with him."

"All right. But you had better tell Aarvan to contact him at once. He is staying at the Danieli."

"I know. I have already told Aarvan to keep an eye on him." Wahl's smile was disarming. "By the way, I may need one of your attic rooms, with a strongly shuttered window. Someplace where we could keep a guest tomorrow evening?"

"Who?" Lenoir was still annoyed with Wahl's interference in the handling of Ballard.

"Fenner's little friend. That should immobilize them both for the next twenty-four hours, quietly, efficiently."

"Quietly? He will go to the police—"

"He will not. Because if he does, he will never see her again. He will be so informed."

"I don't like this—"

"She will never know where she was held, or who was her host. Instruct a servant to guard her room. That's all you have to do. *You* keep out of sight."

"But how—"

"I shall make the arrangements."

Lenoir stared at him. There was no arguing with Wahl in this mood. What had he against this girl?

"That terrace room at the Vittoria would have made everything simpler," Wahl was saying, "but there are other means. Expect her some time after ten o'clock. By the canal door. Don't worry. Just keep out of her sight and hearing."

They had been talking quietly in the center of the round

hall. Now Wahl moved toward the door that opened on the
narrow street, picking up his coat and hat from a chair.

"This way," Lenoir said, pointing to the door that led out
onto the canal.

"I shan't use the gondola. It has waited too long."

"As you wish." Strange man; I shall never know him,
Lenoir was thinking as he followed Wahl across the stone
floor and between the pillars that circled the hall. Suddenly,
he felt alone. Without Sandra, he would be very alone. "Do
you really think that Fenner and Claire Langley are dangerous?" he tried.

Wahl only shrugged his shoulders. He opened the door
slightly, and listened. "I am making sure that they won't be.
That is all." He looked out into the small, narrow street,
sadly lighted by one lamp placed high on a far corner wall.
"Cats," he said contemptuously, as shadows stirred and
snarled to defend the food they had found in a black doorway, "cats and cold spaghetti." He glanced back at Lenoir.
"I may send Aarvan to question the girl," he said softly. He
pulled his hat well over his brow, turned up the collar of his
coat, and stepped into the night. He walked quickly along
the narrow *calle*, past the shuttered windows, still and dark.
The cats were silent again.

Lenoir closed the heavy door. Strange man . . . He had
walked in the direction of the canal, after all. Had he some
other gondola or motorboat waiting for him? He trusts no
one, Lenoir thought. Not even me?

The cats snarled, and two men in a darkened ground-floor
room were sharply alert. Through the inch-wide crack of
shutter, two pairs of eyes watched a man leave the Ca' Longhi.
When he had passed, only an arm's length away, one of them
moved carefully over to a telephone. His voice was low,
English. "Gino? Roger here. Unidentified man just left. Hat
pulled down. Dark coat, collar turned up. About five feet
six. Weight around thirteen stone. That's right, solid construc-
tion but light on his feet. Proceeding toward the canal. You'll
pick him up at the bridge." He put down the receiver.

"Will they?" his companion asked. His voice also was low,
but American. "Listen!" The roar of a motorboat was fun-
neled along the little *calle*, and receded.

American and Englishman both cursed softly.

"Slippery beggar, whoever he was," the Englishman said.
He made his way back to the window. "Any guesses?"

"We didn't see him enter. Must have been there before we got here. That's a long time."

"He sounds important. A motorboat waiting, ready to leave at high speed. Most illegal. The Gondoliers' Association will disapprove."

"Sounds like Wahl," the American said gloomily, "but he is in Switzerland." They settled into boredom again, to wait for the next visitor to Ca' Longhi.

Lenoir locked and bolted the heavy door before he hurried back upstairs. He found Sandra still in the sitting room. She hadn't moved. There were no tears, he noted in relief, no imploring eyes. "I must pack," she said, becoming aware of him. She rose, drawing her cardigan around her, cradling her handbag in her arms. "Or would you take me out to dinner for my last night?"

"You can't be serious!" He was aghast.

"Why not? You and I are known to be in Venice. Weren't we supposed to appear together, to look as if we were on vacation?"

"That was the plan." He emphasized the past tense. But within this last week there had been discovery of Vaugiroud, Roussin. Even Carlson's presence on a train that could take him to Venice had sounded an alarm. Perhaps needlessly. Still—"Be sensible, Sandra! I begin to see why Wahl wanted you recalled."

"Do you?" she asked, and paused at the door.

He frowned, puzzling out her hidden meaning.

"Strange," she murmured, "how everyone who can identify Kalganov is eliminated. Vaugiroud and Roussin. Carlson. They knew, didn't they?"

"Nonsense," he said stiffly.

"They are dead, aren't they?" She looked so wide-eyed and innocent, standing there at the door. "Is Kalganov so important? To whom? I'll tell you: he is important to Kalganov. That is his own private personality cult. You know, *he* could be recalled—for Leftist deviationism."

"Shall I tell him that?" he asked bluntly, and hoped the threat would silence her.

"But you couldn't, without mentioning his real name. You haven't done that once, to his face, in the three years I've known you. Stay clever, Fernand, and keep alive." She laughed unsteadily. "Good night. Or shall I see you again?"

"I have much to do," he said. "Good night, my dear."

He is afraid to see me again, she thought, afraid to listen. "Please try. It's our last evening together." She smiled and was gone. Good night and good-bye, the thought. She climbed the stairs toward the bedroom floor, her face white and haggard.

She heard the echoing clang of a doorbell: Fernand's first visitor. That would give her at least an hour. Until half past nine. She had no plan, but time was more precious than any plan. First, get her coat, money, jewelry. Get away from this house, get out of Venice. She was on her own: Rosenfeld and all his schemes would have to take care of themselves. The hell with him and everything else. On the floor below her, she heard Fernand coming out to greet his visitor. An effusive welcome. Yes, this meeting would last a full hour; the stranger must be important. She wasted no more time, but quickly moved into her bedroom, quietly closed the door, quietly locked it.

TWENTY

AT THE Hotel Vittoria, Bill Fenner unpacked and surveyed his new room. There was not much of a view, but it was a comfortable place, all the more so because Claire was safely next door, and close by two of Rosie's men were installed. So Chris Holland had said. And that compensated for the dull courtyard outside, with its tightly shuttered dead windows.

He had a shower, shaved, and dressed slowly. There was no need to hurry. Claire needed some time to steady herself and be able to face the Piazza San Marco. She had insisted on keeping to his plans for the evening, and he hadn't argued with that. It was important, he knew, to establish the custom of having a drink at Florian's; even more so to stick to the timetable he had given Holland. That was a kind of insurance, he felt. He wondered, as he chose his best blue tie to add some newness to his stand-by dark-gray flannel suit, how many men and women were keeping an eye on their wanderings. "We" was a word that Chris had used constantly. Who were "we"? British and French, as well as Americans? Italians, too? Whoever we are, he decided, we have a comforting sound.

You've come a long way, he told the grave, worried face in the looking glass as he knotted his shantung tie neatly, a long way, indeed. You didn't find Holland's order to change rooms one bit comic or unnecessary. You just acted on it: and your only question is "What did happen in Budapest?"

I wish, he thought as he turned away from the glass to find his jacket, I wish that Claire would develop a howling cold, something to keep her safely in bed and out of all this. Damn Rosie for sending her along. Yet without her, I'd have been lost. In every way.

He checked his pockets. It was twenty-five minutes past six. Time to move. He glanced around the room again, wish-

ing that Sandra had chosen this evening for the meeting instead of tomorrow. Even the idea of another day's waiting
was becoming intolerable.

The telephone rang. He thought it would be Claire, letting
him know she was ready. But it was a man's voice. "Bill?"
it said quickly.

"Speaking."

"Look, can I drop around and see you?"

It was Mike Ballard's voice. Fenner said in astonishment,
"What the hell are you doing in Venice?"

"I flew in an hour ago. Look, Bill—"

"I'm just going out."

"This is so damned urgent—"

"You can't talk on the phone?"

"No." Ballard heaved a worried sigh.

"Why don't you join us at Florian's? We'll be at a table
there, in ten minutes or so."

"Who'll be with you?" Ballard was anxious.

"Claire Langley."

"Just the two of you?" Ballard asked in relief.

"Yes."

"Sorry if I intrude—but I'll take your suggestion."

"You can take it for half an hour. Then get lost," Fenner
said cheerfully.

"Thanks, Bill," Ballard's voice said earnestly. "Thanks a
lot."

"It probably was a mistake. But I was caught at the end of
a telephone, and couldn't think of an excuse," Fenner told
Claire as they walked toward the Piazza. "He sounded so
damned pathetic with that sigh of his." But there was no
doubt that Ballard had made himself a useful topic of conversation. Claire had done her best to look normal: she was as
smartly turned out as ever in a softly flowered dress of
blues and greens, with her blue coat draped over her shoulders; her hair was perfect, brushed high yet neat, gleaming,
smooth; her skin glowed, her make-up was skillful—there was
no sign left of her violent tears; her eyes were clear and
brilliant. This time, Fenner's admiration was not only for
her beauty. He wondered a little, though, if this outward
calm could last. It would not if she had really been in love
with Carlson.

They made their way through a crowded little street filled
with the sound of high heels and soft footsteps, with Sunday

dresses and freshly pressed suits taking their small frills and furbelows for the weekly family stroll. (Walk a little, stop a little, talk a little, a pleasant evening to you and to me and to you, here we are all washed and polished, no work today, no worry, a man can saunter along with the richest of them and be proud of his own.) They squeezed through a cohort of families, and at last had some free space for talking.

"A mistake?" Claire asked quietly, still thinking of Ballard. "No. I don't think we'll drag him into any danger."

"I meant a mistake from my point of view. He'll bend our ear for an hour, try to join us at dinner." Also, Ballard's appearance in Venice at this time could lead to a really big mistake. Tomorrow evening, for instance, and Sandra, and that damned letter. She had suggested Ballard as one of her possible contacts, hadn't she? What if Ballard wandered into the Piazza San Marco tomorrow evening, sat at Florian's just as Sandra came strolling by? Fenner's pulse missed a beat.

"Yes?" asked Claire, sensing his worry. Her interest quickened.

"I'm just thinking of some way to keep Ballard out of the Piazza tomorrow evening."

"That's twenty-four hours away," she reassured him. "Mike may not even be in Venice tomorrow. And if he is, he may not be anywhere near Florian's at half past six on a Monday evening."

"I'd like to make sure of that." My nerves are raw, he thought, if I start worrying about something that could possibly, perhaps, take place if only.

"Then we'll send Chris another little note. And he can send Mike for a motorboat ride all around the lagoon. Or something." She slipped her hand into his, encouragingly. And he relaxed. He could even analyze that attack of excess worry. Tension had caused it, of course—tension over Neill Carlson and Claire He looked at her and took a firmer grip of her hand. "I wonder," she was saying, "why Mike did come to Venice? What's troubling him, do you think?"

He gave her one of the answers only. "He has the idea that I'm out to get his job."

"He's an idiot!"

"Thank you."

"But, Bill—you wouldn't." She was quite decided about that.

"How do you know?" he asked teasingly.

"I know," she told him. He was surprised by the warmth in her eyes as she glanced at him. And that small smile was all for him, too. He entered the Piazza San Marco in the best possible tradition, a general state of mounting euphoria.

The vast rectangle of the Piazza stretched eastward before them, its two long sides edged with unbroken rows of gray Renaissance palaces rising above their arcades, and ended in a sunlit blaze of color, of domes and steeples and turrets resting on a mass of arches and pillars, mosaic and marble and carved stone. Four Greek horses were stepping high above the bronze doorway, giant even from this distance. Angels mounted with golden trumpets, gold banners curled from every point and pinnacle, gold crosses gleamed on every cupola; and Saint Mark himself rose into the sky over the golden lion with outstretched wings. It was more than a cathedral, Fenner thought; it was a shout of joy.

They had both halted involuntarily, before they stepped out of the arched colonnade at this western end of the Piazza and walked, as a thousand or more walked, slowly across the vast stretch of worn marble pavement. Close to the pillared arcades, there was a thick fringe of café tables and chairs, crowded with another thousand people. And another thousand or so were gathered thickly in the center of the Piazza, where the municipal band was giving a Sunday-evening concert and had silenced, temporarily, the sweet and swing music from the newer cafés. Florian's provided no music, having survived very nicely for more than two hundred years on the devotion of its clients and their ability to be amused by others. Its tables, spreading out into the Piazza in neat rows, were densely populated, mostly with well-dressed foreigners, but here and there was a small advance guard of real Venetians, venturing out to recapture their Piazza now that September had arrived.

Claire turned her head away from the mass of tables to look at the band. Very softly, she said, "I see Chris. And not far away is Rosie."

Fenner nodded. So Rosie, looking like a totally unperturbed and harmless tourist—tweed jacket, sports shirt, camera, Blue Guide, and all—had come to see how his two staked lambs were faring. Carlson's death was not only a personal loss; it had been a warning. Rosie, sitting over a drink at a small table, listening to the shimmering crescendos of *Swan Lake*, watching the pigeons soaring as drums ruffled and cymbals clashed, could only mean one thing: urgency.

"We're going to have trouble finding a table," he said, steering her casually past Sir Felix Tarns, who sat with two admiring friends in Florian's front row. Tomorrow night, Fenner thought, we must come here early and be prepared to sit and wait for Sandra. It might be a comic touch to arrive for an assignation and find no table vacant, but it was one that wouldn't appeal much to Rosie's sense of humor. Nor mine, nowadays: I wish to God that Claire was back in Paris.

"We're in luck! Someone is just leaving," she said delightedly.

Luck? Two men were rising from a front-row table just beside them. One was Pietro, starting his way as expertly into the crowd on the Piazza as he had steered his motorboat from the Lido back to Venice. He no longer wore his rakish Captain's hat, or his English tweed coat. His short, dark jacket, with sloping shoulders, was primly buttoned; his legs, thin in narrowly cut trousers, looked like a fencing master's. He and his friend merged perfectly with the hundreds of other dark-haired young men who wandered purposely, pleasantly, around the outcrops of pretty girls. We can use this kind of luck, thought Fenner, and captured the table just ahead of two elegant Frenchwomen, who looked at him with annoyance, waited to see if he would weaken, and at last retreated in an indignation of click-clacking high heels and jangling bracelets. He glanced after one of them briefly, kept surprise out of his face. Yes, that had been Miss Bikini, all right. Their luck in finding a table had been openly established, and very neatly. He saluted Rosie, mentally.

"Difficult to recognize with her clothes on," Claire murmured in agreement, as he helped her slip her coat from her shoulders. She pulled off her white gloves, laid them neatly on her dark-blue purse. Her hand rested briefly on its small, well-filled bulk. He had noticed, but he made no remark at all. "You've changed," she said. "You no longer joke about —" She looked at the purse, resting so innocently beside a mock-silver tray with its used glasses and the lire Pietro had left to cover the waiter's chit.

A joke was a good way to mock reality, to dodge an issue, to escape involvement, to twist an argument, to rout an opponent. Except that his opponents weren't men to be defeated by laughter; the argument ran too straight and deadly for any twisting; he was involved up to his eyebrows, perhaps even over his head; the issue was one that couldn't be dodged; and reality, the lurking face behind the mask of safety, was grim and unrelenting. "Tomorrow night," he told her, "I can start making jokes again." Tomorrow night, he thought, the mask goes back over the face of reality: I'll return to my normal world. "If you'll listen to them," he added.

She almost smiled, and looked away, watching the children playing silent hide-and-seek among the forest of grown-up legs. Fenner could study her unobserved for one long and perfect minute. The glow from the sunset sky fell gently over the Piazza, bathing stone and flesh in its golden shower. But the music ended, a waiter came for their order, voices around them were released from the occasional low murmur into a surge of talk, the children laughed out loud, the massed groups broke loose into whirls and eddies, and high on the clock tower, in one corner of the Piazza, two giant Moors began to strike the hour.

"Seven o'clock. Mike's late," Fenner said, as their booming sledge blows stopped, and the pigeons settled again.

Claire had been watching a round-bottomed two-year-old, well padded under his short white trousers, ankles stoutly held by short white boots, ending his dash for independence in a trip and plump, right at the feet of two tall Municipal Guards, with sashes and epaulettes, cocked hats, swords, and white-gloved hands clasped over the tails of their dark-blue coats. The child yelled as his buttocks and pride were jolted, fell into open-mouthed silence as his eyes traveled all the way up to the cockades on the hats. His father rushed in, to bend and pick up and solve a problem for uniformed dignity. There were smiles and bows all around. Claire's own smile widened, and she laughed. And like the child, she fell silent, staring at Fenner. "I laughed," she said in amazement, "I actually—" She halted, her eyes observing a distant table. "What was that you said about Mike Ballard?"

"He's late, blast him."

Her eyes veered slowly away from what she had noticed. She said softly, "He's here. He was early, I think. And some-one joined him. No, don't turn around, Bill." Her hand had touched his arm before her warning ended, stopping the in-voluntary movement. "His table is at the back, near the arcade, just two rows behind Chris."

Laughter might be a limited weapon, Fenner was thinking, but it was good medicine. Claire was no longer remote, with-drawn: some of her vivacity had returned, and all her quick intelligence. "Who is with him?" he asked.

"A man with very broad shoulders."

"What?"

"Yes. Give me a cigarette, Bill."

"And Chris hasn't recognized him?"

"I wouldn't have," she reminded him, "if you hadn't pointed him out today."

He sat quite silent. At last he said, "We've got to make Chris notice. He's a bright boy. He won't need much of a hint." He lit her cigarette carefully, and his own.

"But how?"

"I think I've got it."

"Bill—" she pleaded.

"Nothing to it," he reassured her. "All I need is a chance to turn around and see Ballard quite naturally."

She looked at him. "All right," she said, and let the cigarette slip from her fingers onto her lap. "Oh!" She half rose, abruptly, brushing the burning ash from her dress. He had risen, too, his chair toppling back with his speed. "It's all right," she assured him, her voice at its natural level. "I jumped just in time." So they could laugh, and she sat down again, saying, "How silly of me!" He turned to pick up his chair and put it back in position. He looked at the curious and amused faces which glanced in their direction. And at the back of the rows of tables, just behind Chris, as she had warned him, he saw Ballard and Jan Aarvan.

"Why, there's Ballard!" he said clearly. "I think I'll let him know we're here. Won't be a minute, Claire." And there wasn't even a minute to waste: the band was tuning up again. Soon, voices wouldn't carry two rows of tables. He made his way quickly toward the arcade. He passed Chris Holland, didn't even glance at him. Aarvan was talking quietly, his back turned to the Piazza. Ballard, lost in his own world of trouble, could only stare blankly at Fenner as he approached them.

"Hello, Mike!" Fenner said. "We found a table at the front, just over there." He gestured toward Claire. "Thought I'd let you know in case you didn't see us arrive."

Aarvan had turned. It was a quick aggressive movement, from a man who thought in terms of danger. Rosie, playing with the view finder on his camera, had noted it. Chris, two rows to the front, could not look around. But he could hear.

"Say, haven't I seen you before?" Fenner asked Aarvan. "On a raft?"

Aarvan's brief show of interest had reverted to a cold stare.

"Yes," Fenner continued cheerfully, "that was it—out at the Lido today. Well—" he looked at the unhappy Ballard who had made no offer of an introduction—"see you later, Mike." He walked briskly away. Chris was examining his check and counting out some lire. Rosie had shut his camera and was waiting for the music to start.

Fenner dropped quietly into his seat as the first bars of *Sicilian Vespers* sounded over a silenced Piazza, noted with thankfulness that the waiter had brought their drinks, and gave Claire a reassuring smile. Why, he thought, in amazement, she was actually worrying about me. About me. Not about the job. About me. And he could calm down, forgetting the nervous tension that had tightened his stomach as he had faced Aarvan. That hadn't been as easy as he had pretended it to be. Now, he could admit that. It was one thing to be an actor, he decided; quite another to make up your lines as you went along. He had to wonder, of course, whether his action had been necessary. Or had he been foolish, had he made a mistake? Some men, judging from their assertions in newspapers and on television, always seemed to believe they were right, knew everything, and had chosen the only intelligent approach to any situation. Fenner could only hope that, out of the several approaches he could have made to this particular situation, he hadn't taken the worst one. It had been an instinctive action, arriving out of nowhere, startling him now as he had time to think about it.

"How was Mike?" asked Claire softly.

"Hopeless."

"If only he would stand up and fight—" She shook her head sadly. "There's no disgrace so great as the one he is heading into. Can't he see that?"

So she knew about Mike Ballard's particular mess of pottage. No need to avoid the topic any longer. "If we could make him see—" He paused, thinking over that, wondering if it could be possible and how.

"If he comes," she suggested.

"Sh!" said a music lover near them, ending their murmuring.

If he comes, Fenner thought morosely, Ballard will be one step farther into the net that Fernand Lenoir has spread for him. He began wondering how Jan Aarvan had entered this picture. Aarvan was Kalganov's man. Was Kalganov in Venice, taking full control?

The band was packing up, dusk was beginning, the balls of light suspended from each arch in the long arcades were being switched on, the crowds were having another stroll before they went home to supper; and Mike Ballard arrived. He had had one drink more than necessary. His manner was too jocular, too determinedly confident. "Well, well, well—" he began, pumped Fenner's hand, kissed Claire on the cheek and patted her arm. "Good to see you. Pretty picture you make, sitting there with Bill. Been admiring you from a distance."

"We thought you had forgotten about us," Claire said. She looked at him anxiously. He wasn't drunk. He could be, though, if he ordered anything more.

"Forgotten you? Never, my love." He pulled a chair over, and sat down. He glanced around him: the tables had become less crowded. Nearby, there were only two smartly dressed girls, with heavy bracelets that jangled as they talked with precise gestures. "French," Ballard noted. "You can always tell. Nothing like the French of that extra *je-ne-sais-quoi* touch of what-you-call-it."

Fenner looked at Miss Bikini and back at Mike Ballard. Let's get down to business, he thought. "What's the trouble, Mike?"

Ballard's eyes flickered away. "Trouble?" he asked vaguely. "Who hasn't got troubles?" His voice became louder. "Where's a waiter—what are you drinking?" He snapped his fingers furiously.

"We're all right," Fenner said. "You order some coffee, and we'll listen."

"Coffee You sound like Eva."

"How is she?"

"And the children?" Claire asked, pressing Fenner's point still farther.

"Fine," Ballard said, avoiding her eyes, "just fine." The bluster left him. He stared down at the table. "They are good kids," he said dejectedly. He let Fenner order coffee without any further resistance. "Well," he said, trying to get back his first burst of enthusiasm, "and how is Venice treating you? Having fun?"

"Everyone has lots of fun in Venice," Fenner said. "Except you, seemingly. What's wrong?"

"Wrong?" Ballard tried a smile. "Nothing's wrong."

"Just over an hour ago, I had a telephone call. Remember? The man who made it sounded pretty worried, worried enough to make me invite him to join us here. But when he arrives, he hasn't a care in the world. He's here on false pretenses." Ballard looked at Fenner quickly. "Scram," Fenner told him with a smile. "Blow, disappear, vanish. Two's company, didn't you know?"

Ballard stared at him, completely off balance. For the last twenty minutes, since the stranger had left, Ballard had sat swallowing three double Scotches, working up his courage, his story, and his bile. He had been tempted to walk right past this table and keep Claire and Fenner out of this mess, or—if he did sit down—to forget the warning that had been sent to him through that cold-eyed stranger, and tell Fenner his troubles. As he had meant to do when he first walked into this Piazza. But that impulse must be choked back. He could sense the stranger's eyes still watching him from some safe distance. Who was he, who were the people who had sent him here? Friends of that beggar Spitzer, certainly. How else could a stranger threaten him so completely? Blackmail. It was blackmail, a quicksand with slobbering lips already sucking at his ankles. He had a return of the impulse to rise and walk away, saying the hell with all their threats. And then he thought of the kids, his job, Eva—and he sat still, trapped and helpless.

"Hold it, Bill," he said, feeling the sickliness of his forced grin after his long silence, "you don't chop off an old friend like that. Do you?" He turned to Claire. "By the way, you seem to have done well with those fashion drawings."

"Thank you," Claire said.

"Not at all. Glad to get you the job. Any time." His coffee arrived, and he gulped it down, scalding as it must have been. He drew out his cigarette case. His lighter matched it. Cuff links for his white silk shirt were of gold, too. Shot-silk tie from Florence. Silk tweed suit from Rome. Shoes, carefully displayed with a crossed leg, from London. Lenoir had supplied Ballard with more than a pretty mistress. Fenner and Claire exchanged a brief glance. He misinterpreted it. "So you are wondering why I'm in Venice? That's easy. There's a story to be dug out. I'm here to dig."

"And who is minding the store meanwhile?" Fenner asked. "Surely not that fellow Spitzer?"

"Oh, I'll be back in Paris tomorrow."

"You left Spitzer in charge?"

"Why not?"

Fenner just shook his head. Perhaps Ballard really did want to commit suicide.

"He's a bit too eager, that's all."

"Yes, eager for your job."

Ballard finished a second cup of coffee.

"Hadn't you thought of that?"

"No," Ballard said shortly. Spitzer and his friends weren't going to take away his job as long as he listened to them. That had been made quite clear. He added, "If so, he isn't the only one." He looked at Fenner.

Claire said. "Nonsense, Mike. You're an awful fool."

There was a pause. "I hope that was a joke," he said. So that's all the thanks I get, he thought bitterly.

"At present, you don't amuse me one bit," she said coldly. "You aren't the Mike Ballard I used to know."

He almost rose, hesitated, tried to laugh it off. "She's spoiling for a fight," he said to Fenner. "Have you been telling her tales about me?" Women always closed ranks against men. Claire was taking Eva's side. As if he hadn't been a good husband, a good provider, when he was in the money. Was all that to be forgotten because of one mistake?

"No need," Fenner said, glancing at the gold cigarette case. We're wasting our time and sympathy on this soft slob who'll persuade himself into believing anything just to hang on to his comforts. "Let's take a walk," he told Claire quietly. She didn't move. Her eyes seemed to say, "Wait, Bill, wait a little. . . ."

"Say, what's come over you two?" Ballard was really worried. Three questions, he remembered in immediate panic, and he hadn't even asked the first one.

"What has come over *you*?" Fenner asked bluntly.

"But—nothing."

"Why did you call me?"

Ballard saw an opening and plunged. "I'm worried. And I think I've good reason to worry. Bill, tell me—why did you come to Venice?" And I'm not just asking this for the stranger, he thought. I want to know the answer to this, too.

"You know why." Fenner was looking at him curiously.

"Those interviews? Bull— Sorry, Claire." He patted her arm and turned to Fenner again. "Does it matter a plugged nickel what a couple of neutralists think? You could write those interviews sitting here, or in Paris."

"I'd rather let them speak their little piece. Much more telling."

"You could have refused this assignment. You're not under any contract to write—"

Fenner cut in. "Who would refuse a week in Venice?"

"You're staying a week?"

"Wouldn't you?"

Ballard looked at Claire. "She'd fight with me," he said with a sudden grin.

Fenner picked up the tab that had been left tactfully under a saucer.

"Hey! What's the rush?"

Fenner said, "Your problems are over, aren't they? I've solved your worry. I'm not in Venice to take any story away from you. It's all yours, Mike. We're off to dinner."

Ballard's grin had faded. "So my problems are over." He looked at the lighted Piazza, at the men and women who walked and talked together, at the laughing children, at the crowds now gathering at one of the cafés opposite where a jazz band was stomping out a new version of *Tiger Rag.* "You two don't need to look so god-damned happy," he said bitterly. "It might do you more good to start looking for that story, Bill. Because you're in it. Somewhere, you're in it."

"In what?"

"You haven't an idea?" Ballard was incredulous.

"Not one."

"Why did Spitzer telephone a report on your plans? Yes . . . just after you left the office yesterday, he picked up the telephone and called Venice."

"He did that, in front of you?"

"Of course not."

"You caught him at it?"

"I'm not such a fool as some people think." Ballard glanced at Claire.

"And you let him get away with it?"

Ballard said testily, "Let me handle Spitzer my way."

"What way is that?" asked Fenner sharply. Ballard fell silent, his false confidence slipping. He looked the unhappiest man in the whole Pizza di San Marco. Which might be true, Fenner thought, and relented. Sympathetically, he added, "Who's behind Spitzer, Mike? Who got him into the office?"

"I hired him. He was highly recommended. Good qualifications, languages, all that. He's thoroughly capable, no doubt about it."

"Recommended by whom?"

"A friend of mine. You can take that look off your face, Bill. My friend had no personal interest in Spitzer, just heard about him. He will be as shocked as I am—"

"Who is this friend?"

"An important guy. Carries a lot of weight, has contacts. Will you listen to me? He's reliable. He has too big a career ahead of him to get mixed up with men like Spitzer. He has got brains, he has got standing."

"Hasn't he got a name? All right, all right. Your friend is an honorable man. He isn't trying to crucify you, in order to keep Spitzer planted in the *Chronicle* office."

Ballard's eyes widened. His lips closed tight. He said angrily, "My God, Bill, if we can't trust our friends, where are we? Look—this man has done a lot for me. He has done a lot for other people, too. You don't believe me? How do you think your wife stayed alive for those last three years? She was a refugee, no money, no friends—"

"Sandra Fane is not my wife."

"That's right." Ballard's eloquence went into high gear. "You and all other Americans were too good for her. When she needed help, did any of us give it? No, it was Lenoir who had the guts to help her start a new life. Would a Communist have done that?"

Claire asked, "Where do Communists come into this, Mike?"

He knitted his brows, tried to pour another cup and found the pot empty. "Perhaps Spitzer—" he began slowly, hesitated. "I don't know. But I'll find out." He looked at Fenner bitterly. "You don't have to go running to old Penneyman with reports that I'm doing nothing. I'll handle this—" He stopped, seeing the anger in Fenner's eyes. His voice eased. "I'll handle this, my way. The *Chronicle* won't suffer."

"Mike!" Claire said. "Of all the spiteful, unfair things to say!" Her eyes still told Fenner: "Wait, Bill, wait a little...."

For Ballard was sorry, and didn't know how to express it. Fenner had his faults, but talebearing wasn't one of them. "I guess I spoke too quickly there," Ballard said at last, flicking his lighter off and on, off and on. He tried to laugh. "I really get her riled when I criticize you, don't I?" He saw the opening for that second question. "Say, how long have you known each other?"

"I know Bill better than you know him," Claire said. "That's obvious."

"But you never mentioned him to me. Funny, isn't it—you knew Bill, I knew him, and—"

"What's funny about that?" Claire asked. "Why should I tell you about my—" She paused delicately, looked embarrassed and amused. "Really, Mike!"

Fenner had dropped enough money on the table to take care of drinks and tip. He pulled the coat around Claire's shoulders. He hadn't looked at Ballard for the last minute. He didn't look at him even as Claire slowly gathered her bag and gloves.

"What have I got, leprosy or something?" Ballard asked angrily. "Why the hell did I bother to telephone you?"

"I keep wondering about that," Fenner said.

"Well—I warned you, didn't I?"

"About what?"

"You know damned well."

"I don't. I don't even believe there is any story—"

"Isn't there? If not, why was Neill Carlson coming to Venice?"

"He likes Venice, I guess," Fenner said. "And who is Neill Carlson?"

"He's some kind of *pro tem* press attaché at the Embassy in Paris. You never met him?"

Fenner looked puzzled. He searched his memory obligingly. Claire said, slipping in quickly to the rescue, "Oh, I remember. I met him at one of your parties, Mike. So Neill Carlson is in Venice?" Her voice was even.

Ballard shook his head, his eyes watching them. "He was killed last night. Fell from a train." So there, Ballard thought, is the answer to that third blasted bloody question. He felt a great relief: they knew nothing about Carlson's movements. And with the relief came a hot flush of embarrassment, a touch of shame as their quiet faces looked at him. He had a compulsion to talk, to explain, to make amends. "A lousy deal," he said. "I don't know what happened. But if it was murder, we'll get the son of a bitch who did it. That's one story I'm going to spread all over the headlines."

"Murder?" Claire asked faintly. That was what she would be expected to ask. But this attack of cold nausea and hot anger was real. Blindly, she stared at Ballard's smooth, well-shaven face and wanted to scream.

Fenner said quickly, "Perhaps you are onto something, Mike after all."

"You bet I am." It was pleasant to be accepted again. Fenner was no longer disbelieving. "Lenoir himself gave me the first steer. Telephoned me this morning. I caught the next plane to Venice." Fenner looked impressed. "You don't know Lenoir, but he is a man with plenty of contacts. When he passes on a tip, it's worth considering."

"Did you go over and talk with him before you left Paris? Or could he give you enough information over the phone?"

"He isn't in Paris. He's here. I'll see him tonight and get more details. This isn't the kind of stuff you talk about on a telephone. Of course," Ballard added quickly, "I'll have to do the work on this story."

"Of course."

"And there will be plenty."

"Want any help?"

Ballard retreated in alarm. "It's my story, Bill."

"Sure. But you can't expect to keep it all to yourself."

Ballard grinned. This was the kind of fencing he understood. "You just stick to your neutralists, and write some of that immortal prose of yours."

"By the way, who was that character who was talking to you before we arrived?"

Ballard's amusement sloughed off. "Just some two-bit journalist."

"Did Lenoir tip him off, too?"

"No connection. He has nothing to do with Lenoir." And Ballard believed that, quite obviously. "Never saw him in my life—until he sat down at my table."

Fenner said nothing. The pattern around Mike Ballard was emerging. And there was nothing Fenner could tell him that wouldn't break security, endanger everyone. Someone else would have to find out why Ballard came in such a rush to Venice: the story Lenoir had promised him wasn't supposed to break for at least four or five days. Yes, thought Fenner, someone else will have to talk with Ballard. And soon. He looked casually around the other tables—neither Rosie nor Chris was there. Out on the Piazza, there was still a dense crowd of people. He saw Pietro and his friend, walking with two smiling Italian girls. He thought he saw Chris Holland, too, feeding some pigeons. And then, strolling slowly back toward the half-emptied tables at Florian's, he saw Jan Aarvan, completely nonchalant, just drifting along on a fine Sunday evening. Aarvan was confident. Aarvan felt secure. He's had too many triumphs recently, Fenner thought: he is swollen with success. But unexpectedly, Aarvan disappeared into a crowd of tourists. Aarvan might be confident but he was still watchful, a clever and cagey operator. "Time to go," Fenner said, rising definitely, glancing over at the big clock across the Piazza. "Quadri's won't keep that window table much past eight o'clock." He pulled back Claire's chair for her.

Ballard looked up at them. "What about dinner tomorrow night, before I leave? And I can tell you about that story—I'll have it filed by then." He studied Claire's face. She hadn't spoken for a long time. "Don't be mad at me, sweetie. I said I was sorry, didn't I? And I still think you're the prettiest girl I've seen in Venice"

He watched them walk away. He thought of ordering a drink. He needed one. High on the clock tower, the big Moors were raising their bronze arms to strike. Tourist stuff, Ballard thought, and eyed the waiting crowds gloomily.

Fenner said quietly as they walked across the Pizza toward the brightly lit arcades on its other side, "How do we get a message to Chris?"

"By way of Pietro, I'd think. It's a risk, Bill."

"Got to be taken." Fenner calculated their course to pass as near Pietro as possible. He and his friend seemed only intent on an animated conversation with their girls.

"I'm dropping a glove," Claire said. "Don't notice."

Indeed he hadn't. It was a most natural accident. "Signorina!" they heard behind them, and stopped. Pietro was brushing off the dust, presenting the glove with a bow. Claire was appropriately startled by her carelessness, thanked him for his kindness. But it was Fenner's quick sentence that Pietro listened to. "He is seeing Lenoir this evening. Deadline tomorrow night."

They walked on, at the same leisurely pace. And paused, like everyone else, to look up at the clock tower when the two Moors bludgeoned the hours. A sea of sound washed over the darkening Piazza into the lighted arcades, drowning the voices and the café music, breaking high into the cool night sky above. A silver cloud of pigeons swirled and settled. "Eight o'clock and all's well," Fenner said wryly. People were moving once more; thinking of dinner, too. Among them were Pietro and his friends, as merry as a Christmas card. What if he doesn't understand English? Fenner thought, and began to worry again. "I think I botched it," he told Claire.

Ballard watched the swirl of pigeons, the people beginning once more to move around. Across the Piazza, he saw Claire's blonde head gleam under an arcade's high lamp, as Fenner led her through the curved arch into Quadri's. But the crowds closed again, and they were hidden from view. The restaurant's second-floor windows were wide open and softly pink, each table glowing warmly with its small shaded lamp. Fenner had all the luck, Ballard thought, staring at the pink lights, and he felt a hideous sense of loneliness. And then, from a group of people strolling past in the darkness, the inquisitor came forward and sat down beside him.

"Well?" the man asked.

"You're damned impatient. What's all the hurry?" He glanced nervously across at Quadri's wondows. Could he be seen from up there?

"What did you learn?"

"Nothing." And thank God for that, Ballard thought. His sense of shame lessened: in a way he had helped clear Fenner of any suspicion. Certainly no harm was done.

"Nothing?" The stranger's cold blue eyes were fixed on Ballard's face as if they could bore their way into the truth.

"Nothing." Ballard's confidence was returning. "Now beat it. You leave me alone."

"And what did you tell them?"

"Nothing."

"You talked a lot. Three small questions did not take so much time." His voice was harsh, skeptical. His words held a new threat.

Ballard's confidence ebbed. There would always be a new threat: no release, no end to the demands. "Damn you to hell, will you leave me alone?"

The man smiled contemptuously and rose. He turned and made one step away. No more. Two quiet men in dark suits blocked his path, and signaled. Two policemen closed in from either side, took a businesslike grip on his arms. There was a spasm of struggle, a brief scuffle, and then the small tight group moved away. Two men exchanging a quick French phrase rose from a table and brought up the rear of the solid little phalanx. The arrest, like the surprise, was complete.

It was so quickly, quietly, expertly done that Ballard wondered if he had dreamed it all. Only a nearby waiter had noticed, only a few people passing closely. There were some shrugs, some remarks about pickpockets, and the incident was over. Except for Ballard. Four men were standing at his table. He stopped staring after the man who had been arrested, looked stupidly up at them. Two policemen in dark-green khaki; a young man, also Italian, judging from his suit, and a man in conservative gray flannels, speaking in an English voice. "You are Ballard of the New York *Chronicle's* Paris Bureau?"

My God, thought Ballard, am I being arrested, too?

TWENTY-ONE

YES, DECIDED Christopher Holland as he saw the complete consternation on Ballard's face, this was the right moment. He nodded to the two policemen, who saluted and strolled on. "Lieutenant Rusconi," he said to the man who accompanied him, as he sat down opposite Ballard, "do you mind?"

"*Niente.*" Lieutenant Rusconi took a chair at the next table, and adopted a severe and thoughtful expression.

Ballard came out of shock. "What happened?" He gestured toward the tight group of men already vanishing into the dark shadows around the base of the Campanile, the bell tower that rose abruptly from the Piazza, well separated from the cathedral. He watched the group disappear around its corner. "Where—where are they taking him?"

"To a motor launch, which in turn will take him to the Prefecture. Your friend has just been arrested—for extradition to France." Holland's voice was businesslike, but not unfriendly. "Why did he come over to your table?"

"He's no friend of mine—never saw him before—" Ballard was starting to rise. "And what business is it of yours?"

"Please sit down, Mr. Ballard. Or else Lieutenant Rusconi, who is now waiting most patiently, will make it *his* business to accompany you to the police station. Perhaps you would rather answer our questions there?"

Ballard glanced at the detective, one of those young eager beavers with a quick eye for promotion, who was watching him with a disapproving frown, and sat back in his chair. Also, the two policemen were still patrolling this side of the Piazza.

"I thought," Holland said, "that you'd find it simpler to talk here. Less formal. And much quicker."

"Why pull me into all this?" Ballard asked angrily. "That man who was arrested—I don't even know his name."

"Who sent him?"

"I don't know. He just stopped to talk to me."

"Twice. He talked to you twice."

"So what?"

"So there is some explanation needed. Especially since the man is being extradited for murder."

"What?" Ballard's aggressiveness vanished.

"His name is Jan Aarvan. Have you ever heard of it?"

"Never." Ballard was worried enough to be honest.

"What did he want?"

Ballard hesitated. He was conscious of the Italian detective's cold watchfulness, of that possible visit to the police station, which would only waste his time, keep him late for his appointment with Lenoir. "He was trying to blackmail me." Ballard noticed that the quiet Englishman wasn't amazed. He had an uncomfortable feeling that more was known about him than just his name.

"I'm glad that you told the truth, Mr. Ballard. It saves so much time all around, doesn't it? Did he ask for money?"

"No."

"A favor?"

"That's about it," Ballard said awkwardly.

"You refused him, of course?"

"I told him to clear out."

"Most courageous of you."

Ballard looked uncomfortable. He glanced sharply at the pleasant face watching him so quietly. Ironical? No, the Englishman was being encouraging, sympathetic. Any minute, he'll offer me a cigarette and establish complete confidence, and have me blabbing out my life story, Ballard thought: I know this type. Well, I'll find out more from him than he'll find out from me. That's for sure. He'd make a good story himself, this guy.

"Are you on holiday, Mr. Ballard?"

"No. Just got here. I'm checking up on a story."

"And you came all the way from Paris? How long will you be in Venice?"

"Until tomorrow night."

So Fenner hadn't made any mistake about that. Tomorrow night. Chris Holland smiled gently and said, "It must be a very short story for such a short stay."

"Interested in it?" Ballard was amused. "You know, you begin to sound like a newspaperman."

"Haven't the brains."

"What are you, anyway? Intelligence?"

"Haven't the stamina."

Ballard's grin broadened. "What's your angle? You aren't French, or Italian. So what's your interest in this fellow Aarvan?"

"He is wanted by the British, too, you know," Holland said smoothly. By this one Briton, certainly.

"Quite an international character?"

"A political criminal. He is employed by Communists. Did you know that?"

Ballard only stared.

"Just what kind of favor did he want from you?"

"Does that matter now?" Aarvan's off my back, Ballard thought. And who sent him, I wonder. Spitzer?

"Mr. Ballard," Holland said very quietly, "I shall ask the questions, and you will give the answers." He paused, and added, "Or else this little interview can drag on for hours. I have no objection. But you?"

"I—I haven't much time to spare. I've an appointment."

So Fenner's message about this evening could have been right. "Well, in that case—the quicker, the sooner. Why are you in Venice?"

"I've just told you."

Holland shook his head sadly. "You disappoint me, Mr. Ballard. You really can't expect us to believe that you yourself would come here for some story or other when you could have sent one of your staff."

"It would have been no use sending any reporter. This story is to be delivered only to me."

"That's the deal, is it?"

Ballard was amused in spite of himself. The Americanism in an English accent was comic. But friendly. He relaxed a little. "Yes, that's why I'm here. Also, the story *is* big. The biggest of the year—that's the tip I got. So I came."

"And you expect to find some scandal in Venice? Dope smuggling among the tourists, adultery by the Adriatic?"

"Nothing like that." Ballard's smile was broadening. "My source of information happens to be in Venice. That's all."

"You must trust him a great deal," Holland murmured. He lit a cigarette, carefully. And how can I warn him about Lenoir? he was thinking. Later. First things first.

"I do." And you aren't going to pry his name and address out of me, either, Ballard thought. That's none of your business bub. Do you think I want a lot of Italian reporters pester-

ing Lenoir? What story would I get then? Or even get in the
future? Ballard glanced at his watch. There was just time
for a quick dinner before he kept his appointment at half
past nine. Lenoir's directions to this Ca' Grande had been
simple enough: it shouldn't be too hard to find. The story must
be really big or Lenoir wouldn't have been so cagey in the
way he gave his address: the house name and street number
when he telephoned Paris; the route itself, but no Ca'
Grande mentioned, in his call to the Danieli. Yes, this story
must be really big, all right. Ballard looked at the Englishman's cigarette, lit one of his own. "Well," he said, "if the
Lieutenant has no objections?" He pocketed his cigarette case
and lighter, preparing to leave.

"I'm afraid he may have," Holland said very gently. "You
haven't been quite frank with us, have you?"

"Look—" began Ballard angrily.

"We are worried about your safety. Can't you understand
that? So please be patient. We still have a few necessary questions to ask. Just what is this remarkable story?"

"Safety?" Ballard's anger subsided into worry. "I don't
know yet."

"You don't *know* what it is? Good heavens, man, how can
you put together an important story like this in one day?"

"I'll have to," admitted Ballard. "Or else the headlines
I never wrote will be screaming at me by tomorrow night.
In this game, you get in ahead of the others, even only by
a couple of hours." He noticed the Englishman was looking
at him, incredulous. "Oh, it's not so difficult—some concentrated work, a little know-how, and the right contacts."

Screaming headlines . . . Holland studied his cigarette. "So
you must expect to get all the details very easily, all
nicely packaged and wrapped up for you? How very pleasant."

"I have to write the story," Ballard reminded him sharply.

"And have it ready when the news breaks? But how can
your informant predict some event—"

"Who is talking about any event? He has collected information—international implications—big stuff. Too big for
him to keep. He's releasing it to the press tomorrow evening.
The Paris papers will have the flash reports, but I'll have
the full details. What's wrong with that?"

"You have it made." Holland's smile was gentle. "But
why should this informant give you such an advantage—such
a break?"

"He happens to be an old friend. That's all."

"And he expects nothing in return? He has no ax to grind?"

Ballard shook his head. He was amused. "And don't ask me his name," he said. "I never give away my sources."

"I didn't ask his name, did I? I just wondered about his politics. Aarvan, after all, must have been told that you had arrived in Venice. Who could have told him?"

Spitzer, thought Ballard, André Spitzer did that. "I think I know," he said grimly. And caught his breath. Spitzer? I didn't tell Spitzer anything about this trip. He might have found out, though. Must have found out. Who else could tip off Aarvan?

"For *your* safety," Holland was saying, very mildly, "I hope you do. You see, Aarvan's attempt at blackmail—" He paused. "Does this interest you?" He didn't have to wait for a reply. Ballard, who was a restless type—his hands had played with cigarette case and lighter, his legs had been crossed and dandled and uncrossed, all through this meeting—was absolutely still. "Aarvan's purpose was to find out if you could be pressured into doing something repugnant to you. That was more important than any information you could have given them. Because his friends would learn, from your reactions, how to manipulate you in future. And you may be sure they are going to apply more pressure. You won't, of course, listen to them. Will you?"

Ballard sat quite silent, not altogether believing, yet wanting to know; like a patient listening to a doctor's diagnosis which he resists but can't ignore either.

Holland's eyes were looking beyond Ballard to another table. "Over there is a good example of what I've been talking about."

Ballard came out of the fog, and glanced around. A group of three men had risen and were making their good-bys. One of them, tall and thin, was wearing a suit whose excellence caught Ballard's attention even at this distance.

"Do you know him? Tarns is his name."

"Sir Felix Tarns? Sure, I remember him. He used to hang around the United Nations. He still goes to the same tailor, I see." Ballard remembered Holland's phrase and repeated it, astounded. "A good example?"

Holland nodded. "In 1944, he was a quiet civil servant, with his father's title and his grandfather's money to help make life agreeable in the Establishment. He liked the ladies—his one human trait, as far as I know. There was a messy adultery, hushed up before it reached the *News of the World*. The Communists discovered it, and applied pressure. He caved in. Then in 1949, one of our traitors skipped to Russia. Sir Felix had carefully nurtured the young man's career, helped place him in a sensitive job. So just before a quiet investigation was started—very quiet; we like to keep those things within the family, you know—Sir Felix resigned. No fuss. No scandal. No headlines. The family congratulated itself, rather blindly. For Sir Felix started another career, as political observer and free-lance journalist. And that has been a most expert snow job." Holland thought, there goes another of Neill Carlson's phrases; and he paused, staring at nothing. He went on. "One small group kept pushing his name into adulatory articles, reviewed his collected essays most favorably, arranged lectures, sponsored important little luncheons. And now honest people are following the same pattern: everyone loves to get into the act, when it comes to celebrities. Yes, it has been one of the best public-relations jobs that the Communists ever put over. Beats your Madison Avenue, any day."

Ballard was absorbed in Sir Felix as he strolled past their table. His attention seemed more on the cut of Tarns's jacket than on Holland's words.

"You don't believe me?" Holland asked, shaking his head. It was always like this. Why had he bothered to waste valuable time? Those whom the gods would destroy, they first make mad, alas. . . .

"Why blame the Communists for everything? Sure, they are a bunch of twisters, but they aren't that smart."

"I didn't blame them for *everything*," Holland said coldly. "I'm blaming them for setting up a man who is a walking, talking lie."

"He has his own point of view." Ballard looked with indulgence at the Englishman sitting beside him. Narrow-minded little squirt, he thought. "I may not agree with it, but that doesn't mean he's a Commie mouthpiece."

"He hasn't any point of view," Holland said. "He only repeats what Fernand Lenoir tells him. Why else do you think he is in Venice, all expenses paid? . . . Dear me, are you leaving? So soon?" He watched Ballard walk away.

To Lieutenant Rusconi, who had moved over to Ballard's vacated chair, he said, "Well, Pietro—what's your guess?"

"You made him sweat a little," Pietro said in genuine

American. "I'd have got nowhere with him." He grinned and added, "Haven't the stamina."

"Did he listen?" Holland was still watching Ballard's retreating back. He was suddenly depressed.

"Well," said Pietro encouragingly, "we got Aarvan, anyway. I just hope the French make that murder rap stick."

"They will. There's a bullet in a man's back that will fit Aarvan's pet revolver." Yes, we got Aarvan, thought Holland. His eyes flickered to the pink lights of the restaurant across the Piazza. "You never can tell, can you?" he asked incredulously. Amateurs rushed in where most professionals feared to tread. It pleased him, somehow, that amateurs could sometimes get away with it, too. His eyes followed the retreating Ballard: no need to make him any angrier. Stir a man up a little, and he could be made to think; but add anger to anger, and a man's mind was sealed tight with blazing emotion. As Ballard, far off, a small dark dwarfed figure walking up a couple of steps into the brightly lit colonnade at the western end of the Piazza, abruptly halted and looked back, Holland shook his head. "No," he told Ballard as he moved between the giant pillars toward the narrow streets of Venice, "we didn't follow you. We're sitting right here where you left us." He said to Pietro, "Time for you to stride off. You are checking with Rosie?"

"I'll call him to report—"

"No. See him. I've got a message for him." Although they had been talking in low voices, Holland dropped his still more. "Can you hear? Good. Tell him that the big blow-up could be tomorrow evening, Monday. Got that?"

Pietro nodded.

"I think it *will* be. That's my own opinion." Holland took a deep breath. He had stuck his neck out, there. His job was to report, not to form any opinion. "Tomorrow evening," he repeated tensely. "All right. Get cracking. But carefully!"

Pietro looked thoughtfully at Holland. "So you got something besides making him sweat?" He rose and left.

"Watch it," Holland told Pietro under his breath, as a middle-aged, sensibly dressed woman stopped mothering the pigeons and stumped after Rusconi. But Pietro was taking no chances. He melted into a large group of sight-seers, the first batch of after-supper visitors drifting back into the Piazza to view the floodlighted cathedral. Even Holland's practiced eye could not be quite sure where he had left them, or in what direction. My turn, Holland thought, rising, and dropped five hundred lire on Ballard's coffee tray as an extra bonus for the tactful waiter who had followed instructions not to disturb this table. He set out at a gentle pace toward the eastern end of the Piazza.

He would be followed. He had asked for that, sitting down quite openly with Ballard. But ever since Fenner's unexpected move at Florian's, a lot of quick decisions and immediate action had developed. And if ever he had been justified in following up Fenner's second surprise, the message that seemed so impossible, he certainly was now: old Rosie would light up like this cathedral, and the austere little Inspector Bernard, all the way back in Paris, would be fizzing off in every direction like a Guy Fawkes rocket, when they got his message.

His problem, at this moment, was not that he was being tailed. (Hello, Neill, still talking over my shoulder? How do you like the way we sewed up Jan Aarvan?) Rather, how was he to make contact with the French agent, André, who had been waiting somewhere in front of the cathedral in case of any emergency? For the message he had given Pietro might not get through: it was crucial enough to be worth sending twice, once to the English and Americans, once to the French themselves. Where, oh where was Bernard's man? Over there, looking very much like a retired Swiss schoolmaster standing among the insomniac pigeons. André had seen Holland, too, for he had begun to move, leisurely and nonchalantly. Which would he choose: the cathedral itself, the clock tower to its left, or the Campanile on its right? The Campanile it was, rising high above all Venice from its own small island at this southeast corner of the Piazza. André vanished inside its doorway along with a thin straggle of tourists.

Holland didn't change his slow pace. He let a group of Austrian students (short leather trousers, and open-necked shirts, even a couple of rucksacks) cluster into the Campanile ahead of him, before he veered up the few steps into a square, stone-floored hall. Speed was essential now. He had a few lire ready, to buy his ride up into the sky.

The students were checking the cost, counting out the small coins worriedly, so Holland could slip ahead of them and enter the big elevator, fairly full, but still waiting for more customers. He had a brief attack of anxiety as a newcomer entered the hall quickly and made straight for the elevator. "Tickets over there!" its attendant said severely, and

pointed. The newcomer protested. The attendant's finger still
pointed, and the man had to obey, but with ill grace. The attendant noticed it, waited for the first six students, said,
"That's all!" and closed the door. Down in the hall, the impatient man was left with the remaining students, who were
keeping him firmly at the tail of their line.

Around Holland, the students were joking about their
friends who were left behind, drawing him good-humoredly
into this small triumph of one-upmanship. He smiled and relaxed. But once he reached the small observation terrace,
which ran around the four sides of the bell tower, he would
have to move quickly, before the next elevator load came up.
André would be startled, probably disapproving. But this was
a night for rules to be broken. This was a night for urgency.
If I can't make contact in two minutes, Holland thought, I
can't make it at all.

The night breeze from the lagoon to the south welcomed
them as they crowded onto the narrow terrace to join those
visitors who were already there. It was dimly lighted, so that
the brilliance of the scene far below them would not be
dulled. There was a jostling for the best view, an exclamation
of voices. André was moving slowly toward the west side of the
Campanile, reconnoitering quietly, expecting, no doubt, to
meet Holland coming around from the other direction. He
froze in complete disbelief as Holland seemingly stumbled
against him in the darkness. "The attempt is tomorrow, Monday night. Get going." That was all. Holland crossed over to
the parapet, near one of its few lights, looking for a view.

He found it, as some visitors decided to take this elevator
down. He heard its door clang shut. He could glance around.
André had gone. So all I have to do now is wait, Holland
thought: I'll wait for fifteen minutes, until almost nine o'clock,
and prove that whoever I was going to meet hasn't shown
up.

The view of Saint Mark's Basin was magnificent, at least.
He waited, hair and tie ruffled by the wind, watching the contrast, far below, of dark waters and sparkling lights. The
elevator made its staid and leisurely return to the terrace. He
looked around at the new arrivals. The delayed Austrians were
joined by a reinforcement. This may be unpleasant, Holland
thought as he let his eyes travel over all the new arrivals with
equal disinterest, and glanced at his watch, but in another way
it is good: the more concentration on me, the safer is that
gentle, self-effacing Swiss schoolmaster.

Holland stayed on the lagoon side of the terrace, observing each batch of visitors that the elevator unloaded, and the two men kept observing him. Twice he glanced at his watch. After fifteen minutes of this, he apparently decided to walk around and check the other sides of the terrace before he gave up waiting. He moved to the eastern balustrade, overlooking the floodlit domes and pinnacles of the cathedral and the pink-and-white palace of the Doges. The Austrian students were gathered here. And suddenly, one of them began to sing. The others joined in. The young, Holland thought, had a genius for the spontaneous gesture. He listened to the gathering strength of their voices: what was that they were singing? Simple, yet complicated. One of those Bach hymns? Or perhaps one of Vivaldi's pieces written for his choir of disfigured orphans who had sung his music down there, in the cathedral, their pitiful faces and crippled limbs forgotten, their clear voices soaring? Holland was thinking of Vienna as he turned the corner to reach the north side of the Campanile, of Vienna in 1947, when he had just met Neill Carlson, of Neill's small room, where his prize Bach records were played almost to death, of death itself among the ruins outside, where peace had brought occupation and cold war, of nine bodies fished out of the gray Danube in one week— some Soviet, some Allied agents, others unrecognizable. Cold war.... He felt a shiver of warning touch his spine lightly. The solitary man standing on this side of the terrace, watching the clock tower across the wide gulf of the Piazza, had turned as he heard Holland's slow footsteps coming over to share the parapet. It was Robert Wahl.

The two men faced each other for a split second before Holland rested his elbows on the parapet and studied the cluster of antlike people far below. Wahl was watching him. He has never seen me before, Holland reminded himself: I am only a name in one of his files. But he will know me again, that's certain. A suspicious type, this Wahl. Or is it Kalganov? Stop speculating, just watch. There he is, and here I am, both leaning elbows on the same wall, not six feet apart. One good shove might save us a lot of bloody history.

Who was Robert Wahl expecting to meet? Perhaps Jan Aarvan? Or was he just reviewing all his plans, taking a Napoleonic view of far horizons? The irony of the situation struck Holland—Wahl must have been here even as he was meeting the Swiss schoolmaster on the other side of the bell tower. Good God, he thought, if I had played the game correctly, we'd have both walked around and met right beside Wahl. He wanted to laugh—the best laughs always occurred when you couldn't enjoy them—as he left the balustrade and walked on. (Supressed laughter was hardly the mood for one good shove. The wall was too high, in any case: it would take two men to heave a body over. Besides, someone below was liable to be hurt or killed. And I'm no Jan Aarvan, Holland thought.)

His pace had quickened as he was about to turn the corner onto the western side of the terrace, wondering if he could reach the Piazza in time to find one of the allied agents there and pass on the word that Robert Wahl was aloft and must descend sometime. He halted abruptly. The two men were blocking his path. They walked down on him, ready to jump him. They were Aarvan's friends, all right. He backed slowly, watching their hands. They moved forward, stopped as they saw Wahl over by the parapet. They hesitated for the fraction of a second that Holland needed. He sprinted back the way he had come, right into the cluster of students. They were too intent on their last harmony to pay attention to the white-faced intruder among them.

He stayed with them, and regained a steady pulse. The two men didn't follow. They might be waiting, but he wouldn't give them another chance to find him alone on a narrow dark terrace, three hundred and twenty-five feet above marble pavement. As for Robert Wahl, he wouldn't wait to be tagged and trailed by Holland's friends—he was probably reaching the Piazza at this very minute. Aarvan's two men had not known who Wahl was, far less Kalganov. In any supersecret organization like theirs, working in enemy territory, the chain of command was carefully concealed. Kalganov's talent for elaborate precaution had saved his own life a hundred times and more. Tonight, thought Holland, with a grim smile, it saved mine.

The students moved off. He kept with them, talking about Vienna, all the way down, all the way across the Piazza San Marco to the labyrinth of narrow streets that spread out behind the clock tower. As they echoed his *"Auf Wiedersehen!"* he had already stepped into a side alley, and was lost in the shadows.

TWENTY-TWO

SANDRA FANE was ready. She carried her handbag, a scarf to cover her head, her darkest coat. And that was all. She combed her hair, made up her face quickly, distributed some of the pieces of jewelry from the bulging bag to her coat's pocket. As for the map—she'd need that to get out of this rabbit warren of a city. A bus or a train? Padua or Milan? And the letter, still secure within the map—she'd throw that into the nearest canal once she was well away from this house. It would take minutes to destroy it here, and there could be scraps of evidence left. Nothing must connect her with that letter. And every second was precious. Every second . . .

At her door, she paused only long enough to make sure that none of the servants were wandering around. (There were three of them, two men and a woman, whom Lenoir had installed, bringing them mysteriously from nowhere: they seemed dull and stupid, but they were no doubt extremely dependable.) But there was no sound. She locked the bedroom door behind her, slipped the key into her pocket, and took off her shoes. Quickly, with sure footsteps and a fluttering heart, she started her silent journey down the curving staircase. Lenoir's door was shut. Thick walls, dim lights, deep shadows . . . The hall below was as empty as a tomb. Her pace increased to a silent run.

She reached the foot of the staircase, and started around the side of the circular hall, using the pillars that supported its dark vaulted ceiling as shelter. She flitted from one to another, passing several ornate doors, all deeply shadowed, all firmly shut—there were several rooms on this floor, but apart from the dining room, the kitchen, and service quarters, no one used them any more. They were too close to the canal level for any comfort. Down here, she could feel the chill of the cool waters outside, even within these thick walls. The flagstone floor turned her feet to ice.

She had half circled the hall. The heavy wooden door that led to the little street was only a few yards away. From the comforting darkness of the last pillar, she glanced back up the staircase. She could see Lenoir's sitting room, closed and quiet. Now! she told herself. She stepped out of the pillar's shadow, her eyes on the street door, studying its massive iron decorations. Which bars locked it, what ones were only part of the elaborate design?

Sharply, the hall's deep silence shivered into fragments. A bell's clanging tongue railed at the house. She jumped. Almost cried out. She retreated behind the pillar, sagged against it for a long moment. Slow, heavy footsteps had come out of a room near the street door as the angry echo died away. That was the servant called Martin, the stupidest of the lot, thank her luck. But she had been stupid herself: she ought to have known that the door to this house would be guarded.

"I have an appointment with Monsieur Lenoir," a man's voice said. "I am early, but I—"

(Whose voice? She knew it. Her thoughts were as jangled as her heartbeats. Whose?)

"—hope he can see me now. Tell him that—"

Lenoir's voice interrupted, from the top of the first flight of stairs. "Who is that? Who is it?"

She did not move. It's Mike Ballard, she thought in amazement. Ballard—here, in Venice?

Footsteps entered farther into the hall. "It's Ballard. I am a little early, I know—"

"A little?" Lenoir was furious. "Forty minutes, to be exact."

"I'm sorry. It's just that I—I had to see you as soon as possible."

"I am busy."

"I'll wait. I have some questions to ask you."

Lenoir's voice changed. "If you don't mind waiting downstairs for half an hour, I'll be able to talk with you. I am engaged at present. You see my difficulty?"

"I'll wait."

"Martin! Make Mr. Ballard comfortable. Take him into the dining room. Give him a Scotch and soda." And stay with him, the words implied. Lenoir's door closed angrily.

Martin's heavy footsteps led Ballard toward the arch at whose side Sandra Fane was standing so still. She slipped on her shoes and off her coat, dropping it out of sight at the base of the pillar, and stepped out to meet them. "Hello, Mike," she said, "how nice that you could come! That's all right, Martin—I'll entertain Mr. Ballard until Monsieur Lenoir is free. Go and have your supper."

The idea attracted Martin. "But—" he began, reluctantly thinking of his orders.

"I am here with Mr. Ballard," Sandra said sharply. She calculated a neatly placed indiscretion. "There is no need for two of us to stay with him."

Martin nodded, and left. She noted that he entered the door leading to the kitchen quarters. That's that, she thought; there remains only Ballard to deal with. Where does he stand, I wonder. Why should he have been invited to Ca' Longhi if he wasn't another Sir Felix Tarns? Yet, as she took him quickly into the dining room and closed the door, his face was a study in amazement.

"Stay with me?" he repeated. "Was that fellow supposed to *watch* me?"

"Fernand trusts no one. Not even me. Why are you here?"

"He didn't tell you?"

"No."

"Then I'd better not," he said, with a touch of humor. He looked in the direction of a chair, but she made no move, simply stood staring at him. She seemed tense; her face was pale, almost haggard. "Are you all right, Sandra?"

"No."

"What's wrong?"

"Are you one of—of us?" Keep the words safe, she told herself: use nothing that he could repeat against you, if he is a secret Communist. And if he is, she thought, he certainly took me in.

"What do you mean?"

"I never guessed you were a sleeper. You really are skillful, Mike."

He repeated, very slowly, "What do you mean?"

"You don't have to keep up the pretense with me."

"I'm not pretending anything," he said angrily, and made a move toward the door.

She had her back against it. Her voice dropped. "Sorry if I've hurt your feelings. You see, there has been such a parade of secret visitors all day." She watched him carefully. "An Italian Communist from Milan, some Cuban on his way back from Moscow—all so important, so secret. And there was Sir Felix Tarns here for luncheon." There was no doubt that she had shocked him. "Robert Wahl, and Jan Aarvan, and—"

She didn't have to go on. He was a man stupefied. He shook his head. Disbelief gave way to anger. "And you have been a Communist all along," he said slowly. "You were the pretender. My God—" He gripped her arm, tried to pull her aside from the door.

"Where do you think you are going?" she asked.

"To see Lenoir—"

"That isn't very smart. You'll blurt out what I've told you, demand an explanation. Either he will have you silenced or —if he can persuade you to do what he wants—he will let you say alive. Why did you come here, anyway?"

"There was some information, an inside story—"

"So that was the bait to get you hooked. But what brought you here ahead of your appointment?"

"I—I had some questions. Some thoughts I had this evening—" He paused, remembering Fenner and that quiet Englishman. "They kept bothering me. I—I just wanted to see Lenoir, ask him—" He looked at her, his eyes suddenly desperate. "What do I do, Sandra? They'll blast my career to pieces."

"Blackmail?" she asked, her voice sad, sympathetic. The stupid, bumbling oaf, she thought. "There is one way to deal with blackmail of that kind, and that is to know more about them than they know about you. I'll give you an inside story that would blast more than their careers."

He stared at her.

"If," she added, "you will help me."

"How?"

"Come," she said quickly, "come!" She tugged at his sleeve. He wasn't moving. "How do I help you?"

"I'll tell you when we get outside. If Martin stops us, say we are taking a short stroll—that we're freezing to death in here." We could get away with that, she thought. Martin was a servant, after all, and a dumb one, too.

But Mike Ballard was still wary.

"Please help me, Mike! They are sending me back to Russia. There's a freighter sailing early tomorrow, and I have to be on board at midnight. All I want you to do is to get me out of here. Hide me. Find Bill Fenner and tell him where I am. He knows where to get help. You won't have to do anything more—except write your story. Look—" Her voice and face had become tense as he stood there, silent. She opened her handbag and pulled out a folded map and thrust it deep into his jacket pocket. "Half of your story is in there—the other half is in what I can tell you. You see I mean what I promise." She took a deep sigh of relief. She felt better, somehow, that she no longer carried that damned letter.

"What is this map?" he wanted to know. He tried to take it out and look at it, but she pushed his hand back into his pocket.

"Oh—of Venice," she said impatiently. "It's only cover for a letter. Keep that safe, Mike. And help me escape. I'll tell you enough to outblackmail any blackmailer."

"What letter?" he asked.

"I'll explain it. I'll tell you its whole background. Come! Hurry!" She was opening the massive door, slowly, just one careful inch.

Ballard stayed where he was. He watched the concentration on her face. I believed her once, he thought; I liked her. I was sorry for her. And all the time she was playing a part, making fools out of all of us. I never would have trusted Lenoir if I hadn't trusted her. And now—she may be telling the truth, but I don't give a damn. They can ship her off to Russia, and good riddance, I'd say. Good riddance if the whole pack got shipped off to Russia, the lying and cunning sons of bitches, all of them, blackmailers and cheats.

"Please, Mike!" she begged quietly, from the door. Her voice trembled, her blue eyes were large and pleading. "This means so much—"

Lenoir's voice asked, "What means so much?" With one arm he thrust the door wide open. In his other hand, he held a dark coat. Behind him was Martin, and the other man servant. He looked at Mike Ballard, who was standing well back from the door, and then at Sandra. She couldn't speak. She only kept staring at her coat.

She told me the truth this time, Ballard thought, she actually told me the truth. The way she stood there, white-faced and hopeless, was too much for him. He said, "Why —Sandra was only trying to get me to take her out to dinner."

"Was she?"

Sandra clutched at Ballard's excuse, even if he had got it wrong. There was some of the old sharpness in her words, but her voice was faint. "I wanted to walk in the fresh air. I wanted to get out of this horrible, hideous house."

"And after dinner? What then?" Lenoir's controlled fury began to slip its leash. He pulled a handful of jewelry from her coat pocket, almost threw it in her face. He looked at Ballard. "Where were you taking her?"

Ballard didn't have to pretend amazement. He stared unbelievingly at the glitter of diamonds and emeralds. "What the—" he began. "Have you two gone crazy or something?"

Lenoir accepted his astonishment. He dropped the coat and the jewels at his feet. He nodded to the two men behind him. "Take over here," he told them. To Ballard, he said, "Come."

Ballard stopped to speak to Sandra. "We'll have dinner another time," he said gently. "I wasn't being ungallant—I just couldn't make it tonight. I've got to take a telephone call at nine-thirty. From New York. Can't miss it."

Lenoir said coldly, "You had an appointment with me at half past nine."

"This one is with my boss."

There was a slight flutter of Lenoir's eyelids.

"That's why I dropped in early. Just took a chance—"

"Well, come upstairs."

"There's scarcely time." Ballard was beginning to enjoy himself. He glanced at his watch. "It's five after nine."

"I ended my other appointment quickly—" began Lenoir angrily.

"Sorry, Fernand. These things happen. Can't stand up old Walter Penneyman. I'll come back after his call. Good night, Sandra." He took her hands, and they were ice-cold. "Have lunch with me tomorrow?" Perhaps she got his message, perhaps she grasped that he was going to get out of this house and find help, and let her be free to walk away, have lunch with him or anyone, as she pleased. Or perhaps not. Her eyes were looking past him at the two men who had entered the room.

"Come," Lenoir said, and gestured to Ballard impatiently. He closed the door behind them. As they walked into the cavern of a hall he was saying unhappily, "Sandra hasn't been at all well. I am sorry you had to witness that little scene." He sighed. "I don't know what to do, frankly. She—she keeps stealing things. You saw the jewels—they are mine, you know, belonged to my mother. Do you know what she was going to do with them? Sell them to anyone she could find. Believe me, my dear fellow, she has done this before. I've had the most enormous trouble getting them back again. Last month, in Paris—oh, well, why bother you with my worries?"

They had almost reached the street door.

Lenoir, still speaking in the same friendly voice, said, "What happened in the Piazza San Marco this evening? I heard there was a small sensation at Florian's."

"A man was arrested." But he knows all that, Ballard thought. Whoever telephoned him the news in the last fifteen minutes gave him all the details. Perhaps that telephone call was the real reason why he had cut short that interview upstairs: suddenly, I was important.

"Who was he?"

"He never told me his name. He came and sat at my table. He was trying to blackmail me." Ballard smiled. "I told him to go to hell."

Lenoir's surprise was real.

"After that, the police arrived. They asked me some questions about him, naturally enough. But I knew nothing."

"Why was he arrested?"

"Blackmailers often get arrested," Ballard said cheerfully. "Good night, Fernand. See you later?"

"Not tonight. Tomorrow."

"I'll be here early. Around nine?"

Lenoir nodded. He was preoccupied. He didn't even pay attention to the scream of pain, distant and faint, that froze Ballard as the heavy door closed behind him and shut him out into the dark, narrow street. A light mist was condensing; the pavement was damp in patches, and the chill from the canal at one end of the short *calle* sent a shiver up his spine. Or maybe it was the memory of that pitiful scream. He set out quickly, walking away from the canal, choosing to plunge back into the labyrinth of Venice by way of the little square. He wasn't being followed; there were no footsteps except the echoes of his. Yet he still had that odd feeling of being watched.

Even as he crossed the sagging pavement of the small square, with its leaning church tower, its closely shuttered houses, its dimly lit café filled with men, the feeling persisted. He resisted breaking into a run, but his pace quickened, and —as the bright shop windows of the next *calle* helped light his way into more crowded streets—he took his first real breath of relief. His brain began to function again.

He chose the lighted doorway of a shoeshop, and stepped out of the stream of people flowing toward the Piazza San

Marco. He pulled the map out of his pocket as if to study
his direction. There was a letter inside—so she hadn't been
lying about that, either—addressed to a Major Christopher
Holland from someone called P. Trouin. He read on, quickly, then folded the letter away in his map and put it carefully back into his pocket. He stared at a row of women's
velvet slippers, red, blue, yellow, pink, beaded and bejeweled, for twelve hundred lire. The letter was like an acid
burning its way into his mind. That was one story, he
sensed, that he never could use: whatever the truth, or the
lie, in that letter, it was far outside his province. Could it
be true? If so, the whole damned world was on the skids,
and his own country was to blame. It couldn't be true—
surely? Or supposing it was a fake, meant to be taken as
true? It would work; it was working on him: he kept
saying it couldn't be true, it couldn't, surely? He knew one
thing definitely: he had been given the hottest package in
Venice to hold. If Lenoir had ordered Martin to search him,
he wouldn't be alive at this minute. Clever little Sandra, and
sucker Mike ... The sooner he got rid of this, the better.
The easy way was to throw it into the next canal he crossed.
The easy way ... Had he become such a yellowbelly as that?

Someone brushed his arm, and he jerked around, ready to
hit back.

"Such darling slippers," the girl was saying, "and only two
dollars! Andy, you must bring me here tomorrow morning
when the shop opens. Just look!"

"I'm looking." Her husband glanced after Ballard. "Say,
we startled that fellow. Who did he think we were, d'you
suppose?"

The girl laughed happily. "Really, Venice is the most
wonderful place. I think I'll have the pink ones."

TWENTY-THREE

UPSTAIRS AT Quadri's, in one of its small softly lighted rooms, with a window wide open beside their table to let them look out over the Piazza, Claire and Bill Fenner dined on red mullet, drank properly chilled Montrachet, and talked. This, he thought as he watched her, had turned out to be a good idea although it had started badly enough.

At first, Claire had been so depressed by Mike Ballard's performance that she had scarely touched her *apéritif*, seemed to have no interest in the tantalizing menu. Even this little table, with its splendid view of the lighted colonnade stretching down the other side of the Piazza, had seemed a mistake, for it had let her see Ballard still sitting over there, talking to Jan Aarvan again.

"I can't bear it," she said quietly. "I just can't bear it. Did we make any mistakes with Ballard, give anything away? Surely he wouldn't—" She bit her lip, looked down at the white cloth and gleaming silver.

"If he does," Fenner said equally quietly, putting his hand over hers, "he won't know he is doing it."

"And that excuses him?" For talking our lives away? She thought bleakly.

"No excuses offered. It's just an explanation."

"It doesn't make me feel any better," she said, trying to smile, failing. She looked back at Florian's. Her eyes widened in disbelief. "We've got him," she said, her voice unsteady with suppressed excitement. "We've got him Bill."

He looked as casually as he could over his shoulder, and saw the end of Aarvan's arrest. He looked back at her. "Now," he said, releasing her hand, "will you drink that Cinzano?"

"Lemon peel and all," she agreed, beginning to laugh.

She raised her glass in a toast. "One down and two to go!" She said very softly.

"I'm glad I'm on your side," he told her. He glanced over his shoulder at Florian's once more. Holland was about to sit down at that distant table. So Pietro *had* understood English. Fenner took a deep breath of relief, and finished his drink.

"All I want is justice," she said, serious again, but no longer unhappy. "Without that, the world is turned upside down, and swamped with bitterness. No thank you—not for me."

"Now I know why the figure of Justice is always shown as a woman," he teased her. "Blindfolded, naturally."

"Naturally?"

"So that in spite of a soft heart, she can play no favorites." He picked up the menu.

"Soft heart or soft head?" she wanted to know. "It's strange, though, that women will say one thing and then do another. We sort of back out, find excuses, hope. . . . In a way, we earn our own disappointments." She looked across the Piazza again.

"Did you earn Mike Ballard?"

"Yes," she said frankly. "I kept hoping he wouldn't, he couldn't. But—well, he did. And that's that." She said it sadly.

"Let's leave him to old Dr. Chris, shall we?"

She studied him thoughtfully. "Men are puzzling," she said. "I had the idea you didn't like—" She glanced around the room. Talking softly like this, they couldn't be overheard. Their window table was isolated from those along the walls. "That you didn't like Chris too much."

"Oh, just a natural reaction. I felt he resented me." Which would be a natural reaction, too: there was I, with Claire, happy and confident and alive; and there was Neill Carlson, dead. He said quickly, to pull her away from that direction of thought, "So men are puzzling? And women aren't?"

"You don't seem too baffled by them."

He shook his head. "If we had forty years together, you'd still keep me guessing."

She looked at him.

"Or fifty," he said smoothly, studying the menu. "What about some red mullet? But first—let's see . . . ."

She watched him as he chose and ordered. She felt a strange warmth, a new sense of relaxing, of light in frightening darkness—light that didn't flicker and vanish, light that held steady and grew. I am tired of walking alone, she thought, of searching and groping and drawing back to past memories. I need someone to lean on, to have with me, and he with; never alone and lost and afraid any more. But that was only a part of the truth, as she knew when his eyes met hers, and stayed, holding hers.

"And wine, signore?" the waiter murmured politely, bringing them back from the long moment of discovery.

"And wine," said Fenner absent-mindedly, forgetting the small pride he took in vineyard and vintage. Tonight, water would have tasted like champagne.

So they dined and talked, their small table an island unto itself, the rest of the room forgotten.

And suddenly Mike Ballard stood beside them, signaling the waiter for another chair. "Do you mind if I join you?" he asked. He was too worried to enjoy the amazement on their faces. "Hello, beautiful," he said to Claire. He was never too worried for that.

"It seems as if you have," Fenner said coldly as Ballard sat down, his back to the room, and switched off the small pink lamp. He waved away the waiter's outheld menu. "Haven't much time."

"Better order something," Claire said. It wasn't only a conditioned reflex springing to work: to make the unusual seem perfectly normal. He's ill, she was thinking. Not drunk, as she had first thought: something was very wrong with Mike Ballard.

He took the menu, placed it in front of him, rested his elbow on it. "Double Scotch and soda," he told the waiter. He looked at Fenner. "I'm taking the first plane I can get back to Paris. But there are two things I've got to do right away." He leaned forward, lowered his voice. "How do we get help to Sandra Fane?"

Fenner recovered quickly. "Why ask me?"

"Cut it out, cut it out," Ballard said irritably. "She told me to get in touch with you if she escaped. She wasn't dousing me with eyewash this time. Not tonight."

Fenner and Claire exchanged a glance. He said, "She escaped? Where is she?"

"She tried to. It didn't work. When I left that place—it's called Ca' Longhi—they had started beating her. Or something." He could still hear the scream. "They are putting her on board a freighter at midnight—it sails tomorrow morning. I guess you don't think you owe her much. Still—she delivered half a story. It could have got me dumped into a canal, it's true," he smiled grimly, "but she did make sure it got out of that house. So you owe her—"

Claire had seen the waiter arriving. "Bill was explaining to me," she cut in quickly, "why he is all in favor of a repertory theater in New York. Don't you agree that if we could alternate a popular play with a classic each week, we could make one pay for the other?" She watched the waiter leaving. "Yes, Mike?" she asked softly.

"So you owe her something," he told Fenner. "That's how I see it." He didn't touch his drink. He had slipped one hand into his pocket and brought out a map. Quietly, he inserted it between the pages of the menu, put his elbow back on top of it. "What about it, Bill?"

Fenner looked at Claire. Is this true? he seemed to be asking her. Can we really take his word?

Claire said, "Couldn't we send the police in?" But on what excuse? she wondered.

"And tell them that a Frenchman is having his mistress beaten up by two servants? They would think it just some new angle in French fun and games. Besides, Lenoir would find an excuse for anything." He stared hard at Fenner. "I've learned," Ballard said bitterly. He looked down at the menu. "Can you help?"

"We'll get word to some people who might be able to."

"That's a promise? You'll get word to them right away?"

Fenner nodded. "You said something about half a story. What is it?"

"A letter. You'll find it inside this menu. Tell me one thing: is it real or is it a fake."

"A fake."

Ballard took a deep breath of relief. "It shook me," he admitted. He picked up his drink and swallowed a large gulp. "Sure, I read it. I thought I might as well know what I was dying for." His smile was brief. "Also, I thought I could use it, perhaps. But"—he shook his head—"half a story could be the wrong story. I'll wait for the whole of it."

"You'll get it," Fenner promised him.

"If it can be told," Ballard said gloomily. But at least, he thought, Bill Fenner can't use it at all. That's certain. He brightened, and finished his drink. "Well—see you in Paris."

"Not if you go back to your hotel," Fenner said very quietly.

"You mean——? But I talked my way out of Ca' Longhi without a slip. And I wasn't tailed. I am pretty sure of that."

"Because Lenoir knows where he can find you." Fenner let that fact sink in, and added, "Wait for us downstairs. Outside. Be careful, Mike. Follow us at a safe distance. We'll take you to our hotel. You can't walk the streets all night, or sit at a café, or try to register at another hotel." His passport would give his name away, and Lenoir's men would soon track him down. "I'll smuggle you up to my room. And I'll pass word to our friends that you may need a little help, too."

Ballard's face was pale. "Me?" He sounded almost indignant.

"Sandra is being questioned right now, isn't she?"

Ballard nodded. "You think she will break?"

Fenner said nothing. Yes, she probably will. She is being interrogated by experts. How much will she tell? Everything? Or just enough to make a deal with Lenoir? We feel we owe her something, but there is one thing certain: Sandra feels no obligation, no loyalty to us.

"I get you," Ballard said dully. "If I tried to check out of my hotel tonight——" He didn't finish. "I get you," he said again, and rose.

He hadn't bargained for that, Fenner thought, as he watched Ballard leave. But he would rally, like the rest of us, when he had got accustomed to the idea of more trouble ahead. Fenner lifted the menu, felt for the map, slid it quietly under his napkin, called for the check, added a handsome tip, and pocketed the map along with his wallet. "How do we reach Rosie?" he asked as he helped Claire slip into her coat.

"Arnaldi's."

The camera shop near the bridge. It was on the way to the Vittoria, thank heaven. "It's twenty minutes of ten," he said as they went down the narrow flight of stairs into the small ground-floor room. "I think we had better cut out that gondola ride."

She nodded. Not many people down here in this room, she noted, and no one who seemed interested in them. No one was hastily calling for his check, leaving his drink unfinished. No one followed them, either, from the brightly lit arcade, except Mike Ballard, who had waited sensibly on the shad-

owed side of one of the arches, and was keeping at a reasonable distance. No one was interested in them at all now.
Why? Were they out of suspicion? Perhaps. It was ironic
that at this point, when they had managed to free themselves
of suspicion, Sandra should have been trapped. What was Bill
thinking, feeling? she wondered. His face was expressionless.
He hadn't spoken since they had come down Quadri's stairs.
He was walking quickly, though, his arm through hers, drawing her along. Sandra, she realized, that's what is driving
him like this. I'll have to start planning for both of us again,
she thought unhappily: emotions, in this job, only led to mistakes.

In silence, Fenner made a cautious detour once they had
left the Piazza, choosing a *calle* that seemed to lead them
away from Arnaldi's shop. But in Venice there was always
another *calle* to lead back. The crowds had thinned out:
most Venetians were already home, thinking of tomorrow's
early start to work. The visitors still window-shopped or
wandered leisurely in a happy daze. No one was following
them, except Mike Ballard. Of that, Claire was sure. And
somehow it worried her. She remembered Bill's good reason
why Mike hadn't been trailed from Ca' Longhi: they knew
where he could be found. That same reason could apply to
us, she thought. As they came back onto the street that would
lead them over the bridge, she said, "Is our hotel safe, Bill?"

"If I see anyone hanging around watching for us, I won't
leave Mike there."

"Then what?" We can't take him near Arnaldi's. That is
definite. We don't even know if his story is true: there may
be no letter inside that map. And yet we've got to assume
the story is real; and hurry; and act, perhaps even rashly. Because of Sandra, because of what she may be suffering.

"I'll think of something," Fenner said worriedly. Perhaps
I'll send him off with Zorzi, and let them drift around the
lagoon for a couple of hours. "First, I'll see you safely into
the shop. You know what to do?"

"Telephone Chris, and have him contact Rosie. When Rosie
comes, I hand over the letter."

"If there is a letter," Fenner said quietly.

"Be careful, Bill," she said, remembering the approach to
the hotel's courtyard. By night, there must be patches of pitch
blackness in that narrow alley. She opened her handbag.
"Take this," she said, slipping her small automatic into his
jacket pocket.

"What—" Then he knew. So she had been thinking, too, of that dark approach to the hotel's back door.

"The Little Comforter," she said, half smiling. She was looking at the camera shop, no more than forty feet ahead of them. "If it's closed, there's a back entrance on an alley. We're just passing it, Bill. See it?"

It was a narrow strip of darkness, wide enough for a lean Venetian to squeeze his way through. He hoped they wouldn't have to use it. You could waste a lot of time searching for the right doorway, or courtyard, or whatever particular whimsy the ingenious architects of Venice had thought up. "We're in luck," he said thankfully. The shop ahead, about to close, was still half open. The boy, Luigi, was fastening a strong grille over its window, already darkened. Fenner's pace slowed, so that Ballard caught up with them. "Walk on," he told him, "to that shoe window over there. Keep inside its doorway. I'll be with you in one minute." He watched to make sure that Ballard didn't look back at them, before he steered Claire quickly into the camera shop. Luigi's bored face brightened as he saw them, but he went on with his job.

Inside, there was one dim light shining down on the counter where Arnaldi, in shirt sleeves, was checking the day's earnings. The rest of the shop was in deep shadow. Fenner chose a corner hidden from the street by a display of photographs. He said, "We have to make an emergency phone call to our friend. Urgent. Most urgent. Can you get him for us? The signora will talk to him. I'm leaving. But I'll be back in ten minutes."

Arnaldi nodded—perhaps in his life he had seen so much that was unexpected that he had reached the limit of surprise —and limped toward the back sitting room.

"Take this." Fenner gave her the map. "Check the letter before you talk with Chris. Tell him Ballard's story, too." He gripped her arms.

"Highest urgency." She looked at his face in the half-darkness. "I know, Bill. And they'll get Sandra out of that house, somehow." She felt his hands tighten on her arms.

"I'm worrying about you," he said quietly.

For a moment, she said nothing. "I'll be safe." Safer than you, she thought miserably.

"Take care—"

"And you take care—"

His arms went around her, holding her close, crushing

her body against his. He kissed her, a long kiss, deep and strong, that took her life and gave her his, a plea and a promise, a beginning. Just as suddenly, he freed her, and was gone.

She heard the door close gently. She stood very still. Then she flung her arms wide, threw her head back, and laughed with sheer joy.

Behind her, Arnaldi cleared his throat. "Your friend is waiting."

She turned, still smiling, but in control of her emotions again, to slip quietly into Arnaldi's back room. He had got the call through quickly, she thought. She still had to check on the letter inside the map. She halted abruptly. "Chris!" she said unbelievingly.

"The bearer of joyful tidings, I see, all rosy and wreathed in smiles and properly tousled. Come in, sweetie, and share this pew, and tell Uncle Chris all about it." He was sitting on the bottom step of a narrow staircase that climbed up the back wall of the room to the bedroom overhead, dressed in wildly striped pajamas and a bright dressing gown, both too loose and long. "Vicente," he addressed Arnaldi, "you go back to your counting-house. And thank you for wakening me so effectively. A cold-water sponge," he explained to Claire. "Never fails." He was making conversation until Arnaldi closed the door.

She took his cue. "Asleep at this hour?" She opened the map and found the letter. She glanced through it quickly, raising an eyebrow as she saw the name of Major Christopher Holland. He wasn't going to like that. She shook her head.

"What else was there to do? I've been quarantined, put out of sight for twenty-four hours. Seemed safer for all of us. I'm hot, my dear; I'm a wanted man. But I scored a little bull's-eye, I think. I hope so. If I guessed wrong, I'll be rusticated permanently—back to the old Finance Division, tracking down dead Nazis' loot." He paused, watching her replace the letter carefully. "All right," he said most seriously. "What's up?"

"Get Rosie here."

"Rosie is having a very busy night, my pet. Must we—"

"Get him, Chris. We have the letter."

He stared at her. "Good God," he said slowly. Then quickly, "How?"

"Telephone, first. I'll explain, once you've tracked down Rosie."

He got up and padded over to the telephone in his bare feet. He hadn't been able to borrow slippers that would fit. As he waited for his call to go through, he eyed the map she held most firmly in her hand. "I couldn't pinch-hit for Rosie, could I?"

She smiled at the mixture of phrase and accent, and reciprocated. "That wouldn't be cricket. He is my boss."

"I can read, too, you know."

"You can't expect to hit the bull's-eye twice in one night."

"Why not?" He conceded his defeat with a grin. "It was a nice try, anyway. Where's your devoted American?" He started to talk into the receiver, something about a fishing boat having docked with a full catch; immediate delivery advisable in this warm weather.

The call was over. "Rosie is on his way," Chris told her. "He won't take long. Is Bill all right?"

"Yes, yes," she said, "he's all right." She was thinking, our job is over. Bill and I are free. The job is over. I give this letter to Rosie, and the job is over.

Chris Holland, watching the emotion on her face, said quietly, "Come along, Scheherazade. Tell me the end of this story. How did you get that letter?"

Fenner found Ballard mesmerized before a window of velvet slippers, beaded and bejeweled, red, blue, green, pink. "Can't make up your mind? Take the blue."

"Sharks," Ballard said, walking on with him. "Three dollars here. I know a place I can get them for two." He sounded more like himself now. "That was the longest minute I ever lived through," he said reproachfully. "Spooky place, Venice, when the crowds leave the streets. Chilly, too." He turned up the collar of his silk tweed jacket.

"The minute stretched a little," Fenner admitted with a grin. "You're lucky I didn't take ten."

"You sound pretty cheerful."

"I am."

Ballard relaxed still more. "You know, Bill—if you had only tipped me off when I met you at Orly, everything could have been simpler for all of us."

Fenner didn't answer. They were starting up the steps of the bridge over the canal. Three men were standing together on its other side, one of them a gondolier. They interrupted their talk as the two Americans came up and over the bridge, and in that brief look, Fenner could feel their surprise. Surprise? I'm getting too damned sensitive, he thought.

As he and Ballard came down the steps, and left the street to turn onto the quay, he saw that the gondolas which usually clustered there were all out on hire except the one that belonged to the gondolier at the bridge. No Zorzi? It was five minutes before ten. Zorzi had possibly picked up another fare. And yet Zorzi had struck him as a man who'd keep his word, just as he'd expect others to keep theirs.

"Something wrong?" Ballard asked, nervous again. On the street, there had been strolling footsteps and talking voices. Down here on this empty quay, which ran briefly along the canal and then dodged under the cover of overhanging houses to become a *sotto portico,* there was nothing but the sound of water slapping idly against stone.

"It's all right," Fenner said reassuringly. He paused beside one of the heavy squat pillars that supported the low, ill-lit arches of the *sotto portico,* to watch a gondola come gliding up from the Grand Canal, floating out of the darkness, passing them silently, the gondolier not even breaking the slow rhythm of his oar as he bent low to slip under the bridge and vanish. Not Zorzi, anyway.

"Come on," Ballard urged. "What has got into you?"

I don't know, Fenner thought, but the sooner I deposit Ballard safely in my room, the sooner I can find out. So quickly he led Ballard away from the canal and the vaulted porch, into the narrow dark alley lined with two rows of shuttered windows. People lived here, for there was music from one room, faint laughter from another, and an occasional ribbon of light where a shutter was left one inch open. But he kept his hand in his pocket.

Ballard was mumbling in a husky whisper, as if the privacy around him was closing in on his voice, too. "As I was saying, if you had only tipped me off when I met you out at Orly—"

"About what?"

"That you were with Intelligence."

"But I wasn't."

Ballard laughed shortly. "That's what they all say. But if you had told me, then we wouldn't be prowling down this godforsaken alley. Because I wouldn't have come to Venice—" He tripped and clutched Fenner for balance. "What's that?"

"A cat. Or your own big feet."

They entered the courtyard. By night, it had a look of

theatrical gloom—a compact stage-set, dimly lighted, for even here the heavy walls seemed to eat up the brightness of the lamps set high on the surrounding houses. By contrast, the hotel's wide doors, opened and welcoming, showed an empty lobby ablaze with gleam and glitter. Fenner's grip on Claire's small automatic loosened, and he took his hand out of his pocket. "Walk straight ahead and use the staircase. Wait for me on the floor above. I'll get the key and take the elevator."

Ballard nodded obediently, and entered the hotel. Fenner followed watchfully. No one around except the night porter, alone at his desk, and an elevator boy. Everyone else was in the bar or the dining room, or out on the town. He could relax a little as he took the slow elevator, and ponder over Ballard's new amenability. Either Ballard felt the edge of danger on which they were all balancing so precariously or he had stopped worrying that Fenner was after his job. Was that what he meant when he said, in his own peculiar form of reasoning, that Fenner had been to blame for his arrival in Venice? Because Fenner was in Venice, and a story was in Venice. But if Fenner was working for Intelligence, he could never use the story and so Ballard could stop worrying. Was that it? Fenner shook his head in wry amusement. He was relieved, at least, that Ballard had stopped glooming around.

But he could wish, when he met Ballard upstairs and noted his rising euphoria, now that they were safe in a brightly lit, comfortable hotel, that Ballard had stayed a little more scared. The edge of danger was a slippery place.

He hurried Ballard into his room, with no one to see them enter. The bed had been turned down, the light left on to welcome him. "Stay here. Keep the door locked. If the telephone rings, wait for an identification before you speak."

"What's the password?" Ballard was highly amused.

"Florian," said Fenner on the spur of the moment. "You won't forget that."

"No," Ballard said abruptly. He chose a comfortable armchair and looked around the room. "So I wait here."

"You wait here." Fenner turned back to the door.

"I could use a drink and a sandwich."

"You'll have them. Just wait, meanwhile." Fenner was getting impatient. "That's little enough to—"

"Do you know who was in the bar? Drinking brandy with his coffee, lucky stiff. Tarns. Sir Felix Tarns."

Fenner halted. "Did he see you?"

"No." Ballard was irritated. "Would that matter?" Tarns was a stinker, but not the Jan Aarvan type. His mood was back to high amusement. "You know, I was thinking how we could shake him a little. Just enough to—"

"You keep away from that telephone!" Fenner said angrily, making a quick guess.

"Okay, okay."

"All set?"

"Any cigarettes? I'm all out." Ballard caught the pack that Fenner had tossed over on his way to the door. "Stay for a couple of minutes, Bill. Claire has given the alarm about Sandra, hasn't she? So what's the rush?"

"You are part of it," Fenner reminded him, opening the door.

"When do I get bailed out?"

"Soon."

"How soon is soon? One hour? Two? Am I just to sit—"

"You'll find a couple of books on top of the dresser," Fenner said.

"Hey!" But Fenner had closed the door firmly. Ballard heard its lock snap tight. He stared angrily at the door, lit a cigarette. Not that he wasn't grateful to Bill for getting him off the streets. But all those cloak-and-dagger boys were too damned mysterious. Part of the act, no doubt. Made them feel important. It wasn't as difficult a job as they made it seem, though. Hadn't he talked his way very neatly out of Ca' Longhi? Hadn't he brought them the letter? He, a rank amateur, had done what they couldn't do. Not bad for old Mike, not bad at all. Finesse and quick wits, a little daring, that was all you needed in this or any other sport.

He smoked two cigarettes, started walking around the room. There was nothing to drink. The books on the dresser didn't interest him. (They seemed dull compared to the excitement he had been going through. Who wanted to read about Faulkner's Mississippi or the White Nile on a night like this?) The window looked out onto a blank courtyard. Quiet, restful. He turned the door's lock cautiously, glanced into the corridor. Quiet and restful, too. Not so expensive a hotel as the Danieli, but not bad. Comfortable and respectable. He watched a well-dressed, elderly couple go into a room not far away. Near the staircase, a middle-aged maid ended her gossip with a white-haired servant in a green apron and striped waistcoat. The corridor was empty again. This was the kind of hotel where Mama could let her eighteen-year-old daughter stay without a chaperone, and only have to sigh over the bill. A dull and virtuous place, cosy and safe.

He could fix the lock so that the door would open from the outside. And he did. He was thirsty, he was hungry. The bar was a quiet place. He could have his sandwich and Scotch, and the pleasure of watching Sir Felix Tarns lose a little of that stiff-necked composure, too. It was time that someone administered a little shock treatment to that quiet-faced stinker: that could have saved his wizened little soul, before now.

Mike the missionary, he thought, as he entered the small bar, paneled, softly lighted, its velvet chairs around polished-wood tables mostly empty, and ordered a double Scotch and a couple of chicken sandwiches. Mike the avenging angel, he added grimly, thinking suddenly of Lenoir as he saw Tarns's head bent over a newspaper. Finesse, just a little finesse, could hurt Lenoir where he didn't expect it. Ballard slid off the bar stool as the solitary attendant telephoned the kitchen for the sandwiches, and walked across the room.

"Sir Felix Tarns? You are a friend of Sandra Fane, I believe?"

Sir Felix looked up at him blankly.

"Sandra told me you visited her today. Was she all right then?" Ballard dropped his voice still more, to an appropriate conspiratorial murmur.

Sir Felix said icily, "I don't believe I know you—"

"Doesn't matter. It is Sandra we have to worry about. I saw her this evening. She's ill. I don't think she is going to last until morning, in fact."

Tarns's handsome, gaunt face whitened. "I beg your pardon?"

"She wants to talk with you. She needs your help. I think you'd better get over to Ca' Longhi right away. Lenoir is having her shipped off to Russia."

There was a definite pause. Sir Felix rose to his feet. "I do not know who you are. I do not know why you should tell me this fantastic story. But I do know that I do not have to listen to it." He walked quickly out of the bar, his head up, eyes cold, nostrils pinched. He had been shaken enough, though, to leave his newspaper behind him and his brandy unfinished.

Ballard enjoyed his sandwiches and his drink. Tarns was a womanizer—that had been the start of his troubles—and any womanizer had a definite drift toward Sandra Fane. I ought to know, Ballard thought. Tarns could pretend he had never heard of Sandra or Lenoir. But he had listened, all right. Now let him go to Lenoir, let him at least stop Sandra screaming.

The trouble with the bright boys like Fenner, Ballard reflected, was that they had to plan and prepare and wait and tie themselves up in double talk and high signs. Fenner's pals would have to rack their brains to find a way into Ca' Longhi. It would take them at least a couple of hours to get organized. The place was a fortress. You just didn't climb in a window. Not in Ca' Longhi. But I've got inside: I've sent Sir Felix Tarns, no less. And when he insists on seeing Sandra, and Lenoir has to start sweet-talking—well, that could hold up Sandra's questioning for a couple of hours. It could even delay her being taken on board the freighter.

How's that for an idea, Fenner?

It wasn't altogether like that, though.

Sir Felix was definitely alarmed, but he did not go to Ca' Longhi. He compromised. He telephoned, instead.

Lenoir was, in turn, astounded—indignant—amused. Sandra couldn't be in better health. She had already retired for the night—she had an early start tomorrow. Yes, she was going to visit Moscow. The invitation had only arrived this evening, and Sandra had accepted it with great excitement. Naturally.

"Naturally," Sir Felix agreed. *Shipped off to Russia*—what hysterical phrases those Americans used. "I envy her. This is such a pleasant time of year in Moscow. I am sorry I shan't see her before she leaves."

"That's possible, if you could join us for breakfast tomorrow. At six, I'm afraid. That might be a very pleasant send-off for her."

"A little early for my own plans," Tarns excused himself quickly. "But you will give Sandra my best wishes? I hope to see her in Paris when she returns. She is returning?"

"At the end of October. By the way, whoever told you this nonsense about her illness?"

"I have no idea. Just an American in one of those appalling silk suits. He said he called on you this evening. Otherwise, I should never have telephoned."

"I'm glad you did. Otherwise, my dear Felix, you would

have been worried unnecessarily. Is the American staying at your hotel?"

"I suppose so. At least, he was ordering sandwiches in the bar. He is no doubt eating them there at this minute. Peculiar habits they have, I must say."

"And a peculiar sense of humor. Until tomorrow evening, as arranged? Have a pleasant night!"

The call ended. It was really indiscreet of Fernand, Sir Felix thought in annoyance, to mention my plans in that tone of voice. Surely how I choose to spend the next eight hours is entirely my business? Bridling over Fernand's slight raising of the whip, Sir Felix prepared to leave the hotel for his pleasant night. Sandra Fane was already forgotten.

TWENTY-FOUR

BILL FENNER left the hotel casually. He crossed the courtyard briskly. He passed through the alley at a light run. But as he reached the *sotto portico,* he dropped back into a quick walk as he saw a man and woman, arm in arm, sauntering toward him. They passed him, American they were by clothes and voice, seemingly bound for the alley. He halted in the shadows of one of the squat pillars at the canal's edge that held up the low ceiling of the covered way. Ahead was the short stretch of open quay, and then the street that traversed the bridge. It was fairly quiet at this hour, with only occasional tourists drifting around. The gondolier was still there. So were the two men. They weren't talking now. Just standing together.

To his surprise, as he was about to walk on, two other men stepped out of a recessed doorway near the street and joined the group at the bridge. Had they been there all along? Perhaps, Fenner admitted worriedly: the doorway was deep and dark; he could have missed them when he and Ballard came this way—he had been too busy looking at the canal for Zorzi. As he waited, puzzled (the two newcomers had looked at their watches, said a few words, moved slowly back into the doorway), he heard the voices of the American couple retreating from the alley.

The man was saying, "But it won't lead anywhere."

"It looks romantic. You never can tell—"

"It's a dead end," the man said flatly, and won. Their footsteps came back into the *sotto portico.*

"Isn't this a funny old place?" the woman asked as she halted. "Sort of an arcade. Where does it lead, d'you think? Perhaps down to the Grand Canal. Come on, Milt. Let's see!"

"There's no exit that way."

"How do we know until we try it?" High heels clacked

308

lightly, the man's steps followed slowly, toward the far end of the *sotto portico,* a place of deepening shadow turning into black depth. "Romantic, isn't it?" the woman's voice drifted back, a little uncertainly.

"We're nuts," her husband said, balking. "There's no street down here—just a dock where they bring in supplies. Come on, Sue, let's get to the Piazza."

His voice, raised in annoyance, had carried as far as the recessed doorway near the bridge. One of the men stepped out onto the lighted quay, and started toward the voices. The gondolier's two friends had looked quickly in their direction, also. But the American couple, retracing their steps, had passed Fenner and were reaching the open quay. The man halted, went back to his doorway. "Funny, isn't it," the woman was saying, "gondolas instead of trucks."

"Funnier if they tried to float a truck."

"I just never thought how they got supplies to the shops and restaurants. You know, Milt, it must be strange to house-keep here." Their voices faded into a murmur. At the bridge, they hesitated, and took the wrong direction for the Piazza San Marco. The men on the bridge paid no more attention. The gondolier, in fact, had decided to go down to his craft, which was moored so close to the bridge that half of it disappeared into black shadow.

Fenner was about to move on. He was puzzled. He hesitated. He looked over his shoulder, to the far end of the dark and deserted *sotto portico.* Just what had worried those men when Sue and Milt had gone exploring down there?

Carefully retreating from the shelter of one pillar to another, Fenner tried some exploring himself. Quickly, he made his way back through the shadows into the black depths of the *sotto portico* and ended, as the practical Milt had predicted, at a house wall where the ground floor of the building pushed out to reach the canal. There was, also, as his eyes became accustomed to the various depths of shadows cast by a far-off and meager lamp, a heavy doorway, closed; barred windows, unlit; a coil of rope on the paving stones; some basket-covered kegs; two barrels; a crate. And on the canal side, cradled darkly against the edge of the *sotto portico,* was a heavy gondola, neatly tarpaulined and shipshape, waiting for tomorrow's workday. Nothing, no one here.

Fenner almost turned away. Then he noticed that there were two shapes of tarpaulin deep in the well of the gondola. Amidships, one was squared off neatly, stretched over the square bulk of its cargo, roped in a businesslike way, but the smaller tarpaulin-covered shape seemed loose, ill-secured, as if the workmen had been in a hurry and had dumped the last load in a bundle. It wasn't their way, though: the neatness of the rest of the gondola, and of the miniature wharf to which it was so securely moored—Fenner stopped speculating and stepped carefully into the gondola, keeping his body bent, his head low, using the bulk of the well-stowed cargo as a shield against any watchful eyes from the distant street. He felt the lilt of the canal send the gondola swaying gently with his weight. He steadied himself, paused just long enough to let the gondola right itself. He was down in the broad deep well of the boat, and invisible from the bridge up the canal. He moved carefully, reached out to the small bundle of tarpaulin. It was tightly wrapped but un-roped, pliable to his touch. It stirred with a small feeble movement, felt more than seen.

Quickly, he searched for an opening in the tarpaulin, wrenched it apart. A man's eyes stared up at him wildly. His mouth was tightly covered with a broad strip of adhesive, his hands and feet tied with wire. Cautiously, Fenner flicked on his lighter briefly, shielding it with his hand. It was Zorzi.

Fenner tried to ease the cruel bandage from Zorzi's cheeks, and the staring eyes closed. But the gondolier's pulse, though weak, was still countable. There had been no sign of any blood, so Zorzi had probably been hit on the head, or at the base of the neck. Enticed near here on some pretext, and struck from behind? Fenner worked frantically at the band-age and wrenched it loose. The wires around the wrists and ankles were not so easily removed. He could feel blood there, where Zorzi must have tried to struggle free. And the more he had struggled, the more the several strands of wire had been pulled, almost welded, together. Impossible to unravel. Fenner's penknife was useless, too. He needed pincers. He needed some light to work by. He needed help, and quickly. Police, in this case, would be the simple solution. But that was all that was simple. Normally, he would have stood up and yelled, until a passer-by in the street came running, but not with those men at the bridge. He could guess what kind of help they'd give him. No, he would have to walk past them, in his search for a policeman, and if he couldn't see any around, he would have to get to Arnaldi's shop by its rear entrance—only not by a direct approach, for the waiting men might see him branch off the street into the side alley.

He disliked the idea of leaving Zorzi, trussed up like this, to regain consciousness by himself in the darkness. But there was no choice. And just as he was about to hoist himself onto the covered wharf, he heard the sound, the soft silklike sound of a gondola speeding smoothly down the little canal. He crouched instinctively, and glimpsed the two men from the bridge sitting erect and motionless as they swept past. The gondolier standing high behind them might have seen Zorzi lying free of the tarpaulin, but if he did, his only response was to increase speed. He shouted a warning to some approaching gondola coming up from the Grand Canal, and that was all.

Fenner pulled himself onto the paving stones of the *sotto portico* and broke into a run. Ahead of him, the street was peaceful and almost empty. He glanced at the recessed doorway on the quay as he ran past. There was no one there. The men had got tired of waiting and left. Or perhaps they had seen the flicker of his lighter in the freight gondola, and decided that flight was wise. As he reached the bridge, he remembered Zorzi, this noon, standing down there in his gondola, shouting up to Claire and himself. Ten o'clock ... Their arrangement had been no secret. Now he knew why the five men had waited, why Zorzi had been eliminated, why his gondola had been taken. Instead of cursing Mike Ballard as a general nuisance and delay, he ought to be giving him special thanks for changing their arrangements.

He halted on the crest of the bridge and looked both ways along the street. There was no policeman in sight. Near him were two Italians walking quickly home, a small group of Austrian students hiking along. He tried some Italian on both, and received only puzzled frowns in return. Thankfully, he saw the American couple retracing their sadly wandered steps. "There's a man in a gondola down there!" he yelled to them, and pointed. "He has been mugged. Will you wait with him? I'll telephone the police."

He ran on, leaving Milt staring, and the students translating his words. There was a quick clatter of metal heels as the young men surged down onto the quay. (Milt, to his credit, was dragging Sue along, too, saying gloomily, "Might as well be back in New York.") The students would find Zorzi, all right. He could hear them whooping into the *sotto portico,* as he approached Arnaldi's shop. He passed it, his eyes searching for the alley. He was relieved to see the boy, Luigi, stationed near its dark entrance as if he had been waiting for him.

"Did you—" Luigi began, but Fenner was already in the alley. Luigi didn't follow him at once. He stood looking along the *calle* toward the bridge. The students' clatter had probably made him curious, Fenner thought as he concentrated on the alley. It twisted abruptly to his right. The light, at the corner wall, was worse than meager. He counted three doors ahead of him, and then noticed a fourth in a very dark patch of shadow. Was that Arnaldi's back entrance? As he hesitated, he heard Luigi's light steps running after him. The boy brushed past him, his face worried, his eyes questioning. But he kept silent, only knocked gently on that fourth door; repeated the knock; waited; knocked again. The door opened quietly; Luigi and Fenner slipped inside. Arnaldi nodded to them and switched on the light as he locked the heavy door behind them.

They were standing in a large cluttered space, half storage, half workroom, with a small stove in one corner for bachelor cooking. There was a pleasant smell of freshly made coffee. And from the next room, through its firmly closed door, came laughter and a voice (Rosie's?) raised jokingly. The mood was merry, Fenner thought, and some of his tensions left. "Get the police," he told Luigi. "Take them to the big gondola moored at the far end of the *sotto portico*, on the other side of the bridge. They'll find a man there, badly hurt."

But Luigi wasn't listening. He was talking Italian, far too quickly for Fenner to follow. Arnaldi, his smile of welcome vanishing, burst into a vehement flow of angry words. Luigi nodded, avoided Fenner's eyes, and left. "What is it?" Fenner asked sharply. "What is it?"

The door to the other room opened. "Fenner?" Rosie called to him. "Come in, come in. D'you know the lucky guy who was to receive the letter? Old Chris, here. Come and see his face." Christopher Holland, in pajamas and dressing gown was standing at a table spread with some papers and a large map of Venice, studying a sheet of paper. "Very funny, very funny," he was saying bitingly. There were two other men in the room: a small, neat Frenchman with an upraised eyebrow and an amused smile; a larger, rounder man—Italian, by his clothes—pursing his genial lips, shaking his head in sympathy even as he restrained his laughter. "Joke is over," Rosie agreed. "Any trouble with Ballard?" he asked Fenner as he entered.

"He is in my room. I told him to wait there until you sent someone. The password is 'Florian.' "

"It is, is it?"

"There has been bad trouble near the bridge. Better call the police. Where's Claire? Upstairs?"

Four faces stared at him blankly for a second. Rosie, as if he couldn't believe Fenner's question, moved into the storage room, looked quickly around it and back at Arnaldi. "Where is—" he began.

Arnaldi burst into a stream of explanation.

"Marco—" Rosie called to the Italian Intelligence officer, "what's he saying? That she *left?*"

Marco nodded. "Not long ago—perhaps seven, eight minutes, no more. She walked to the bridge to cancel an arrangement with someone called Zorzi. Also she hoped to meet Mr. Fenner. He was late, and she was worried. Women—" Marco shrugged his shoulders. Women worried about such small things. "Arnaldi has now sent Luigi to find her and tell her that Mr. Fenner is safely here."

Fenner was already in the storeroom, making for the back door. Holland darted after him and caught hold of his shoulder.

"Wait!" Rosie moved quickly and gripped Fenner by the wrist. As Fenner tried to pull free, Rosie twisted it behind his back. "Stop it, Bill, stop it! You'll break your arm. Listen, man—listen! You can't run out there."

"Don't be a bloody fool," Holland told him. "Rosie's right. We can't go dashing in and out of that alley."

"Zorzi is tied up, unconscious," Fenner shouted at him. "They took his gondola—I saw them leave. Claire—"

"Pipe down, Bill! Do you want everyone out there to hear?"

"Come away from the door," Rosie said. "Come on, Bill. Tell us everything. Then we'll know what is to be done." He looked at the Italian, whose face was grave. "Police?" he queried softly.

Marco asked quickly, "A gondolier was attacked? His gondola stolen?" That was indeed bad business.

Fenner said tensely, restraining his impatience, "Yes. I found him in a freight gondola, at the *sotto portico* just below the bridge."

Marco moved to the telephone.

"Come on, Bill," Rosie said, releasing his wrist, getting

him back into the sitting room, closing its door. "Now tell
us—"

"They've got Claire." His anger was rising again, along
with the hideous feeling of complete helplessness. "Claire
is—"

"We don't know that. She may walk back in here with
Luigi. Could you have missed her on the street to the
bridge?"

"No!"

"She may have walked on to the hotel when she didn't
find Zorzi. Could you have missed her while you were in
that *sotto portico?*"

Yes, that was possible. It was a slim hope, but Fenner
grasped at it. His voice became more controlled. So did his
mind. Quickly, he told them about the waiting men, and
Zorzi. But as he talked, the slim hope vanished. He knew.
He knew they had Claire.

The others listened intently, exchanged a brief glance as
he ended.

"*C'est Kalganov,*" the Frenchman said. His eyes held no
illusions.

Marco, whose call to the police was over, lifted the telephone receiver again. "I shall tell our men to block the Ca'
Longhi canal. They could stop the gondola. Quietly, of
course."

Rosie nodded. If, he added to that, Kalganov has had her
taken there. Kalganov? This had his touch, all right. He has
dropped the Robert Wahl pattern of action. But why? Why
take such a daring risk at this stage? Was he so sure of success that risks could be taken? If so, he could not know
how close he was to failure, to complete discovery. He could
not know that Claire had friends here in Venice, powerful
friends, ready to act. That was certain, Rosie decided. For
once, we will surprise Kalganov. "Marco—can you advance
your plans?"

"To what time?" Marco asked worriedly, pausing in his
telephone call.

"Eleven-thirty."

Marco did some quick mental calculations. "Yes, all the
material is ready, all the preparations. Just a matter of final
instruction. I shall have to leave here very quickly."

"We'll all be leaving. Very quickly."

Marco nodded, began speaking urgently into the telephone.

"Will you all wait until Luigi gets back?" Christopher Holland asked the room angrily. First they said that Claire was probably safe, and then they all started talking of Kalganov, and advancing plans for the assault on Ca' Longhi. Not that he had much hope, himself. No, the more you thought of Fenner's story, the worse everything looked. "I blame myself," Holland said, giving Fenner something else to think about. "We were having a conference in here, so I asked Claire to brew us a pot of coffee." That had been a tactful excuse to get her out of the room where subjects were being discussed that weren't for Claire to hear. Her job was over, finished. ("Fancy loose and foot free," she had told Holland, holding up the letter, laughing. "Assignment over, isn't it?") Yes, her job was over with the delivery of the letter to Rosie. And she had dropped her guard. As we all do, Holland thought, when tension ends. I ought to have remembered that, but with all the excitement—the letter, Marco's plan, the arrangements— "I'm sorry, Bill," Holland said awkwardly.

Fenner wasn't listening. He moved to the door. Luigi was here. And he came alone. In his hand, he held a small blue bag.

"Where did you find it?" Rosie asked. Chris Holland was already hurrying upstairs.

"Near the bridge. Down beside—"

"Why did you let her go there?" Fenner burst out.

"I was at my post." Luigi was hurt. "I couldn't leave it."

Fenner caught control of himself. "Sorry. Sorry, Luigi. It wasn't your fault." He looked at Rosie.

"Yes," Rosie said, "the fault is mine. It goes back a long way—to Saigon." Some new speculation formed in his quick, dark eyes. "Saigon," he repeated, as if that answered a question.

The Frenchman, who had spent the last five minutes studying the letter, looked up to say impatiently, "The fault is with Kalganov. And with Lenoir. None of us would be here in Venice tonight if it were not for those men." His cold logic was salutary. The surge of emotion was over in the tense room.

"Better get back to your posts. We start leaving soon," Rosie told Arnaldi and his son. He closed the room door behind them.

"Then what?" Fenner demanded.

"Chris will brief you," Rosie said, as Holland, some clothes on his back, the rest in his hand, came at a rattling run down the steep stairs. He turned quickly to Marco, who had just finished giving his last instructions over the telephone. "All set?"

"Completely," Marco told him, putting down the receiver with a flourish. He was a beaming picture of confidence. "Have no fear, my friend. It has been well prepared. We are ready. At half past eleven—" Marco made an expressive gesture with up-flung arms—"and we call the fireboat. We will give you some excitement," he promised. He was buttoning his neat dark jacket, picking up his black Homburg, gray suède gloves, silver-headed stick. He looked like a sedately prosperous civil servant, returning from a Sunday visit to his grandchildren. He knew more about arson than the terrorists he had tracked down in the course of duty. Tonight, thought Rosie, we depend completely on Marco and the skill he has learned from the men he has caught. Thank God, too, for men like Marco, who aren't vote-catching politicians co-operating with allies only when it suits the climate of opinion. Without Marco, where would we be tonight?

He grasped Marco's hand, gave it a firm grip. "Thank you. And good luck." Marco left, with a wave for everyone. "You're next to go, Jules," Rosie told the Frenchman.

Jules had already looked at his watch. Three minutes, and he would leave. "I shall report to Paris that we have the letter. After that, I shall join you at Ca' Longhi. Just about the time when our wine merchant is being flown out of Zurich." The idea pleased Jules.

"No one knows of his arrest?" That was important. One hint of Trouin's extradition, and Kalganov would be warned.

"Not even his little Communist secretary."

"By bedtime, she may begin to wonder where he is."

"By bedtime, she will have other worries." The Frenchman looked at the letter on the table. "That could be very useful to make Trouin start talking."

Rosie shook his head. "You can have one of the copies that Fernand Lenoir must have at Ca' Longhi."

"He may destroy them when Marco's little excitement starts."

"I doubt if there will be time." Rosie was polite, but obdurate.

The Frenchman looked with regret at the letter. "A pity. It would certainly loosen Trouin's tongue."

"He will talk, in any case. He is no Jan Aarvan."

The Frenchman nodded. He glanced at his watch and

moved to the door. "*À bientôt!* And please leave Monsieur Fernand Lenoir to me."

"He is all yours. At half past eleven!"

With a polite bow, the Frenchman left. Rosie said to Holland, "You're next, in four minutes." He turned back to the telephone. Once he made contact, he began speaking quickly, giving seemingly precise directions, but nothing he was saying made sense to Fenner.

"You see," Holland said, drawing Fenner's attention to him, as he knotted his tie and pulled on his jacket, "it is less than six minutes since Luigi got back, and everything is moving."

"I see." Six minutes ... six hours, six days.

"Cut out the bitterness. It gets us nowhere," Holland said sharply.

"I can be bitter with myself, can't I?"

"No—you can't afford any emotions whatsoever. We're going into action. Keep your mind cold, your reflexes quick."

Fenner found a cigarette, lit it, took a deep long drag. "What's the action?" His voice and face were hard.

"A little fire. Nothing dangerous, mostly a nice cloud of black smoke. Marco will see that the fireboat is there at once. And, of course, the firemen will have to go through Ca' Longhi to make sure nothing is smoldering. There will be a number of volunteers who'll push in with them. Like to be one?"

Fenner said nothing. But his eyes held new interest.

"The police will enter then, too. Tricky business to arrange. If we simply sent the police knocking at the door, there would be some delay in getting it opened—a lot of talk back and forth about illegal entry and search—enough delay, at least, to allow Lenoir to get rid of any evidence and let the Grand Canal take the blame for two deaths." He had used the callous phrase purposely. He was watching Fenner. Damned, Holland was thinking, if I'll risk taking anyone along with me on any action unless he has a good grip on himself. But the American had taken his advice: he was in tight control of his emotions.

"Sandra Fane," Holland went on, in the same quiet voice, "is in a pretty bad spot. But Claire? No. I don't think so. If Kalganov had wanted her killed, she would have been found under the bridge instead of her handbag. She could be a hostage, held to blackmail you—keep you immobilized."

"But why? We gave nothing away. They had even stopped paying attention to us."

"Lenoir stopped paying attention. But Kalganov—" Holland shrugged. "He always has some reason. But this time, I rather think he has made a mistake."

Bill Fenner looked at his watch.

"We *all* make mistakes," Holland insisted, "even Kalganov."

Cold, cold comfort. Fenner stirred restlessly, his eyes on his watch. "Do we have to wait?" he asked impatiently.

"Yes," Holland said most definitely. "We wait. We can make no move against Ca' Longhi until Marco's men are ready. Surprise—that's our strongest weapon, Bill. Calm down, calm down. We'll get Kalganov. He's in Venice. A general alert has been sent out." He glanced over at Rosie, who was finishing his long call. "This is the first time we've ever been ahead of Kalganov. We'll get him."

"So you have all decided to call him Kalganov," Fenner said grimly. That might sharpen their morale, but it only plunged him into deeper depression. Kalganov. And Claire . . . What chance did she have with him?

"It's his name. We are sure of that now."

Fenner raised his eyes from his watch. "How?"

"Through Neill Carlson. He finished a report on Robert Wahl shortly before he left Paris—a study of time and place in Wahl's travels abroad, coinciding with outbreaks of violence and terror. That report was compared yesterday with our files on Kalganov's known activities. The times and places matched."

"That won't be enough evidence for a trial."

"No. And so he will be arrested and tried as Robert Wahl, conspirator in an assassination attempt. But in our minds, it will be Kalganov who is sentenced. That's one file we can close, at last."

"*If* Wahl is executed," Fenner said savagely. There was going to be a lot of sympathy stirred up for a poor unsuspecting film producer who had been used by crooked politicians. "You'd be more sure of closing that file if you could have him tried as Kalganov." The man who stated, fifteen years ago, that he had killed over two thousand men. . . .

"We may manage that," Holland said very quietly.

"But no one can identify him as Kalganov except Jan Aarvan." And he wouldn't talk. Nor would Lenoir.

"Or perhaps Sandra Fane?"

Fenner's lips tightened. Ironical, he thought, that Sandra was, at this moment, more important to Rosie and his friends than Claire. He looked at his watch again. "Time to go."

"Still a minute left." Holland had picked up the letter as Rosie left the telephone. "What do you plan to do with this little document?"

Rosie came out of his own thoughts. "Burn it."

"Couldn't agree more," Holland said. "May I?" He had his lighter ready.

"It's addressed to you, isn't it?"

Holland watched the flaming paper curl. "I'm sorry to disappoint Jules. He wanted it. But it's too good—a masterly job, one I wouldn't even trust to most-secret, triple-locked files." His foot stamped on the black gleaming ashes, pounding them into a smear of charcoal dust on the floor. "Arnaldi will give me hell," he said, smiling.

"Come on," Fenner told him from the door. He looked at a strangely silent Rosie. "Did you get any report about the gondola? Was the canal blocked in time?"

Rosie shook his head. "Two gondolas reached Ca' Longhi just before Marco's orders got through. One brought a visitor—"

"Who?" asked Holland quickly.

"Couldn't be recognized in the darkness. He was expected: he didn't have to wait at the door. Just slipped in—"

"And Claire?" Fenner asked. "She was in the other gondola?"

"Yes. At least, two men carried something—"

"Come on!" Fenner said savagely, and left.

"Keep with him," Rosie told Holland. "He's in an ugly mood." He paused and added angrily, "Why the hell wasn't I told that he and Claire—"

"They weren't. It must be one of those first-take, fast developers. That does happen."

"But why *now*, of all times?"

"Something always goes wrong," Holland said philosophically. "You ought to know that, old boy. Coming!" he called to Fenner, who had shouted back to him. "And I thought I had got him all quietened down," he told Rosie as he left. "See you at the café on the square; just before eleven-thirty?" And then the balloon goes up, he thought, as he hurried through the storeroom. Fenner was waiting, grimfaced and silent. But he did listen to Holland's quick instructions on how they'd leave separately, and where they'd meet.

Something always goes wrong, Rosie thought as he folded up the map of Venice, gathered together the sheets of paper on the table and began tearing them to shreds. Because people were people, not to be arranged like schedules. Such as this one he held in his hand. He studied it for the last time: nothing forgotten, nothing omitted. He tore it up and burned it with the rest of the scraps of paper.

Arnaldi had come back into the room. "They have both gone," he told Rosie. He was still upset. He didn't even notice the black ashes. "The young lady—I thought she left under orders. I am sorry. It was my fault."

"The fault is mine. I didn't give her orders to stay with you. Don't worry, Vicente, we'll find her. She'll return. Keep her purse until she comes. Right?"

We'll find her, he repeated to himself as he stepped out into the alley. Will we? Good God, why did this have to happen? Her mission was accomplished with the delivery of the letter. By this time, Claire and Fenner ought to have been back at the Hotel Vittoria, enjoying a nightcap in the bar. That's the way it should have been. The Hotel Vittoria ... Ballard!

I mustn't forget him, Rosie reminded himself. He is safe enough in Fenner's room with the door locked; a damned sight safer and happier than Fenner will be this twisted night. If we have a minute to spare before the fireworks start, I'll get Marco to call the tourist police, tell them to pick up Ballard and take him to their station, keep him there until I can turn up. By that time, all going well, he will be free of Fernand Lenoir—but for good.

The end of the alley was in sight. Luigi had seen him. He gave no warning signal. All was well—so far. He passed Luigi silently, gave the boy a broad wink to make him feel better, and set out on his detour to the little piazza behind Ca' Longhi. It wasn't far away. Marco would already be there. Jules, too, perhaps. And Chris, with Fenner, should now be taking the water route.

Cautiously does it, Rosie told himself, entering a long narrow street of closed shops, quiet and peaceful. Abandoning all worries, all thoughts, his mind only responded to each second, commanded only his ears and eyes.

TWENTY-FIVE

THEY HAD left Arnaldi's shop separately, Holland walking ahead, Fenner following at a little distance. Holland was leading him away from the direction of Ca' Longhi, Fenner realized, but there was nothing he could do about it except hope that there was safety in this madness. They were almost back at the Piazza San Marco before Holland cut down toward the Grand Canal and reached a considerable cluster of gondolas. To Fenner's further doubts and dismay, Holland stepped into the first gondola he reached. Once Fenner joined him, they were quickly away. Even so, it was a leisurely method to travel up the broad curve of water. Fenner looked at the *vaporetti* still bustling up and down the Grand Canal, cutting through its dark ripples with a steady, soft-sounding swish. He said nothing, just set his mouth more grimly. Holland was the expert, but damn his eyes all the same.

Holland guessed his thought. *"Festina lente,"* he said quietly. "We can talk here without being noticed." He looked at one of the water-buses, all lit up like a Christmas tree, passengers clearly visible inside its glass windows. "I thought you ought, first of all, to look at Ca' Longhi from its canal side. Here is the setup briefly." He began a clear, concise description of its immediate surroundings and entrances. And then he gave an exact account of its interior.

"How did you get a man inside?" Fenner asked quickly. If one man had got in, he could.

"We didn't. The place is a citadel. Marco got the information."

"But how?" Fenner insisted.

"Through the servants who were discharged. Lenoir brought his own." Holland was scanning the right bank of the canal, studying the façades of the houses which formed a continuous row with occasionally a walled garden, a small indented piazza, the mouth of a *rio*, or a landing stage to break the line of buildings. The sparkling edge of hotels had been left behind. The houses were more somberly lit, some almost in darkness except for the steady glow of lanterns at their water-washed front steps. "They are all so different, and yet so—" Not alike, certainly. A mixture of centuries, Holland thought. Perhaps it was their variety of detail that made it so easy to pass over one that was less distinguished, to travel beyond it. Suddenly, he nodded. "There it is!" He signaled to their gondolier to draw toward the left bank of the canal, opposite Ca' Longhi.

"Which?" Fenner asked. Over there, he could see a narrow waterway joining the Grand Canal, with large houses rising on both corners. Gothic, or Renaissance with nineteenth-century restoration? His eyes, accustomed to the dark half-lights of the canal, picked out the house that seemed more closed than the others. Not a light from any window, no lamp on its solid wall. "That one," he said softly. "Three floors above the water line, four attic windows jutting up from its roof. No front entrance."

Holland nodded. So he did listen to me, he thought in relief. He called back to the gondolier, "Slowly, slowly! We want to admire the architecture."

"Venice is the place for architects," the man shouted back. "They have not lived until they see Venice."

"How true. Perhaps we could stop for two minutes? Let us see the view?"

The gondolier swung them expertly out of the way of traffic, brought them close to the left bank and rested in the dark shadow of a large palace-museum.

"Keep looking at the whole sweep of the canal," Holland advised Fenner, "not just at one house. That's the idea. And let's go over the interior of Ca' Longhi again. First the cellar—" He paused, waiting.

"Partially submerged, not in use any more. Above that, first floor, with three entrances: one, at the side, on that small canal over there; one at the back, on a narrow street; one a service entrance, near a small piazza linked to the canal by the narrow street. The hall is circular, with pillars. . . ." His voice went on with the quiet recitation, floor by floor, particular by particular, and ended with "—Then the attic. Four small rooms, once occupied by servants, now used as storerooms."

Yes, he had listened, thought Holland. He is ready and fit to go along with us: his mind is working, his emotions are in control.

"How many men have they got?" Fenner asked. He was studying the façade of Ca' Longhi, its second-floor balconies, its upper-floor decorations. If I could get in—by one of those windows—

"Two men servants—one is now a colonel in Intelligence," and, remembered Holland, well trained by the old MVD. But he didn't mention that. "Kalganov slipped him in."

"He doesn't even trust Lenoir?"

"He trusts nobody. Then there is the cook—a woman, but she could be counted as a man—a Kalganov agent, just to keep an eye on the colonel, no doubt. And there are the two men who abducted Claire. And there is Lenoir's visitor, unless he has left. And Lenoir himself. That makes possibly seven, certainly six, inside the house. Outside, they have two on patrol—one near the side canal, one on the small square. We've spotted them. We'll deal with them before we make our first move. Seen enough?"

"Almost." Fenner's eyes were studying the roof of the adjacent house. "The next house—its back overlooks the little piazza? And do some of the houses on that square run up to it? The roofs are continuous?"

"Yes"—Holland was watching him curiously—"with some ups and downs, of course."

"But no gaps? That house, adjoining Ca' Longhi, really forms one side of the little square?"

"Bill," Holland said worriedly, "this isn't in our plans. Better stick to—"

"It could be done," Fenner said softly. From some house top on the small piazza, he could reach Ca' Longhi's neighbor. It could be done. The roofs had varied pitches, but all of them were sloped gently. The tiles would be fluted. There were wide chimneys, decorated gutters to help block any fall. "There is some kind of a balcony in front of the attic windows, isn't there?"

"Only a ledge—"

"But with a fairly high balustrade. It's safe enough, Chris."

"Not so easy. It looks simpler from here—"

"The moon's just right." A quarter-moon, its light not too strong, but sufficient. Clouds were small, dimming the moon only briefly. Above the vagrant clouds, the sky was dark and clear with bright stars.

"Have you a head for heights?"

"I'll manage. I've done some rock-climbing."

Damn, thought Holland, and searched for another reason to dissuade Fenner. "We can't really have anyone clambering around the front of that roof, being seen from the Grand Canal. Can we? And we certainly are not going to have anyone skittering over the roof, raising any alarm in that house to give them warning of trouble to come. The only alarm is the big one. Throw them completely off balance. Without that—"

"Calm down. I won't raise any alarm. I'll get up there and wait. Until half past eleven. That's zero hour, isn't it? Then I'll go in. Okay?"

"You'll have to clear it with Marco. He's in charge of this operation." Holland was both annoyed and sympathetic. And in a way, he even liked the idea. If it didn't raise any bloody alarm, he thought. He tried again. "Why aim for the attic? There are plenty of closed rooms in that house. The ones on the ground floor—" He caught himself in time. If Lenoir had time to eliminate evidence, a body could be dropped very simply into the dark waters of the canal, only six feet below those ground-floor windows. "They may be holding Claire down there. It's logical."

"If they expected attack, which they don't," Fenner said. His eyes were still studying the roofs, as if he were already choosing his route across them.

Holland called softly to the gondolier, who had been back-oaring gently to keep the gondola close to the museum's wall without scraping against it, "Take us across the other side. No, not that *rio* opposite! Take us to the one just above it." And we can walk from there in one minute to that small piazza, Holland thought as he glanced at his watch. They were in good time: not too early, not to late. To Fenner, he said gloomily, "You'll end up in the canal, old boy. One glissade, and I'll have to fish you out. Miss all the fun."

Fenner didn't answer. He was staring up at the attic windows. "Thought I saw a light. Just a thin sliver—a crack in the shutters."

Holland looked quickly. There was nothing to see.

Their gondola was slowing up to avoid the rush of water from a *vaporetto* on its quick way up the canal. Sharply, there sounded a warning hoot from its siren. Floating down toward the water-bus, in the middle of the canal, was an island of gay lights and music. The water-bus altered course slightly, with a last pay-attention blast on its siren, and passed the two decorated gondolas, roped together, crowded, their three-piece orchestra throbbing into *O sole mio* under a canopy of colored lights and flowers. See Venice by night. Indeed, yes. Fenner watched the shimmering drift of the linked gondolas, listened to the music as it floated along, looked back at the attic window. I'm going in that way, he decided. How strong are the shutters?

"Bellissimo!" their gondolier shouted to encourage everyone's enjoyment, and began his rhythmical sway once more on the flat-topped stern, judging the backwash of the *vaporetto* skillfully, rowing his way in earnest now across the canal.

"Bellissimo!" Holland agreed, tactfully. He started as Fenner's arm grasped his. Fenner was staring up at the roof of Ca' Longhi.

Holland looked, too. He saw a thin edge of light from the second attic window. Then it vanished.

"Watch!" Fenner told him.

The light came on again. It went off. On again. Off. On.

Their gondola was drawing closer to the bank, up canal. They could no longer see the attic window.

That might not be Claire, Holland thought. It could be Sandra Fane. But all he said was, "That's what I like about women. They never give up, do they?" He added, "You'll have company on the roof. Two of Marco's specialists."

Fenner looked at him swiftly.

"Did you notice those nice big Renaissance chimneys, filled with soot? No, don't ask how they'll do it. Just guess. You'll come near enough the truth."

They both half smiled, fell silent.

Had that been Claire, Holland wondered again, or Sandra? He was too old a hand at this kind of work to hope for anything: you did you best, made the most of every small advantage, and that was that.

It was Claire, thought Bill Fenner, it was Claire.

Claire drifted out of the black sleep of unconsciousness into blind suffocation. She couldn't see, couldn't hear, couldn't breathe. Her hands went up to her face, pushing, pulling, and she came free of the long dark cloak that had been twisted around her.

She was lying on a narrow bed in a square-shaped room with a light, one naked bulb dangling from the ceiling, setting her head throbbing as she looked up at its knife-sharp gleam. She looked away, to the other side of the room. It was filled with a mass of old furniture, trunks, crates. She pulled the cloak's cocoon-like wrapping away from her thighs, freed her legs, and sat up slowly. The thin straw mattress crackled; the rickety bed creaked and trembled. From the cluttered side of this boxlike room came the scrabble and skitter of mice back into the wainscoting. If I frightened you, you frightened me, she told them silently; and rose unsteadily. Wooden floor, dusty. One door, very closed, in the center of the wall that faced the window. A single window, stoutly shuttered on the outside. And silence. Silence complete. Where was she? At Ca' Longhi? It was only a guess: she had no way of knowing. She had seen nothing, heard nothing, since she had come down the bridge onto the quay to talk to Zorzi, waiting half asleep in his gondola.

The gondola had certainly been Zorzi's. From the bridge above, she had seen about two thirds of it clearly and recognized the brightly polished dolphins that held up its black side cords, the black leather cushions with their bobbed red fringes, the red rug at the feet of the two upright armchairs. She ran down the steps and saw Zorzi stretched along the stern under the shadow of the bridge, resting gondolier-style on his back, knees raised, one leg dangling over the other, hands behind his head, hat tilted over his brow. But it wasn't Zorzi.

The man had a ready explanation as he rose and came forward to where she stood by the side of the gondola. Zorzi's little boy was ill: Zorzi had asked him to take his place tonight. As she quickly searched in her purse to give the man some lire and ease the broken appointment, she heard quiet footsteps behind her. And sensed danger. She had snapped her bag shut, turned to see who this was—two men, pleasant-faced, smiling. But across the quay, in a dark doorway, were standing two other men, one looking along the lighted street, raising his hand. As a signal? Before she could scream, the gondolier behind her had struck a sharp blow against the back of her neck. She had dropped her bag as she felt the pain, the paralysis that turned the scream into a moan. And then blackness complete. And nothing more.

Where was she?

She walked over to the casement window. It opened inward, showing a deep recess between it and the shutters. No problem there. But the board shutters were another matter. They were sturdy, unpainted, weathered by age. They met together tightly, as if sealed by sun and rain. And they were most definitely secured: a combination of hasp over staple was clinched by a padlock. The hasp and staple were of black iron, antique in design, massive. The padlock was new, small, made of steel. She looked as it in dismay. Then she noticed the contrast between the large staple, made for some heavy ancient lock, and the padlock's slender link. There was a lot of room to spare there, enough to give the hasp some free play.

She reached up, across the deep stone sill, and pulled the hasp toward her as far as the padlock would allow. This would permit the shutters—if she could force them apart—to open for at least one inch. One good inch of view. That was all she needed. She would know where this window faced—a courtyard, a canal, a street. She could scream for help. Her throbbing head might split open, but she would like to scream right now. Useless, though; unless she knew there were other houses, other people near enough to hear her cries, she would only give warning to her captors that she had to be gagged and bound.

But she couldn't force the shutters apart. She pulled and tugged. They should open inward, obviously, judging by the depth of the stone sill. But they didn't move. She could get no grip, no fingerhold on their closely met edge. They were jammed. Warped? Too long unopened? She stepped back, letting her tired arms rest, easing the hard pressure of the sill against her waist. She stared at the shutters helplessly. And in that moment, she felt her complete loneliness.

Where was Bill? Was he safe? The two men in that dark doorway had made no move toward her—only signaled that the lighted street near them was clear, that no one was about to reach the bridge. Had they been sent to deal with Bill? Would they have taken him, too? Or left him there in some dark corner? Was he lying somewhere near that alley?.

Rosie, Chris, Marco, the Frenchman they called Jules—where were they? Had her handbag been found? She didn't even know if it had fallen on the quay or been kicked into the canal in the quick scuffle. If it had been discovered, and she *must* believe it would be or else she'd be paralyzed by helplessness, the search was on. Her optimism was qualified,

though: the first search must be for Sandra Fane. Her escape
was vital if Kalganov was ever to be tracked down. When
Ca' Longhi was raided (and Marco had plans all made and
ready, hadn't he? That was when she had been asked to
leave them in peace while they talked, to make coffee—tactful Chris . . .), Lenoir would certainly be caught. But Kalganov, where was he to be found? So Rosie and Chris—they had
to concentrate on Sandra, free her, protect her, get her
tongue unlocked, find Kalganov before he could change his
plans again, perhaps even pull a victory out of threatened
defeat.

Strange that Sandra was the one who would escape.
Where was justice now? Very much there, she realized sadly:
Justice, blindfolded, so that she would play no favorites, and
Kalganov could be caught. You'll have to settle for that, she
told herself: what is unfair to you is fair to others. How else
would people be able to go on spending pleasant Sundays in
their free-walking, free-talking, free-thinking world? Kalganov, uncaught, would end all that: if not this time, the next
time, some time. He had the will, and he had the cunning,
and he was gathering the power. Strange, she thought, the
Russians may yet be thankful to us—although they'll never
admit it—if we can stop Kalganov. Unless, of course, they
want a return to Stalin the Awful . . . Ivan the Terrible . . .
Kalganov the Frightful.

All right, she told herself, you've talked yourself into accepting Sandra's importance. She comes first. You're a poor
second. As far as the Kaganov problem goes.

Strange, though, so many things are strange. . . . For eight
years, you've had no personal need to survive. Since Jim's
death, no real meaning in your own life. All you wanted
was the cause of Jim's death removed, the cause of those
other murders exposed, the blackmail of terrorism and the
threat of violence gutted out—the way cancer is destroyed
before it runs through the whole body. And you had fine
words to speak: you said you'd die happy if, in one small
way, you could help. You told Rosie that. You meant it, too.
You still mean it. Only now, today, you would like to have
helped and stayed alive, too. Strange . . . on the day you found
life anew, you may lose it.

She closed her eyes. She allowed herself one long, unhap-
py sigh. The mice rustled. She came back to the room again.
She stared at the shutters. How long shall I be kept here?
How long have I been here?

She couldn't even tell that. Her watch had been taken off her wrist. Regrets and sad thoughts vanished. She was suddenly angered by the very meanness, the calculation of that theft: she was to know neither place nor time. She stopped staring hopelessly at the shutters and looked around for something to use on them.

Spindle-leg chairs, a broken marble table, cracked or spotted mirrors in gilded frames, antiquated footstools, a carved chest, chipped golden cupids, a high old-fashioned trunk with curved lid, smaller trunks of battered tin, an elaborately carved candlestick with broken feet and a chunk of wax still in its holder, uncovered boxes exposing a clutter of yellow-paged books half fallen from crumbling bindings, a music stand tra-la, a do-re-me recorder, two repellent busts of Roman matrons, inlaid trays, broken chessmen . . .

Her eyes traveled again over the most likely objects. Quietly, she moved through the crush of junk. She was searching for something strong enough to act as a lever, force the shutters apart; something sharp enough to try to turn the padlock. Everything was made of wood, or marble, or plaster, or glass, or tin. Inside the large trunk, she found faded brocades and silks. She picked up the tall candlestick—wood, too, but a solid piece of carving—and studied the remains of its broad candle. The wax was so hardened by age that even a mountaineering mouse had only fretted its edge with gnawings. Possible?

She hit the squat chunk of wax against the edge of the marble table. It split after three quick, hard blows, and the candle could be gouged away from its holder. She found what she had hoped for: a metal point almost two inches long onto which the original candle, tall and heavy, had been jammed for safe anchorage. She found, too, something she didn't want: after the sound of the blows, someone outside the door had walked a few heavy paces, and stood listening. She waited. The footsteps receded again, and silence returned. The guard must have sat down on a chair; the guard, by the footsteps, must be a man. So she knew what was outside in that direction. She would have to work cautiously.

She carried the largest footstool over to the window to give her ten more inches of height. She examined the padlock more closely. Its keyhole was too small for the thick point of the candle holder. That was a bad disappointment. She would have to concentrate on the shutters. It should have been a simple job, but it wasn't. The candlestick wasn't too

heavy, but it was cumbersome to handle. Its spike, once she
had managed to insert it between the two shutters, refused
to catch on either wooden edge to give her enough leverage.
It slipped, held, slipped, almost caught again, slipped. If she
could have risked noise, it would have been easier. She was
almost weeping in frustration when she felt the point hold as
if, this time, it meant to keep its grip. She pressed, pressed.
One shutter trembled for an instant, sighed, and moved free.

She pulled it inward, as far as it would come. She had her
full inch of view. Of black nothing. Idiot, she told herself,
kicking off her shoes and running over to the light switch
near the door. She remembered the guard outside, looked
down at the gap of door above the threshold. Not always an
idiot, she thought, as she dropped her coat along the edge
of the door, and switched off the light. She could see what
lay outside.

It was a view of night sky, black suffused with red. So she
was in Venice—that was a city's glow—and not in some
remote house far out on the shores of the lagoon. Stars, bright
when the light clouds drifted away from them. A small piece
of moon. Some distance away, directly opposite her, there
were roofs, a row of them, broken in silhouette, possibly
belonging to large and handsome buildings. But she could
only see their unlighted upper floors—her downward view of
them was blocked by some kind of balcony outside this window. Did they rest on water, or on some broad piazza near
water? (She had been brought here by gondola, hadn't she?)
To see the ground floor of that row of houses, she would have
to stand higher, be able to look down over the high balustrade that cut the view in half. She would have to drag apart
some of the clutter behind her, pull that marble-topped table
to the window.

The idea, when she had switched on the light again and
could study the table, defeated her. She couldn't move it
six inches. She stood there, dispirited, looking down at the
silks and satins in the opened trunk. It was made of light
wood, covered with leather. The lid felt thin to her touch.
Perhaps she could empty the trunk, drag it gently over to the
window. But even as she pulled at a piece of heavy brocade,
white turned yellow, she knew she was too tired, too weak.
She sat down on a low chest beside the trunk, her hand fall-
en on the silks. She'd rest for a little. Opening those shutters
had been harder work than she had thought at the time. Or
else she had hope then; and now it was slipping away.

Bill—what had happened to him? Where was he? Her thoughts kept being forced back to him, as if they were being drawn. . . .

She raised her head. From the silent darkness outside there had come a ship's warning traveling over water—not the heavy blast from a liner or freighter, but the peremptory little siren she had heard today on a water-bus traveling to the Lido. Could that be a *vaporetto* plying its way up the Grand Canal? She rose, moved quickly to the door, switched off the light, returned to the window. The shutters had swung closed again. She forced the inch of space open. As if to answer her question, she heard music floating toward her, at first faint, louder, very loud; less loud, decreasing, passing. *O sole mio*. So it was the Grand Canal down there, far below her. And there were gondolas, with their people looking up to admire the view on either side. And even if the dark houses far opposite were museums or offices, closed for the night, there were other houses near them where people lived and stepped out onto their balconies to look at the night. People . . .

She picked up a shoe and wedged its toe into the little opening between the shutters. That would hold them. She ran to the light switch, her exhaustion forgotten.

She flicked the switch on. And waited. She flicked it off. Count a slow five, switch on. Count a slow five, switch off. Count; on. Count; off . . .

That was all she could do. That, and hope.

TWENTY-SIX

HURRYING, BUT not too alarmed, Robert Wahl had made his quiet return to Ca' Longhi. A black gondola in a small dark canal, an unlighted door waiting to open for him, and he was safely inside the heavy walls. He was more annoyed than worried. Lenoir's guarded telephone call only told him that there was trouble with Sandra, that he was needed. He arrived, expecting to stay for ten minutes, blaming Lenoir for any difficulty that had arisen: Sandra Fane had been obedient enough when he had left her.

Then he heard the details. The problem had developed a different dimension. The quiet, understanding, wisely tolerant smile of film producer Wahl was wiped out; the handsome face became Kalganov's mask, eyes narrowed and calculating, mouth grim and unrelenting. The voice changed, too, from ironical innuendo to savage contempt, goading Lenoir into a flood of self-justification.

The situation was not out of hand, Lenoir insisted at the end of his detailed report. Sandra had realized her situation was hopeless. She had confessed. She was in the library, next door—writing out a statement of her guilt. Martin was guarding her.

Kalganov listened impatiently. "And what have you done about Ballard?"

"Tarns reported he was in the Vittoria bar. I took immediate action, of course."

"Such as?"

"I had a man pick him up at the hotel."

"How?"

"He met Ballard coming out of the bar. He persuaded him to walk to the front door."

"With what?"

"A gun concealed under a raincoat over his arm. It was

discreetly done. Ballard made no trouble. He was taken completely by surprise." Lenoir's temper was shortening, his voice became more clipped.

"And at the front door?"

"I had a motorboat waiting." Lenoir paused. "Naturally."

"And the letter? Did Ballard have the letter?"

"I am waiting for a telephone call about that."

Kalganov's silence lasted a long minute. At last, he said, "They will not find it. He will swear he never saw it. That is why he walked out so quietly from the hotel. Nothing could be proved against him, and so he felt safe."

"He also felt the gun hard at his ribs." Lenoir eased his voice. "I think he still has the letter. That could be the only reason why he was in the Vittoria bar—to meet Fenner and give him the letter."

"Fenner," Kalganov said very softly, and frightened even Lenoir.

Nervously he glanced at the telephone. "We'll soon know whether Ballard has the letter or not. Meanwhile, we have to deal with Sandra's written confession. It is important to us."

"To you, particularly. The first question that Moscow will ask when they hear of her treason will be, 'How did Comrade Lenoir live with this woman for three years and not notice anything wrong?' You are in trouble, Comrade, if she does not confess correctly."

And so are you, Lenoir thought. "I am aware of that," he said coldly.

"I hope you have instructed her adequately."

Lenoir almost smiled. "Certainly, I persuaded her to leave out the reason for her defection. She blames you for that, Comrade Wahl."

"She has put the party in jeopardy, and you make jokes?"

Lenoir's amusement died away. "It was no joke." His voice was bitter.

Kalganov stared at him. "I shall see her. I am taking charge here. Your part of the operation is over. Without the letter—" He snapped his fingers.

"There can still be a campaign of rumors and newspaper speculation. It worked last April."

"And failed, because we had no evidence. This time we had evidence. And we let it slip."

"Along with the ten-thousand-dollar bills," Lenoir reminded him. That had been Kalganov's project. Its failure had not been emphasized, Lenoir couldn't help remembering.

Kalganov changed the subject, and his manner, abruptly. In a more normal tone, he said, "Fortunately, the main operation goes through. That is what counts, anyway. The essential action—that is the heart of the matter."

"Fortunately, too," Lenoir suggested, "I did not mention De Gaulle's name in the letter, nor the actual time and date of the assassination." He paused, waiting for some recognition of his skill in the letter's wording: it would make clear sense once the event had taken place. Its careful phrases only implicated, meanwhile, the Americans and the British go-betweens in some cynical and devious plot holding an enormous threat against France. "I shall concentrate instead on the cooperation of progressive newspapers. You still need their headlines in order to give some reasonable cause for Trouin's panic and suicide." My part in this operation is not over, he thought: Kalganov needs me. He relaxed. "You agree?"

Kalganov was scarcely listening.

"You agree?" Lenoir insisted.

Kalganov said slowly, "Are you sure she did not tell Ballard about the assassination?"

"Martin examined her thoroughly on that point. She insisted she had told Ballard nothing. She had simply given him the letter to pass on to Fenner."

"Did she tell Fenner about the assassination?"

"How could she? She hasn't seen him yet. She was to meet him tomorrow night."

"Who made this arrangement with Fenner?"

"Ballard. She asked Ballard to make contact with Fenner in Paris—and he did, as we know from André Spitzer's report."

"She asked Ballard? Why?"

Lenoir hesitated. "She had discovered you were having her recalled."

"You told her?"

"Not I." Lenoir returned Kalganov's cold stare and hoped he was believed. If she learned from me by subterfuge, he thought, that was not a calculated error on my part: it was a personal betrayal on hers. "She was afraid, because she did not know the reason for her recall," he went on quickly. "She says she was driven into an attempt to escape. She thought Fenner would help her. She used the letter only to bargain for help."

"You believe her?" Kalganov did not.

"Who can believe a traitor?" Lenoir asked diplomatically.

"We have other ways of learning how much Fenner knows. Where is the woman, this Mrs. James Langley?"

Why should he speak so bitterly of that name? Lenoir wondered. He said, "She is upstairs. A pity—" He paused delicately.

"What is?"

"That you did not have Fenner brought here, too," he said innocently. And that is one mistake for which I cannot be blamed.

Kalganov moved to the library door. "We are wasting time. I have business of my own tonight," he reminded Lenoir. Aarvan's arrest had to be investigated, thoroughly, and this fool had brought him here. "I'll deal with the confession and with Langley. After that, I go." This house smelled of stupidity and bungling, of evasions and excuses. . . . Kalganov's instincts urged him to finish what had to be done and leave. Quickly. Too many unanswered questions, too many imponderables. More might lie behind Aarvan's arrest than just some mistake Aarvan had made on the Simplon Express. The mistake could have been Fenner, Fenner the seemingly negligible. . . . Kalganov looked at Lenoir bitterly as he paused at the door. These intellectuals were all the same: elaborate little plans, fussy attention to small perfections, and then, when something went wrong because of their inborn blindness, they screamed frantically for help, for someone else to act. To do. To complete. "We shall see how well you have instructed Fane," he said bluntly, and entered the library.

Lenoir had been right about one thing though. Sandra Fane was without any hope at all. It was possible, Kalganov thought as he looked at her, that she would confess everything sooner than he had expected. Despair was the necessary catalyst to produce satisfactory obedience.

She was sitting at the table, staring down at what she had written on a piece of paper. She had cried. Tears were still half dried on her cheeks. Crying from pain? Or crying because she was defeated? He congratulated Martin on leaving so little evidence of his work. She looked almost normal except for the fear in her cringing body.

He picked up the confession and read it. "Totally inadequate," he said, letting it drop.

She looked at him, put a hand over her aching mouth.

She took a deep breath. "What do you want me to write?" she asked faintly.

"The truth."

She picked up the pen, waiting for him to dictate. "Yes?" she asked. He eyed her coldly. Was she still capable of insulting him?

"You forgot to mention that your ex-husband, William Fenner, has been an agent of American Intelligence since Korea; that you kept this secret, deceiving your comrades in New York, Mexico, Prague, even in Moscow itself. Because you knew that this fact would damage your career."

So, she thought slowly, I not only deceived Kalganov, I deceived everyone. Everyone must share the blame. The more blame shared, the less for him. Cunning, clever Kalganov, so generous in sharing.

"Why," he was demanding, "didn't you mention the fact that Fenner made secret contact with you as soon as you came to Paris?"

"Three years ago?" Her eyes, half closed with the knifelike pain that jabbed inside her left shoulder, opened in wonder.

"Three years ago. He pretended he was still in love with you, didn't he? Poor Sandra—you believed him. Because you are still in love with him. Aren't you?"

His voice was gentle, suddenly, like the first touch of a wire loose against her throat. His eyes narrowed, watching her face. The wire noose seemed to tighten.

"Complete the confession," he said. "Add one more page to what you have written. Give the facts. All the facts. The blame for your treason lies with Fenner. And with you, for your weakness." His eyes were satisfied now. He laid a fresh sheet of paper in front of her, and turned away. "I shall see you in fifteen minutes. If it is not correct—" He looked across the room at Martin. The wire noose, which had slackened, tightened again. "But if you write the truth, Moscow will take your honest remorse into consideration. You might even stay alive."

He left, stopping to tell Martin something she couldn't hear. Martin nodded and looked at her. Her hand fell away from her painful mouth, and the pen began to write. Martin, big and slow and thorough, studied her with amusement, as if he were admiring the artistry of his persuasive powers.

The door closed behind Kalganov.

He found a frowning Lenoir standing beside the telephone. "She will confess the truth," Kalganov said, "the whole truth, this time. I'm going upstairs. You would like to be present, of course, when I question Claire Langley?" His heavy sarcasm ended. "What's wrong?" he asked testily as Lenoir's frown deepened.

Lenoir gestured toward the telephone. "Ballard—he hasn't got the letter."

"So he has already passed it to Fenner!"

"He would not tell us."

"He did not talk?" Kalganov was scandalized.

"No," Lenoir said quietly, "he didn't talk this time. Odd, isn't it? He was the biggest talker I ever met."

Kalganov was outraged. "They did not keep him alive to talk?" he asked unbelievingly.

"There was an emergency. He tried to escape." Lenoir waited for Kalganov's outburst, but it didn't come.

"I know one who will talk," Kalganov said very quietly, and moved to the door. He waited there for Lenoir.

"I am going to call Zurich, to find out if Trouin has been arrested," Lenoir said quickly. Kalganov's methods are his; mine are mine, he thought. I will not go upstairs. I will not go into that library next door.

"I did not forget Trouin. But there is a quicker way of finding out if the assassination plan has been discovered by Fenner. The answer to that question lies no farther away than your attic room. Are you coming?"

"First," Lenoir said evasively, "I must send out a general alert for Fenner. He may still have the letter."

"Scrap that letter! Forget it! It's lost to us—for good!"

"I want Fenner," Lenoir said grimly.

"And so do I." But, thought Kalganov, I do not use that as a subterfuge to evade what has to be done. These intellectuals are always the same: they talk of sending in the tanks to shoot down rebellion, of using firing squads and bulldozers to plow traitors into massed graves, of forcing prisoners into screaming insanity for the sake of information, but they do it from the end of a telephone, from the committee table, from the anonymous distance. There he is, Comrade Lenoir, about to order torture if need be, death eventually, for the American called Fenner. But he will command it from this quiet room, among his books and records. And he is looking at me as if I were the monster. "Are you coming?" Kalganov demanded, opening the door onto the landing.

"Shortly," Lenoir said. "I have to—"

"Indeed you have," Kalganov said contemptuously. He walked out. Lenoir was picking up the telephone receiver with a great flourish of urgency.

Kalganov passed the library door, halted—that was Martin's voice, raised in anger—and retraced his steps. More trouble, was it? He entered quickly. Yes, more trouble. Martin was standing over the desk, threatening. Sandra Fane was cowering back, yet strangely determined.

Kalganov picked up the confession. One paragraph was all she had added, a very bald statement, but adequate enough. The names were there. That was what mattered. Fenner would never escape from that indictment. Even if, tonight, he slipped out of reach, his name would stand on file. Fenner's end was only a matter of time and convenience. His death was written on this sheet of paper. But there was no signature. "You have forgotten something," he said, too gently.

"I'll sign it when I reach Moscow." Her voice was still faint, but her eyes were sullen, steady. He won't kill me until it is signed, she thought again. And when I reach Moscow, I'll write a new confession. I'll denounce him as a Stalinist, a Leftist deviationist, terroristic opportunist, dogmatist. There are plenty of phrases to pin on Kalganov. I'll pin them all.

Still planning to escape, Kalganov thought as he watched her. He glanced pointedly at the clock. Twenty-three minutes past eleven o'clock. "Sign it," he said, smiling. He drew a revolver from inside his jacket. "If you wish to sail from Venice, Sandra, you must sign." His voice was most reasonable.

She looked at the revolver. She saw its strong barrel. She remembered Lenoir telling her in amusement about it: specially made, custom built like Robert Wahl's suits, to shoot the terrible bullet with the grim name: Jugular—a Harvey Jugular bullet. And Lenoir and she had laughed: Kalganov and his fads; Kalganov, the great producer of real-life dramas, action guaranteed.

"After all," he was saying, "a signature is a mere formality. The confession is in your handwriting, isn't it?" He glanced over at Martin. "I won't shoot you if you sign. I shan't touch you. You will rise from that desk and walk away. I promise you. I keep my promises. And my threats. You know that."

Yes, he kept his threats. She looked at the revolver, so casually held, so deadly. And he had kept promises, too. Something about this promise seemed—seemed—what? She was too tired, too cold, too sick, to hold on to the small warning. It faded; she couldn't even remember what had troubled her. He had promised: he wouldn't shoot her; she could rise and walk away. She picked up the pen, fumbling, and signed her name.

Kalganov nodded, slipped the revolver back into its hiding place, lifted the two sheets of paper, folded them neatly, placed them in an inside pocket. "Thank you, Sandra. You can go to your room. Martin will put you on board the ship at midnight."

The blue eyes, once so beautiful, so confident, looked up at him thankfully. She rose, began her slow painful walk toward the door. Martin was waiting for her. He held out his arm as if to help her. She saw something like a black fountain pen in his hand, pointed at her face; and suddenly, a little cloud of vapor, of—

That was all she ever knew. She dropped where she stood.

There was a slight, bitter odor in the room. Martin opened the window quickly, flung back the outside shutters. "It soon dissipates," he said reassuringly. He smiled. "I'll put her on board the motorboat at midnight."

Kalganov had clamped a handkerchief over his mouth and nose. He knelt to feel Sandra Fane's pulse, to make sure.

"Fatal heart attack," Martin said, "you can depend on it. And you don't need that handkerchief. It is only the first impact that is deadly."

Kalganov rose. "Quick and efficient." He glanced for the last time at Sandra Fane. "Too quick," he said, "for a traitor." He avoided the door near which she lay. He didn't have Martin's trust in the rapid dissipation of that gas. "You did a good job, Comrade Colonel," he told him as he left by way of the sitting room.

Lenoir was still at the telephone. He seemed to be waiting for his call to be answered.

As Kalganov passed through the room, he said, "I'm expecting you upstairs. Don't forget that!" He paused at the door. "Come up in ten minutes. And bring the news that Fenner has admitted everything."

Lenoir stared at him.

"We've caught Fenner, didn't you know?" Kalganov smiled widely. "I'll tell her that. She'll try not to believe me. But your news will add just the right pressure. Psychologically—"

"Yes, yes," Lenoir said irritably. He looked at the receiver. "It's this damned connection to Milan. I seem to have been cut off. I'll have to try again. I am extending the alert on Fenner. I think he has left Venice. But he can't have got very far."

"You are wasting time," Kalganov said sharply. "The answer is upstairs. Ten minutes?"

Lenoir was complaining into the telephone. He nodded to Kalganov, and glanced at his watch to check the hour. It as almost half past eleven. No, Fenner could not have run very far, as yet.

TWENTY-SEVEN

FENNER SAID softly, "One minute to go." He edged his way carefully over the crest of Ca' Longhi's roof toward the concealing shadow of a large and ornate chimney on the Grand Canal side of the house.

"Keep off the sky line," Holland whispered warningly. He gave a brief wave to the men, Marco's experts, who were waiting farther back, by the kitchen chimney. They were too busy to acknowledge. They had been warned by their miniature radio anyway, to expect two more on the roof. The blessings of scientific invention, thought Holland; a pity that there were no similar aids to crossing three roofs, climbing a parapet, dropping down a short gable end. He shook his head, remembering how he had slipped in spite of his rubber-soled shoes. Dirt-colored sand shoes they were, compliments of Marco, along with the old dungarees he had provided—Fenner called them sneakers and overalls. Logical enough: the shoes sneaked along, the one-piece outfit went over all. But words aside, Fenner's actions were quick, instinctive. Holland had not ended in a bottom-down slide into the canal. And I came to keep an eye on him, Holland thought, and grinned. Also, Marco wasn't going to let Fenner climb up alone. Also, I still like Fenner's idea. So here we are, up on the roof of Ca' Longhi, slightly bruised and bleeding at the knuckles, and two minutes to go.

Either Fenner's watch was fast or he was just forcing the time as he had forced the pace. He was still forcing it. He left the chimney and started along the red fluted tiles, silvered into faint pink by the moonlight. Dammit, he should have waited for that large batch of light clouds to start sailing over the quarter-moon, Holland thought. That might take too long, though. And Fenner was moving slowly, being careful (as Marco had warned them) not to scrabble above the attic corridor, where there might be someone on guard outside the room.

The attic windows had their own small roofs emerging out of the gently sloping tiles. Fenner's plan was good. He had approached the second room at the point where it met the pitch of the main roof. He was sliding onto it, taking shelter behind the decorated arch that jutted up over the window beneath him. From the canal, he would not be noticed.

Not bad, thought Holland approvingly, not bad at all; the only bad thing is getting there. He set out, following Fenner's route. And the part that had looked the easiest, that small slide onto the attic's roof was, astonishingly, the worst. But Fenner may have had the same experience, for although there was a welcoming grin on his face, there were beads of sweat on his brow as he blocked Holland's unexpected momentum.

"The immediate problem," Holland whispered, regaining control, feeling a sharp edge of tile bite into one knee as he braced his hands gingerly against the back of the window arch, "is whether this holds." It felt solid enough. It was only the elaborate curlicues and cutouts of stone that had given this piece of Venetian Gothic its fragile look. He sucked his skinned knuckles and studied Fenner's next move with sympathy. "We must look like a couple of gargoyles," he added as they raised their shoulders cautiously to look over and down.

Fenner was noting the two pillars that decorated each side of the window beneath him and pretended to hold up its arch. They were slender, and fluted twistingly. They would give him enough grip as he pulled himself onto the narrow balcony from the slope of the main roof. He couldn't drop directly onto the balcony from where he knelt. There wasn't enough breadth on that glorified ledge to allow for any lost balance. It had a balustrade, but that could have developed a weak patch or two in the last four hundred years; and below it there was only a short stretch of sloping tiles to the roof's edge. No, he would have to back up to the main roof—thank God its slope was gentle—and come down it by the side of this outcrop of attic, and then swing around its front corner, holding that pillar, onto the balcony's balustrade. After that, it was simple. The balcony was narrow, but there was room to maneuver.

He sign-languaged his plan quickly to Holland. "It's only

a dormer window with some fancy trappings," he added to encourage himself.

"That's all. Nothing to it," Holland agreed with a small smile. His whisper strengthened in alarm. "Hey, wait! Still seventy seconds to go."

"It's time." Fenner was already backing onto the main roof.

"Take this—" Holland unbuttoned a pocket.

"I've got one," Fenner whispered up, as he started down the side of the attic roof.

"What caliber?" Holland leaned over and gripped his arm.

"A .25. It's Claire's."

"You may need more than that peashooter." Holland passed down a .38/32 Smith and Wesson. "Straight and true," he murmured. "You may need this to shoot out the lock on the shutters. You'll only have time for one shot if there is any guard around to hear it." He watched Fenner stick the short-barreled revolver deep into a pocket, button it. "Slowly does it," he whispered as Fenner moved on. He spread-eagled his body, face down, on the slope of attic roof, dug in his toes, leaned over near its front corner, held on with one hand, held out the other for an emergency grip as Fenner worked his way toward the pillar. He tried to keep his eyes fixed on the top of Fenner's head, descending step by step down the main roof, his hands flat against the rising attic wall. Fenner was reaching up for Holland's hand. He grasped it, and their two arms, fully extended, let him swing around the corner to catch hold of the pillar.

My God, how I hate heights, Holland thought as his body strained against the pulling arm and he felt his eyes drawn down to the canal far below. He closed them quickly; Fenner released his grip, whispering, "Okay, okay," and Holland could have both his hands to clamp on those comforting curlicues of carved stone. From away behind him, on the other side of the roof, came a long, clear whistle. He called softly down to Fenner, "Thar she blows!" Eleven-thirty it was. He settled back contentedly on the tiles. He was imagining, with considerable enjoyment, the little scene from hell that was now bursting into Ca' Longhi's kitchen.

Fenner caught his breath and balance. This was a devil of a time, he thought, as he held onto the pillar, to discover he had lost his head for heights. But if he had got this far, the return could be managed: climbing up was always easier than coming down, and Holland would be there to grip Claire's hand. He moved carefully along the narrow balcony —it shook a little under his weight, but held. There was no light from the small opening in the shutters. The fear he felt now was for Claire. Had they taken her away? Was she no longer— At that instant, the room light flashed on. And it was Claire he saw. Claire. Thank God.

She was standing opposite the window, her hand on a light switch. Her coat, thrown on the floor at the door beside her, covered the threshold. So there was a guard, outside in the corridor.

Gently, he rattled the shutters, called, "Claire!" softly. She seemed to freeze against the wall. Her eyes stared at the window with disbelief, her face tense and white, so tense and white and exhausted. Then she was running toward him. She slipped her fingers between the shutters. "Bill?"

He touched them. "It's Bill." That was all he could say.

From somewhere, not too far distant in the house, there came a roaring shout.

"They've found out!" she whispered in anguish. She glanced back at the door, expecting to hear the key turn in the lock, the guard burst in. There was a movement in the corridor, but the footsteps weren't coming here. They were running away from the room. Another shout, fainter. . . .

"No. It's a fire," Fenner said quickly. "What's holding these shutters?" A large black iron band was all he could see. "Is there a padlock behind this thing?" He tried to grope for it.

"It is tight up against the hasp to let the shutters open."

"Take this and shoot its lock out." He pushed Holland's revolver between the shutters. It stuck. It wouldn't go all the way through. It needed another half-inch for clearance. He tried to force the shutters farther apart. They wouldn't move. "Take your automatic, Claire. Shoot twice, quickly." Would twice be enough?

She whispered, "The guard is coming back. I hear his footsteps."

"I'll keep the door covered with the thirty-eight. Shoot quickly."

"Stand away from the shutter," she told him anxiously. "It's dangerous—"

"Shut up. And I love you, too."

She gave a smothered laugh, and looked at the automatic as she raised it. It was so small, so light, not even comforting any more. The padlock was small, strong. Would two bullets be enough? Perhaps three? She wished her hand would stop this nervous trembling.

It is always the same, thought Fenner grimly; if anything can go wrong, it will. Always? No. There was another side to that coin: if something could go right, it might. It just might. "Quick," he whispered as he heard the piercing shriek of a fireboat's siren, far below in the Grand Canal. "Hurry, Claire!"

It was Kalganov who had shouted.

He had reached the third floor of Ca' Longhi on his climb to the attic. He was still thinking contemptuously about Lenoir. The Frenchman ought to have handled that confession himself. He should have dealt with Sandra Fane. Instead, he hadn't even asked what had happened to her. He knew, all right, but he wanted no share of the responsibility; so he hadn't asked. Lenoir would never—

What was that? Some disturbance. Far downstairs.

He looked over the yellow marble balustrade. He heard the cries more clearly: "Fire!" Down in the hall, a billow of black smoke gushed from the kitchen quarters; it spread and thickened, pouring over the flagstone floor far below him. As he stared at the forming cloud, the cook came running out from the kitchen corridor still screaming, "Fire, fire!" The cloud enveloped her, and turned her scream to a choking cough.

Kalganov shouted.

The guard, posted outside the girl's door, started to his feet and came running along the attic's corridor. Kalganov, turning to race downstairs, signaled to him to stay where he was. He shouted again, bringing Lenoir away from his precious telephone and Martin out of the library. Lenoir stared over the balustrade. "Fire!" he cried, as if he had discovered it. "Look! Fire!" He pointed down to the hall.

"You amaze me," Kalganov said bitingly as he passed Lenoir at a run. Then he halted, really amazed, when Lenoir didn't follow: just stood, hands on the balustrade, looking over into the hall. There were three figures down there now, running around in the cloud of smoke like chickens with their heads chopped off. "Get them organized," he told Lenoir sharply. "Come on, get moving! It's only a kitchen fire. We can deal with it."

"It's spreading!" Lenoir cried, pointing down to another

room where a thick ooze of smoke soaked its way into the
hall from under the closed door. "That whole wing—"

"Don't open it!" Kalganov yelled down to the hall, "don't
open that door!" But one of the men had already thrown the
room door open, and was entering. "Don't open any windows, you fool!" Kalganov was screaming after him. "Do
you want people outside to give an alarm?" He was clattering
down the last flight of stairs, a handkerchief covering his
mouth and nose. Martin was at his heels.

Who was the fool? Lenoir wondered, following more slowly.
Windows had to be opened to get rid of that smoke. No one
could breathe. The shouts had become gasping coughs. He
choked into his handkerchief—burning grease, obnoxious,
sickening—and retreated a step.

"Fire extinguishers—" Kalganov was yelling. "Where are
they?" he shouted up to Lenoir.

"I—I don't know. How could I?" Lenoir kept his voice as
normal as possible. This screaming was grotesque. This speed
of action was close to panic.

"Water!" Kalganov shouted, now. "Buckets—"

"Water makes the smoke worse," the cook called to him,
groping her way to the staircase, her eyes white in a blackened face, hair soot-heavy.

"Whose carelessness?"

She shook her head helplessly. "The fireplace was filled
with flames. They just—"

"How far have they spread?" Kalganov stared at her.
"The fireplace? That's all?" He turned to Martin. "Take
charge. It's nothing serious. A chimney fire. Use salt—" He
broke off, listening. Far distant came the high wail of a
fireboat's siren. Loud, louder, nearer and nearer.

But it's less than a minute since Kalganov's first shout,
Lenoir thought in complete amazement, much less. How quick
they are!

Too quick, Kalganov thought grimly, and started back up
the staircase, pausing only to yell down to the startled faces
in the hall, "Keep the doors barred! Tell them the fire is
under control!" But his voice was lost in the siren's hideous
scream, blaring into the small canal. As it sobbed into silence, heavy pounding began on the street door.

Lenoir caught Kalganov's arm. "We must let them in—it's
the law! They've seen the smoke." Someone has to use his intelligence, he thought, but he wondered why Kalganov was
looking at him with such a strange small smile. "I'll keep
them downstairs—"

There was a shot, light, muffled by distance. Another. And another. They came from the attic.

Kalganov pushed Lenoir aside, and was racing along the first landing to the next sweep of stairs.

"Open the doors!" Lenoir called out. "Open the door, at once!" If the firemen had to use axes to get in, there would be questions, suspicions, a search. Show no panic, Lenoir told himself as he started downstaris. This is a matter of tact and reason.

Again there was a shot. Only one, this time, sounding loud and clear from overhead.

Lenoir halted in surprise. Kalganov hadn't yet reached the attic stairs. He was only on the second landing, racing past the bedroom doors. That must have been the guard who had fired, Lenoir thought worriedly. But those three lighter shots? The girl had carried no gun, no weapon of any kind. So the men who brought her here had reported. Or had they blundered? Let Kalganov puzzle that out. Upstairs is his problem. Mine is here.

Lenoir looked down at the shadowy figures who were moving into the swirling cloud in the hall. The cool air from the wide-open door cut through the black smoke, dissolving it into thin gray wisps. The number of men alarmed him. He raised his voice, "The fire was only in the kitchen. It has been confined. No need—" He broke off as four men came running up the staircase. "Gentlemen!" he insisted. "There is no need whatsoever—" He stared at them. These men were not firemen. And behind them were policemen. Suddenly he remembered Kalganov's small smile. Kalganov had guessed, Kalganov had escaped.

Lenoir caught his bitterness, choked it off. Kalganov would do more than escape: he would eliminate all evidence. Lenoir blocked the path of the men as they reached him. "Get out! Get out, all of you! Do you hear me? The fire is over. You have no right—"

"Don't we?" asked an American, a dark-haired man with angry dark eyes. He shoved Lenoir aside. "He's all yours, Jules," he said over his shoulder, hurrying on, two others at his heels.

Jules nodded with grim satisfaction, and stepped aside politely to let the Italian policemen make the arrest.

Lenoir didn't even listen to them. He was watching the American and the two men, spreading out out along the landing, opening doors, searching. "Here, Rosie!" one called urgently from the library. Lenoir almost panicked. Sandra . . .

He glanced quickly down at the hall. Martin was there, handcuffed, watching the search, too. But he had no alarm on that stolid face, upturned to the library door. There could be no sign of bullet or knife in Sandra's body. Lenoir relaxed. He stared at the handcuffs closing on his wrists. "What is their ridiculous charge?" he asked.

"Abduction," Jules said. He added, with a thin smile, "Meanwhile."

"Abduction?" repeated Lenoir unbelievingly. Three more men pushed their way past him to help with the search upstairs. The man called Rosie had come out of the library, and was signaling to the others to follow. But I have given Kalganov time, Lenoir thought rapidly; without evidence, what can be proved? I've given Kalganov at least two minutes. The strong attic door would give him more: locked and barricaded, it could stop the search for many minutes; more than enough to let Kalganov go free. He wouldn't leave the girl, either. No evidence—no proof; only guesses and suppositions. A body found floating in the Grand Canal was proof of nothing except death. "Whose abduction?" Lenoir demanded with an appropriate show of anger.

Jules did not answer. His hand tightened on Lenoir's arm. "Start moving!" he said. Then the little group on the staircase halted, looked up. One shot, distant yet clear, echoed down from far above.

One shot, definite in every way, thought Lenoir. The American with the ridiculous name had not even reached the attic staircase. He was racing now, the other men clattering wildly after him. Too late, Lenoir's mocking eyes told the backs of the running men, too late. By this time Kalganov is out on the roof. The girl is gone. Kalganov will escape.

And so shall I, Lenoir thought. Since when has propaganda become a felony? He looked at the Frenchman beside him, coldly. "You are making a grave mistake."

"You must tell that to Trouin, the wine merchant," Jules said with his thin smile. He tightened his grip on Lenoir's elbow as another shot rang out, and Lenoir's indignant innocence crumbled in blank silence.

The siren had screamed high as the fireboat curved from the Grand Canal into the *rio*, swooped down two full octaves, and stopped.

Claire started when the shrill note blared into the attic. Then, as it ended abruptly, she took a deep breath, steadied her nerves, and took aim once more at the padlock. "Hurry, Claire!" Bill's whisper urged her from the balcony.

"Three shots," she warned him. Three to make sure. She fired rapidly. And accurately. For when she wrenched at the padlock, it broke loose. Fenner smashed the shutters open, jumped down beside her.

"Out!" he told her, regaining his balance, a revolver pointing at the door, his eyes glancing around the room. His free hand steadied her as she began to raise herself over the window sill. She heard the guard's footsteps, the heavy key turning in the lock. We'll never make it, she thought, and dropped back onto the floor, turning to face the door with Bill. He caught her, swung her to the side, sent her tumbling, sliding over toward the heavy, carved chest. She fell prone behind it as the door crashed open. There was a shot. One shot.

Cold with fear, she raised herself on her elbow, her automatic ready. But Bill was all right. He was looking at an empty doorway. She pulled herself to her knees, and saw that the guard had fallen backward across the threshold, half in, half out of the room. He was clutching a shattered right shoulder, and beginning to moan.

Bill had heard something else, for he moved quickly to the door, kicking aside the guard's pistol, switching off the light. "Keep down!" he said softly, and she obeyed him, letting herself drop back again onto the dust-coated floor.

Running footsteps, that was what Fenner had heard. And so had the guard. For he made an attempt to rise and lunge forward with his one good arm. Fenner smashed down at the upraised head with his revolver, sent the man toppling back into the corridor. He pulled the large key from its outside lock, tried to close the door, found that it jammed on the man's leg, lying stiff and straight over the threshold. From the far end of the corridor, the light was switched off.

The footsteps, careful, no longer running, were coming close. Too close. No time to clear the threshold, get the key into this side of the lock. No time to do anything at all except step behind the gaping door, and wait. He glanced over at the chest. Claire could be seen from the threshold if she didn't keep herself flat on the floor. Keep down, Claire! he told her silently, for God's sake, keep down.

Any minute, now . . .

He waited, spine pulled taut against the door in the hope that he couldn't be seen through the close-angled crack at its hinges, left hand lightly holding its knob to sense any touch on it from outside, right arm close across his ribs with the revolver's two-inch barrel pointing just where someone would step across the guard's ankle.

But the man was waiting, too. His breathing, audible at first, had been controlled. There was only silence in the blackness of the corridor. Neither breath nor footstep. A clever type, thought Fenner: not one who came bursting into a room with his gun blazing. What was he waiting for? Reinforcements? Or was he studying what he could see of the room from the gaping door? If so, he would see that the shutters had been burst open, for a stream of faint moonlight stretched obliquely toward the crowded furniture, played over it gently, set two dark mirrors gleaming, turned a golden cherub into silver, shimmered over the silks and satins lying in an opened trunk near the chest where Claire lay so still, whitened floor and walls, sharpened shadows.

Why didn't he move? He knew he had little time.

He is more than a clever type, thought Fenner tensely, eyes now fixed on the edge of the opened door. He isn't just standing somewhere in that corridor (and I wish to God I knew exactly where), waiting for someone to make a false move: he is goading us into one. Us? He doesn't know I am here. He didn't see who was trying to close the door. He can't see me standing here. That's the only good thing about this position: he can't see me. But if he throws this door wide open, he could fling me off balance for one second. And seconds can mean everything—for proof, just look at that damned foot lying wedged across the threshold. So that's one advantage he has. There is another, too: he is in a black corridor looking into a moonlit room. Or now and again moonlit. For the light, ebbing and flowing, was once more veiled by a passing cloud.

Fenner heard the first careful movement from the other side of the door. Here it comes, Fenner thought, here it comes, whatever it is. He braced himself, waiting for the darkness to end once the cloud had passed over. The pale, uncertain light began to flow back into the room. He gave one quick glance in Claire's direction, for the low chest had worried him:

unless she lay absolutely still, she might be seen. Invisible, thank God. Then, as the light played briefly over the mass of furniture, he froze. That mirror tilted drunkenly forward from the wall, that mirror catching a beam of moonlight— He stared at Claire's trapped image. She had moved behind the trunk, using its up-raised lid as a shield. Abruptly, the moonlight fled; Claire's reflection vanished. He was left staring at a jumble of dark shadows. But the position of her head and shoulders behind the trunk's lid as she knelt, motionless, waiting, her automatic ready, would be marked and remembered. From the corridor, he heard another careful movement, the slight scrape of metal on metal (a silencer, perhaps?), a small click of readiness. When the light strengthened again —but Fenner didn't wait for that.

He wrenched the door open, dropped to the floor. The man just beyond the threshold swerved his aim from trunk to door's edge, and fired silently into the darkness. The bullet smashed savagely into the wall behind Fenner as he shot from the floor at the black shadow emerging from the corridor. It gasped and fell, lay motionless. The moonlight was spreading across the room again, sending the mirror glancing.

"Don't move, Claire!" he called warningly. He began to rise, and stopped, watching the man's still body. A clever type, Fenner remembered. He could be faking. And his aim was good. If I had been standing as he expected, his aim would have been very good.

"Look out!" Holland shouted from the window, and fired. The man's long revolver, grotesque and grim with its silencer, lifting slowly, painfully, clattered back to the floor.

Holland jumped into the room, side-stepped out of the flow of moonlight, circled toward the door like an alert and capable terrier flushing out a rat. "He's had it," Holland said very softly. "No more strain." He took a deep breath. As Fenner rose, he switched on the light. They stood half blinded by the naked bulb's jagged glare. "It's Kalganov," Holland said unbelievingly. He looked at the doorway, where Rosie stood, revolver ready, his breath coming in sharp gasps. "Kalganov," Chris Holland told Rosie. "It's Kalganov!"

Fenner looked down at the man who had almost ended their lives. He had died badly. The handsome face was distorted with his rage to win, the clever eyes staring with savage hate, fanatical refusal; declaring a perpetual war; damning all and everyone to everlasting hell. As it might have been, Fenner thought, as it could have been if this man had won. If the moment of death was the moment of truth, then in Kalganov's truth there was nothing but menace.

He turned away, started toward Claire. She had not moved.

Holland was saying quietly, "It was a close thing, a damned close thing." He had picked up Kalganov's revolver, which he was examining with interest. He shook his head over the bullet he had ejected into his palm. Silently, he showed it to Rosie. Outside in the corridor, there were many footsteps, voices. Let Rosie and Chris deal with all that, Fenner thought as he made his way toward Claire. He felt no triumph in Kalganov's death. Only a sense of warning. The Kalganovs died, the Kalganovs lived. No end? No peace? Yet this one had been defeated. This one, at least. He wasn't the first to have been defeated, either. He wouldn't be the last. They were not invincible—if you knew they existed. If you knew, and faced them.

He stepped over a footstool, pulled aside a chair. His movements were slow, exhausted, deliberate. And at last he reached Claire.

She had started to rise, and then, as all strength left her body, sank behind the trunk again, her shoulders drooping, her hand—still clutching the automatic—lying inert on her thigh. Her head rested against the lid of the trunk; disheveled hair fell over her white face. She had been crying; slow tears still escaped from the dark curve of eyelashes, down over the dust-streaked cheeks.

She heard his footsteps now. She looked up at him; tried to smile, but she couldn't. He loosened the tight clasp of her fingers from the little automatic, slipped it into his pocket. That's all over, he thought, all over. He reached down and gripped her waist, raised her slowly to her feet. She said, "Oh, Bill—I thought you were dead. For one whole minute, I thought you were—"

He caught her, drawing her close to him. Their arms encircled each other, and held.